OF REALMS AND FATE

CHELSEA BANNING

CONTENTS

Pronunciation Guide

- Bradán- brah-DAWN

- Muirne – Myr-NAH

- Garbhan- Gar-vhon

- Dohmnall – Donnal

- Garanwyn – Gah-RAHN-Win

- Grainne-GRAW-nyuh

- Teamhair na Rí – CHOW-er na REE

- Ceridwen – Care·uh·dwen

- Myfanwy -Me-VAN-wee

- Dafydd -DAH-vith

To everyone who never stopped believing in me...

CHAPTER ONE

MORGANA

"Hello, Mother."

Morgana blinked, barely able to process the sight before her. Her son, her dead son, stood on her porch, regarding her with a soft expression, as if he had only been away a few months. Morgana gripped the door to keep herself upright. So they had done it. Her gaze shifted over to Nimue, narrowing. Despite Morgana's warnings, Nimue had done the forbidden. No wonder the world had shifted. Morgana had felt it. It was why she had returned home from the Isle of Sky.

Nimue was pale, with vibrant purple shadows under her eyes. Her skin had lost its usual glimmer and her hair was limp and stringy. She leaned heavily on Mordred, who had a tight grip around her waist.

"What have you done?" Morgana whispered.

"Can we save it for later? Nimue needs care." Mordred gently pulled the cloak from Nimue's shoulder, exposing a blackened spot with shadowed veins reaching toward her neck. Morgana grimaced at the sight of it. Under the black, the skin was red and swollen.

She knew she should send them away, let them live with the consequences of resurrecting the dead, but her own morals as a healer would not let her. Gritting her jaw, Morgana stepped aside and let them into the cottage.

Cafall barked at them and Morgana hushed him, pointing to the bedroom. The dog followed her finger and curled up on the bed with a whine.

Mordred helped Nimue into the chair by the fire, where Morgana had been sewing new socks for the winter. She busied herself gathering ingredients from her shelves, hoping to calm her nerves before she got to work.

Her hands shook as she pulled out her supplies: salves, ointments, clean towels. She glanced at Mordred. He looked the same, if not better, than he had the last time Morgana had seen him. She had gone to him then, begged him not to start a battle with Arthur, having Seen it would only end in tragedy. Mordred had refused. His anger at losing the title of heir to the throne had sent him over the edge, ending the relationship between the once inseparable uncle and nephew. And with her, once he found out how she had helped Guinevere conceive.

Morgana drew in a breath to steady herself and crossed the room to Nimue, where she carefully peeled away her shirt. The wound was ugly, and the rot had set in. Iron was deadly to mere fae, but Nimue was born of both god and fae, what they called

Ellyth. Nimue should have healed from this wound after only a day or so.

"You could not heal this on your own?" Morgana asked, wetting a clean cloth in the water basin.

"We ran out of medicine," said Mordred, glancing about the cabin. "I did the best I could. I slowed the infection."

Morgana huffed, but went to work grinding herbs and cleaning the wound. She gave instructions to Mordred, who obeyed quietly. A memory flashed in Morgana's mind. One of a small Mordred helping her in the infirmary at Camelot. He had been happy as a boy, if not mischievous. But he had loved to watch and help her work. He absorbed information like a rag with water, never forgetting once he learned.

She gently dabbed some paste onto Nimue's wound. "Why do this, Nimue?"

Nimue's lip curled. "You know why."

"Fae and humans have always been at odds. It is nothing new."

"We are being slaughtered!" Nimue snapped, yanking her arm from Morgana. "Chased from mountain to shore! I will not stand by as the Christian zealots destroy what we have built. Magic is dying. The humans are forgetting the gods and fae for this new Christian way of life. You once stood with me to save our people. Or have you forgotten your fae blood?"

"I did not forget," Morgana snapped. "But fighting fire with fire has only ever made things worse! Although you never seemed to understand that."

"Don't patronize me!"

Morgana ripped off a bandage from her roll. Cafall barked and Morgana hushed him.

"Why bring Mordred back?" Morgana wrapped the bandage as best she could around the wound. Mordred had now gone off to wander around the cabin, looking in drawers and inspecting what she had inside. "What have you sacrificed to make this impossibility happen?"

"I told you before," Nimue said through gritted teeth. "I vowed I'd come back for him."

"You never told me how you escaped," Morgana said. Nimue had come to her first. And Nimue had appeared at her door, barely able to stand. Morgana had nursed her back to health for months, begging her to tell what had happened, but Nimue had refused, asking instead if Morgana knew of any ways to bring a soul back from the In-Between. Then Nimue had left in the middle of the night without a word.

Nimue looked at Morgana for a long moment. Mordred had stopped fumbling around in cabinets, and silence fell. For a moment, Morgana thought Nimue would not answer.

"My soul was—" Nimue swallowed, closing her eyes. "I was being pulled in both directions. Death or life. I fought for life. Kept fighting. Kept reaching for the light. I knew Arawn wanted to come for me, but I kept out of his reach. One day, I...woke up back home. To life. I could hear Mordred's voice sometimes when I was down there...I tried to take him with me, but when

I couldn't, I promised I'd come back for him. If I could do it myself, I could get him out too."

"How?"

"It took time," said Nimue. "But I found what I needed to pull him out, no thanks to you." Her eyes were sharp as she glared at Morgana. "I found someone who knew how to summon a soul. I spent the last few years gathering what I needed."

"Yes, I heard," Morgana said, folding her arms. "Burning abbeys in your wake, killing humans, and stealing relics."

"They deserved it," Nimue growled. "And those relics belong to the fae."

"Arawn will not like that both you and Mordred escaped his grasp."

"We were not *dead*," Nimue growled. "How many times to do I have to explain this?"

"The In-Between is dead enough for the God of the Underworld," said Morgana. "He will come for you."

"He got another soul out of it," Mordred said. "Melara."

Nimue glared at him, her gaze enough to shatter a soul.

Morgana knew Melara. They had been priestesses of Avalon together. Melara and Nimue had grown up together.

"Oh, Nimue," Morgana said, closing her eyes.

"When I cast the spell, I had to give something in return," said Nimue quietly, her voice cracking. "I had planned it to be the boy Pendragon. But it took Melara."

Morgana shook her head. "No, Nimue. You sent Melara to her death with your blatant disregard for anyone but yourself!"

Nimue looked away, anger flushing her cheeks.

"So, what do you plan to do now?" Morgana asked. "Now that you have Mordred back, what is your plan? Do you wish to start yet another doomed war?"

"We will return these lands to the fae," said Nimue. "They are ours by right. We built them; we welcomed humans to them to live peacefully. And look what they have done! No more."

"You won't win, Nimue," Morgana said quietly. "The fae that remain are leaving for the Otherworld. They *prefer* it there."

"You speak as if you know us," Nimue hissed, disgusted. "And yet, do you? When is the last time you have gone home, Morgana *le Fey?* Do not presume to tell me what *my kind* wants."

"I know who and what I am," Morgana growled. "But do you, Nimue? This path you are on will only lead to more death. Look what happened last time."

"I was too hasty in my attempt last time," interrupted Mordred, biting into a slice of bread he had swiped from the table. "This time, however, we will be more careful. I have a new goal. It is not about the injustices of Arthur, but of all the prejudices these new humans hold. We used to live in harmony, humans and fae. They respected us, feared us even. Now all they see are demons from this Hell because of this new Christian god. It is time to restore Briton to its old glory. And we need your help, Mother."

"My help?" Morgana scoffed. "I did not stand with you before. What makes you think I will change my mind? I do not take part in war, Mordred."

Even if he was her son, war was not something Morgana could support. Yes, it was inevitable in life, even with fae. Morgana had gone to the battlefield once with her first husband, King Urien, when she was young, barely nineteen. Her stepfather had married her off as soon as he could to get her away from court, away from him and her mother, Igraine. Men became savage animals on the battlefield, killing without thinking, without seeing. It was a powerful drug that infiltrated the blood and gripped the mind. When war mixed with power, there was no undoing the hold.

"I admit, I was hurt," Mordred said. "You are my mother. I had thought you would be by my side at the battle, and when you weren't, I assumed you were with Arthur."

"I wasn't there, like I told you I wouldn't be," said Morgana. "Neither of you would listen to reason, and I couldn't bear to watch—"

"Well, you can be with me now."

"To do what?" Morgana asked with a sigh.

"To rebuild, of course," said Mordred, throwing his arms out. "A new and brighter future. Tintagel and Cornwall will be yours. As it should be! They are your birthright."

Morgana shook her head. "Mordred, I cannot and *will not* aid you in vengeance and revenge. It is not my way."

He scoffed. "Your way? Look what your *way* has gotten you—a hovel in the forest. Hiding your powers out of fear. I am giving you a chance to atone for your mistakes." Mordred crossed the room and took Morgana by the arms.

"Mistakes?" Morgana took a step back and shrugged his hands off. His touch was cold, even through her wool dress.

"Yes," said Mordred. "If not for you, the Twin Pendragons would not exist."

Morgana clenched her jaw.

"And you would be on the High Throne?" That was what he had always wanted. Power. "That's what this is still about? Not the fae. You want the throne."

Mordred smirked, and it didn't go past Morgana's notice that he avoided Nimue's eye. He stopped in front of the pile of cloaks and boots on top of an old trunk in the corner.

"What I want," said Mordred, "is for what is ours to stop being taken. First Briton, then Tintagel, Camelot. You should be a queen, Mother. And yet you live in disgrace."

"I *was* a queen once," Morgana said. "And I never wanted it. I prefer to live *here*. In peace."

"You should be ruling over Dumnonia!" Mordred snapped, shoving the cloak and boots off the trunk. "Not that blubbering idiot, Constantine."

"Put those back! And Constantine is your family," said Morgana. "His mother was my mother's sister, your great-aunt—or did you forget that? The laws of man state that the firstborn—"

"Half-sister," Mordred mumbled, opening the trunk. "And fully human."

"Human blood runs through both our veins," Morgana reminded him, but he had pulled fabric out of the trunk.

"You live here with someone," Mordred said. He unraveled a red and white striped banner and froze. He was so utterly still, as if a statue.

Morgana braced herself for the fight. If there had been one person Mordred hated more than Arthur, it was—

"Lancelot?" he whispered with fury as cold as ice. "You live here with *Lancelot*?" He spit the last word out as if it were poison on his tongue.

Morgana struggled with words. Once upon a time, she, too, had loathed Lancelot. But war and loss and time change a person, and two people can share common griefs. Before Morgana could say anything, though, Mordred threw the banner down and was right in front of her, gripping her arm. She hissed in pain, struggling against his hold.

"I should have known," Mordred spat at her. "You gave birth to me, but you've never truly been my mother. You've done nothing but put Arthur and his precious knights before *me*, your own son!"

His bellowed words echoed in her ear. Mordred grabbed Nimue and half dragged her to the door. Nimue cried out in protest and tried to break from him, but Mordred ignored her.

"Mordred, wait! You're hurting her!" Morgana followed them. "Mordred! She needs to recover!"

Mordred whirled around on her. "I will not stay any longer in his house. You know what he has done! He who turned his back on his own people! He who gave up his magic to live fully human."

"You will march toward your deaths," said Morgana as they reached the porch. "Both of you. You cannot bring back the dead without upsetting the balance of the world. Of life. The world has already shifted. I can feel it."

"You're such a hypocrite!" Nimue hissed, holding her arm. "You, who gave Arthur fertility when he had none? You who gave Guinevere not one, but two babies not supposed to exist, and yet you lecture me!?"

"That is not the same as resurrecting it!" The fire in the hearth burst up through the chimney. Cafall barked from the bedroom doorway. "You well know this, Nimue, or have you forgotten the laws of magic?"

"Enough." Mordred put an arm around Nimue's waist. "We are wasting time arguing."

"Mordred, I cannot let you do this."

Mordred whirled on her, and his eyes blazed. "And what will you do to stop me, hmm? Will you go crying to Lancelot? Someday you will understand that I am doing this for us. For all of us."

Morgana kept her face neutral, but the fire that burned in Mordred's ice-blue eyes was not of the living world. He was just as she suspected. Too far gone. She did not recognize her son in this face twisted with fury and hate. Mordred had always been arrogant and prejudiced, but he could be reasoned with. This Mordred... Morgana could see that humanity was leaving him, if it had not disappeared already.

"You will regret this fight," Morgana whispered.

Mordred smirked. "You will see, Mother. Once we have made this new world, you will see. But it would be wise not to try and stop us."

"And what will you do this time, Mordred?" she asked, needing to stall them. Give herself time to call upon her magic. It had been so long since she had used it. "How are you going to create this new world?"

"Well, for a start, by getting rid of the Pendragons once and for all."

"No."

Mordred scoffed. "Do you truly think you can stop me? I will not allow the love I once held for you to protect you anymore, Mother. I will strike you down with the rest."

"My son died twenty years ago," Morgana whispered, the surrounding air charged as if with lightning waiting to strike. "And you are not him."

Something twitched in Mordred's eye, and he pushed his hand forward. Without him making contact, Morgana was shoved into the air, slamming into the wall behind her. Cafall barked and growled and ran after Mordred, but he and Nimue were gone in a tendril of black shadows. Morgana's head swam and her vision blurred. Cafall licked and nudged her, whining.

She groaned and pushed herself up, scooting back against the wall.

Morgana felt her head. It hurt, but there was no blood. "Cafall. Bag. Bag."

Cafall immediately obeyed, running across the room to drag a leather satchel from the table. "Good boy," she whispered, fumbling through it until she pulled out a small vial with yellow liquid. She downed all of it and scratched Cafall on the head. The effects of the tincture were near immediate. The pain in her head faded, and the dizziness went away.

She glared at the spot on her floor where the black tendrils of shadow had left a mark. She knew those shadows, knew where Mordred and Nimue had fled to.

After penning a letter to Lancelot and one of her ravens flying off with it, she dropped Cafall off with a friend at the closest village and left for Avalon.

CHAPTER TWO

Nimue

Nimue cried in pain as they landed. Mordred caught her, but his grip was too tight on her injured arm. He shifted his arm to her waist, and she leaned in to him.

"We made it," Mordred mumbled, looking around.

Yes, they did, thank the gods. She hadn't had time to stop Mordred before he got them out of there. He had never been strong enough to travel through realms with his own magic before.

They stood on a dark pathway under trees so thick, the sunlight struggled to break through. In front of them was a moongate formed by trees, vines, and purple and blue flowers.

"Come." Mordred urged her through the gate. They stepped through and were instantly inside a dark marble castle. The walls were tall, decorated with vines, art, and a few statues. Minotaur guards lined the doorways and one grunted at them, smoke coming from his nose.

Nimue sighed, relief washing over her body. Home. The fae-lands. The air was so thick with magic, she could feel it on her skin like a spring mist. She took in a deep breath, letting the magic fill her lungs. The pain in her arm even faded a little.

"Her Majesty is awaiting you," the largest Minotaur said in a deep voice that reverberated around them. He beckoned them to follow, using his giant spear like a walking stick.

Fae of all kinds—small, large, winged, scaled, furry— passed by them in the corridors, and outside the windows shone a night sky with more stars than anyone could ever think to see in the human realms. Lights and galaxies shimmered over the mountains as if the sky itself was alive.

They were taken to a greenhouse, where the only occupant was busy pruning flowers. Her shimmering blue and purple hair tumbled down her back in loose curls, and she wore a simple black dress and thick gloves. Her gossamer wings were tucked down her back like a cape on her dress. Nimue had never seen her look so plain before.

"Your guests, Your Majesty." The Minotaur bowed.

"Thank you," she said, her voice like a whisper. The Mino-taur let out a soft growl before leaving them alone.

Queen Mab finally turned around, her shining teal eyes in-stantly falling on Nimue's shoulder. She hissed and glided across the room, yanking the gloves off to reveal silvery gray skin, that glimmered in the moonlight. She took hold of Nimue's arm, causing Nimue to grimace as pain shot up through her arm. Nimue grimaced as pain shot up through her arm. Mab's berry lips pursed as she carefully pulled away the neckline of Nimue's tunic.

"The brat of a princess stabbed me," Nimue growled.

"You should have healed by now," Mab whispered, her voice floating around the room. "But it would seem magic is taking its price. Your powers."

"Can you help?" Nimue asked.

"I can try," said Mab. "But first, let me congratulate you." Her eyes traveled to Mordred. "Taking a soul from Arawn is no easy task."

Nimue furrowed her eyebrows. "Mordred wasn't in the Underworld."

Mab raised an eyebrow at Mordred. Nimue followed Mab's gaze to Mordred, who was staring at Mab, his face blank.

"Mordred?" Nimue said.

"You had taken too long," he said, still not meeting her gaze. "I had moved on."

Nimue stepped away from him, heart racing. "No." She shook her head. "I took you from the In-Between. I cannot take a soul from Arawn. No one can."

"You did," said Mab. "And your friend was the trade."

Nimue shook her head again, not daring to believe Mab's words. Arawn would be furious. Nimue shuddered. Morgana was right. He would come for her. He would come for Mordred; he was the most powerful of all the gods. Nimue turned to Mordred, seeing him in a new light.

"How could you not tell me?" she hissed.

"I did not want you to worry." He reached for her, but Nimue jolted away from him.

"You lied," she hissed. "You lied to me!"

"I did not want to worry you—"

"Worry!" Nimue threw a potted plant at him, which he ducked. It shattered on the floor behind him. She cried out as her arm throbbed. "How dare you! You've marked us! You've doomed us both!"

She lunged at Mordred, tears spilling down her cheeks, but Mab held her back.

"You must not damage your arm further!" Mab scolded. "And Arawn is the least of your worries at the moment. Many of your allies have fled. Word has spread of what you have done."

"I didn't know!" Nimue screeched.

"Your love has blinded you Nimue," said Mab, her eyes flashing. "You have lost your allies. You cannot wage a war against Camelot now."

Nimue snarled at Mordred, a growl bubbling in her throat.

"We'll rebuild," he said. "Those that fled weren't loyal, anyway. It is good we know who we can trust now."

Nimue scoffed. "Do not talk of loyalty and trust."

Mordred's nostrils flared, his jaw clenched.

"Humans are simple," he continued, his voice slightly breaking. "We can use them. Agravaine, I'm sure, is itching for a reason to invade Briton."

Nimue snorted. Agravaine. The weakest of Morgause Pendragon's sons. A spoiled brat, only on the throne because his brothers did not want it. He was a snake. They could not trust him; he'd turned tail as soon as he realized Mordred was dead at Camlann. Cowardly bastard.

"Well, rebuilding will have to wait until Nimue is healed," Mab said. "She is not strong enough. I—wait." Mab let go of Nimue and sniffed at Mordred. "I smell something in you. It is not only your blood flowing through your veins. You smell of Pendragon. Of Merlin's old magic."

"Nimue used the boy Pendragon's blood," said Mordred.

Nimue sank down on a stool, cradling her arm to her chest. It was suddenly cold in the greenhouse.

"Yes, but it should not have—" Mab crossed over to a small firepit in the back corner. Mumbling under her breath, she tossed some herbs onto it and flames burst to life. Mab stared at them for a moment. "Your fate is now tied to his. If he dies, so do you. If he lives, so do you."

Nimue's heart dropped to her stomach. "What?" she gasped. "No! That cannot be right. I followed your instructions, Mab!"

"It was not supposed to happen," Mab said, her gaze not leaving Mordred. "What happened in the Underworld, Mordred?"

Mordred shrugged. "Nothing. I was merely there, like other dead souls, until I heard Nimue calling me. But let us speak of this another time. You are right, Mab. Nimue needs to heal."

"Arawn will come for you, though," Mab warned. "I am surprised he let you go in the first place."

"Arawn isn't as powerful as he used to be," said Mordred. "None of the gods are."

Mab raised an eyebrow. "Only a fool would believe that."

"I've seen him," said Mordred. "He grows weak. Magic is leaving, even in these realms."

Mab stared at Mordred for a long time. "You put us all in a dangerous situation," she said. "Arawn's wrath will extend to us once he finds out. You will not find many allies—humans or fae—if Arawn has marked you."

"The Underworld is dying," said Mordred. "Along with the Otherworld, with Avalon. With us. I know you can feel it too!"

"Yes, I know. I have felt it for decades!" Mab hissed.

Mordred glared at her, his lip upturning in a snarl.

"Leave me." Mab waved her hands at them. "I must think." She turned to Nimue. "And you must rest. I will call the best healers and witches to tend to you."

"What, I—"

"You are in no shape to do anything for a good long while," said Mab. "Rest here."

"Nimue"—Mordred took her hands in his—"you need to heal. We cannot claim our victory if you are not at your best."

Nimue snarled at him, but even that was weak. She would not forgive Mordred so easily, but unfortunately, he was right. She needed rest.

"Fine. Fine. We will rest."

Mordred kissed her hands. "Yes. Rest, my love. And then we shall have our glory."

CHAPTER THREE

MORDRED

Mordred waited until the full effects of the sleeping tonic had taken hold of Nimue before he slipped out of the bedroom. Mab had sent her best healer to escort them to a large bedroom that overlooked the mountains. The healer had gotten to work immediately and Mordred had stood back, letting the Dryad change the bandages. Nimue had reopened the wound when she threw that plant at him.

Nimue, at first, had refused the sleeping draft, but the healer was insistent that she needed to sleep so her body could recuperate. And that was perfect for Mordred. He had an errand to attend to.

He slipped as silently as he could down Mab's corridors, ignoring the Minotaur guards and fae that passed by.

He came to a small, deserted hallway and, after making sure there were no eyes to see him, he spun and disappeared. It was easy now to walk between worlds in the blink of an eye. While he had waited for Nimue, he had made good use of his time in the Underworld, for she *had* taken too long and his soul had passed to the dead. Arawn had been easy to fool. Between his weakened state and the dead coming in by the droves, Mordred had slipped into the god's personal library and taken just the thing he needed.

He had not planned to tell Nimue yet, of course, but Mab's loose lips had destroyed that notion. Idiot. Now there would be tension between him and Nimue. He'd lost her trust. He'd have to build it back, carefully.

With a rush of air into his lungs, Mordred appeared at the edge of a cliff, where waves crashed hard onto the rocks below. Gulls cried overhead and the smell of salt and fish filled the heavy air. The wind was bitterly cold, slapping across his face with mists of salt water. The moon was bright overhead, reflecting in the dark waters.

A castle fortress sat ahead, towering over the seaside. A castle Mordred should have known well, should have grown up in, running through its corridors as a young lad. But now blue banners flew with King Constantine's sigil.

A sneer pulled at his lips. He eyed the guards at the towers and turrets. None at the ground, and less than he expected. Good. Easier to take them all out.

Mordred made his way to the castle, climbing up the back wall and hoisting himself over the side. He crept toward a guard, and one hand around the man's neck was all it took for him to slump to the ground. Same for the other. He tossed their bodies off the battlement and hurried inside the other tower.

His footsteps were silent on the winding stone steps. The corridors were empty, cold, but thick with magic. An old, ancient magic. It filled Mordred, sending shivers through his limbs.

It smelled like his mother. Even after all these years, her presence lingered in the walls that rightfully belonged to her. To Mordred.

Footsteps echoed, and Mordred paused, listening. They grew louder, stopped, then a door creaked open and closed. Silence met his ears; whoever it was must have entered a room.

After a couple of turns, Mordred spied an old man in a heavy dressing gown and fur slippers.

He took his arm and whirled him around, covering his mouth with a hand and sticking a dagger to his throat.

"Where is Constantine?" he asked.

The man tried to scream behind Mordred's hand, but he dug the tip into his neck.

"Answer the question, old man." Mordred loosened the hand over his mouth.

"H-his chambers," the old man gasped.

Mordred pulled the dagger away and snapped the man's neck. He slumped to the ground and Mordred stepped over him.

Two guards stood outside of the king's chambers, and Mordred dispatched them quickly and silently. He pushed the door open and immediately felt the need to retch. The stench of drink and the odor of someone who had not washed in gods knew how long hit him like a brick. The room itself was a mess, with dirty dishes, clothing, an overturned desk, and books scattered about. Mordred yanked a handkerchief from his pouch and pressed it over his nose.

The king sat in a chair by the window, looking out at the sea. Constantine didn't even look back as Mordred stepped into the room and closed the door behind him. His hair was a mess and his clothing rumpled.

When Mordred approached the king, he spied a dagger in Constantine's hands.

"The taking of one's own life is a mortal sin," Constantine wheezed, still not looking at Mordred. "Doing so condemns one's soul to an eternity of torture and hellfire—of which I am already living. But do I endure it for the rest of my mortal life for a chance at salvation? Am I strong enough? Or do I rid myself of this pain on earth and hope that God will take mercy upon my soul?"

"You will not rid yourself of this earth," Mordred said. "I have need of you, cousin."

Constantine finally turned his head, and what color was left on his face drained.

"No," he whispered. "It cannot be."

Mordred grinned.

CHAPTER FOUR

MORGANA

Morgana had sworn she would never set foot in Avalon again after she and Vivienne had that fight. But here she was, on the shores of the lake once more. She felt like a young girl again, Vivienne at her side, waiting for her to open the veil for the first time. She stared out over the icy water, hugging herself against the cold that seeped through her heavy furs.

The pulse of magic was weak—faint, barely there. This place used to vibrate with magic, ready to burst through anyone who could wield it. It would wake up her senses and call her home. But now it felt tired, almost dead.

She stepped onto the sand and halted when a vision flashed in front of her eyes. *Blood soaked the sands. Mordred screamed with rage as he released a power beyond any fae. Gawaine and Percival fell, their eyes lifeless. A girl with striking red hair ran into the forest.*

Morgana fell to her knees, screaming out in pain. She had not had a vision in decades. A cold wind blew, and with it, the vision and pain faded. But the tears still streaked down her cheeks. Morgana pushed herself to her feet and, with a new determination, stepped into the biting water. She held out her hands, taking a deep breath, trying to feel any ounce of magic. She called to the mists, asking to let her pass, but the mists only grew stronger, the water colder. An icy wind bit through the air and Morgana leaped out of the water, her feet burning from the cold.

"Vivienne?" she called, her voice echoing. "Vivienne, can you hear me? What has happened?" Her voice bounced around the trees and rocks. She waited, but nothing happened. Heartbroken, she turned to leave. But the wind shifted direction and a small boat glided to the shore, with a lone figure in it that Morgana immediately recognized. A female fae with small antlers, dark brown hair, tawny skin, and bright brown eyes. Relief washed over Morgana.

"Eilonwy?" she asked. "Is it you?"

Eilonwy held a finger to her lips and held out her other hand. She pulled Morgana into the boat where a warming sensation fell over her. Her clothes dried and her fingers tingled.

"What—"

"We will speak at the Isle," Eilonwy said, and the boat moved on its own toward Avalon.

The journey was not as Morgana remembered. The mist was thick and lingered. Before, the mists would roll away and the Isle would greet her with its song and beauty as the boat sailed smoothly through the crystal waters. But now, Morgana could barely see in front of her. She kept silent on the ride, as Eilonwy didn't even glance back at her.

Only when the boat bumped into the Isle's shore did she know they had arrived. It was dark, and a chill hung in the air. Warmer than back at Glastonbury's edge, but still cold. The trees had lost their leaves, reflecting an ugly winter's day. No snow shimmered on the ground. Just cold, dead earth.

The private lodgings of the priestesses were dark and covered to keep out the cold and trap heat within. The temples and statues of the gods were barely noticeable. It was silent. Not even a song from a bird, or chirping from squirrels. Despite this, Morgana felt a sense of coming home.

Eilonwy took Morgana to the very center of the Isle, to Vivienne's own temple, where fires were lit in all the hearths and heavy woolen blankets covered the windows. All the priestesses stood guard around the temple, dressed not in their blue robes, but in armor and weapons. The breath left Morgana's lungs. Avalon had been a sanctuary, a haven, the safest point where the realms met. And now destruction had taken hold. It caused her physical pain. She had forgotten her attachment to this land.

A priestess with hair and skin the same golden color sniffed at Morgana and patted her down.

"Migina, you know me," said Morgana.

"I thought I knew Nimue," she growled and stared into Morgana's eyes for a long time. "We can trust her."

"I know," Eilonwy said. "I would not have brought her here otherwise."

Eilonwy beckoned for Morgana to follow her. Migina stayed close behind her, weaving through the pillars and statues and under the curtains and fabric that hung on the doorways until they came to Vivienne's private quarters. It was a faint, bittersweet shadow of how Morgana remembered it. All the plant life that Vivienne loved to surround herself with was withered and dried.

Vivienne lay on the bed, her skin dull and pale. Her hair stuck to her forehead, but her eyes were open. She turned to them as they entered, her eyes widening as her gaze fell on Morgana.

Eilonwy bowed her head. "It is good to see you awake again, sister."

A small smile formed on Vivienne's lips. "Thank you, Eilonwy." Vivienne's gaze landed on Morgana again and she reached out a hand. Morgana immediately went to her, falling on her knees beside the bed and bowing her head over Vivienne's hand.

"I am so sorry, Vivienne." Morgana's shoulders shook. She couldn't contain her tears any longer.

"I felt you coming," Vivienne said, petting Morgana's hair. "You are troubled."

"Mordred and Nimue just left my house. It is all my fault," said Morgana. "If I had been here sooner, if I hadn't—"

"No," said Vivienne. "We cannot battle the past and the future. We must be in the present. Your choices have all been made because you thought they were the right ones. That is all that matters."

"Vivienne, Nimue has done something."

"I know," said Vivienne. "She killed Alfdis and Creiddylad. I had to use most of my power to seal Avalon from her."

"Is that why the island is…?" Morgana trailed off, not capable of speaking the words.

"Yes. I gave all power to the protection wards," said Vivienne. She pushed herself to a seated position and held out her hands to Morgana.

"How can I help?"

Vivienne smiled at her. "Oh, my little raven. As happy as I am to see you home, your destiny does not lie in Avalon."

"What?"

"You must go to Camelot," said Vivienne. "Your fate lies there."

"Camelot?" Morgana said. "Vivienne, you know how I left."

"Yes," Vivienne said. "It is time you stopped hiding, Morgana. Your family needs you."

"My family," Morgana whispered, choking up.

Vivienne put a hand on her cheek before she lost herself to memories.

"Mordred is coming for Anwil," Vivienne said. "He will need your guidance."

"I do not think I am strong enough," Morgana said.

"Have faith in yourself," Vivienne told her. "I know it is a hard task I ask of you. Mordred is your son."

Morgana shook her head. "My son is dead," she whispered. "The longer his soul is here in the world of the living, the more the balance shifts."

"I feel it too," said Vivienne. "You must rest before you go. Stay a night or two, but then you must go to Camelot."

"Vivienne, I—" Morgana cut herself off, ashamed. "I do not know if—if I can still use my powers. It's been so long."

Vivienne put a hand on her cheek. "I see you are weary in mind and body," she said quietly. "I see now you must stay awhile and rebuild your strength."

"Thank you," Morgana said.

"But do not lose your way," Vivienne said, her voice growing hard. "Your nephew needs you. I fear he may not have much time."

"What do you mean?"

"Nimue used his blood in her spell," Vivienne said. "Used it to reawaken Mordred. There is something between them now that ties them together. I do not know what, but it pulls at Anwil. Weakening him."

"What?"

Vivienne's hand slipped from Morgana's face and she shook her head, closing her eyes.

"I cannot See as well anymore," Vivienne said. "Their fate lies in shadow. But it must be *you* who guides Anwil and Ariadne to their destiny."

"I do not even know where to begin." Morgana hung her head, resting her forehead on Vivienne's hands.

"When you go to Camelot," said Vivienne, "find Merlin's study. He hid away some books in his study of forbidden and long forgotten magics. You may find something there to break this tie between Mordred and Anwil."

Morgana stiffened. She had a complicated relationship with the old wizard.

"Merlin is not there," Vivienne said with a knowing look. "Nimue has gotten to him, too."

"He's dead?" Morgana gasped.

Vivienne shook her head, her eyes sad. "No. But his mind is lost. He lives with the goddess Ceridwen now. His grandmother."

Morgana let out a breath. "I am sorry, Vivienne. I know you loved him."

Vivienne brushed stray hair from Morgana's face. "My dear girl," she said softly. "I am glad you returned to us. If the Pendragons do not sit on the throne, I fear magic will be lost to this world. They are the last tie between humans and fae."

Morgana squeezed her eyes shut, her mind racing.

"I will do my best," Morgana whispered. "But I have not used my magic in so long. I fear I have lost it."

Vivienne lifted Morgana's head. "It is still there," she said. "We will help you find it again."

"Thank you, Vivienne."

"Get some rest, my raven," said Vivienne. "We have much work to do."

CHAPTER FIVE

ANWIL

Anwil stared at himself in the full-length mirror and felt like an impostor. The full weight of the coronation regalia crashed down upon him. The red velvet cloak was heavy on his neck, even though the gold chain that held it together was pinned neatly to his scarlet tunic. A two-day celebration awaited to crown him High King of Briton. But Anwil didn't feel like celebrating. They had just buried those closest to him not two months ago. His wife, mother, father figure, friend.

He turned away from the mirror before he gave in to the urge to throw it to the ground and watch it shatter into a thousand pieces. Anwil stared around his chambers—the king's chambers. The servants had cleared away all traces of Yvanne, and he was all alone in these large rooms. She should have been here next to him in a radiant gold gown, shimmering like the sun itself. But she was buried in the cold earth, her body wasting away.

He left his chambers to find Lohengrin waiting for him in the cold hallway. Lohengrin looked exhausted as well. Both he and Anwil had many late nights the past month, working on tightening the security and safety around the castle and the city. He and Lohengrin were similar in that they threw themselves into work to stay busy. To keep the grief of their losses at bay, if but for a moment.

"Let's get this over with," Anwil mumbled, slipping his gloves on. The corridors were always cold in the winter months, no matter how many fires they lit, but now they felt frozen, as if all the heat from the surfaces had been sucked away.

Lohengrin merely nodded, and guards trailed behind them as they made their way down into the castle proper. The corridors were empty of people save for the guards at nearly every entry-way.

They stopped at the great hall's doors, guarded by two men with spears on either side. They bowed and Lohengrin turned to Anwil.

"By your leave," he said, bowing.

Anwil nodded, and the two guards opened the doors. Before Anwil could even breathe, trumpets blared. The Knights of the Round Table were waiting for him just inside the doors, all wearing matching red and gold tunics and shining maille. Anwil stepped into the hall and took his place in front of them.

Nobles and peasants alike were packed into the annex, shoulder to shoulder, standing on either side of a red velvet carpet that stretched up to the dais where the Druid High Council and the Priests of Glastonbury waited.

Anwil took in a deep breath and slowly made his way down the aisle. He kept his eyes on the Pendragon banners that hung on the wall behind the priests. Trumpets blared again as Anwil kneeled on the gold pillow in front of the dais.

"Anwil Pendragon," Lord Dafydd, the new Druid chieftain, boomed throughout the hall. "Do you solemnly swear to protect all people—human and fae alike—of Briton and uphold chivalry and justice?"

"I do so solemnly swear," Anwil repeated.

"And do you, Anwil Pendragon," Father Bowen said, "solemnly swear to uphold all the religions of this land so that we may coexist in peace and prosperity?"

"I do so solemnly swear," said Anwil.

The priests and Druids each recited a prayer, and both Dafydd and Father Bowen placed the heavy golden crown on Anwil's head. Anwil got to his feet and pulled the ceremonial sword from his scabbard. Dafydd took the sword and handed Anwil Excalibur. Father Bowen handed Anwil a heavy wooden cross. Two powerful symbols of equal measure in Briton. Excalibur hummed in his hand and he could hear it ringing in his ears. He slowly turned to face the crowd.

As one, the crowd kneeled.

"All hail the king!" Lord Roland called out.

"All hail the king!" the crowd repeated after him.

Anwil bowed to the crowd, a tradition Arthur had started. A king serves his people. Anwil recited the speech he had written, swearing to be merciful and just, and to protect the lands. He spoke the words without hearing them and thought it felt too rehearsed and canned, but the crowd burst into thunderous applause anyway.

Anwil let the clapping die down and turned to his gathered knights. He caught Lohengrin's eye and nodded. Lohengrin took Ariadne's hand, escorting her toward the dais. Anwil handed the cross back to Father Bowen as Ariadne stepped in front of him. She looked at him curiously. This had not been done in the rehearsal, but Anwil had been planning it for some time.

"Kneel, sister," Anwil said, and Ariadne looked even more confused. But she picked up the heavy skirts of her red and gold damask gown and knelt on the golden pillows.

Anwil held out Excalibur. A small gasp echoed around the hall.

"Ariadne Pendragon," Anwil said. "Daughter of Guinevere and Arthur and princess of Camelot and Briton; for your bravery and your heart, I, King Anwil Pendragon, High King of Briton, do knight thee with a seat at the Round Table." Anwil tapped her lightly on each shoulder with the blade. "You shall henceforth be known as Dame Ariadne Pendragon, Knight of the Round Table."

Anwil sheathed Excalibur and held out his hand to Ariadne. Her eyes glistened with tears as she took his hand to echoing applause. Anwil smiled at her, his first one in a long time. But his sister deserved this. She'd fought to rescue him: fought against Nimue and dealt the killing blow to the traitorous Cerdic and Bors. She had proved herself more than worthy of the title and honor.

Ariadne crossed a fist over her heart and said, in a slightly shaking voice, "My sword is yours. I vow to protect the kingdom and maintain justice. I will show mercy and compassion and uphold honor. As long as I draw breath, this will be my vow."

Anwil bowed his head and gestured for her to take her place with the knights. Ariadne curtsied low and stood with the other Knights of the Round Table, who all congratulated her.

Anwil stepped up onto the dais and turned to the crowd. Lord Roland led them in a chant. *"Long Live the King!"*

In a daze, Anwil stood at the drink table and watched the crowd. He had just finished a round of dancing with the fourth young noblewoman thrust at him by overbearing mothers, and he had finally made his way away for a moment. The crowd was joyous, laughing, dancing, and drinking. As if they hadn't just come out of an entire season's worth of catastrophes.

Someone tapped Anwil's shoulder and he looked up from his empty drink to see Lady Ellyn pouring herself one.

"You all right?" she asked, turning to him.

"Fine," he mumbled.

But Ellyn gave him a knowing look. "Well, I can't speak for your mother, but I did know Sir Percival well." She plucked his goblet from his hand and refilled it. "And I know he would want us to find some joy in the darkness. He told that to Lohengrin when Ulrich and Gaheris passed. Think of this as more of a slap in the face to Nimue. As hard as she tried, she failed. You still became king, which is what they all fought for. We are still here to live and celebrate our lives."

She handed him back his drink, and he smiled at her.

"I suppose you're right," he said, though he was unsure if he could heed her words. "Lohengrin is lucky to have you, you know."

"Damn right I am," Lohengrin appeared behind her and kissed her hair. Ellyn's smile brightened as he slipped his hands around her waist.

"To our loved ones who cannot be here with us tonight." Ellyn raised her goblet, and they followed. "May they live forever in our hearts and memories."

Anwil gulped down the mulled wine. It warmed his insides, a pleasant feeling even though the great hall was warm from the bodies and the fire roaring in the hearth.

"Another mother and her daughter coming up behind you," Lohengrin said, glancing over his shoulder.

Anwil held back a groan. He did not wish to dance anymore.

"Your Grace," Ellyn said loudly and slid her arm through Anwil's. "My mother is hoping to update you on the hounds she's been training."

"Please," Anwil said and gave a nod to the disappointed mother and daughter as they passed.

Ellyn led Anwil over to Lady Tessa and spoke about how she was training dogs to help soothe the injured. It was rather fascinating and Anwil was hoping to learn more, but Lord Leontius, the ambassador from Byzantium, found him soon afterward. Anwil was grateful to hear that the Byzantium king still wished to uphold their new alliance.

On his way back to the Table, Lady Laudine caught him and told a story of how Merlin once turned another wizard into a toad. Anwil wasn't sure if she had made that up or not.

Ellyn, thankfully, was able to pull Anwil away before Lady Laudine fully launched into another tale—this time about a lion and a Scottish church harper. Anwil mumbled a thank you to Ellyn, as Lohengrin had been roped into a debate with King Elyion and Sir Xiang.

"Don't thank me just yet." Ellyn subtly nodded to something over his shoulder. A rather large group of young ladies of the court had gathered with their mothers or fathers, eyeing him.

"I can't avoid them forever," he said.

One by one, Ellyn introduced them all, knowing all by name and title. Anwil greeted each one. He kept himself polite, but aloof. He was not ready to replace Yvanne yet. It had only been two months since her funeral. The hurt was still fresh, and propriety dictated at least six months before he even thought about another marriage.

"You have your pick of the litter and yet you dismiss them all," a voice behind him said as Anwil turned away from the small crowd. His cousin, Gingalain, was sipping from his goblet, watching the group of ladies finally disperse. Ellyn excused herself with a quick, but hard look at Gingalain, and hurried off.

"Beg pardon?" Anwil said.

"The most eligible and beautiful women of the kingdom are throwing themselves at your feet," said Gingalain. "And you have no interest. If I were you, I'd take my time getting to know *each* and *every* one of them."

"Now is not the time, cousin," said Anwil.

"Now is the perfect time," Gingalain clapped him on the shoulder. "You can choose any of them, or even all of them! You're the king. Even after you get married, you can have your pick. No one can tell you no."

Anwil shoved Gingalain's arm off his shoulder. "That isn't how it works."

Gingalain scoffed and rolled his eyes, but Anwil was done with him. He excused himself and made his way back to the high table, where Lancelot was now sitting.

"Everything all right?" Lancelot asked.

"Fine," said Anwil, sliding into his chair. But Anwil didn't get to enjoy much of the reprieve the high table gave him. Mirah was making her way toward him, her red and gold dress fanning out behind her as she nearly ran toward the high table.

She stopped to bow before approaching.

"Anwil," Mirah pleaded quietly, "*please* dance with me. Lady Laudine wants to show me a rash on her feet."

Lancelot barked a laugh as Anwil pulled a face and hurriedly got up.

"Gladly," he said, taking her hand and weaving through bodies to the dance floor.

Anwil wasn't much of a dancer, but with Mirah, he had never felt that his dancing shortcomings were an issue. He felt an ease with her he didn't feel with anyone else. Except perhaps with Yvanne.

Anwil would never forget how the dagger sliced through her neck and the wave of crimson that fell down her body as she slumped to the ground. Nor forget the scream of agony that had released from her father, King Constantine. Anwil had sworn his heart had stopped beating that day.

As the minstrels started a new song, Anwil remembered Yvanne on their wedding day. Her bright smile and infectious laugh as she guided him through the steps and didn't mind when he stepped on her foot. She had been radiant. He remembered the blues and golds of her eyes glittering like the morning sun on water.

"No, you go under this time!" Mirah's voice broke through the noise and thoughts in his head and he ducked under her arm.

Mirah laughed and spun back to him and despite the swirling thoughts in his head, Anwil smiled too.

When they switched partners and his sister spun toward him, she gave his hand their familiar squeeze before she spun away again and Mirah was back in his arms, her brown eyes shining up at him.

CHAPTER SIX

ARIADNE

Ariadne slumped down at the high table, breathing hard. She had finally made herself free of the dance floor after Mirah had pulled her in for what was supposed to have been one dance that turned into three.

Ariadne poured herself a goblet of mulled wine. She couldn't get the day's events out of her mind. She was knighted. A knight. A Knight of the Round Table. The only thing she had ever wanted in life, all she had worked for. And now that she had it, it almost felt empty. As if she didn't deserve it, didn't earn it. She had led Gawaine, Lyrion, and Percival to their deaths. Their blood was on her hands, and it would never wash off. And yet, she also found herself free. Free to seek revenge.

Laughter echoed, and Ariadne blinked. The roar of celebration of Anwil's coronation came rushing back to her. It was also Yule, which used to be one of Ariadne's favorite holidays. Yuletide had always been a mass celebration that lasted a full week in Camelot, a tradition that had begun not long into

Arthur's reign. Guinevere had loved Yuletide and made every single one special when Ariadne and Anwil were children.

Hollies, berries, and green garlands lined the hall along with the Pendragon banners. Pies lined one full table, but were already half-eaten. A wine fountain stood at the far end of the hall, and candied fruits were scattered about the tables. The smell was so sweet, but mixed with the wine and sweat from the guests, it made Ariadne's stomach turn.

She leaned back in her chair. She was not alone at the high table, but it was nearly empty. Anwil was still out on the floor, dancing with Mirah, and...laughing. She hadn't seen him laugh in months. Ariadne hadn't laughed since then, either. Another roar of laughter washed toward her, and Ariadne's chest tightened, twisting. All around the hall, people were smiling and laughing. As if they were mocking her. Mocking the dead. Her blood boiled.

"If you grip that goblet any harder, it might crack."

Ariadne jumped at the sound of Lancelot's voice next to her ear. He had moved, and was sitting next to her now, watching her carefully. He had kept a close eye on both her and Anwil since returning with them.

"Are you well?" he asked.

"Fine," she answered, placing the goblet onto the table as gently as possible. The entire court had fawned over Sir Lancelot when he arrived. The legendary Sir Lancelot, greatest of the Knights of the Round Table, returned to Camelot after twenty-five years. But Ariadne wasn't sure what to make of him. And she very much did not wish to speak to him right now.

"Your brother—"

"If you say how much he reminds you of Arthur, please spare it," said Ariadne, glaring at her cup. "We've heard enough of that all our lives."

Lancelot raised an eyebrow. "I was going to say he did well today. As did you."

"I didn't do anything." She also did not need his approval, but she kept that to herself.

"You did, though," said Lancelot, pouring himself wine. "You accepted the knighthood with grace and stood by his side. That sent a message, loud and clear."

"What message?"

"Loyalty," said Lancelot. "And strength. Which is exactly what Camelot needs to show at the moment. It was well done."

Ariadne didn't know how to reply to that, so she said nothing.

"I know you care little for me," said Lancelot, and that made Ariadne look at him. "But you have my word that I will do all that I can to help and protect you and your brother."

Ariadne stared at him, and he held her gaze. His eyes were the fiercest blue. They reminded her of Mordred's. Ariadne turned away from him.

Lancelot sighed and left the table to mingle in the crowd. She stayed at the table for a few more moments, watching the crowd again. The dancing had stopped, the musicians taking a break, but the crowd broke up into smaller groups, still laughing and talking and drinking, and eating. Ariadne had had enough. She downed the rest of her wine and made her way through the crowd to Anwil, who was with Mirah, talking to King Elyion. More laughing.

Ariadne needed air. She tore from the great hall and into the cold corridors. The guards had the decency not to approach her as she leaned against the cool stone of the wall and took a few deep breaths.

"Escaping as well, I see?"

Ariadne jumped at the voice. Sitting on the bench below her was Lady Laudine. Ariadne hadn't seen her in the shadows. She was bundled with furs and rested her hands on her cane.

"It was rather stuffy in there for me," said the older woman. "And that is saying something. Come. Sit."

Lady Laudine patted the spot next to her, and Ariadne knew better than to make an excuse. The last time she did, Lady Laudine had rapped her ankles with her cane.

"What brings you out here?" Lady Laudine asked.

"It was stuffy," Ariadne said with a slight smirk.

Lady Laudine gave her a look. "I may be old, Your Highness, but I am not stupid. Come, tell me. I do have some wisdom that comes with near eighty years of age. Perhaps I can apply some of it to you."

Ariadne hesitated. "They're all dead," she said quietly after a few moments. "It's only been two months and we're expected to move on like it never happened. To smile and work and just…replace them."

Ariadne sniffed, feeling the sting of tears warm her eyes. Lady Laudine handed her a handkerchief.

"Yes," said Lady Laudine. "The world does not stop for anyone. Especially for royalty. We must be better than letting ourselves be consumed with silly human emotions like grief. At least, that is how it feels, is it not?"

Ariadne nodded, surprised at how accurately Lady Laudine described her turmoil.

"But no one expects you to forget," Lady Laudine continued. "You lost quite a few pieces of your heart, and that is no little thing. While it is harder in this world for a woman to show her emotions, no one is expecting you to move on and forget so quickly, my dear. While a coronation needed to be rushed, your grief does not."

Ariadne hurriedly wiped at the tears on her cheeks.

"And I'll let you in on a secret," said Lady Laudine, leaning toward her. "Having a good day or something to smile about is not a forgetfulness of those we have lost. In fact, quite the opposite."

Ariadne tilted her head in question.

"She raised you and your brother, did she not?" Lady Laudine said with a small shrug. "She prepared Anwil for this day, as she did for you. That is what mothers do. We help nurture our children into who they are meant to become. And now Anwil is king and you are a Knight of the Round Table. Celebrate tonight by honoring her accomplishments in you. And I know Sir Gawaine would be the loudest amongst those cheering for your knighthood. In fact, now that he is gone, I have no guilt for admitting he would be a blubbering mess. He really was soft at heart, you know, especially when it came to his children. And you and Anwil were as good as. So, cry it out a moment, Your Highness, and get back in there. They would not want you sulking all night in the corridors with an old woman like me. "

Ariadne was silent. She had never expected Lady Laudine, of all people, to be right.

"Thank you," Ariadne said, handing her handkerchief back. "Truly."

Lady Laudine waved her hand. "If you see Treven, send him out for me. He's being paid far too much to enjoy himself tonight."

Ariadne composed herself a moment more and re-entered the Hall. Music and the rumble of voices hit her as soon as the door opened, but now the night seemed less daunting.

CHAPTER SEVEN

MIRAH

The first lesson Mirah's mother, Nazrine, had taught her about being a healer was that it was impossible to save everyone. Sometimes, no matter what one did, no matter what magic or remedies were used, a life would fade away. However, no matter how often Mirah reminded herself, it did not make it hurt less. But she had perfected the art of putting on a strong face for all who came through the infirmary doors.

She had become a healer because she enjoyed helping people and was fascinated by the human body. How it worked, how it ailed, and how she could make it better. Healing was in her blood. So she let herself mourn a few days before picking herself back up and getting back to work.

"Make sure you take a spoonful three times a day," Mirah said to her most recent patient and last of the day, the youngest son of Lord Garanwyn. "And no traveling home until you are well. Tell your father that is Mirah's orders."

"Yes, my lady. Thank you," the boy said, pocketing the vial of tonic and shuffling out of the infirmary.

After recording the visit into her log book and cleaning up, Mirah was the last to leave the infirmary. Master Cassius had left hours earlier, as had most of the other apprentices. She had stayed behind and was doing more research when the young noble boy wandered in. She didn't mind. It took her away from the roadblock she had hit with her notes.

"You should be in bed." A voice startled her, and Mirah whirled around in the dark corridor.

"As should you," she told the figure.

Lohengrin approached her, the candle in his hand making it seem as if his hair was aglow.

"I couldn't sleep," he said. "So, I thought a walk might help."

"Do you want a sleep tonic?"

"Thank you," he said. "But honestly, they make me feel terrible in the mornings, like I've had too much to drink the night before."

Mirah grimaced. "I know; I'm sorry. I'm still working on that side effect. Perhaps some valerian root tea, instead?"

"Can I counteroffer escorting you to your chambers?" Lohengrin said, smiling. "You know, I did put orders out that no one was to be alone in the corridors at night."

Mirah bit her lip. "Sorry. I had some late patients."

Lohengrin eyed her but offered his arm.

"Between you and those Pendragons, sometimes I think I'm going to have an aneurism," he grumbled as she took his arm.

Mirah bit her lip to hide her laugh. "Was Ariadne caught sneaking into the kitchens again?"

"Anwil in the library," he answered.

"No surprise there," she said. "I must say, though, a trip to the kitchens sounds tempting. I could go for some of that blackberry pie the cook made…"

Lohengrin shot her a look, and she laughed.

"I'm surprised there's any left," he said as they turned a corner. "Seeing as how I caught people nearly fighting over it at the reception feast."

"I think Cook saved some just for her few favorites."

"You mean Ari and Anwil?"

"I might have asked her to bake an extra or two." Mirah grinned. "It's *my* favorite."

Lohengrin shook his head, but a smile played at his lips.

"Don't judge." She nudged him with her shoulder. "It's a good treat after a long day."

"I can't argue that," he said.

"How is your wedding planning coming along?" Mirah asked cautiously. It was a sore subject for him and Ellyn as of late.

"Fine," he said stiffly. "We picked a new date. The Summer Solstice."

"Oh, the veils are thin on the solstices. You could make an offering to Arawn in honor of your father and brother," she suggested carefully.

He swallowed. "Yes," he said quietly. "We plan to."

Mirah halted her steps and took Lohengrin's arm. "Lo—"

He shook his head. They had reached Mirah's door.

She sighed and gave his arm a gentle squeeze. "Try to get some sleep, yes?"

"You first," Lohengrin said, and they bid each other good-night.

Mirah entered her chambers to find a fire roaring in the hearth. She would have to thank her maid in the morning. She dropped her bag on her writing desk and hurried into the washroom, wanting to sleep for days.

But her sleep was interrupted.

Flashes of a woman, a priestess, judging by the color of her eyes.

A crown sat on the king's chair, broken in half.

Ariadne on a battlefield, bloody and bruised, reached for a bloody axe.

Anwil, but his eyes were a cold, piercing blue.

Camelot burned.

The Round Table cracked in half.

Mirah jerked awake, her curls plastered to her face with sweat.

The fire had burned down and judging by the moonlight pouring through her window, it was well past midnight. She reached for the journal on her nightstand and scribbled down what she had dreamed. Once she finished, she padded to the small table in the corner and poured herself a cup of water, gulping it down and willing her heart to slow.

She threw another log onto the fire and poked at it, just for something to do with her shaking hands. After the fire roared back to life, Mirah picked up the journal and read through what she had written. She was sure this had been some sort of vision, as her dreams had never felt so real, so horrifying before.

How she wished Merlin was around, if he was even still alive. No one had been able to find him, not even after Anwil had told them what he had heard Nimue say. Merlin was gone.

Mirah would have to talk to her father or aunt, Anipe. She didn't want to do either, however, as her father had been overprotective lately. He had been going back and forth over Mirah returning to their family estate, Evanshire. Whether it would be safer for Mirah to be outside Camelot or inside the city with all the guards and wards.

But if Mirah told him this, he would surely order her back to Evanshire, and she did not wish to go. Camelot was her home.

If she told her aunt, Anipe would surely tell Jabir.

Mirah sighed and tossed the journal back down and crawled into bed, throwing the covers over her face and curling against one of her pillows, groaning.

CHAPTER EIGHT

CONNOR

Sweat dripped down his forehead despite the chill in the air. Bodies littered the surrounding ground, lying atop blood-stained snow and mud. Connor kneeled, listening—waiting. Even his breath was quiet. And then he heard it. Faint pounding on the earth.

He shot up, twisting around and swinging his axe through the invader who had tried to sneak up on him. The blade embedded itself in the invader's chest, and Connor yanked it out with a kick to the man's pelvis. The man's body tumbled to the ground as his friends roared and came after Connor. Bradán and Domhnall were immediately at his side, fighting off any who dared come near.

They had been chasing these invaders for days, always a few hours behind, finding village after village burned to the ground. The Irish were a warrior people, strong and formidable, but whoever these invaders were... to slaughter Connor's people in mere hours... He gave orders to his soldiers to show no mercy.

Connor stabbed the handle of his axe straight into the face of a man charging at him and then swiped at his legs with the blade, cutting him off at the knees.

Grainne, his second-in-command, ran her sword through the throat of another man who tried to sneak up on Connor. He nodded his thanks to her and looked around. The invaders were finally dwindling. His soldiers—what was left of them—were rounding up the ones still alive, or putting them out of their misery.

Grainne shoved another man to his knees in front of Connor. Her white-blonde hair was soaked red with blood and mud splattered across her face. The invader glared up at Connor and growled in a language Connor didn't understand. He must have been a lord, as his furs, bloody as they were, were fine, and he wore bright colors under his cloak, and jewelry. His hair was long, dotted with beads and small braids.

"Don't think any of them speak Irish or even Latin," said Grainne, her voice rough. "They're not Britons or Picts."

"Who are you?" Connor tried in Latin.

The man said nothing. He repeated the question again in Breton. Nothing.

"Kill him with the rest," Connor told Grainne and went to find his uncle.

The large man was sitting on a boulder, drinking from his waterskin, the battle winding down.

"Any survivors from the villages?" he asked Garbhan.

"Mostly women and children," Garbhan grunted, wiping his bald head with a rag he pulled from his belt. "But they're either injured or terrified. Or both."

"We'll take them with us," Connor said. "We can't leave them here on their own. I'll have Lady Éabha gather her men and start on rebuilding the villages when spring comes."

Three whole villages had burned to the ground thanks to whoever these gods damned foreign invaders were. And whoever they were, Connor was going to find out.

Garbhan just grunted in response.

"Do you have any idea who they are?"

His uncle shrugged. "No. Never heard their language before."

Connor kneeled down next to one of the dead invaders and yanked off the pendant around his neck. It was an odd-looking hammer with swirls and strange runes.

"Sink all their ships. I don't want any chance of survivors sailing back and bringing reinforcements."

Garbhan gave another grunt, and Connor left him to find his cousins, Bradán and Domhnall. They were talking to an older woman, her lip bloody and her eye turning purple. Her brown hair had fallen from its braid and she clutched a shawl over her shoulders. Her jewelry indicated she was a clan leader.

"Mistress Aoife," said Domhnall, when Connor approached. "Of Clan O'Neill. Her husband died in the raids."

"I'm sorry, mistress," said Connor. "We'll send help to rebuild the villages."

"Did you kill them?" she growled.

"Aye."

"Good." She held her chin out. "Too old to fight, myself. As was my husband. Stubborn mule that he was, though. Tried to fight. Always told him that bad knee would be the death of him."

She sniffed, trying hard to keep her tears from falling. Connor put a gentle hand on her elbow.

"Any survivors who wish to come with us back to Teamhair na Ri, they can," he told her.

"Thank you, Prince Connor," she said gently. "But if it's all the same to you, I was born here and I will die here. We'll take back what we can from their bodies and then burn them. Gods know they've taken enough gold. You make sure you make any survivors pay, you hear me?"

A smile tugged at Connor's mouth. "Aye, mistress."

Mistress Aoife gave a stern nod and turned back to her village, beckoning at a young child.

"Have we gotten any more information?" Connor asked hours later as they settled down for camp. He, Bradán, Domhnall, and Grainne huddled around a large fire with a few others, eating a bit of bland but hot soup and dried meat.

"One of them spoke a bit of Latin," said Rory, a young soldier. "Got a few words. Came from east of the north, past Lothian."

"Norsemen," Garbhan growled, plopping hard on the log across from Connor. "They're known invaders, apparently. Found a lad they took as a slave when they pillaged Lothian."

"How'd it go there?" Grainne asked.

"Not well for them," Garbhan answered. "Agravaine chased them away pretty quick. So, they came here. Lad knew little else."

"What were their numbers? Did they lose many before coming here?"

"The lad didn't know," Garbhan snapped at her. "Do I need to keep repeating myself?"

Grainne made a rude gesture at him, and Rory sniggered. Garbhan shifted his flare to Rory, who ducked his head, finishing his food.

"I'll send a letter to Lothian," Connor said before a fight could break out between them. "See if they're willing to give any information."

Garbhan snorted. "Good luck. King Agravaine's a right ol' bastard."

"Aye, well, so are you." Connor finished the last of his soup and left the fire before Garbhan could make any retorts. He'd pay for that line later, but Connor was not in the mood for his uncle.

He stepped over dead bodies and fallen weapons all the way to the infirmary tent where his older sister, Muirne, was working on wrapping a soldier's arm. Only a quarter of his fighters were left, and Connor worried most of them wouldn't survive the journey back home. A small fire burned in the tent, the smoke drifting straight through the small hole in the top. Kettles of water sat around it, and injured soldiers occupied the few cots..

The soldier Muirne was working on tried to stand as Connor came in, but Muirne stopped him.

"I said don't move," she snapped at him.

The soldier looked down, his cheeks flushing.

"It's all right, lad," Connor said to him. He crossed the tent and poured warm water from the kettle by the fire into an empty basin and wiped his face off. Other healer-priestesses from Muirne's order were helping the other injured.

"How are you faring?" Muirne asked Connor as she carefully tied the bandage on the soldier's arm.

Connor didn't answer her as he dried off his face.

"Connor," said Muirne. "Talk to me."

He glanced at her patient, and she tapped the soldier lightly on the shoulder. "You're good to go. Make sure you keep that wound clean or else infection will set in."

"Aye, Your Highness," he said to her and bowed before scurrying out of the tent.

Connor sank down on the log the soldier had been using. "We lost so many," he said, his voice breaking. "If I would have just—"

"No," Murine said sternly. "Don't do that. You did the best you could. No one expects this in winter. I'm surprised their ships even made it through the waters in this weather."

Connor hung his head, running a hand through his hair. "Father's going to be livid."

"Aye, most likely," Muirne agreed. "But let me handle Father this time."

"No, this is on me," Connor said, standing up. "I failed to get our forces here in time. And now three villages are gone. It's my damned fault."

"If you would have left during that snowstorm, none of you would have made it," Murine said, her eyes flashing.

"I need a drink," Connor grumbled.

Muirne rolled her eyes but shoved a flask in his hand. Connor drank all of it. The liquid burned his throat, but he didn't care. He needed to feel something.

"Easy, brother. You'll need your wits about you." She snatched the now empty flask from his hand.

But Connor didn't want his wits about him. He wanted to forget the hell he had just seen.

"We set up a larger tent just past the hill for the mortally wounded, to ease their passing. Come. They need you."

Connor silently asked The Dagda for strength to get through the night and followed his sister to his fallen warriors.

CHAPTER NINE

ARIADNE

The days passed slowly, heavily, as if trudging through water. Some days, Ariadne burned hot, wanting to plunge her sword through anyone who moved, and other days she just sat and stared at nothing, her eyes raw and depleted of tears. Winter came with heavy snow and violent winds and sleet, as if the gods were angry too.

No one could do anything but sit in the castle and wait for warmer weather. Merlin's mirrors had been packed up or destroyed, for fear of Nimue getting a hold of one. Travel was near impossible without them, the weather too harsh to risk the horses and their own lives.

There was no news of Nimue and Mordred. No word, no sightings, nothing. More than likely, they were in hiding. And plotting. Perhaps recuperating. Ariadne had badly injured Nimue with her iron dagger. She hoped it had been fatal, but word on if Nimue was alive or dead was silent. Rumors of fae attacks in the outer villages swept through the city and while a few Knights of the Round Table were dispersed to check on the villages, they weren't able to make it far before needing to turn around.

Ariadne spent the mornings she wasn't on duty in the training hall, working with Brionna and Malcolm. She became stronger, faster, but with that came more disdain from the squires and the noblemen who were passed over to be a Knight of the Round Table. But no one held more contempt than Gingalain, Gawaine's only son. Especially when Lancelot had become general in Gawaine's stead. Ariadne and Gingalain were cordial to each other before, usually staying out of the other's way, but now Gingalain had a snide remark or insult to throw her way any chance he got. He blamed her for Gawaine's death, and Ariadne could not bring herself to challenge him on that.

When spring finally broke, the days were gray and rainy, the resulting mud presenting problems for the rebuilding of the market. Ariadne found herself in the city most days, helping the workers and setting up temporary tents so the shops could still sell their wares while their buildings were being fixed.

When Ariadne wasn't in the city, she was back in the training fields, where, unfortunately, old whispers still followed.

A princess shouldn't fight.

A woman *shouldn't fight. Ever since that Greek woman came, the world has gone upside down. Women everywhere think they do a man's rightful role.*

She's a girl. I can't learn from her.

She should get married and make a match to benefit the king-dom.

Ariadne ignored them. She had gotten rather good at ignoring the whispers, reminding herself what Brionna had always told her: to not let them doubt who and what she was.

Ariadne was unwrapping her hands one morning on the training field after an already vigorous session when Brionna approached the fields with Lohengrin. They were followed, unfortunately, by Gingalain. It was rare for him to be seen at training, especially so early in the morning. Ariadne contemplated calling it an early day until Gingalain picked up a training sword and approached her.

"Cousin," he said—or spat, rather. "Let's spar."

Ariadne shoved the wraps in her satchel. "I don't think so."

"Oh, come now. Let's see what all that *training* has taught you," he sneered. "Let's have a real fight."

"No," Ariadne said again.

Gingalain laughed. "I knew you'd be a coward."

Ariadne clenched her fists, counted to ten. She could feel Brionna's gaze—and that of everyone else in the fields-on her. She wouldn't take Gingalain's bait. He wasn't worth her time, and she didn't have the energy for it today.

"I will not fight you," said Ariadne, turning away from him. "I have other things to do."

"Other things? Like what? Whoring around with another squire, or perhaps leading my mother to her death, too?"

Ariadne saw red. Gasps and exclamations of shock came from the others, but Gingalain ignored them. In the corner of her vision, Lohengrin lunged for Gingalain, but Brionna held him back.

Ariadne kept still. Kept her temper in check. He was trying to make her angry. She would not let him. She would not give him the satisfaction.

"However you may feel about me," she said as calmly as she could, "I am still sister to the king. You will not address me with such disrespect again, or you will face punishment."

Gingalain did not answer, and Ariadne was relieved for this to be the end of it. Her relief was short-lived though, as the faint sound of boots shifting in the dirt and Ariadne ducked just in time to miss Gingalain's sword.

Yells broke out across the field.

Brionna barked Gingalain's name, but he came after Ariadne again.

He swiped at her and she dodged left, then right, backing away from him.

"I won't fight you," Ariadne said, tossing her satchel to the side. "You're too angry."

"Damn right I'm angry," Gingalain hissed.

Over his shoulder, Brionna eyed them, ready to interfere. Ariadne gave a slight shake of her head. She needed to handle this on her own.

"My father is dead!" Gingalain continued. "And it's *your* fault."

Gingalain charged. Ariadne stepped to the side and elbowed him in the face. He stumbled, and she used the opportunity to break his hold on his sword and yanked it from his grip. She twisted his arm around his back and kneed him in the lower back, sending him to his knees. Gingalain struggled and spat curses.

Lohengrin, Brionna, and Malcolm swarmed. Lohengrin got to him first, his face red with rage.

"We do not attack anyone with their backs turned," Lohengrin growled, his voice lethal. He yanked Gingalain to his feet by the neck of his tunic. "If you want to know why you aren't on the Round Table, that's why. *Leave*." Lohengrin shoved him so hard, Gingalain fell into the sand.

Gingalain glared up at him. "You don't get to tell me what to do," he snarled. "Not when you cozy up to that traitorous fae bastard who—"

"Finish that sentence," said Malcolm, "and you lose what knighthood you have."

Gingalain shifted, glared at Malcolm but said nothing, and got to his feet.

"Disrespect Ariadne like that again, and you *will* be stripped of your title," Lohengrin snarled. "Report for squire duty tomorrow at dawn."

"I am a knight!" Gingalain snapped.

"Then act like it," Lohengrin hissed.

Gingalain glared at him, his lips twitching as if he were fighting not to say something. But he whirled on his heel and stormed away.

"Are you all right?" Brionna asked Ariadne quietly.

Ariadne stuck Gingalain's training sword back on the rack. "I'm fine," she said, and then turned to Lohengrin. "I had him handled."

"He needs to learn his place," Lohengrin said. "He's too comfortable thinking he can get away with whatever he wants. Besides, you are our princess. In case you forgot. He *cannot* speak to you that way."

Ariadne sighed and picked up her satchel. "He's not wrong, though. I did lead Gawaine to his death. And your father. And Lyrion." Her voice broke on Lyrion's name.

"No," Lohengrin turned her toward him. His eyes were bloodshot, either from sleepless nights or crying; Ariadne didn't know. "I told you before: It was not your fault. They died doing what they had sworn to do. To protect Camelot. To protect you. Now get to *your* duty."

Without waiting for a reply, Lohengrin too stormed off. Ariadne watched him go, too stunned to move.

"He and Ellyn had a fight last night," Malcolm said quietly. "He's been like this ever since."

"About what?" Ariadne asked, but Malcolm shrugged.

"Follow him, please?" she said to Malcolm.

He nodded and hurried off after Lohengrin.

"Come," Brionna said, tugging at Ariadne's arm. "Master Owen needs help with his shop. The door fell again."

"I'm fairly certain he is doing this on purpose because he fancies you," Ariadne said, falling into step with her.

"As he should," Brionna chuckled. "Look at me. I am stunning. Xiang tells me everyday."

Despite her mood, Ariadne let out a laugh and nudged Brionna with her shoulder.

CHAPTER TEN

ANWIL

Anwil was hidden behind a mountain of paperwork, all waiting for his signature. He had holed himself up in the in the king's study to finish as much as he could without the interruptions that working in the throne room invariably brought.

When he first began working in the study, Anwil had felt like an intruder. His mother hadn't changed a thing when Arthur died, not even using it herself. The quill and ink bottle that Arthur had used last had still been sitting in the middle of the desk next to a half-written note. One of Arthur's cloaks had still hung on the back of the chair, and a portrait of him and Guinevere had hung above the hearth.

Anwil immediately had it redecorated. He moved the portrait to the family wing's common room and had a bookshelf put in and even had the curtains changed.

Sighing and dropping the quill, Anwil leaned back in his chair. Sunlight streamed through the window, glinting off the mantel where Excalibur sat.

Anwil glanced at the sword. It rested neatly atop the hearth, on a plain wooden mount. The blade itself was simple, no jewels or inscriptions. It had no need to be gaudy.

The Lady of the Lake herself ordered Excalibur created for someone worthy to protect Briton and all those who lived in it. That honor was not given lightly. Arthur was the first human gifted the right to wield the magical sword. Returned upon his death, it had been stolen by Nimue and used to bring her lost lover back to life.

Anwil had wanted to return Excalibur to Avalon, as it hadn't been given to him. But the island was still sealed shut and travel was dangerous. No one had any idea where Nimue and Mordred had fled. Nimue's old refuge had been abandoned, with no clues or hints to where they might have gone.

Anwil turned away from the sword and peered out the window to find the sun setting. He had worked through supper again, losing track of time. He pushed himself from the chair, knowing he was about to hear an earful from Mirah. She had been on him about not working himself to the bone, but it was the only way he could get through the days.

He poured himself a cup of water and drank it all in one gulp before snuffing out the small fire in the hearth and locking up the study.

"Fair warning, Your Grace," the guard outside the door said. "Five council members came to talk about the king's meeting next month. I sent them all away, but I'm sure they're waiting to bombard you in the corridors."

Anwil suppressed a groan. "Thank you, Tom."

Tom bowed his head and Anwil pocketed his key ring, heading down the hallway. Nobles bowed and greeted him as he passed, and he murmured polite hellos to all of them but kept his pace fast, not wanting to be stopped.

When he saw Lady Sura, the council treasurer, he ducked behind a statue of Sir Kay until she passed. A servant caught him, eyes wide, and Anwil put a finger to his lips. They scurried away and Anwil breathed a sigh of relief when he made it to the private wing's winding staircase.

It was much quieter in the family wing and he felt like he could finally breathe. A cart of covered food waited for him in the common room.

Ariadne was there as well, finishing her own supper. She was curled up on the armchair, legs tucked underneath her and her boots on the floor next to the chair.

"Don't worry," she said when Anwil crossed the room. "I won't tell Mirah you worked through supper again. It's probably cold by now, though."

"I'm too hungry to care," Anwil said, plucking a lid off of the tray. He ate the meat pie quickly, barely tasting it. When he finished, he realized Ariadne had been staring into the fire the entire time, barely moving, her eyes glazed over.

"You all right?" he asked, putting the bowl back on the tray.

"Gingalain's an ass."

Anwil snorted. "Aye, well, nothing unusual there."

Ariadne cleared her throat and put her empty bowl on the cart. "He caused a spectacle this morning," she said. "I handed him his ass though. So did Lohengrin."

Anwil laughed. "Good. He needs it."

"Are you ever going to join us in training?" Ariadne poured a mug of wine and handed it to Anwil before pouring one for herself.

"I've been working with Lancelot all winter," Anwil said.

"Yes, but you should come to the fields every once in a while," said Ariadne. "It would do the squires some good to see you."

"I'll embarrass myself," Anwil mumbled.

"You're not as bad as you think."

Anwil shot her a look.

"You're not," Ariadne insisted. "You can hold your own. Sometimes."

Anwil rolled his eyes and changed the subject. "I've been thinking," he said. "We should check in on King Constantine. He hasn't answered any letters, and rumor is he won't leave his room, nor speak to anyone."

Ariadne sighed. "I've heard that too. Who will you send?"

"You," Anwil answered, and Ariadne's eyebrows shot up.

"Me?" she said. "You don't think that's too dangerous to send out your only heir?"

"It is dangerous," Anwil agreed. "But it needs to be one of us. He blames me, though, for Yvanne's death, so if I go, it'll only end in disaster. It has to be you."

"Her death wasn't your fault," Ariadne said quietly.

"I know." Anwil took a drink of his wine.

"Who can I take with me?"

"I recommend Lancelot," Anwil said. "He and Constantine were friends once. And Jabir."

"Mirah?" Ariadne suggested. "Maybe she can give Constantine something to help."

"If she wishes," Anwil said tightly. He didn't like the thought of Mirah on the open roads.

Ariadne gulped down the rest of her wine. "I should get some sleep, then. I assume we'll leave soon?"

"Day after tomorrow?"

Ariadne nodded and, after putting her goblet on the cart, kissed Anwil's cheek and bid him goodnight.

Anwil left soon after and breathed a sigh of relief when he entered his chambers. A fire was crackling in the hearth, and Leofwine had turned down the covers and put a warming pan under them. Anwil told his groom he didn't have to, but on days like this, it was nice to crawl into the warm bed.

He quickly washed his face and teeth and, as he was undressing, he caught sight of himself in the mirror. The black, shadowy veins on his chest were getting worse.

CHAPTER ELEVEN

Mirah

Mirah loved spring in Camelot; it was her favorite time of year. And this year, the city market was bursting with life around the reconstruction, as if the city itself were waking up after a long sleep. There was a happiness present that wasn't found in the other seasons. A hope filled the air of the year to come, even if it rained most days.

"Good morrow, Lady Mirah!" Mistress Catriona called from behind her stand. "Any yarn I could interest you with today?"

"Not today," Mirah said, even though a lovely saffron color caught her eye. "I'm on an errand."

Mirah left the stand reluctantly, weaving through the crowd and clutching her basket close. She nearly ran over a loose chicken, was almost accosted by the melon lady, and had to duck under a plank of wood, but she finally made it to the apothecary.

A man with green-tinged skin and dark brown hair sat behind the dark wood counter. He looked up and grinned, showing slightly pointed teeth.

"Ah, Lady Mirah," he said, opening his arms. "It is good to see you."

"You as well, Master Rune," she said, returning his smile. "I hope business has been good?"

Rune's smile faltered. "Yes," he said. "What can I help you with today?"

Mirah's heart sank. She knew he was lying, but she didn't wish to push the subject. Though he hid it well, she could see the pain behind his eyes. She always had a knack for knowing when someone was lying to her.

So instead, she handed him her list. "Are you able to get this?"

His brown eyebrows shot up under his hair.

"This is rare, indeed," he said. "What will you need it for?"

"A patient," said Mirah. "I cannot say much else. It is highly confidential."

"I see," said Rune. "Well, I don't have any in stock, but the next full moon, I could make a trip to the Otherworld if you are in no hurry."

"I do not wish to inconvenience you," said Mirah politely, even though she needed the ingredients to help Anwil with his odd fatigue.

"I need to go anyway to see my family," said Rune, waving a hand. "However, it will be expensive."

"I am not worried about the cost," she said. "Send the bill to the royal infirmary. I can count on you to be discreet, yes?"

"You have my word." Rune waved his hand and her list disappeared.

"Thank you," said Mirah, her shoulders sagging in relief.

"Of course, my lady," Rune said, his tone gentler. "Was that all?"

"No, I have another list for you." Mirah handed him the list and he read it over quickly.

"Are you traveling somewhere?" he asked.

"To Cornwall," Mirah said. "King Constantine isn't doing well, and I'm accompanying Princess Ariadne to check on him."

"Ah," Rune said, his face falling. "I didn't see it happen, but I heard his scream. I'm not a father myself, but..." He shook his head. "Forgive me. I'll gather these for you right away."

Rune ducked through the curtain to the back room, and Mirah wandered the shop to distract herself. It was her favorite in Camelot, filled to the brim with all kinds of magical herbs and medical supplies, as well as charms, talismans, and other spell supplies.

She picked up a vial of sparkling pink dust, examining it closely. It was labeled in an elegant red script with a word she did not recognize. But there was a little heart drawn in the corner.

"Be careful with that one," Rune said, returning to the counter with an armload. "Mighty powerful aphrodisiac."

Mirah carefully put the vial back.

"Thank you." She set her basket on the table and scooped the bottles, herbs, papers, and powders into her basket. "How's your husband, by the way? Is his leg still bothering him?"

Rune grinned. "No, he's back to running the farm and running around with the animals," he chuckled. "It's been good to see him so happy again."

"I'm so glad," Mirah said with a grin of her own. "Hopefully he won't get shoved over by a cow again."

Rune laughed. "Now that he's better, he will never live it down."

"Of course not," said Mirah, chuckling. "Thank you again."

"Don't forget this." Rune held out his hand and a purple and blue rose bloomed in his palm.

"Oh, that's beautiful," Mirah said, gently taking it by the stem. "Thank you."

"Anything for my favorite customer."

"You're such a charmer," Mirah said, shaking her head. She handed him a bag of coins. "Can you send a note to me when you're able to get the others?"

"As you wish, my lady," he said, giving a bow.

Mirah left the shop, savoring the sweet scent of the rose. She took her time heading back to the castle, stopping to talk or look at wares. The clouds had broken and the sun peeked through, and Mirah savored the fine weather. She bought a beautifully painted glass vase for the rose, and a book of poetry written by various fae and humans who lived in the city.

And when she passed Mistress Catriona's stand again, she bought that saffron yarn.

"Letter for you, my lady!" a page boy waved a letter at her as she made her way into the castle.

Mirah thanked him and broke open the green seal of her family's crest.

It was from her aunt, Anipe. She read over the letter, frowning. Anipe, who managed Evanshire while Mirah and Jabir were kept in the city, had written of some trouble at the family estate.

She wrote that a roof had fallen on one of the renter's cottages and the stables needed updating. Not to mention a leaky roof at the manor house. Her aunt finished the letter by saying she would arrive in Camelot soon to speak to Jabir about the issues, and looked forward to visiting with her favorite niece. Mirah chuckled at that, as she was Anipe's only niece.

Mirah stuffed the letter into her pouch and hurried on to the infirmary, where she found Master Cassius in their shared office. It was messy, with scrolls, vials, and instruments strewn everywhere.

"Mirah, my girl!" said the old physician, looking up from the book he was reading. "It is your day off. Is something the matter?"

"I just need to gather a few things before I leave." She plopped her basket on her desk. She filled the vase with some water from the decanter by the hearth and stuck the rose inside.

"Oh, a secret admirer?" Cassius wiggled his bushy eyebrows.

Mirah almost snorted. "No, just Rune." She sat the vase in the sunlight on her desk and set about organizing the supplies she had bought. She had never traveled as far as Cornwall to treat a patient, and looking at her now covered desk, she may have overpacked.

Mirah put her hands on her hips, assessing everything. Her gaze landed on her journal. She had tried to forget about her vision, trying to convince herself it was just a nightmare, but she had dreamed of it again just last night.

"Cassius, do you know anything about visions?"

Cassius' eyebrows shot up. "Visions? Why do you ask? Have you had one?"

"I think so," she said. "But I've never had one before, so I'm not quite sure."

"Well," Master Cassius put his book down and took off his spectacles. "I fear I know little about them myself. Master Merlin and Morgana le Fey had them all the time, however."

"Morgana le Fey?"

"Oh yes," Master Cassius said. "She was Camelot's royal physician once upon a time. Royal advisor as well. She taught me to heal when I was young. If you can believe I was ever a young man." He chuckled.

"In ancient times, yes?" Mirah teased.

"Ho ho, you ghastly girl!" Cassius laughed. "Now, what did you see?"

"Just flashes, really," she said and told him about the broken crown, Ariadne and the bloody axe, Anwil's eyes and the broken Table.

Master Cassius frowned. "I see." He stroked his beard.

"Do they always come true?" Mirah asked quietly.

"From what Merlin and Morgana have said, sometimes visions are metaphors of possible outcomes," Cassius said slowly. "And some can be right on the nose. They are glimpses of the future from the gods, given to point us in the direction they wish us to go."

"So, they will come to pass?" Mirah urged.

"That I do not know, my dear girl," Master Cassius said solemnly. "Even Merlin and Morgana did not know if their visions would come true or not."

Mirah put a shaking hand over her stomach and slid into her chair.

"I wish I could be of more help," said Master Cassius. "Perhaps you could talk to your father?"

"You know what his reaction would be," Mirah said quietly.

Master Cassius replaced his spectacles on his nose.

"Fathers worry," he said. "He only wishes to protect you. Although, you can talk to the Druids. Lord Dafydd is still here."

"Perhaps," Mirah whispered. She did not know any of them well and didn't want this sort of vision to be well known. "Well, thank you."

"Any time, any time," he said, picking up his quill. "Safe travels to Cornwall, my dear. I'd hate to have to replace you. I'm too old to teach anyone else."

Mirah chuckled. "Oh come now. Aurelius can surely take my place."

Cassius glared at her over his spectacles.

CHAPTER TWELVE

NIMUE

Nimue healed slowly. She refused to see Mordred, to even let him in her chambers, which she did not leave. She was too angry. The one male, the one *being*, Nimue trusted fully had shattered what trust she had left. If she hadn't been weak from this damned wound, she would have torn him apart. But she still barely made it out of bed for the first few days and slept most of the time. Nimue hated being weak. And if she spent one more day cooped up in this bedroom, she would scream.

The only solace of freedom she had was the balcony, giving her a magnificent view of the mountains of the Unseelie Court, the small kingdom that Mab ruled over. Here, all the fae deemed unworthy, too gruesome, too fearsome, too unusual, even in the fae world, came to live.

This was where Nimue came when Vivienne banished her from Avalon, when her own sister cast her aside for merely trying to help their own kind. Cruel, Vivienne had called her, for taking revenge on those who had murdered the fae. Betraying her vows of peace. But what good was peace when it caused them to turn a blind eye to bloodshed? The priestesses were supposed to be protectors of the fae, but they had forgotten what that meant. So, if Nimue had to be cast out of Avalon for doing what she had been born to do, then so be it.

"Mordred has returned," Mab said one morning as Nimue dressed. She had been at Mab's castle for months, and only recently had she been able to dress herself without pain in her arm.

"Where did he go?" Nimue asked, slipping on her sandals.

"Many places." Mab handed Nimue her brush. "He wishes to speak to you about it."

"I have no desire to talk to him."

"I understand," Mab said. "But you need him."

"I cannot trust him."

"You never should have in the first place, but here we are," Mab said, throwing her hands up. "He is a skilled warrior, and you need him to lead your armies."

"You said we had no armies," Nimue growled. "That our allies had fled."

"Many have," said Mab. "But you can make more. Camelot has many human enemies. You should be making friends with them."

"Friends with humans?" Nimue barked a laugh.

"The enemy of your enemy is your friend," Mab said. "Besides, you can always do away with them once you've defeated Camelot. Make nice with them. Offer them something they can't refuse."

"Like what?"

"Humans are simple." Mab waved a hand. "Gold, kingdoms, someone for the bed..."

"Why would I give humans kingdoms when we are trying to defeat the human kingdoms?"

Mab gave her a pitying look. "Nimue, you are smarter than this. You only need to make them think they'll have kingdoms."

"And we'll need Mordred for that," Nimue said through gritted teeth.

Mab nodded. "I also came to tell you that the girl Pendragon has left Camelot."

Nimue whirled on her. "Why didn't you say that first? Where is she?"

"She is traveling to Cornwall." Mab beckoned her to follow her inside and to the scrying bowl by the hearth.

She waved a hand over it, and Ariadne Pendragon's face came into view in the water. She traveled by horseback with Lancelot, the young witch, and Sir Palomedes' son.

"Why are they going to Cornwall?"

"According to Mordred," Mab said, "the human king Constantine is ill."

"How does he know?" Nimue snapped.

"Ask him yourself." Mab waved her hand over the bowl and Ariadne disappeared. "I will not be a messenger between the two of you. I only came because I do not wish to see you waste away in this room."

Without waiting for a reply, Mab swept from the bedroom. Nimue threw herself into her vanity chair, huffing. Mab was right. Damnit. She needed to get back to work. She brushed her hair and tossed it into a braid before heading into the corridors.

"Where is he?" she asked one of the Minotaur guards.

"Study," he growled.

He was indeed in the study, leaning over the desk, flipping through a small book. He looked up when Nimue came in, and smiled.

"My love," he said, rounding the desk and taking her hands in his. They were cold. "You are beautiful. And looking much better than before. Mab said your wound has healed."

"Where did you go?" Nimue asked, slipping her hands from his and crossing the room to pour herself a goblet of wine.

Mordred chuckled. "Straight to the point, as usual. I've returned from Dinas Emrys most recently."

"And Cornwall?" Nimue sipped on the chilled wine.

"Yes, there too," Mordred's smile turned into a smirk. "I paid my cousin a visit. He is ill."

"How so?" Nimue asked, perching on the arm of the fat armchair.

"Ill of mind," Mordred answered. "The death of his beloved Yvanne sent him into a stupor."

Nimue couldn't help but let out a laugh. "A stupor?"

"Aye." Mordred sat in the chair and pulled her into his lap. "It made him much more agreeable."

"To what?" Nimue shifted on his lap.

"To do my bidding," Mordred grinned. "We now have a fantastic inside look into Camelot."

"And just how exactly, did you get him to agree to be your spy?"

"I promised to bring his darling little daughter back from the dead," Mordred said.

Nimue's eyebrows shot up.

"Of course," Mordred continued, "I'm not going to do it. But he needn't know that."

"Well." Nimue raised her glass. "I must congratulate you. That was well done."

Mordred kissed her and Nimue stiffened but let him. She pulled away, however, when his hands slid around her waist. She removed herself from his lap.

"You're not still angry with me, are you?" he asked.

"Of course I am," Nimue snapped. "You lied to me. How can I trust you?"

"I am sorry." Mordred got up and took the goblet from her hands. He set it down to take her into his arms. "I should not have. I only thought the fear of Arawn would turn you away."

It would have, Nimue thought. For good reason; the god of death was not to be trifled with.

"But I am here now," Mordred said, trailing a finger down her cheek. "And I am on your side."

Nimue wished she could believe him. "Where else have you been?"

"All over," he said. "With Mab's help, I've convinced fae to our side, and sent letters to old human enemies of Arthur's."

"Aren't they all dead?" Nimue asked.

"Most, their descendants, though, are itching for revenge. If we plan this correctly, Briton's throne will be ours by Samhain."

"That soon?"

"That soon," Mordred said, taking her hand and kissing her fingers.

She pulled her hand away. "Then we better get to work."

CHAPTER THIRTEEN

CONNOR

Prince Connor of Clannig and Ireland stared at the newly built castle, with its towers and flags. A castle modeled after Camelot, which his father, King Connig, had become obsessed with. Before, the High Kings of Ireland didn't live in stone castles larger than needed, but Connig had to be different. He wanted power like Camelot held over Briton, and he was well on his way. The rebellion against the previous king only amplified support for Connig. The old High King had been a tyrant, waging war against both his own kin and *tuatha*-king-dom. Connig, who was a chieftain rich in trade in Southern Ireland, seized the opportunity to maintain the guise of *for the people*, conveniently helping anyone in need of supplies and food—especially those who were wronged by the old king. So when Connig rebelled, support was easy to come by. They defeated the old king easily and Connig was crowned and moved immediately north to Teamhair na Ri.

But Connor hated The Seat of Tara. His home was the sea and the ports and the ships.

Connor did not want this new life. Trapped behind these endless stone walls with secrets and plotting, it was suffocating.

He turned back to his soldiers. They were well worn and eager to return to their families after spending the winter up north. Connor urged them on as they approached the village of Teamhair na Ri that surrounded the new castle.

There was no joy in their return. No victorious cheers from the people as Connor dismissed his men to their homes.

Bradán and Domhnall followed Connor into the castle courtyard. Garbhan had slunk ahead, no doubt to speak to Connig first.

"Your father wishes to speak to you, Highness." Senach, a Druid priest and Connig's most trusted adviser, met them in the courtyard.

"My father can wait," said Connor, trudging through the mud.

Senach looked strained, but nodded. Muirne turned up at his shoulder.

"I can meet with him," she said, her gray eyes weary.

"Welcome home, lady priestess." Senach gave a low bow and escorted Muirne into the castle.

Connor sighed and headed straight for his rooms. He barked an order a bit too harshly at the first servant he saw to draw him a bath and to not have anyone disturb him. The young lad jumped and scurried away. Connor dropped his pack down in the corner and wanted so badly to just sink into his bed, but he stank. Thankfully, it wasn't long before servants brought hot water for his bath in the small adjoining room.

The water was a relief on his aching muscles, but he only gave himself a few minutes to soak before scrubbing the grime and dried blood off until his skin was raw and the water cold. Without bothering to get dressed, he crawled under the furs on his bed and slept almost as soon as his head hit the pillows.

"How kind of you to grace us with your presence, son," Connig growled as Connor walked in late to the dining hall two days later.

After sleeping for most of the day of his return, Connor had wandered to the tavern and drank himself into the night. He had woken up with a splitting headache, tangled in the sheets and the barmaid asking if he would visit her again.

Connig sat at the head of the long table, papers and his *feis*-council surrounding him. Normally, the *feis* only met once per third Samhain. Connig must have summoned them about the invaders.

Connig's ice blue eyes stared holes into Connor, and Connor stared right back as he pulled out a chair at the table, spun it around, and sat.

"Apologies, Da," Connor said, putting a smirk on his face that he knew his father would hate. "I needed to catch up on my beauty sleep." He sent a wink to Lady Caoimhe across from him. The older woman blushed and looked away from him.

"By spending the night in a tavern?" Connig hissed. "Getting yourself pissed?"

Connor held his father's glare and poured himself some of the mead on the table, but Garbhan appeared behind him and snatched the cup out of his hands.

Connor grabbed Garbhan's tankard and downed it in one gulp. Garbhan snarled at him.

"You will mind your manners, boy," Connig growled. "We have work to do. Our coffers are running low. Dismally low."

Connor's fist twitched. He had promised the northern villages they would send aid. He should have known Connig wouldn't intend to keep that promise.

"So, you will go to Camelot and make an offer for the princess's hand in marriage."

Connor blinked and then laughed. "Come again?"

"I do detest repeating myself." Connig leaned back in his chair. "You will go to Camelot and do whatever you can to get the Pendragon girl to marry you. We need her dowry, and opening trade to Camelot will benefit Ireland for years to come."

"You can't be serious," Connor said.

"I am," said Connig. He handed down a scroll. "The princess will be hard won, so I am sending you under the pretense of becoming a Knight of the Round Table. Earn her favor."

Connor's jaw dropped. "A Knight of the—Father, I already lead your battles. I don't need—"

Connig folded his hands over his belly. The thick gold circlet on his hairless head glinted in the sunlight streaming in from the windows.

"Aren't they at war themselves?" Connor asked, not able to help himself. "Is it wise to send your only heir to a country on the brink of war?"

"It's the perfect time," said Connig. "They'll be desperate for allies. I have no doubt you can fend for yourself. But we need Camelot's power and money if Ireland is to survive."

Bastard. If he hadn't bankrupted them in the first place, they wouldn't be in this mess.

"When do I leave?" Connor asked through gritted teeth. He knew there was no more arguing.

"Just after Beltane. Garbhan will accompany you. And take your cousins."

"What do you mean Knight of the Round Table?" Bradán questioned, spoon halfway to his mouth. Connor had found him in the pub, needing to get out of the castle and with a good drink in hand. Bradán had beaten him there.

"I mean what I just said," said Connor. "My father is sending me to Camelot to become a Knight of the Round Table and woo the princess to marriage."

"But that could take years," said Domhnall. "Or...never. What if they kick you back home?"

"Then I better not come home," Connor mumbled into his mead.

"Who's going to command the armies if more invaders come?"

"Grainne," said Connor without hesitation. "She's the best. Taught me everything I know."

"Isn't Briton in a war?" Domhnall asked. "Their queen was assassinated last Samhain, wasn't she?"

Connor nodded.

"Well, we'll come with you," said Domhnall.

"We'll what?" Bradán's jaw dropped.

"You have to," Connor said. "Connig's orders."

Bradán looked from Domhnall to Connor and back again. "But—"

"We wouldn't have let you go to the dragons alone anyhow," said Domhnall, interrupting Bradán's protests. "Besides, someone needs to have your back when you say something stupid."

Connor let out a weak snort. "Perhaps you should go for the princess."

A hand fell on his shoulder and he looked up to see the blacksmith he had had a good time with before he had left north.

"Welcome home," he said with a smooth grin.

Connor sighed. "Not tonight," he mumbled, and the grin fell from the blacksmith's face. He didn't say anything as he left Connor's table. Domhnall raised his eyebrows and Connor just shook his head. He wasn't feeling up to anything at the moment, not even a drink. In fact, a night alone was more tempting.

"I'll see you tomorrow." Connor tossed a few gold coins on the table and left the tavern, heading not to his rooms, but to the Druids Groves. It was the only place he knew he could find some peace in this hellish castle.

CHAPTER FOURTEEN

ARIADNE

Ariadne had never seen the ocean before, and she was utterly mesmerized. The power of the waves crashing against the cliffs and the gulls squawking overhead filled her senses. She urged Nerys to a stop to take it all in. Tintagel Castle sat on the edge of the cliff, Constantine's flags waving violently in the sea wind. Ariadne had an urge to jump off her horse and leap off the cliffs into the raging waves.

"We'll need to continue on foot," Lancelot said, yanking Ariadne away from her thoughts. "Around there are the stables. And from there, the bridge."

Ariadne followed his pointing hand to a see the wooden barns and fence just behind a small hill. It was so open here in Tintagel. So different from Camelot, where the crowds of people could get so packed, it was hard to move in the streets.

To see such open air and ground was almost unnerving. And yet, a sense of peace fell over her.

"Where is everyone?" Mirah asked.

"Apparently they all left," Ariadne said. "Or were dismissed. I doubt there's even a stable-hand anymore."

"Someone would have stayed for the horses," said Jabir, dismounting.

Someone had indeed stayed for the horses, an old stable-master and his grandson—although the stables were worse for wear. The barn needed cleaning, and many of the stalls weren't mucked either. Ariadne gritted her teeth. If the stables were like this, what was the state of the castle?

"We're the only ones left, my lord," said the stablemaster as he showed them to empty stalls for their horses. "Everyone else left after the pay stopped. But I couldn't abandon the horses."

As if on cue, one of the horses banged on their wall.

"It is all right," said Lancelot. "If all goes well, you shall have more help soon. And we will care for our own horses."

"But my lord—"

"Please do not worry yourself," Ariadne told him softly. "It is no trouble. Can you let the castle know we are here?"

"Aye, I'll send Ruan. I'll have him take your bags as well," he said and walked off, leaning heavily on his cane.

"This doesn't bode well," Mirah said to Ariadne.

"No, it doesn't," she agreed.

"Have you ever been to Cornwall, Sir Lancelot?" Mirah asked him as they made their way down the winding path to the castle. Jabir hovered close to her, as he had for their entire journey to Tintagel.

"Once," Lancelot answered. "With Arthur. We toured Briton for two years, visiting each king at their home. Constantine was still a knight with us and his father ruled Dumnonia."

As they continued their conversation, Ariadne let herself fall behind, admiring the ocean. She couldn't take her eyes off it. It was beautiful. And powerful. Ariadne pictured ships rocking against those waves and being consumed by them. She hurried along, and when they stepped off the bridge to the courtyard of the castle, a shiver passed down her spine.

The castle was nowhere near the size of Camelot's, but there was something familiar about it. Ariadne had never seen these turrets and towers, but they called to her. As if welcoming her home. But how could home be a place she had never visited?

The air was thicker the closer they came to the castle. They were the only ones in the courtyard.

Even the entryway was void of anyone. Not even servants. Ariadne paused on the threshold, her head spinning.

"Ari?" Mirah was at her side. "What is it?"

Ariadne shook her head. "I don't know," she said, putting a hand on the wall to steady herself. As soon as her skin touched stone, a sensation like a limb falling asleep shot through her arm. She couldn't move. The world around her faded, and figures of people appeared to her as if in a dream.

A young girl with long black hair ran through the halls, her laugh echoing off the stone. A man and woman greeted the girl with enthusiasm, picking her up and twirling her around.

Then it turned dark. Raining. A storm blazed. The same man entered the halls, but he wasn't right. Something was off about him. The girl was older now, yelling at the man. Ariadne couldn't make out her words.

"Ari!"

Ariadne was yanked away from the wall, heart pounding in her chest. Mirah held her as her knees shook.

"What the hell was that?" she rasped.

"What was what? You just stood there," Mirah said. "Panting."

"I saw... things."

"What things?" Mirah asked, and Ariadne relayed what she had seen.

"You had a vision," Lancelot said. "There is old magic here at Tintagel. And you have familial ties. Your father was born here. Perhaps the magic recognized you."

Ariadne yanked her waterskin off her belt and drank deeply. She didn't like having visions.

Mirah gave her a peculiar look, and she was about to ask about it she became aware of hurried footsteps along the right corridor, and a maid stepped into the light.

"Forgive me," she said, breathing hard and dipping into a curtsy. "I was in the kitchens. My name is Edith, and I can show you to your rooms."

"Where is King Constantine?" Lancelot asked her.

The maid hesitated. "He, er, he's in his rooms, my lord. He doesn't like visitors anymore."

"Take us to him," Ariadne ordered, and the maid flushed.

"Yes, Your Highness. This way."

They followed Edith through the dark corridors and up the winding stairs. Every stone, every step, Ariadne felt the castle calling her, as if it were tugging on her clothes. The higher they climbed, the more suffocated Ariadne felt.

She breathed a sigh of relief when the maid took them to a door at the far end of the corridor, and knocked.

"My lord?" she called. "The Princess Ariadne and Knights of the Round Table are here to see you."

There was no answer, and the maid sighed. "He never replies anymore."

She pushed the door open and stepped aside.

The first thing that hit Ariadne was the smell. Odor, bad food, and urine mixed in her nostrils and she wanted to vomit. She yanked a rag from her pouch and held it over her mouth as the others did the same.

Ariadne peered inside the room.

The chambers were a mess. Plates of untouched, moldy food littered the floor, along with clothing. The writing desk was overturned and ink stained the floor. Papers were everywhere, as were pillows. The curtains on the bed were ripped and barely hanging on.

Constantine was sitting by the window in an armchair.

"Why has this not been cleaned?" Lancelot asked the maid.

"He will not let us, my lord," the maid answered, her face red.

Ariadne stepped inside, careful to not step on any food or clothing. Constantine had lost weight and his hair was thinner. His clothing smelled as if it had not been changed for a while, and he held a dagger in his hands.

"My lord?" Ariadne said through the rag. Her eyes watered. The rag was not much help.

"Go away," Constantine wheezed.

"My lord, we are here to—"

"I said go away!"

Ariadne put a hand on the back of the chair. "My lord, you cannot live like this."

"I am not living," he said, his voice full of despair.

"Con," Lancelot said gently, but Constantine turned away from him. Lancelot's eyes were filled with sadness as he turned to Ariadne. "Perhaps I—"

"The taking of one's own life is a mortal sin," Constantine said, his gaze fixed out the window. He turned the dagger in his hands. "Doing so condemns one's soul to an eternity of torture and hellfire. But this life without Yvanne, without Lowena, is torture." He turned to Lancelot, fresh tears in his eyes. "Do I endure this for the rest of my mortal life for a chance at salvation? Or do I rid myself of this pain on earth and hope that God will take mercy upon my soul? I've been at war with myself for so long. Staring out the window, hoping to see her return."

Ariadne gently took the dagger from Constantine's hands. He didn't fight her.

"Yvanne would not want this of you," she said gently. But Constantine whirled around in his chair, snarling at her.

"Don't talk of Yvanne," he snapped. "Not when you're the reason she is dead!"

Ariadne flinched and Constantine continued.

"You and your brother," he yelled. "They were after you! They killed her to hurt you! I never should have agreed to the damned marriage. She'd still be here! You failed her! We failed her! I...failed her."

Constantine's head fell into his hands and he sobbed.

"Ariadne," Lancelot said, but she whirled on her heel and hurried from the room.

"Get him in a bath and clean clothes," Ariadne told Edith. "And clean this room."

"My lady, there's only two of us left," she said. "We've tried to get him—"

Ariadne yanked the small coin purse from her belt and shoved it in the maid's hands. "Find people."

The maid's eyes widened and her lip trembled, but she dipped a curtsy. "Yes, Your Highness."

"I'll make a tea to calm him," Mirah offered. "It should make things easier. Can you show me to the kitchens?"

Edith glanced inside Constantine's room, where Lancelot was kneeling in front of Constantine, then at Ariadne and back to Mirah.

"Yes, my lady," she said. "This way."

"I'll see what I can do," Mirah told Ariadne before following Edith.

"I had no idea it was this bad," Ariadne said once Lancelot had closed Constantine's door behind him. "All the letters we sent were returned unopened. We assumed he was angry and hurt, but this..."

"I do not wish to imagine the pain," Jabir said, "of watching your child murdered in front of you. I do not think he will come out of this."

"Well, the least we can do is give him some dignity back," Ariadne said. "We'll have to find the steward and see if we can convince him to return."

"Constantine had always been a gentle soul," Lancelot said quietly. "He was not cut out to be a knight. He wasn't a fighter. He felt everything too much. I think you're right, Jabir. I do not think he'll come out of this."

"We'll have to find his heir," Ariadne said.

"Who is that?" Jabir asked.

"A nephew in Ireland," Ariadne said. "His younger sister married an Irish lord and had one son. She died giving birth, but the son, we think, is still alive."

"Tegen," Lancelot said. "I remember her well. I did not know she had passed."

"Do you know the Irish Lord?" Jabir asked.

"Yes," said Ariadne. "But after their last war, we lost track of him. I was hoping the steward knew."

"We'll find him," Lancelot said. "For now, we should rest. We have a lot of work on our hands."

CHAPTER FIFTEEN

ANWIL

A nwil carried a large stack of parchment and letters. His hands were still stained with ink from the late night he'd had, signing, rewriting, answering, amending. Lord Roland walked with him, impeccably dressed as always, with a dashing new hat. It was the first Meeting of Kings with Anwil as High King and it was the most important meeting of his life. This would set the stage for him and his reign. If he did anything wrong here, it could taint his reputation and any respect the kings had for him. He had been busy over the past couple of months, planning funerals, overseeing repairs to the city in the unusually harsh winter conditions, appointing new kings to replace Caradoc and Bors III.

Lord Roland cleared his throat and the guards opened the doors to the great hall. It was decorated with banners from all kingdoms, and a roaring fire burned brightly in the hearth, along with candles and sconces scattered about. The kings, except King Constantine, were already there with their queens, and they stood and bowed as Anwil entered. Anwil nodded back and gestured for them to sit.

He carefully set all the papers down and was grateful to see a quill, inkpot, and a steaming mug of what was becoming his new favorite drink, coffee. He clasped his hands behind his back and addressed the Table.

"Good morrow," he said. "And thank you all for coming. Before we begin, I want to extend a welcome to the new kings of Gwent and Sussex."

The kings pounded their fists against the table and their wives politely clapped. The two kings bowed their heads.

"And I also wish to say a few words," Anwil continued. His chest tightened, but he ignored the feeling. "Many of you knew my father, the renowned King Arthur. He was a great warrior, strong and righteous, and he inspired others to create our kingdom of Camelot. And all here knew my mother, Queen Guinevere. She, too, was a notable leader, resilient and fair. She spread peace far beyond Camelot, making it home to all. Now, I am no warrior like my father, and do not yet have the experience like my mother, but I am ready to accept my role as King of Briton. I assembled you today so that we may continue to rule together, in harmony. I offer you myself, and a promise to rule with the strength of my father, the resilience of my mother, and the knowledge that I have gained through studying these two beloved rulers. Together, we are untouchable. In this time of darkness, I will do all that I can to keep Briton and Camelot on a steady path to greatness and glory."

Silence met his speech, and Anwil stiffened. Perhaps that had been a mistake, but when King Elyion pounded on the table, giving out a cheer, the others followed suit. Queen Beatrice, Elyion's wife, gave him a warm smile, and Anwil's shoulders sagged with relief. Lord Roland patted him on the shoulder as he sank into his chair. He pulled the mug of coffee to him and drank, savoring the smooth taste. He needed the drink today. He hadn't slept and his fatigue was worsening.

The first hour was spent on the usual reports, which Anwil and Lord Roland took a lead over. Taxes, trade, and the state of Gwent and Sussex were the first things on the list.

The new king of Gwent, Bors's nephew, Owain, wasn't much older than Anwil, but hadn't supported his uncle in the coup last autumn. And Sussex's new king, Tolan, was a distant relation to Caradoc and Cerdic. He was the Baron of Sussex, an old title, and had happily taken to his new role. He was old but had a few sons who did well, and Anwil hoped they would not cause any trouble.

Once they had gotten through reports and took a quick break to eat, Anwil was more exhausted than ever. He had to fight yawning all morning and was already on his third cup of coffee. He was always exhausted lately. Feeling drained, as if he could never rest no matter how much he slept.

When lunch chatter died down, attention was turned back to Anwil. It was the moment of the meeting he was dreading.

Talking about Mordred and Nimue and revisiting the unfortunate memories of the past few months.

Anwil held out his hand to Lord Roland, who handed him the papers they had prepared for this.

"As you know, Nimue, a former priestess of Avalon, and the Lady of the Lake's sister, has been wreaking havoc across Briton the past year to bring Mordred back from the dead. She kidnapped me to use my blood to revive him and succeeded in her mission.

"Now, their mission is to finish what they started with Mordred's rebellion at the Battle of Camlann. Mordred rebelled against my father for disagreeing with his reign and because he would no longer be heir by the birth of my sister and me. Nimue joined because she was his lover, but she also had her own agenda, involving opening the veils between worlds and letting the fae take over the lands. One of the promises my father made when he was crowned, as did I in my own coronation, was to both fae and human alike, that this land belongs to all of us, together. Not one lording over the other.

"However, Nimue does not see it that way. She and Mordred wish to open the veils and rid this land of humans completely. Their first mission is to rid the Pendragon reign and destroy Camelot. We are their biggest obstacle. So, my lords, as High King, I ask you. Will you join forces, together, and help us stop Nimue and Mordred from destroying Briton?"

King Elyion was the first to stand. "You have my allegiance." King Caewlin, leaning heavily on his cane, stood next. And one by one, the kings stood, followed by their queens, and offered their armies.

"Thank you," said Anwil, and motioned them to sit. "Lord Roland, will you call for Sir Lancelot? We have much to discuss."

"Well done today, Your Grace," Queen Beatrice said quietly to Anwil as the kings and queens filed out of the now closed meeting. "Well done, indeed."

"Thank you, my lady."

He bid them all farewell and once they were gone, fell back into his seat and ran his hands over his face.

Lord Roland chuckled.

"Take a break, Your Grace," he said. "You've earned it."

"There's still so much to do," Anwil mumbled from behind his hands.

Roland looked over his spectacles at him. "And it will still be here, waiting for you on the morrow. Your mother knew how much a balanced life was needed, especially as a monarch."

Anwil lowered his hands from his face, and a flash of his mother's dying face fell across his mind. Anger, guilt, and pain shot through him like arrows through his chest.

He grabbed at his chest, taking in a sharp breath. His heart pounded beneath his palm.

"Are you all right, Your Grace?" Roland asked.

Anwil's vision blurred. Mordred's face materialized in his mind.

Fire blazed behind his eyes.

He couldn't breathe.

"I think I will rest." Anwil forced the words through a clenched jaw.

Anwil barely waited for Roland's response as he bolted from the hall. The sun had already set, the winter days short and cold.

Lancelot followed him into the corridor, where Lohengrin was talking with other guards.

"Anwil!" Lohengrin called after him.

But he couldn't answer. He bolted around them, ignoring their calls.

He climbed the winding stairs leading up to the private wing, but slowed with each one, nausea bubbling over. He didn't make it to the top stairs before the pain in his head grew worse. His vision blackened and he vomited on the stairs.

Mordred laughed, the sound grating in Anwil's ears. The pain worsened. He saw fire. So much fire. It burned hot. Too hot.

"Anwil," someone far away said. "Anwil!"

Anwil tried to open his eyes, but it hurt. Everything hurt. His back landed on something soft. His bed.

Someone called his name again, but he slipped into unconsciousness.

Anwil gently awakened to a cool breeze over his face. A fire crackled in the hearth, and someone was lightly snoring. The pain had subsided, but he felt sore, as if he had spent the entire day training in the ring with Lancelot. He opened his eyes. He was in his bedroom, the blankets under him soaked and his hair stuck to his face.

A water pitcher and cup sat beside his bed and Anwil managed to push himself up enough to pour some water. He was parched. He drank it all in one go. Putting the cup back, he noticed he was in a sleep shirt. His heart fell, realizing someone had changed him. They would have seen the mark on his chest. Cursing to himself, he burrowed back into bed and it wasn't long before he slipped back to sleep.

Bright sunlight woke Anwil in the morning, along with the sound of curtains being flung open. He groaned and forced his eyes open, blinking in the light. Lohengrin stood over his bed, glaring at him.

"Don't look at me like that," Anwil grumbled.

"According to Cassius, this is the third time this has happened," Lohengrin said. "Anwil—"

"I'm fine," said Anwil.

Lohengrin scoffed. "Not according to Cassius."

Anwil's stomach dropped. "What did he say?"

"That you've lost weight," Lohengrin said. "Your heart rate is all over the place, you had a fever, and you threw up everything in your stomach. When were you going to say you're sick?"

"When I figured out what the fuck was wrong with me," Anwil snapped. "Because neither Mirah nor Cassius have any bloody clue."

Lohengrin swore under his breath. "Are you dying?"

Anwil blinked. "What?"

"Please don't make me repeat that question."

"No," Anwil said. "At least, I don't think so."

A shadow passed over Lohengrin's face. "Does anyone else know?"

Anwil shook his head. "Did the kings find out what happened?"

"No," Lohengrin said. "But they're wondering why you haven't left your room in two days."

"Two days!?" Anwil ran his hands through his hair. "Shit. I'll tell them I ate some bad fish or something. I'll have to meet with them later."

"You need to tell Ari."

Anwil looked back at Lohengrin. "What? No. I'm fine. We don't need to worry her."

"She's your sister."

"The less Ari knows about this, the better. You know how she is."

"Aye, I do. So I know what she'll do to you when she finds out you've been keeping this from her."

Anwil sighed, the pain coming back to his head. He hated to admit it, but Lohengrin was probably right. At first, Anwil had attributed it to the strains of his new role as king, but perhaps he could no longer pretend to himself that the dreams and sickness weren't something else.

"Fine," he said.

"Good," said Lohengrin, his shoulders slumping in relief. "And you better figure this out, because I refuse to lose another brother."

CHAPTER SIXTEEN

ARIADNE

"There's nothing after Yule," Ariadne said as they looked through Constantine's ledgers. It was their third day, and Constantine still refused to come out of his room, but he did not bark at anyone who brought food or cleaned. The maid, Edith, was able to find a few workers to clean and help in the stables temporarily, and already the castle looked better.

"Did he steal any money and run off?" Mirah suggested, looking up from the paper she had been reading. She, Ariadne, and Sir Jabir were holed up in the steward's old study, to see what sort of state Dumnonia was in.

"He died," Lancelot said grimly, handing a paper to Ariadne. "Was found dead in the middle of the night last winter. Neck snapped."

"What?," Ariadne exclaimed, reading over the note. It was from the head housekeeper, writing down what she had found. They never found who killed him.

"Someone murdered Constantine's steward and no one informed us?" Jabir took the note from Ariadne. "Did Constantine even look into it?"

Lancelot looked through more papers, and shook his head.

"He is so far gone," Mirah whispered, eyes shining with tears. "to not even look into his own staff's murder."

"Something doesn't feel right," Ariadne said.

"Of course not, Ari," Mirah said. "A father had to watch his daughter murdered. Of course he isn't right."

"No, I mean, more than that," said Ariadne.

"I'll keep looking," Lancelot said, shuffling through more papers.

"And he didn't even bother with a replacement," Ariadne said, rubbing her forehead. "Well, we can send one from Camelot. One of the council members could do it until they find a new one. I'm sure Lord Garanwyn would love it."

Jabir, who was sat next to Mirah, let out a soft snort, and Ariadne raised an eyebrow.

"Come now, Sir Jabir," she said with a small smirk. "Surely you don't think ill of the mighty Sir Kay's son? Not in front of the great Sir Lancelot."

Lancelot snorted but said nothing, picking up a leather-bound scroll from the shelf.

Jabir shot Ariadne a look and she bit her lip to compress a giggle.

"I would not trust Garanwyn to do this," said Sir Jabir. "Perhaps Lady Sura? She is honest and good with numbers."

"She's head of Camelot's treasury," Ariadne said. "She can't be spared. What about—"

Ariadne stopped. A woman appeared in the doorway, but she was wrong. Ariadne could almost see right through her. Her long hair was dark, and her clothing was almost a century out of date. She stepped into the room, peering up at the shelves. The curve of her ears had a slight point to them. She reached for something on the bookshelf, and a small girl ran inside, holding a doll. The woman turned and picked up the girl, hugging her close. They spoke, but Ariadne could not hear them. The woman smoothed out the girl's black hair and smiled at something she said. She showed the doll's arm to the woman, revealing a tear. They spoke again, and the woman carried the girl out of the study, disappearing.

"Ari!"

Ariadne sucked in a breath of air, and the noise of the wind and waves came crashing back. She stumbled back into a chair, breathing hard.

"Did you see her?" Ariadne asked as they all hovered around her.

"See who?" Mirah asked.

"There was a woman," Ariadne said. "I think she was a ghost, or... or a spirit. I could see through her."

"What did she look like?" Mirah asked.

When Ariadne explained, an odd look came across Lancelot's face.

"What?" she asked him.

"You saw Igraine, your grandmother," he said softly. "With her daughter, Morgana."

"Morgana le Fey?"

Lancelot nodded. "The stones recognize you."

"There's a portrait of her," Mirah piped up. "In the gallery."

"Show me."

Mirah took her to a small room with paintings that covered the walls. Mirah didn't need to point out which was Igraine.

The painting was exquisite.

Igraine sat in front of a handsome man wearing a fine green coat and a thick gold circlet over his yellow hair. His expression was hard, commanding, but the hand on Igraine's shoulder was painted softly his thumb resting on the exposed skin of Igraine's neckline as if in mid-caress. Her head was slightly turned toward his hand, and her mouth turned up in a soft smile. Ariadne could almost feel the warm affection between the two.

When her eyes traveled down to Igraine's green dress, her heart flipped. Ariadne knew that dress. Threaded with gold embroidery and long, billowing sleeves, Ariadne had seen it before. On her mother.

She reached out a trembling hand to the portrait, her fingers caressing the painted folds in the skirt.

"Mother had this dress," she whispered.

"Arthur gave it to her as a gift." Lancelot's voice startled Ariadne.

She whirled around to find him hovering in the doorway.

"After Arthur's birth," Lancelot said, stepping into the room, "Uther moved and married Igraine so quickly, most of her possessions were left behind. She died before she could recover them. When Constantine's father was placed as the new duke, his wife saved Igraine's things and gave them to Arthur when he ascended the throne."

"She tried to get me to wear that dress so many times," Ariadne said. "But she never said it was Igraine's."

"Why wouldn't you wear it? It's beautiful," Mirah asked, nudging her shoulder.

"I'm told all the time how I should wear green because it complements my hair, so I refuse to wear it," Ariadne answered.

Mirah snorted. "You're ridiculous. When we get back, you're wearing that dress."

"Why am I seeing her, though?" Ariadne said. "Igraine, I mean. "

"I think you are seeing memories," Lancelot answered. "The ancient magic here recognizes your blood. I feel it as well, but as I have no connection here, it does not affect me as much."

Ariadne took in Igraine's features. The painter had put amazing detail into the portrait. Her warm, brown eyes were flecked with gold, very much like Ariadne and Anwil's own. Igraine leaned slightly into her husband's hand on his shoulder. He was bent forward just a bit, as if he did not wish to be too far away from her. A couple in love.

And then Ariadne's grandfather, Uther, tore them apart.

Ariadne tore her eyes away from the portrait and put her head in her hands.

But why exactly was she seeing them? Camelot held memories and magic too, and Ariadne had never seen the dead before.

She shook her head. "We should get back to work."

Without waiting for a reply, she slipped out of the study and back to the steward's office.

****

Ariadne's dreams were not safe from the memories either. Ariadne saw Igraine again, but this time, Igraine looked worried. Scared. It was storming and she sat on a bed, the young girl curled in her lap. Lightning and thunder cracked outside but Igraine rocked the girl, singing to her.

Ariadne saw Uther, recognizing him by his red hair. He was outside Tintagel Castle, a large army behind him. And next to him stood Merlin.

Then Igraine was on the bed, screaming, her belly swollen. Women surrounded her and the girl paced outside the room. A baby was born. Igraine held him once, and then he was taken. Igraine called for him. Pleaded. But they never brought the baby back.

Ariadne woke with the sun, soaked with sweat. Every night for a week, she saw the same thing. Uther seizing Cornwall, Arthur's birth, and Igraine.

"Why? Why are you showing me these terrible memories?" Ariadne said out loud.

She pushed herself off the bed and went to the water basin by the window. Washing herself off, she wished for her tub and plumbing back at Camelot; a full bath right now would be perfect. But they were leaving Tintagel soon and there was no time to heat and carry water.

Once dressed, Ariadne checked on Constantine. He was back by the window, but at least he was clean.

"My lord?" Ariadne said cautiously. "How are you feeling?"

Constantine did not answer her.

"We found a temporary steward," Ariadne continued. "Anwil is sending one from Camelot to rehire the staff and get the castle in order again."

Again, no reply.

Ariadne had carried a set of papers for Constantine, and she set them on his desk. "Well, here's the plans," she said. "We're returning to Camelot now. Goodbye, my lord."

She waited a moment, but still he did not reply. Ariadne left him alone and met the others in the courtyard, where new stable-hands had brought their horses.

"No luck," Ariadne said.

"I left the kitchens some tea recipes," Mirah said. "And spoke with the local healer. I don't know what else we can do for him, though. The trauma he's had…"

"We've all had trauma lately," Ariadne grumbled. "I watched my own mother die, and I didn't throw myself into a stupor."

"You are stronger than he is," Lancelot said. "Come; we must leave now before the storm comes."

Ariadne glanced at Tintagel once more, a sadness welling in her belly as if she were leaving home, but she urged Nerys on, back to Camelot.

CHAPTER SEVENTEEN

MORGANA

Time did not pass in Avalon as it did in the human realm. It could pass in a blink in Avalon, and yet hundreds of years could have passed in Briton, or it could drag on and on and feel like years, but only minutes had passed outside of it. Morgana had forgotten what that had felt like. She did not know how much time had passed since she had returned to Avalon. The days were long, yet passed quickly. The island slowly regained life as Vivienne recovered. Each day, the grass was greener, flowers budded and bloomed, and leaves grew. Slowly, animals returned from their hibernation and the air warmed.

Once, she would have hated to admit it, but she had missed life in Avalon. Her calling was here; there was no denying it. Not anymore. Morgana remembered back to her younger days and how much joy she had felt waking up every morning in Avalon and going about her duties, practicing magic, speaking with the fae and the gods.

But Morgana hadn't spoken to the gods in a long time. She had turned her back on them, as they had turned their backs on the world.

"I have Seen something," a frantic Vivienne said to Morgana one morning.

The days had passed with Vivienne taking Morgana through the priestess training, the same she had as a young woman when she first came to Avalon. It was an odd feeling, returning to the training she had nearly forgotten, but it felt good. As if stretching a sore muscle. When she wasn't training, she was visiting the Otherworld, looking for any signs of Mordred and Nimue.

Morgana shot up from her place on the ground, where she had been relaxing against an ancient stone. "What?"

"Nimue has bound Mordred and Anwil together," Vivienne said. "Their souls, they are tethered. One cannot live without the other. If one dies...so does the other."

Morgana's heart dropped into her stomach and she put a hand on the stone to steady herself.

"How can that be?" Morgana gasped. "It's not possible."

"Well, Nimue has done it," Vivienne said, her jaw tense. "You must find a way to undo it."

"Me? Can't you?"

"I cannot leave Avalon," Vivienne said. "There isn't much I can do from here. But Merlin—"

Morgana clenched her fists. "No. I will not go to him."

"Then Anwil dies," Vivienne snapped. "Mordred will not last long in this world. Even now, his body decays and his soul tries to part itself from it. You must push whatever feelings you have for Merlin away and save Anwil."

Morgana squeezed her eyes shut. "Where is he?"

"With Ceridwen," Vivienne answered, "his grandmother, in the Otherworld. But his mind is lost. However, he may have something in his books in his study at Camelot. He studied dark magic to understand it."

Morgana relaxed a little. If she did not have to see the man who led to her mother's ruin, the better.

"All right. I'll leave for Camelot," Morgana said.

"The boat is already waiting,"

Once Morgana was packed, Vivienne escorted her to the shores.

Morgana turned to Vivienne, who now looked as she once had, glowing silvery skin and sparkling violet eyes with shimmering black hair. The other priestesses stood behind Vivienne as Morgana said her goodbyes.

Vivienne took Morgana's face in her hands and kissed her forehead. "Have courage, my raven, and know that I have loved you like a daughter," she said softly. "It was an honor and privilege to know you, Lady Morgana of Cornwall."

Morgana closed her eyes at her oldest and first title. She hadn't gone by that since she was a girl. A girl who had been long forgotten. Morgana engulfed Vivienne in a tight hug, which the priestess returned, holding her as a mother did a hurting child.

Vivienne whispered an old blessing in her ear and gently nudged her toward the boat. Morgana raised a goodbye to the priestesses, who bowed.

With one last look at the enchanted isle, Morgana turned away as the boat glided through the crystal waters, back to Briton. Back to Camelot.

Camelot came into view as Morgana rode to the top of the hill on the King's Road. Her gray mare, Boudicca, had been waiting for her when the boat bumped into the shores of Glastonbury.

It was a quiet journey, even though she had met many travelers along the road. None of them paid her any mind, an odd experience for Morgana. Once, she could not travel anywhere without being recognized.

A kind family on a wagon, though, shared a midday meal with her when she had sat down on the side of the road to eat her own food. They did not recognize her, nor even so much as blink when she said her name was Morgana.

Smiling, Morgana had listened to the tales they spun about how Princess Ariadne stopped a coup by cutting down two mighty lords of Briton single-handedly, and that King Anwil had gone on a quest and found the legendary Sir Lancelot living as a crazed hermit in a cave. (She laughed for hours afterward about that one, impatient to tell Lancelot).

Pulling herself from her thoughts, Morgana pulled Boudicca to a halt as the gleaming city came into view. It was more than she had ever expected. Camelot, as she remembered, had been a humble but proud city.

But this.

This was nothing like she ever could have imagined.

Tears welled into her eyes with her thoughts of her brother and if he could only see what Guinevere had built. Arthur's dream sat in front of her, with red and gold banners at every tower. It was magnificent. And it was full of people. Even from her spot on the road, she could see them spilling into the city.

Hearing the pounding of hooves and wheels behind her, Morgana urged Boudicca forward to Camelot.

As she approached, the power of the wards around the city nearly knocked her off the horse. She felt the magic like tendrils reaching out to her. It whispered in her ear, slid around her legs, her arms.

I am not here to harm, she told the magic.

It pulled away, as if shocked she dare speak to it. But it let her through, though the guards at the city gates stopped her and asked for her to dismount.

"Is there a problem, sirs?" Morgana asked once her feet were on the ground.

"Standard procedure, mistress," the younger one said.

"Are you human or fae?" the older one growled at her.

Morgana stiffened. "Why would it matter?"

"Can't have fae spies comin' in to kill our king, now can we?" he said, puffing his chest out. Morgana took him in. He was perhaps half a foot taller than her, with pale skin, brown hair, and a neatly trimmed beard. He looked to be in good shape and his hand itched toward the sword at his belt. To have such a weapon would mean he held some high rank. The other guards at the gates only had spears.

"I have fae blood from my mother," Morgana answered truthfully. "But I am no spy."

The younger one, a thin, brown-skinned man with a clean-shaven face and locks, pulled out a scroll and graphite. "Name?"

Morgana turned back to the mouthy older one and locked her gaze with his.

"Morgana le Fey."

The graphite fell out of the guard's fingers.

They both stared at her, slack-jawed. She would have found it funny, if not for the absurd screening they wished to put her through. A shadow of fear passed over Mouthy's face and he went to yank the sword from his belt. But Morgana smirked and the guard found that he could not pull the blade from its sheath. His eyes widened.

"Perhaps you should send for Sir Lancelot," Morgana suggested.

The younger one came out of his stupor and nudged Mouthy.

Mouthy shot Morgana a glare and called for another guard, who, after a few whispered words, ran into the city.

Mouthy glared at Morgana and pulled iron chains from his waist.

"If you dare try," Morgana hissed, "I will gut you."

"If my memory is right," he said. "You're King Arthur's evil sister. And aren't you Lord Mordred's mother? From what I hear, that's the man trying to kill our king. So you either put these on quietly or I'll have the archers shoot you down."

Morgana raised an eyebrow and looked up and down. His uniform was familiar, and while he had a sword at his waist, he was assumedly still an ordinary guardsman and not a knight or lord.

"You don't have the rank to order that."

"Protecting our king is my duty," he growled. "And if I have to slit your throat—"

"No one will be slitting anyone's throat!" came a bark.

It was not Sir Lancelot who came to the gates, but a young man with light brown hair. Clad in black and red and a gleaming hauberk, his demeanor told Morgana he was the one in charge. A sword hung on his belt, along with a couple of daggers at his hips and boots.

"My lord—"

"You're dismissed," he said to the two guards.

Mouthy glared at the knight, his jaw clenched, but the knight stared him down, as if daring him to challenge the order.

Grumbling, Mouthy fell behind the gates, and the knight turned to Morgana.

"My lady," he said. "I am Sir Malcolm. Please come with me."

He gave her no option but to follow him. So, she tugged on Boudicca's reins and stepped into Camelot behind him.

To say what greeted Morgana was unexpected was grossly understated. Camelot was a bustling city with colorful people, buildings, and animals. People in all manner of dress and accessories hurried along the cobbled streets, laughing, talking. They passed churches, schools, an orphanage, and private houses.

Morgana was sure she would hurt her neck trying to take it all in. But she had to keep her focus on the knight she was following so as not to lose him in the crowd.

When they came to the market, an amalgamation of smells hit Morgana, and her mouth watered. Smoked meat, sweet treats, fresh fruit were all around, and Morgana had to yank Boudicca away from three booths. Tears threatened her eyes to see it all, to see Arthur's dream come to full fruition.

After a while of pushing through the crowds, she and Sir Malcolm came to the castle gates, a sight more familiar to her.

They halted at the gates again, and the young man told her to wait. She leaned against Boudicca's shoulder, scratching her neck. The mare nuzzled into her and blew hard out of her nose.

"I know," Morgana mumbled. "You can rest soon."

After a short while, a familiar voice reached Morgana's ears. She peered around Boudicca to find Lancelot, resplendent in red and maille, hurrying toward them from the courtyard.

Morgana grinned at him. "There's my mad hermit."

Lancelot halted in his steps. "Your what?"

CHAPTER EIGHTEEN

MORGANA

Poor Sir Malcolm looked as if he were fighting a laugh as Lancelot stuck his hands on his hips.

"What do you mean, mad hermit?"

"It's a wonderful story that I cannot wait to tell you," Morgana teased. "But sadly, you *will* have to wait. I have news from Vivienne."

"Judging by the look on your face, I'd say it isn't good," Lancelot mumbled.

Morgana shook her head and glanced at Sir Malcolm, who was watching them closely.

"Malcolm"—Lancelot turned to him—"will you inform the king that Lady Morgana is here?"

Malcolm bowed and left.

"Follow me," Lancelot told Morgana, and once again, she followed a knight through a gate of Camelot.

Morgana followed Lancelot down an unfamiliar corridor, taking in the portraits, tapestries, statues, and art that hung along the walls. Servants wearing matching red surcoats and tabards passed by, along with nobility in all kinds of dress from around the world. And not one of them gave her a second glance.

Once, they would part or turn the other way when she passed in the halls, but to be so invisible in the castle was not something she had expected.

"I've only just returned myself," Lancelot said. "Last night."

Morgana raised her eyebrows.

"Cornwall." Lancelot lowered his voice. "Constantine is...well...I'll tell you about that later. I'm sure you want to rest first."

"A bath would be lovely, honestly," Morgana admitted.

"I figured," Lancelot said. "I have my old quarters back. Lady Reya has retired at Joyous Guard with her sister-in-law, Lynette."

"I Saw Gawaine's death," Morgana said, slipping an arm through his. "When I returned to Avalon. I am sorry, Lance. You loved him well."

"I said my goodbyes when I left Camelot," Lancelot said. "He died honorably, protecting the princess."

"You mentioned Lynette is with Reya?" Morgana asked. Neither woman had cared for Morgana, though. Her last memories of the two were the horrid lies they had spread of Morgana without remorse: She was a harpy, a siren, a whore. That she was a traitor who brought Arthur's downfall and helped Mordred kill him on the battlefield.

"Gaheris passed just a year ago," Lancelot told her, bringing her back from her memories. "At the fire in Glastonbury. Along with Sir Ulrich."

Morgana took in a sharp breath. Gaheris had been a close friend once. A good man. She wondered how many more had died in her absence. Morgana whispered a blessing and Lancelot took her hand, but Morgana spotted a familiar figure just ahead.

"Blanchefleur?" Morgana called to her, and immediately regretted it. Did Blanchefleur hate her now too? It had been so long. Was it even her?

The woman turned around. She looked very much the same as the last time Morgana had seen her. The same periwinkle blue eyes and pale, yellow hair, although wisps of white shone in the blonde and laugh lines had been etched on her face and around her eyes.

"Morgana?" She put a hand to her heart as Morgana and Lancelot approached.

"Do my eyes deceive me?" Blanchefleur looked Morgana over.

"They do not, old friend," said Morgana, and for a moment, neither of them moved. But then Blanchefleur's arms were around Morgana who sighed in relief, holding her friend close.

"Oh, Morgana, how I have missed you," Blanchefleur said.

"And I you." Morgana pulled back and brushed some hair from Blanchefleur's face.

"What brings you back?" Blanchefleur asked, looking from Morgana to Lancelot.

"Mordred," Morgana answered.

Blanchefleur's face fell and darkened.

"I know he is your son, Morgana," said Blanchefleur. "But he killed my husband and my baby and I cannot—" A sob choked out of her.

Morgana took her hands in hers.

"I do not blame you for your feelings against him," said Morgana. "Mordred is lost to me. He is no longer my son."

Blanchefleur looked up at her with red eyes. "We have both lost sons," she whispered.

"I am sorry about Percival," Morgana whispered. "And your boy."

Blanchefleur gave her a sad smile. "His name was Lyrion," she said. "He was my baby. My youngest. Percival died defending him, but Mordred was too much." She squeezed her eyes shut. "Percival was a true knight. I've always known he would die protecting us. I never took one day for granted. Not one. I have another son, Lohengrin. I live for him now."

"I do not blame you if this causes a rift—"

Blanchefleur shook her head. "We well know no one controls Mordred except Mordred. I do not blame you. I have never blamed you for Mordred's sins."

Morgana let out a breath of relief. "It is good to see you, Blanchefleur."

"Welcome home, Morgana."

A warmth spread in Morgana's heart. Home.

Blanchefleur kissed her cheek and disappeared around a corner.

Lancelot put a hand on Morgana's back and led her to A familiar corridor. Lancelot explained the castle had undergone four additions and the original castle was now the royal family's private wing. Only the Pendragons, their close family, and some very close friends lived in the old castle.

These halls, Morgana knew. She could feel the old magic Merlin had woven into the stone and wood. The tapestries, while worn now, told familiar stories, and she even saw herself in some.

Lancelot's chambers were unfamiliar to her, as they had not gotten along then and she had only visited them once when he had fallen ill in the early years of Arthur's reign. Lancelot led her directly to the washroom, where a young girl was setting out soaps and towels. She bowed and scurried away when they entered.

"Why do they all wear the same clothes?"

Lancelot chuckled. "The servant's uniform," he said. "I thought it odd myself. The crown provides them with the surcoats to help keep their own clothes from getting worn."

Morgana blinked. "I've never heard such a thing."

"It was Guinevere's idea," said Lancelot, crossing the room to the large tub. "They are easily identifiable."

Morgana smiled. "That sounds like her."

She picked up a bar of soap and inspected it. It was a musky, spiced scent that warmed her nose.

"So much has changed," she said, more to herself.

Lancelot leaned over the tub and turned a handle on the wall. Water spilled out of the spigot and Morgana gasped.

"Come feel it." Lancelot waved her over, and she stuck her hand under the water.

"It's warm!" she exclaimed.

"Takes after the Roman aqueducts," he said.

"But how is it warm?"

"The water is heated below the castle," Lancelot explained. "An invention of Merlin's, apparently, run by magic. If you wish it warmer, however, you'll have to light a fire under the tub."

Morgana peered under the tub, where a small portion of the floor was dug out for coals. "I wish Arthur could see this."

Lancelot got that look on his face that told Morgana he was getting lost in his memories.

"Anwil and Ariadne are wonderful," he said. "They are just like them—Arthur and Guin. Ariadne is more like her father than Anwil is. Anwil has Guin's gentle soul."

"Not a good thing for a warrior king to have." Morgana frowned.

Lancelot shook his head, taking Morgana's cloak from her.

"He is like Arthur in some ways. In that, he ignores his feelings and buries himself in his work." Lancelot turned the water off. "He is a good man, but perhaps too good."

Lancelot knelt to take off her boots.

Morgana's own heart sank. "This world is going to tear him apart."

"I don't think it will," said Lancelot, looking up at her, his dark blue eyes shining. "He has strength. He just needs to recognize it. I think he's exactly what this world needs."

Morgana chuckled quietly.

"What?"

"You sound like your mother."

"That's not an insult." Lancelot pulled her tunic off. "And speaking of my mother. We've gotten distracted. What is this news?"

Morgana took hold of Lancelot's arms. There was no easy way to deliver this kind of news, so she got straight to the point.

"Anwil is dying."

CHAPTER NINETEEN

ANWIL

Anwil was sore. His training lesson with Lancelot that morning had been brutal. The knight said he was improving, but Anwil wasn't sure. It was becoming harder and harder to keep up with each lesson. He tired more easily than ever, and the muscles he had built over the winter when he had started the lessons were shrinking. The spot on his chest was bigger than ever and soon, he wouldn't be able to hide it under his tunics. It creeped toward his neck, moving higher every day.

Anwil signed his name and stamped the royal seal with his ring on the bottom of the document and leaned back in his chair with a grunt. He stretched his shoulders and rubbed his wrist before rolling the document and carefully encasing it into a leather tube, tying and sealing that with the royal seal as well.

No one knew he had written this, not even Lord Roland. But it was done. Just in case.

Ariadne would be taken care of in case the kings threw out the inheritance laws Anwil had signed a few months ago. While the kingdom was stable, the death of a king always threw everything off balance. And the British people, especially the kings, were battle hungry. After nearly twenty years of peace—besides the odd raider skirmishes—the kings were itching for battle. Anwil could sense it in the new kings. They were eager to raise arms against Nimue, ready to take their glory.

Anwil had been relieved when they all finally took their leave of Camelot a few days ago. They had been driving him mad.

Someone knocked on his study door, and Anwil called for them to enter.

It was his sister. He sat up.

"Surprised you're awake," he teased.

She narrowed her eyes but plopped down on the sofa. "Did you get my letters?"

"I did," Anwil said, joining her. "But they were vague."

Ariadne sighed. "It's not good at all," she mumbled. "He hadn't bathed in months, won't speak, barely even moves from this chair in front of the window. It overlooks the path to the castle and I wonder if he stares at it, hoping to see Yvanne..."

Anwil took in an unsteady breath.

"He let his room stay clean while we were there," Ariadne continued, "but he won't speak. After the outburst I wrote to you about, he hasn't acknowledged anyone, won't even look at anyone. Mirah left some teas and tonics for the kitchens, but...I don't know if he can come out of this."

Anwil pushed off the couch and crossed the room to the pitcher of wine and poured some for himself and Ariadne.

She mumbled a thanks as he handed her the goblet.

"It's ridiculous," Ariadne hissed. "As if we didn't see our mother die, as if she didn't bleed out in our arms! You also saw—you held Yvanne! And Gawaine, and Percival, and Lyrion...we've lost too! And yet, he acts as if his loss was greatest!"

"Ari," Anwil said quietly. "We cannot compare loss. Loss is loss, and for some, the grief *is* all-consuming."

"That's what Mirah and Lancelot said, too," Ariadne grumbled. "But he is a king, though! His people need him. Look at us! We're not wallowing away in our chambers. We're making sure the kingdom is run! Thousands count on us, on him and—"

Ariadne gripped her goblet so hard, Anwil feared it would break. He took it carefully from her and set it down on the table. He then wordlessly pulled his sister to him and held her as she took in a shattering breath, and broke.

After a while, Ariadne pulled away, wiping the tear tracks from her cheeks. Anwil gave her his handkerchief.

"I'm sorry," she mumbled.

"Don't be," he said. She looked away from him, her cheeks red, so he asked, "What was that other thing you wished to talk about? That you didn't want to put in a letter."

"Oh," she grunted and grabbed her goblet, taking a long drink. "Apparently I see ghosts."

Anwil wasn't quite sure he heard her right. "Beg pardon?"

"Lancelot and Mirah said there's ancient magic at Tintagel." Ariadne rubbed at her face. "And that because you and I have familial ties and were born of magic, it affected me more. I *saw* them, in the halls, interacting with each other. As if they were still alive, but they weren't quite all there. And I dreamed of them."

Anwil sat back, trying to wrap his mind around it. "Saw who?"

"Igraine," Ariadne said. "And her husband, Gorlois. And then Uther. And Morgana le Fey. As a child."

Anwil let out a breath.

"I don't know why I saw them," she continued. "Or precisely what it means, but...I needed to tell you."

"What did the others say?"

Ariadne shrugged. "Not much. Just like I said before. That the magic recognized me. We didn't speak of it on the way back. Lancelot said it wasn't safe."

Someone knocked again and Anwil called for them to enter and Sir Malcolm stepped inside.

"Forgive the interruption," he said. "But Morgana le Fey just arrived."

Ariadne's goblet slipped from her hands and tumbled onto the stone floor.

"Well, looks like you can ask Morgana herself why you saw her," Anwil said to her.

He was met with a look of bewilderment.

Morgana was not as Anwil expected. He expected someone like Lady Vivienne, with shimmering hair and long robes, an ethereal presence about her. But Morgana le Fey was none of those things. If Anwil had seen her in the corridors or in the city, he likely wouldn't have noticed her at all. Her gray-touched black hair fell in a tight braid over her shoulder, her dress was a plain green linen, and her pale skin dotted with light freckles.

She was so utterly...human. Except her eyes. They were the same purple as Lady Vivienne and Nimue's.

Morgana looked up from the Round Table as the doors shut behind him and put a hand to her chest, gasping.

"Forgive me," she said. "Lancelot said how much you look like Arthur, but I didn't expect..."

"Welcome back to Camelot, my lady," Anwil said to her and gestured for her to sit. All of the Knights of the Round Table were there as well, various forms of emotions on their faces.

Ariadne grabbed his wrist. "What are you doing?" she whispered.

"Wait a moment," he replied.

Ariadne opened her mouth to answer back, but Anwil stepped away, toward an empty chair. As he sat, the knights looked from him to Morgana.

"I can see in your faces you have plenty of questions," he said to them.

"Questions?" Lohengrin snapped. "Yes, questions. How about how the fuck can you let the mother of the man who killed my father and brother—"

"Lohengrin!" Brionna grabbed him by the shoulder and yanked him back from the Table before Anwil even had a chance to reply. "Do you forget that this is your king you speak to?"

"A king I also thought was my brother," Lohengrin snarled.

"That's uncalled for!" Ariadne shot to her feet, slamming her hands on the table.

"She's the enemy!"

"Lady Morgana is not our enemy, Lohengrin," Anwil barked back at him. "I understand you are angry—"

"Angry!" Lohengrin exclaimed, trying to yank himself from Brionna, but she held tight to his arm. "Mordred brutalized them. In front of me. Laughing as he slit their throats. And his mother is here as a welcomed guest?"

"You are out of line, Sir Knight," Ariadne hissed through gritted teeth. "Sit down."

Lohengrin sent her an astonished look but slid back into his seat. Brionna let go of his arm but did not back away.

"You are my closest friend, Lohengrin," Anwil said. "But I will not tolerate another outburst like that."

Lohengrin bowed his head. "Forgive me, Your Grace."

"Forgiven," Anwil said.

Ariadne slowly sat back down.

"Why is she here, though?" she asked.

"Because she has been our spy in the Otherworld since winter," Anwil explained.

It was so quiet, Anwil could almost hear the birds chirp outside the windows.

"What!?"

"Lancelot, do you want to start at the beginning?" Anwil turned to him.

Lancelot exchanged a look with Lady Morgana, and she nodded.

"I have known Morgana for over fifty years," Lancelot said. "Ever since she returned to Camelot after King Urien's death. And I have only ever questioned her loyalty to Arthur once. We were wary, as you are, when she came to Camelot. Morgana had every right to hate Arthur. Uther killed her father, did horrible things to her mother, but never once did Morgana blame Arthur for any of it. Nor did she ever covet his crown. She advised and cared deeply for Arthur until his last breath. It was Morgana who helped Bedievere carry his body to Avalon after Camlann. It was Morgana who cleaned his wounds and dressed him, so his return to Camelot—even in death—was done with dignity. Not once did Morgana's loyalty to Arthur break when Mordred rebelled.

"When our time in Camelot was at an end, we found each other again and created a new life. Together. I give you my word that Morgana is here as an ally."

Silence hung in the air. Anwil looked at Morgana, who had let Lancelot speak. Her eyes were on her folded hands on the table, her expression the same blank look Anwil had seen in his mother when she did not wish her thoughts to betray her.

"You chose your brother over your own son?" Xiang asked quietly.

Morgana looked up at him, a shadow of regret passing on her face.

"I was not a good mother," she said. "I was still a priestess when I fell pregnant with Mordred, and I could not be both. Babies are not welcome in Avalon and when you are a priestess of The Modron, that is *all* you are. You cannot be split. So I gave Mordred away. I naively thought Morgause a friend. I thought we had bonded over how badly Uther treated our mothers, but I was wrong. Because Mordred's father was fae, Morgause wanted his magic. So she raised him for herself, for power, and into someone who held no love for me. I understood. I gave him up. When he became a knight, I tried to repair our relationship, and I thought I had, but Mordred never wanted it. He is incapable of love. He doesn't understand it. He only sees it as something he can manipulate. I gave birth to him, yes, but...". Lancelot took one of her hands in his. "Besides, what Mordred is now is not natural. He died at Camlann and should still be dead now."

Anwil's heart lurched at her tale. He and Lancelot had spoken of Morgana during training, but Lancelot had held off on the heavy details, claiming they were not his to tell. Anwil saw why. Even Lohengrin seemed moved by Morgana's words, as his glare had softened.

"Well, I for one am glad if Lady Morgana is on our side," said Brom. "If the tales are true, she's one powerful witch."

"Brom!" Ariadne snapped.

"What?"

Morgana chuckled. "It is all right," she said. "I have been called many things in my life, witch being the most common."

"His Grace said you have been in the Otherworld, my lady?" Jabir said.

"Yes," Morgana answered. "Mostly in Avalon with Vivienne. She is why I am here now."

"Is she dead?" Ariadne asked. "I saw her last Autumn. She was so ill."

"She is much recovered," Morgana said with a small smile. "But there is grave news." She glanced at Anwil, who did not like the look on her face. "When Nimue resurrected Mordred, she used your blood. Because of this, the spell fused a bond between the two of you. Often a tether can be used in simple protection or bonding spells, but something different happened in Nimue's spell. Your souls have been bound."

Ariadne gasped. "What? What does that... what does that mean?"

"It means if we do not break the tether, Anwil will die," Morgana said quietly.

Anwil's chest tightened. His heartbeat roared in his ears. Lohengrin looked at him, his expression full of pain.

"Die?" Brom said.

"Mordred's soul belongs to the dead," Morgana explained. "It is not long for this world. Eventually, he will die. Again. Taking Anwil's soul with him."

Anwil bowed his head and squeezed his eyes shut. Morgana had just confirmed what he had already been thinking. He was dying.

"*Can* we break it?" he rasped.

"That is why I am here," Morgana said. "Vivienne believes Merlin may have the answers. He is indisposed, not of his mind, but the books in his study could have answers."

"How long do I have?" Anwil asked quietly, staring at the table.

"I don't know," Morgana said softly.

Ariadne slammed her fist on the table. "No!" she cried. "No, Anwil is not dying. He's not!"

"Ari," Anwil said. "Please."

"I will do everything in my power to keep your brother from this fate," Morgana said to Ariadne. "On my life, I swear it."

Ariadne said nothing, but her eyes were watery.

Anwil pinched his nose. "Who else knows?"

"Outside of this room," said Morgana, "Vivienne, and I would assume Mordred and Nimue."

"Do we know where they are, Lady Morgana?" Lord Roland asked.

"They are somewhere in the Otherworld," Morgana answered. "But as to specifics, I do not know."

"My lady," Jabir asked. "Will breaking the tether harm the king?"

"Vivienne said breaking the tether is the only way to save him," Morgana answered. "He will not die, but as to any pain, I cannot say."

"Anwil—"

He brushed his sister's hand away.

"Use whatever you need," he said to Morgana. "Do whatever you can to free me of this."

She met his eye. "I will."

"Good," Anwil replied, standing up. "I'm sure you're tired and hungry after your journey. We can talk more tomorrow."

The knights and Morgana stood without argument and filed out. Ariadne hesitated by him, but he shook his head. He caught her eyes watering but looked away and heard her storm from the room.

When Lohengrin passed him, though, Anwil caught his arm. He waited until they were alone before speaking.

"You're angry and hurt. I understand," Anwil said, speaking in low, quiet tones. "But do *not* speak to me like that again, especially in front of others."

Lohengrin shot him a look, his face flushing, but gave a curt nod and Anwil let go of his arm, watching him leave.

Anwil slumped back down in his chair and let out a shuttered breath, clutching at his chest.

CHAPTER TWENTY

ARIADNE

Anwil avoided all contact the rest of the day and the next morning, locking himself in his chambers. Ariadne tried to goad him out before she went on her patrol, but he wouldn't answer. So she left for duty, grateful she had something to distract herself with.

Lancelot had taken Morgana directly to his chambers, as word had gotten out and she was bombarded with questions and accusations as soon as she stepped into the corridors after the king's meeting. And then Ariadne was carted off by Brionna, despite her protests, to the training fields.

"No, we have to do something. We can't—" Ariadne had argued, but Brionna shushed her and stuck a sword in her hand and sparred with she until she couldn't get up anymore. Later, she realized it was exactly what she had needed.

"If Lady Vivienne trusts her, so should we," Mirah told her late that night when Ariadne filled her in. "Lady Morgana is even more powerful than Merlin. If this tether can be broken, she can do it."

So, despite her grievances, Ariadne accepted it. Until she knew more about Morgana, though, Ariadne would be cautious, and told the guards to keep a good eye on her.

Patrol kept her mind distracted, and just an hour into it, the skies opened and dumped heavy rain into the city. Ariadne and Brionna, who had just finished hearing complaints about the woman selling melons, were soaked within minutes.

The cold seeped into her skin through her clothing and leathers. No matter how often it rained, Ariadne hated it. She hated being wet. Unless she was swimming or in a bath, of course, but to be out in the city in the rain, the mud, the puddles, the cold... Ariadne shoved a soaked, stray curl from her face, grumbling to herself.

Her mother used to love rain-filled days, saying it made the world calmer, and perhaps she was right. But Camelot was coming to life despite the weather. Shop owners were readying for the day's market and the influx of travelers the warm weather had brought. Ariadne could see them through their windows, bustling about. Some braved the weather, hurrying along the cobbled streets to run their errands.

She had awoken that morning to a shining new hauberk and tabard waiting for her. The knight's tabard. Scarlet red with a rampant gold dragon on the chest. Ariadne had picked it up with shaking hands, hardly believing it was finally hers and waiting for the joy. But it didn't come. Couldn't come. Not when Morgana le Fey had arrived in Camelot and told her that her brother was dying.

Ariadne hadn't slept. Had barely functioned for the rest of the day after meeting with Morgana. She had tried to talk with Anwil, but he didn't wish to see anyone and closed himself off in his chambers.

Ariadne hadn't the strength to speak to anyone, either. So she asked Lord Roland to have Morgana shown to Merlin's study. Instead of her chambers, though, Ariadne went to the training fields and hit a dummy until her knuckles were bruised and bleeding.

"Oh, beg pardon, Your Highness!"

Ariadne halted in her steps, nearly knocking into Mistress Claudia. Ariadne had been so lost in her thoughts, she hadn't seen her trying to cross the street.

"My apologies, Mistress," Ariadne called over the rain.

"I'm actually glad to see you," said Mistress Claudia, the half-fae modiste. "I have something for you. Can you stop by the shop?"

Ariadne looked at Brionna, who nodded and followed the seamstress to her shop. The bell tinkled as they hurried inside, water soaking the wooden floor. It was a small shop, crammed to the brim with fabrics, hats, gloves, cloaks, and projects in the making.

"I cannot believe this weather lately," Mistress Claudia said, lighting a few candles with her fingers. "The gods must be angry about something. Now, I know it must be hard for you, and I waited to send it, but it can't very well go to waste in my storage room."

She disappeared through a curtain and returned a moment later carrying a regal dress. Red silk shimmered in the candlelight, and embroidered golden dragons lined the hem, the sleeves, and neckline.

"Queen Guinevere commissioned it for His Grace's original coronation this summer," Mistress Claudia said somberly. "But I hadn't the chance to finish it over the winter. I fell ill, you see. Well...it's done now and I think you should have it."

Ariadne stared at the dress, eyes stinging. "I-I don't..." she shook her head.

"I know how hard it is to lose one's mother," said Mistress Claudia. "I lost mine when I was fourteen. The hurt never really goes away. But it's good to remember. I still remember my mother's voice, and how she was so patient teaching me needlework. I'm sure you have wonderful memories of your mother as well."

Ariadne nodded, not able to find her voice.

"Shall I send this to the castle when the rain clears?" Mistress Claudia asked quietly.

Ariadne took in a deep breath and let her fingers trail over the wide sleeve of the dress. "Yes, thank you."

"Your mother will live on," said Mistress Claudia. "With you, with your brother, and through the legacy she left behind. She built something only believable in dreams. She will not be forgotten. Not in a thousand years."

"Thank you," Ariadne said, her throat catching.

"Of course, Your Highness." Mistress Claudia bowed and returned to her storage room.

"Ari," Brionna said from behind her.

Ariadne hurriedly wiped at her eyes and cleared her throat. "Right. Back to patrols."

"Is everything—" But Brionna didn't get to finish her sentence, as a screech pierced the air. Immediately, Brionna and Ariadne tore from the shop and toward the sound.

They skidded to a halt in front of one of the smithies, where a fae female was holding her blackened hand. Her golden skin was flushed with red, and her yellow eyes burned hot.

"You bastard!" she screeched at a young man in a thick apron just inside the entrance. "I'll kill you!"

Ariadne jumped in between them, nearly slipping in a puddle. "What happened?" she asked.

"He did it on purpose!" the fae spat around her. "He's trying to kill me. But I'll kill him first!" She tried to step around Ariadne, but Ariadne grabbed her waist.

"I did no such thing!" the younger man said. "It was an accident, I swear!"

A crowd had formed, despite the still steady rain. Brionna tried to shoo them away, but they were reluctant to go.

"You gave me iron!" the fae female lunged for him, but Ariadne held her tight.

"No killing, no maiming," Ariadne said to her, and then glanced at the crowd. "You may all go now."

A few heads turned, but no one moved.

"That was an order," Ariadne growled at them and reluctantly, the crowd dispersed.

Brionna ushered them under a tent covering lumber for the city's rebuilding efforts. The fae still held her wounded hand, shadowlike veins now crawling up her arm.

"What happened?" Ariadne asked more gently.

The fae female hissed at the blacksmith's apprentice, who still hovered by the smithy's entrance.

"I came for my order," the fae female said. "But he gave me the wrong thing and handed me iron."

Ariadne turned to the apprentice.

"I didn't! I swear!"

"You knew my order was gardening tools! Not a dagger!"

"We cannot have deliberate attacks against the fae," Ariadne said to the apprentice, and then turned to the fae. "What is your name?"

"Nerissa," she said.

"As he said, it was an accident." The blacksmith, a large man in a dirty apron, appeared at the door. "We've got iron all around. She shouldn't even be here."

The fae growled. "I've been a customer for years, but no longer. I'll be going to Master Brenwick's from now on."

Before the blacksmith could reply, Ariadne held up a hand. "Mistress Nerissa will be treated at the castle infirmary, and her tools will be given to her at no charge."

The blacksmith glared at Ariadne. "I can't afford to—"

"At. No. Charge."

The blacksmith's face turned a brighter shade of red, but he just stomped back into the shop, pulling his apprentice with him.

Brionna followed them inside and retrieved a set of gardening tools.

"Thank you," Nerissa said as Brionna handed them to her. "But I could have handled it."

"You threatened to kill him," said Ariadne. "That's not handling it."

"This isn't the first time something like this has happened to us," Nerissa said, taking her tools. "Many of the fae in this city are being treated with more hostility."

"I know. I'm sorry," said Ariadne. "We are doing what we can, passing new laws, declarations. Nimue is only making everything worse."

"Human minds are stubborn," said Nerissa. "They let fear and ignorance control them. This city is better than most human dwellings, but I fear Nimue may be right about one thing."

Ariadne suddenly felt cold. "What?"

"That humans and fae cannot live harmoniously," she said, shaking her head. "Thank you for today. But I can find my way to the infirmary from here."

She left Brionna and Ariadne to watch her go. Ariadne whirled on her heel, ready to head into the smithy, but Brionna grabbed the back of her tunic.

"Do not," Brionna hissed. "You'll make it worse."

"But they—"

"I know," said Brionna. "But it will be hard to prove. If it happens again, harsher punishment will be dealt. You cannot beat sense into people. Unfortunately."

"If only," Ariadne mumbled. "It would make life easier."

CHAPTER TWENTY-ONE

MIRAH

Mirah shuffled into her chambers, tired after a long day in the infirmary. A stomach sickness had been making its way through the city of late, and as soon as they had arrived home from Cornwall, Mirah had been swept back to the infirmary to help. After nearly a hundred patients and a lot of mopping, they finally narrowed it down to some bad fish from one of the taverns.

As Mirah closed the door, she noticed a kettle over the hearth and the sound of footsteps growing louder.

Her maid, Yasmin, came out of the washroom, drying her hands on a cloth.

"I drew a bath for you, my lady," she said. "I heard about the bad fish."

"Have I told you how wonderful you are lately?" Mirah mumbled, raising a laugh from Yasmin.

"Just yesterday, but I don't mind hearing it. Does good for my ego," Yasmin teased. "Go on and bathe, and I'll have your tea ready."

"Bless you," Mirah mumbled and did just that.

She stayed in the lavender-filled water until it turned cold. When she emerged from the bathing room, dried and changed into her nightdress, Yasmin was pouring her a cup of tea.

"Goddess," Mirah said, sinking down on the sofa, clutching the mug. "You are a goddess."

"If only," Yasmin chuckled. "Is there anything else?"

"No, thank you." Mirah sipped on the tea. "This is delicious. Do you want to stay for some?"

"Thank you, but I should sleep, myself," Yasmin said. "Good night, my lady." She bobbed a curtsy and left Mirah alone.

Mirah laid her head back on the sofa, relishing in the quiet. Only the comforting crackle of the fire filled the air. She stayed that way for a while, just sitting on the couch, sipping her tea in the quiet, letting her mind relax. When she finished the tea, she fished out the old, battered copy of the Avesta that used to belong to her mother's family. It was a religious book Nazrine used to read to her Mirah had grown up with the Mazdayasna teachings and followed them. Since coming of age and devoting her time to healing and court duties, she had lost track, however.

Mirah sank back onto the sofa and flipped through the book, the pages familiar under her fingers. Her mother's handwriting was in the margins, along with that of other family members Mirah never got to meet.

Mirah trailed her fingers over her mother's words on the inside of the front cover, *humata, huxta, huvarshta*. Good thoughts, good words, good deeds. The Threefold Path the prophet Zoroaster taught.

Mirah read through the familiar words, hearing them in her mother's voice. Soon, she dozed off, the book slipping from her hands and landing with a hard smack against the floor. Mirah jumped and bent to pick it up, but something made the hair on her arms stand up. Like something or someone was watching her. Mirah slowly picked the book up and stood, turning—and she nearly screamed.

But her voice was taken from her. Standing in front of her, with skin shining like moonlight, was a goddess. The goddess. The Modron. The Mother. Her face slipped from maid, to mother, to crone and back again as she towered over Mirah.

"Daughter," the Modron said in a soothing voice. Her face settled as the mother. Not young nor old, but a face full of wisdom and comfort. "Do not fear."

"Why have you come?" Mirah whispered. Her voice returned. But she was rooted to the spot, clutching the Avesta to her chest.

"I gave you gifts far beyond healing, child," the Modron said. "It is time you start using them."

"What do you mean?" Mirah asked.

The Modron pointed to the hearth, and the flames burst to a roar. Mirah saw herself, older, eyes blinding white, swirls of power around her, a crown of white light around her head.

"What does that mean?" Mirah turned back to The Modron. Her face had changed to the old crone.

"The strings of fate are woven for you," The Modron said.

"What strings? Wait; my path is already laid out? Why can I not choose—no, don't leave!" Mirah tried, but the Modron was gone in swirls of white smoke, the fire dying down to coals.

Mirah slumped back to her sofa, shaking, still holding the Avesta. It took her awhile to calm her breathing and move her limbs. When she could lift her arms, she patted and pinched at herself, making sure she was actually awake and it wasn't a dream.

The Modron herself had visited her. Was in her room. And talking of her fate.

"What the hells?" Mirah said out loud, letting out a long breath. She shoved herself off the couch and scurried into the washroom to splash water on her face.

She slid down the stone wall, curling her knees to her chest.

"Mama, I wish you were here," she whispered. "I need you. I don't know what this means and I'm scared."

Mirah bowed her head into her legs and cried.

Mirah did not like the new coffee drink that had been given to Camelot at Anwil's wedding, but she drained two cups the next morning. She hadn't slept at all, and infusing magic in her usual morning tea for a boost in a state like this was a bad idea. Her mind was still racing, and any spell she cast had the potential to go wrong. It was one of the first things her mother, and Merlin, had taught her about magic: One needed a calm mind to produce the best results.

Her mind was not calm. She could barely concentrate on anything. But she needed something to do. She couldn't sit still.

Instead of the infirmary, however, Mirah had gone to Merlin's study to find anything in his books about The Modron and fate.

She hadn't expected, however, for the study to already be occupied.

A woman was flipping through a small book in front of the many stuffed shelves. She looked up when Mirah burst in and nearly stumbled down the steps. Power. The air was thick with it. More so than she had ever felt in Merlin's presence.

The woman put the book aside and smiled at her. "Hello," she said. "Lady Mirah, I presume?"

Mirah could only nod.

"I am Morgana," the woman said. "It's a pleasure to meet you. I've already heard great things."

"Oh?" Mirah managed. She couldn't possibly imagine who would have spoken to Morgana le Fey about her. She was a legend, one of the most powerful women in centuries. Mirah had always looked up to her, never believing she was evil. Her mother had spoken highly of her, using Morgana's findings and spells in her own healing.

Morgana's smiled widened. "Your father," she said. "And His Grace."

Mirah's cheeks flushed. Anwil had spoken to Morgana about her?

"I am—er—I'm one of the royal physicians. And I... apprenticed under Merlin. I had wanted—that is—er—" She cleared her throat, her cheeks burning. She never stumbled over her words like this.

"I do apologize if I startled you," Morgana said, cautiously crossing the study. "His Grace gave me a key to Merlin's rooms. I've just come from Avalon and need to look through Merlin's books."

Anwil must already trust Morgana if he had given her a key to Merlin's study. Only she and Anwil had ever had carried one since Merlin's disappearance.

"Good luck," she said. "He was very disorganized."

Morgana laughed softly. "Yes, I remember. Have I interrupted your tasks for the day? I can come back later."

"No, I was just..." Mirah trailed off and cleared her throat. "You're not interrupting anything."

"Well, don't let my presence deter you," Morgana said. "I'm a quiet companion."

"You're a priestess," Mirah blurted, and Morgana halted midturn.

"I was." She nodded.

"Of Avalon," Mirah said and Morgana nodded again, regarding her curiously. "So you worked with The Modron? Have you...has she...ever visited you?"

Morgana didn't answer right away. She took Mirah in, and Mirah felt as if she was trying to look into her soul.

"Why don't we sit down?" Morgana gestured to the mismatched armchairs by Merlin's desk. "It seems you have much on your mind."

As soon as Mirah sat down, she found herself spilling everything to Morgana. From the first dream a few weeks ago to the visit from The Modron last night. Guilt panged in her stomach. Here she was telling a stranger her deepest secrets when she couldn't even bring herself to talk to her father about it.

"I don't know what any of it means," Mirah finished.

"It means The Modron chose your fate from the moment you were born," Morgana said, a slight bite to her voice. "The gods like to do that every once in a while. They tried to do it to me."

"Tried?"

"I'm not good at following orders," Morgana said with a wink. "But by veering off the path they wanted for me, I suffered the consequences."

Mirah's heart sped.

"Do not fear," Morgana said, leaning toward her. "Now, the dream. Visions are rare. There's only a handful of us who have them. They aren't always what we think they are and could be any endless possibilities. The hard part is learning how to decipher them. Sometimes they are warnings of what could happen; sometimes they are what will happen."

"I'm very confused," Mirah admitted.

"May I have your hands?" Morgana held hers out and Mirah took them. "Magic doesn't always make sense. Sometimes it contradicts itself. Visions are one of those times. Yours feels like a warning. With The Modron's visit to you last night, I believe she is telling you that you will have a great part in Camelot's future. Much more than servicing the sick. You have great power, Lady Mirah. I can feel it." Morgana squeezed Mirah's hands. "But know that you and only you are in control of your fate. The gods may have a chosen path for you, but you do not need to follow it."

"You said there were consequences," Mirah whispered.

"Yes," Morgana said. "When you defy the gods, they tend to get angry, but we have free will. Remember that. If you do not wish to have a part in Camelot's future, you do not need to. You can continue your work to be just a healer if that is your heart's desire."

Tears threatened Mirah's eyes. All her life, she had wanted to follow in her mother's footsteps. healing the sick, tending the injured. It brought Mirah joy, gave her a purpose in life besides marrying a rich lord and continuing a bloodline.

Camelot gave her that ability. It welcomed her with open arms. She was apprenticed not only under Master Cassius, but Merlin, the greatest wizard to ever live, himself. She was able to learn so much more than she ever expected. How the body works, how it lives and dies.

Camelot also gave her a second family. With Ariadne and Anwil. And Ellyn and Lohengrin.

And not to mention all the people within the city.

If her visions were telling her that her home was in danger, then she wanted to fight for it.

"I want to help," she said. "I want to fight for Camelot."

Morgana grinned. "Good," she said. "You can start by helping me organize this mess."

Mirah couldn't help but bark a laugh.

CHAPTER TWENTY-TWO

Morgana

Morgana hated Merlin's study. It was so disorganized and chaotic, it made her skin crawl. She and Mirah tried to find some sense of order and organize, but they gave up on that early on. All they ended with was a pile of books they had already looked through, and ones they needed to look through. The books contained a plethora of information about nearly everything except the one thing they were looking for. It shocked Morgana that Merlin did not have any research or notes, or even journal entries about necromancy. There were plenty of books about the dead—how bodies decompose, how different cultures and religions view the dead—but nothing that could help them.

Frowning, Morgana put aside a small book on how to make parchment and stretched in her chair. She was growing frustrated. The more time they spent looking through these books was time taken from Anwil. They would have to look somewhere else.

She glanced out the window to find the sun had nearly set. Turning back, her gaze landed on Mirah, who was asleep in the armchair, a book dangling from her hands.

Morgana gently shook her awake.

"You should go to bed," she said. "It's been a long day."

Mirah blinked up at her. Her eyes were red. She looked around the room and let out a breath. "We're never going to find anything, are we?"

"We will find something," Morgana said. "I promise you that. Tomorrow, we will look for possible hidden books. He may have hidden some of the forbidden books behind spells or secret doors. If we do not find anything after that, we'll start a new direction."

Mirah stood up and wiped her hands on her apron. "What will we do if we can't find anything?"

"There is also another possibility," said Morgana. "I had hoped to avoid it, as it may not afford much luck, but we could visit Merlin in the Otherworld. Vivienne said his mind is lost, but we might be able to get something out of him."

"We?" Mirah said. "I can come with you?"

Morgana nodded. "If you wish, yes. It'll be dangerous, though."

"I'll be fine," said Mirah, standing and knocking over the book she had been holding. "As long as—"

But both Morgana and Mirah stared at the book that had just toppled. Hitting the floor, it had broken into two books. Morgana picked up the book that had fallen from the other one. It was worn, the brown leather broken in spots. She flipped through it and gasped.

"This is Merlin's private diary," she whispered.

"What does it say?" Mirah peered over her shoulder as Morgana read aloud.

June 24, 551

Guinevere and the twins are both resting comfortably after a somewhat difficult labor. The children are healthy. Strong. Perhaps too strong. I felt a surge of power throughout the castle when the first child, a girl, arrived. And again, when the second, a boy and heir. The last time I felt a surge like this was when Arthur was born. Guinevere will not admit to it, but I know she went to Morgana for the children. What this means for the children, I do not yet know. I will remain by their sides to protect and guide them, as I have done with Arthur. They are of him; I am sure of i t.

"A surge of power?" Mirah asked. "What does that mean?"

Morgana thought back. She hadn't felt any surges of power from what she remembered. Perhaps she had been too far from Camelot to have felt it, too wrapped up in her own grief. Morgana continued reading.

January 5, 553

The twins grow healthy and strong. They have shown no signs of magic, nor anything else out of the ordinary for human chil-

dren. But there is something special about them, just as there was about Arthur. They are intelligent and kind, the boy especially so. Guinevere has done well not to spoil them with riches.

I have asked Vivienne to come to Camelot and assess them..
March 2, 553

Vivienne has spent the last two days with Anwil and Ariadne. They do not show signs of being able to wield magic, but magic surrounds them. It is in their blood. Vivienne believes they are tied to the lands; they are part of the balance of our worlds, the human and the fae. They have a small amount of fae blood from Queen Igraine, and mixed with the spell Morgana used to help Guinevere, there is an odd kind of magic in their veins. Guinevere will not let me take a sample of their blood for testing, however, so I will just have to observe.

"I felt something in Ari before," Mirah whispered. "When we went to Avalon last autumn. The magic...it told me it needed Ari. I didn't—still don't—know what that meant. I had forgotten about it with everything going on."

"Let's see what else..."

June, 10, 568

The twins have still not shown any signs of magic, but Vivienne has returned for Anwil's wedding. She has come with grave news. Their fate has changed. A storm like no other is coming. Only one may survive.

"It stops there," Morgana mumbled, flipping through the book once more.

"That was the night before Anwil's wedding," Mirah said. "He left with Lady Vivienne a few days later."

Morgana sighed. Now there were even more questions to answer.

CHAPTER TWENTY-THREE

ANWIL

Morgana le Fey had only been in Camelot two days and there were already fights about her arrival. Anwil had to mediate between council members. Ariadne broke up three physical altercations in the corridors, and now Anwil was waiting on the clergy, who had requested an immediate meeting.

"Father Ifan," Anwil greeted the old priest as the clergy filed into the throne room. "It is good to see you recovered."

Father Ifan gave him a warm smile and took his hand. "And you, Your High...I mean, Your Grace. Forgive me for old habits."

Father Ifan turned as Ariadne returned from the drink cart with a steaming mug.

"Your Highness, I have not yet congratulated you on becoming a Knight of the Round Table."

"Thank you, Father," Ariadne said, beaming.

A monk at the table let out a *harrumph*. "A woman should not be a knight," he said. "It is not their place. I do hope you reconsider your choices, Your Highness."

"Brother Felix," Father Ifan said, a tone of warning in his voice. "That is not the way to speak to the princess."

"I speak for God," said Brother Felix. "And a woman's place is not gallivanting around with a sword."

Anwil put a hand on Ariadne's arm before she said anything. He could see her face reddening.

"You are very opinionated, Brother Felix," Anwil said. "Here in Camelot, we celebrate differences. However, speak like that to my sister again, and you will not be welcome back at court."

Brother Felix's face turned a slight shade of purple, but he did not retort.

"Shall we get started?" Anwil gestured for them all to sit.

"Thank you, Your Grace," Father Ifan said, taking a seat next to him. "And I thank you for accepting our request to meet. I am sure you understand our concern for Camelot's new guest."

Brother Felix shifted in his chair but didn't speak.

"Yes," Anwil said. "And there is no need to be concerned. Lady Morgana is here as an ally and friend."

"If I may? Morgana le Fey has a dubious reputation, Sire," Father Ifan said. "Is it perhaps wise to have her back? Her loyalty to Camelot was questioned so heavily, and then her disappearance, well, it does not look good."

"I know of my aunt's reputation," Anwil said. "It is false. Lady Morgana is loyal to Camelot."

"But her son has now been raised from the dead," Father Ifan said. "A blasphemy most evil. And now *her* return. I fear it challenges your loyalty to the Christian church."

"Are you suggesting *we* raised Mordred from the dead?" Ariadne asked, arms folded across her chest.

"Of course not, Your Highness," Father Ifan said carefully. "However, you have been favoring the fae lately."

"We have a war with the fae looming over our heads," Ariadne said. "If we wish to fight them and win, we need magic."

"You should pray," Brother Felix said. "Pray to the Lord High God and he will grant you favor."

"Pray for what, Brother?" Ariadne asked. "For God to kill all the fae? That's genocide. I do not think God would approve. Or maybe he would. He drowned the world in a temper tantrum, did he not?"

Brother Felix's eyes bulged so far out of his head, Anwil was afraid they would fall onto the table. He lightly kicked his sister under the table. She winced, but didn't reply.

"You speak in blasphemy, Your Highness!"

"Enough!" Anwil snapped. "We are not here to argue faith. Camelot has always and will always honor both the old and the new ways. The people of Briton are both fae and human alike, and I will not condone the ridding of either."

Brother Felix leaned back in his seat, his upper lip twitching.

"Now," Anwil said. "Unless there is anything else, we can begin."

"Actually," Father Ifan said, leaning forward. "We have had an uptick in fae attacks on a few abbeys just north of Bath. The locals have tried everything they could. Perhaps a Druid would be willing to assist?"

"Isn't there a local chapter in Bath?" Ariadne asked.

"There used to be," Father Ifan said. "But they have since moved on."

"As they should," Brother Felix said. "It is sinful you wish for those heretics' help, Ifan."

"Why have you come, Felix?" Ariadne asked. "Because if it is only to argue, you can leave."

"I beg your pardon?" he said, eyebrows nearing his hairline.

"You have been nothing but rude since you sat down. So unless you mind your tongue, the door is right there." She pointed to the double doors.

"I see we won't be making any progress today." Anwil stood up, having had enough. "Thank you, gentlemen, but we shall have to reconvene at a later time when we can all speak civilly."

The clergy thankfully left silently without protest, but not before Father Ifan glanced Anwil's way as if he wished to say more, but Anwil turned away. Once the double door shut, he whirled on Ariadne.

"I could have handled myself," he hissed.

"What?" Ariadne asked. "What do you mean?"

"I didn't need you to defend me," he said. "All you managed was to rile Felix up. Especially after the genocide comment.

Now you've given them a reason to think we are favoring the Old Ways."

Ariadne's eyebrows shot up. "He was out of line! He has no right to speak to you that way. You're the king. And if you've forgotten, it's my job to defend you."

"Physically," Anwil said. "But I need to speak up for myself or no one will respect me."

Ariadne startled. "People respect you," she said quietly.

"Obviously not enough," Anwil said. "This meeting was an example of that. Look, I know you have issues with the new ways, but you were out of line."

"If you're looking for an apology, I won't give it," Ariadne said. "Because I am not sorry for defending you, physically or not."

She brushed past him and stormed from the throne room. Anwil slumped back into his chair and rubbed his hands over his face.

That was an absolute disaster, which would surely bring ramifications. Anwil would have to speak with Lord Roland to figure out some sort of damage control.

"Long day?"

Anwil sat up as Mirah peeked through the doors.

"I just saw Ariadne. She looked angry."

"Mirah," he said, his heart jumping.

She stepped inside, gently closing the door behind her.

"I'm sorry I haven't said hello since I've returned," she said, crossing the room. "But with the bad fish illnesses and meeting Morgana, it's been a whirlwind."

"You don't have to be sorry," Anwil said. "I heard you're helping Morgana go through Merlin's books."

"I am," she said, sliding into the seat next to him. "But, Anwil, is it true you're dying?"

Anwil blinked. "I... er—" He cleared his throat. "I don't know. If we can't break this tether...possibly."

Mirah reached over the table and put her hand over his, and his breath caught. His skin tingled where they touched.

"Anwil," she said, her eyes wide with concern.

"I'll be fine," he said. "We'll break this. With you and Morgana working on it, I have no doubt." He flipped their hands and laced his fingers with hers.

Mirah frowned. "Anwil."

He shook his head. "I'll be fine. I have faith in you and Morgana. Now, tell me about your progress with Merlin's books. I remember how you used to complain about his organizational skills."

"We haven't gotten much done other than cleaning, honestly," Mirah said and bit her lip. "We've looked through a pile, but nothing helpful yet."

"Isn't there some sort of spell you can use to find the book you need?" Anwil asked.

Mirah laughed. "No," she said. "If I knew which book it was already, yes, but magic isn't that specific."

"Well, I tried," Anwil said.

Mirah laughed again, but her smile faltered. She looked at their joined hands. "Anwil, I—"

But the doors opened again and Mirah jumped away from him, her cheeks red.

A guard stepped into the room and bowed. "Beg pardon, Your Grace, but Lady Sura is wishing to speak with you."

"I'll go," Mirah said, standing up. "I'll keep you updated on our progress." She sent him a small smile and left the throne room as Lady Sura entered carrying a large stack of papers.

CHAPTER TWENTY-FOUR

NIMUE

Nimue returned to Mab's court with a company of near one hundred warriors. She guided them to the camp Mab had set up at the base of the mountain. Mab's own court was eager to march on the human world, but she had to be careful. She could not interfere with humans, per some punishment by The Modron centuries ago, but her court could make the choice for themselves.

"Not bad," Mordred said as she led the warriors into the camp.

"We need at least five thousand more," Nimue said. "With Morgana in Camelot and the damned Druids recruiting fae themselves, we need to outnumber them."

"Agravaine can add at least two thousand to our numbers," Mordred said.

"Humans," Nimue scoffed. "Not very formidable against fae."

"But formidable against humans," Mordred pointed out. "Most of Briton's armies are human."

Nimue glanced around the camp. Fae of all kinds walked about the tents and the fires. Weapons and armor hung on racks, and a makeshift forge was bustling away, creating more.

"They won't enjoy allying with humans," Nimue said. "It would feel counterproductive."

"Not when we send the humans out first," Mordred said. "Conquer the petty kingdoms one by one and let loose the fae on Camelot. They will have no backup to help defend them once the kingdoms have fallen."

Nimue contemplated his words. It was clever; she hated to admit that. And the fae might buy it. Sacrifice the humans first, let them kill each other. It would be the only way the fae would ally themselves with humans.

"Very well," Nimue said. "Have you spoken with Agravaine lately?"

"He is itching to take his revenge on Camelot," said Mordred with a small smirk. "We should visit him soon."

"We?" Nimue raised an eyebrow.

"Of course, we," Mordred said smoothly. "We are still in this together, are we not? Or have you not yet forgiven me?"

"I haven't decided yet," Nimue lied. No. She would never forgive him. But she would need his experience to lead the battles. So, for now, they were together.

"What if I told you," Mordred said, slipping an arm around her waist, "that I found hot springs in the mountains and I could take you there right now? Do you remember our last night in a hot spring?"

Nimue remembered it well, as did her body, which betrayed her. Mordred nipped at her ear, his fingers trailing down her arm, the other gripping her waist. A warmth spread through her, pooling between her legs. Her body needed him. The traitor. Nimue stepped out of his embrace, heart pounding.

"We do not have the time," she said. "I'm going to my chambers to retire. Don't bother me until tomorrow."

She brushed past him without waiting for him to respond.

CHAPTER TWENTY-FIVE

ARIADNE

Ariadne kept her hand on the pommel of her sword as she weaved her way through the packed streets of Camelot with Brionna, Lohengrin, and Sir Xiang. They were on the hunt for a group of thieves and had gotten a tip from one of Lohengrin's informants as they patrolled the streets. A string of robberies had popped up the past week, and they were rounding up all the culprits.

"They're in here," Xiang said, slowing his pace.

He gestured to a small inn that got little attention except from those with something to hide. Ariadne didn't come to this part of the city much, as pickpockets and drunkards made their homes here. It did pang her heart to see this street in such disarray, though, and she made a mental note to see if there could be anything done about it.

As Xiang peered into the window, Brionna set herself up by the front door, pressing her back along the old wood next to it. Ariadne and Lohengrin crept around back to the door in the alleyway. She stepped around piles of water and stale vomit, and waited. Lohengrin planted himself on the other side of the door.

Sir Xiang's yell echoed, and an immediate commotion broke out inside. Shouts, bangs and even a crash and glass breaking. Ariadne dug her feet into the ground, ready. Heavy footsteps rang out and Ariadne and Lohengrin smirked at each other as the door flew open and three men tried to run out but stopped dead, eyes wide.

"Hello," said Lohengrin. "Nice weather we're having."

One pulled out a dagger and ran for Ariadne. She disarmed him easily, kicking the backs of his knees, and driving him to the ground. Lohengrin had little trouble with the second, as well.

The third, wide-eyed and puffy from drink, turned on his heel and ran back inside, but Xiang blocked his way. He tried to dart around him, but Xiang grabbed him by the shirt and threw him through the door, landing in a puddle as Brionna came around the corner, holding a man already in irons. Ariadne clasped her man in identical irons as he snarled and threw curses at her. She patted him on the shoulder as she heaved him to his feet.

"You had a good try," she said, but that only made him angrier. He tried to elbow her in the face, but she was faster. She leaned out of the way and had him back on the ground in the next second. She sat on him and he tried to kick and buck her off, but his attempts were weak.

"I can stay here all day," she told him. He cursed at her again.

"Looks like all of them," said Brionna.

"Aye," said Lohengrin, hoisting his man up from the ground and shackling his arms behind his back. "That's all. Your fun is officially over, my friends."

Xiang shackled the feet of the man Ariadne was sitting on. He grunted and cursed at them some more. Ariadne snorted.

"So eloquent," she said, and stood and hoisted him to his feet. He struggled but stood. "You'll have some time in the dungeons before your trial. Perhaps you can write a book while you're there."

He glared at her but said nothing.

"Come on, then." She gave him a push, and they followed the others around the corner.

Lohengrin turned to them once everyone was loaded into a caged wagon.

"What do you all say to some lunch, eh? I'm starving."

They ended up in The Crown and Dragon, Camelot's most popular inn and tavern. The owner, Myfanwy, waved at them and had warm cider for them almost immediately. Her bright green eyes sparkled, matching her smile, and her slightly pointed ears poked out from her golden hair.

"We've a pork roast today," she said, "if you're hungry. It'll be on the house."

"Myfanwy, you know we pay," said Brionna.

"Oh, posh," said the innkeeper, waving a hand at them. "You look like you've had quite the morning. I'll be back with plates for each of you."

Before they could protest, she was gone.

"I could go for pork roast," Xiang said.

Ariadne sipped at her cider, relishing the perfectly spiced flavor. Although the weather was comfortable, a roaring fire crackled. There were no minstrels at this time of day, but once the evening hit, these people would be roaring along with the fire.

"Oh, almost forgot. We got a letter this morning." Lohengrin pulled a folded paper from his pocket and handed it to Ariadne. "You're not going to like it."

She glanced through it, her jaw dropping. "Prince Connor of Ireland is to be a Knight of the Round Table?"

Xiang plucked the note from her hand as she stared at Lohengrin. "Enacted the Prince's Right," he mumbled. "I thought we weren't doing that anymore?"

"We are," said Lohengrin. "It just hasn't been requested since Arthur."

"But why Prince Connor?" Ariadne asked.

Before she could say anything further, Myfanwy appeared with their plates. The food smelled delicious as per usual, and Ariadne took a bite of the tender roast and held back a moan of pleasure. It was delicious.

"Not much explanation other than it's his father's wishes," said Lohengrin, digging into his food. "King Connig wrote a letter to Anwil not too long ago."

"And we're going to let him?" Ariadne asked, annoyed that her brother hadn't mentioned it to her.

"He's a prince," said Lohengrin with a shrug. "A prince of a kingdom we need an alliance with. So yes. He's a good fighter, apparently. Leads his own battalion."

"We can't let him be a Knight of the Round Table," Ariadne hissed. "He has a horrible reputation."

"How do you know?" Xiang asked.

"We have correspondence from Ireland regularly," Ariadne explained. "And any mention of Prince Connor is followed by how frequently he visits brothels."

"We should not judge before we meet him," said Xiang.

"Isn't one of the requirements to have an impeccable reputation?" Ariadne hissed. "His is terrible! Womanizing, lazy—"

"You of all people should understand how rumors spin out of control." Lohengrin said.

Ariane snapped her jaw shut. Because he did have a point. Annoyingly.

"If visiting brothels is the worst thing the prince has done," said Brionna, "then he is no different than most men here in Camelot."

Xiang and Lohengrin immediately protested.

"Of course, I do not mean you two." Brionna kissed her husband on the cheek.

"He'll need to squire before he can be knighted," said Xiang. "Perhaps he should be yours, Ariadne."

Ariadne's jaw dropped open. "I... what?"

"That's a good idea, my love," said Brionna, smirking.

Ariadne wanted to jump across the table and wipe the grin from Lohengrin's face. But the urge didn't last long, as a slight spark had returned to his eye. So she held her tongue and went back to her food, keeping her grumbles to herself.

Ariadne refused to speak to any of them as they made their way back to the castle, wrestling with her own feelings.

To bestow one of the highest honors on Camelot onto a foreign prince with a horrid reputation could tarnish the credibility of the Round Table. And yet, as Lohengrin had said, his reputation could be exaggerated by rumor.

Ariadne pushed all thoughts of Prince Connor out of her head by the time they made it up the courtyard steps. She had plans to check in on Mirah and Morgana's progress. It killed her to just wait around as they read through books. It felt like wasting time. Time Anwil most likely did not have.

But she didn't have to go far, as Mirah found her in the corridor, face drained of color.

"What is it?" Ariadne asked as she pulled them behind a statue of Sir Galahad with the Holy Grail.

"King Constantine is here," Mirah said quietly. "But something is wrong. He feels different."

"What do you mean?" Ariadne whispered.

Mirah wrung her hands. "I can't explain it. Something is...off about him."

"I don't understand."

Mirah sighed in frustration. "I don't know how to explain it. He just feels wrong."

Ariadne looked at Mirah curiously, but nodded. She knew Mirah well enough to take heed of these kinds of warnings. Mirah had good instincts.

"Where is he?" Ariadne asked.

"With the other kings in the throne room."

Ariadne nearly groaned. She had forgotten about the kings' summer solstice meeting.

"Have you spoken to Anwil about this?" Ariadne asked as they made their way there.

Mirah shook her head. "Not yet. I haven't been able to get him alone."

The kings and Anwil were seated at the Round Table, papers everywhere, empty cups of tea and coffee strewn about. Mirah curtsied to all of them before whispering a quick request for Ariadne to meet her later and leaving the room.

"Ari," Anwil said with some relief in his voice as she walked in. "Congratulations on catching those thieves."

"Word travels fast," Ariadne took a seat next to Anwil. Her attention landed on King Constantine.

He did look different. Healthier. He had gained a bit of weight back and color had returned to his face. His navy cloak and matching tunic were neat and pressed.

"King Constantine." Ariadne greeted him with a bow of her head. "Welcome back to Camelot."

Constantine gave a curt bow of his head, but said nothing. He looked as if he'd rather be anywhere else but here.

The meeting went on as reports came in from each king. Constantine did nothing out of the ordinary, and Ariadne eventually stopped watching him. It was a rather uneventful meeting. Not one mentioned Morgana. They must have already spoken about it.

But then Anwil proposed a new decree, naming Ariadne his heir apparent and regent in case the need came up.

King Owain of Gwent was the first to oppose it. "The law states a direct male heir," he said. "And if no male heir exists, we the petty kings vote. That is our right."

Ariadne was unsurprised at the opposition. She was quite used to it.

"And it is my right as High King to declare an heir," said Anwil. "The law needs to be changed. My mother ruled for twenty years and ruled well. Why should women be overlooked when they are just as capable of ruling?"

"When our forefathers came together to unite Briton's kingdoms," said King Caewlin of Mercia, "the laws were voted upon. We have upheld those laws at great cost. While Queen

Guinevere was a fine ruler, she was only regent until you came of age, Your Grace. The people will not accept another queen."

"The people, or you?" asked King Tolan, Sussex's new king. "Do you remember Queen Boudicca of the Iceni? Who led troops into the biggest opposition Rome faced when they invaded our lands? Women ruled equally amongst the men for thousands of years in the old lands until the Christians began their preaching of Eve's sin."

Ariadne raised her eyebrow at that. She had not expected a defender in Tolan. She'd had suspicions about his relationship to Cerdic.

"Many of us kings are Christians, my lord." King Caewlin sent a hard look at Tolan.

"Take a vote," Constantine said, his voice flat. "Instead of arguing and getting nothing done."

Caewlin glared at him, but the other kings seemed to be in agreement.

"The next male closest in kin is Lord Gingalain," Caewlin said to Anwil. "*He* should be your heir apparent."

Ariadne clenched her fists under the table. No. Gingalain was too unpredictable, too impulsive. And he was an ass. He would ruin Camelot.

"I declare Ariadne as my heir apparent and regent," said Anwil. "If you should like to vote, so be it. But I will not declare Gingalain as such."

"All for Princess Ariadne?" Tolan said and his, Elyion, and Anwil's hands went up. "Nays?"

Owain, Caewlin, and Constantine's hands went up. A tie.

"As High King," said Anwil, "I have the rights to break the tie. Ariadne is my heir apparent and regent. It is done."

Anwil poured the wax onto the paper and pressed his ring into it before signing his name. Ariadne kept still, her face neutral. She did not wish to give the kings any fuel to their fire. She was surprised, herself. She had never expected to be the heir to the throne, nor regent and wasn't sure how to feel about it. She let out a shaking breath.

Anwil slid the new decree over to her and she signed her name below her brother's. The kings reluctantly signed, and as soon as Caewlin scribbled his name, he excused himself. The rest soon followed after him, Constantine not looking at either her or Anwil as he left.

Soon it was just Anwil and Ariadne in the throne room. Anwil put his head in his hands and sighed. He looked tired.

"Do you think they'll try to put Gingalain on the throne?" Ariadne asked quietly.

Anwil slowly slid his hands from his face. "I want to say no, but we should prepare for it, anyway."

"How was Constantine?" she asked.

"Same as how you saw him," Anwil said. "Barely said a word. We were all shocked to see him. He didn't reply to the summons, so I hadn't expected him."

"Mirah said something is off about him," she said.

"He watched his daughter bleed out in my arms," Anwil said stiffly. "I wouldn't be comfortable here either."

"No," said Ariadne. "Not like that. She's worried."

"Well, keep an eye on him then," Anwil mumbled, gathering papers. "I have to meet with Lord Garanwyn."

"Why?"

"Skirmishes in his lands," he answered, heading toward the door.

"Wait. What did they say about Morgana?" Ariadne jogged up to him.

"They were not happy," Anwil snapped and Ariadne took a step back. "Sorry. I'm tired. We'll talk later."

He left through the doors, leaving Ariadne to stare after him.

CHAPTER TWENTY-SIX

CONNOR

"Shite. That's the biggest castle I've ever seen."

Connor snickered when Bradán's jaw dropped but he wasn't wrong. The castle of Camelot towered high over them, with six towers and at least four different levels. Each tower held a giant red flag bearing the gold crest of a dragon, as did many buildings in the city below the castle.

"It sure is something, isn't it?" Connor said as he took it all in, himself. From their point on the road, they could see almost the entire city.

It was protected behind a tall stone gate patrolled by guards and packed full of buildings of stone, wood, and brick. The streets wound around and up to the castle's main courtyard. And then there was another structure that led to the city from the west. Two layers of archways were stacked on top of each other, the top layer much smaller than the bottom

"Ridiculous, if you ask me," Garbhan grunted, and Connor bit his tongue.

"What are those?" Bradán pointed to an arch structure.

"Aqueducts," Domhnall answered. "It looks as if they continued using the Romans' inventions. They bring water to cities and villages. The base starts at a river or lake, and it takes water from there into the city. See that over there, where it leads to? That is called a castellum, where the water is then stored and distributed throughout the city."

"I thought the Romans left Briton ages ago?" Connor asked.

"They did," he answered. "But it looks as if Camelot has borrowed much of their architecture. Can't blame them, though. The Romans were genius in their—"

"Conquering bastards if you ask me," Garbhan said, shifting in his saddle.

"Well, that too," Connor said. "Pretty clever though, don't you think? Using your enemy's ideas against them. Where did you learn this?"

"Senach's obsessive book collection," Domhnall chuckled.

Garbhan grunted again. "Clever or not, let's get a move on. I don't want to spend more time than we have to in this city."

Connor reluctantly urged his horse to follow his uncle. The gates to the city were closed and guarded, with men on the ground and on the battlements.

"Greetings," Connor called to them in their Briton language. "I am Prince Connor of Ireland. And with me are my cousins,

Bradán and Domhnall of Clannig. And my uncle, Lord Garbhan. We are here to visit with King Anwil. We are expected."

Connor pulled out the letter from King Anwil he had tucked in his hidden pocket, and handed it to one of the guards, who read it over carefully and showed the other.

They nodded to each other and one of them disappeared through a narrow door in the wall.

"My lords," another guard said, "welcome." He turned and whistled. With a groan, the iron gate slowly lifted.

As soon as they rode through, a wave of noise from a grand, bustling city hit. People hurried back and forth on foot or in carts, guards marched by, there was an occasional loose animal, and—Connor nearly halted his horse—fae. Fae walking and talking to humans as if it were normal.

Senach had told him that the fae were different in Ireland, but Connor had not expected this. Back home, they did not mingle. The fae were more feared. Something not to trust, to stay away from.

"Move on," Garbhan called to him.

Connor picked up his pace but couldn't help but take it all in.

The buildings were packed on top of each other and were all kinds of colors and sizes, as were the people. He wondered how well protected the streets were, given how packed they were. Pickpocketing must be a problem.

Tall spears poked out from above the crowds, carried by more guards in red tabards, so either their presence was a deterrent or they kept an iron watch on things.

They wound around the cobbled roads until they came to the castle's curtain wall. Two watch towers sat on either side of another iron gate, again crawling with guards in red.

As they approached, the guards on the ground bowed and the gate was lifted.

Bradán gave a low whistle as they crossed into a well-kept courtyard. A winding path of white stone circled a patch of green, low-cut grass and a fountain. A rampant marble dragon spewed water in the center.

The courtyard wasn't as crowded as the city streets and Connor breathed a sigh of relief.

"Your father wasn't kidding when he said they had money," Bradán whispered in Connor's ear.

A nobleman with a blond mustache and a young woman with shockingly bright red hair were making their way toward them.

It was the older gentleman's clothes that caught Connor's eye first. He wore a cream tunic embellished with red embroidery that matched his cloak and hat. A jeweled sword rested at his hip, and his boots bore buttons that matched the red of his tunic. Connor had never seen such intricate fashion before. The jewelry, he was used to, as it was custom back home to showcase wealth with jewels, but clothing was practical, except for the rare celebration or ceremony. But even then, they had nothing like what this man wore.

The man bowed deeply as the woman looked him up and down; her face was hard to read. But when he looked at her a bit longer and took in the freckles and hair, he knew. Princess Ariadne. The rumors of her looks had done her wrong. She was stunning.

Connor took in her clothes, a maille shirt under a green tunic and trousers. A sword was belted to her waist, along with a couple of daggers. And Connor was willing to bet there were a few more hidden on her person somewhere.

So the rumors of her fighting prowess must be true then. He felt himself grinning. She caught him staring, though, and raised an eyebrow. He quickly turned his attention back to the older man.

"Welcome, my lords," said the older gentleman, "to Camelot. It is wondrous well to see you, Your Highness. I am Lord Roland of Bath, High Chancellor to His Grace, King Anwil, and Knight of the Round Table."

"Thank you, my lord," Connor said.

"May I present Her Highness, Princess Ariadne of Camelot and Briton, and Knight of the Round Table?"

"Princess," Connor said, bowing.

"Prince Connor," she said, folding her arms across her chest. "I do hope your reputation does not precede you."

Connor's eyebrows shot up. "And what exactly is my reputation here, Princess?"

"Besides a formidable fighter," she said, stepping up to him. They were nearly the same height. "It is said you love to enjoy women above everything else. Including duty."

Connor gave her a wolfish grin. "That's because women are goddesses here on earth, Princess."

Bradán snickered and Domhnall subtly elbowed him in the stomach.

Princess Ariadne scoffed lightly. "I see it does. That's unfortunate."

She stepped away as Lord Roland cleared his throat.

"I am sure you are tired from your journey, my lords," he said. "Her Highness has graciously agreed to escort you to the Guest Wing. The squires here"—Lord Roland gestured to a couple boys who had approached—"are ready to take your horses and your things."

"We can mind our own things," Garbhan growled.

"I am very sure you can, my lord," said Lord Roland without a pause. "But we want to extend our greatest hospitality to all of our welcomed guests."

Connor handed the reins of his horse to one of the squires and thanked him. "I'll care for my own weapons, though, if you don't mind."

"Of course, of course," said Lord Roland. "I would not have expected otherwise. I shall, unfortunately, have to take my leave of you. Please do enjoy the newly renovated guest wing. It is truly marvelous." He bowed and left them, Garbhan muttering under his breath in Irish.

More squires took their bags and bundles off the horses and hurried away in the opposite direction, toward the castle.

"This way," Ariadne said.

She took them east across the courtyard to what looked like a newer part of the castle, where the stone was less weathered. It did not have the tall towers or floors of the main castle. It, in fact, looked as if a manor had been attached. Soldiers jogged past them, calling to each other. Others bustled past, as well, but they appeared to be both servants and nobles

Guards opened the door and Princess Ariadne stepped inside, turning right down the corridor. A wide hallway with doors lining the walls wound both ways. Sconces were lit, and tapestries and portraits decorated the walls.

"The rooms with the open doors are yours," said the princess. "Each is equipped with its own washroom and—"

Garbhan brushed past her without a word and stormed into one of the open rooms. The door slammed shut behind him.

"Apologies," Connor said, glaring after his uncle. "My uncle is...difficult."

Ariadne gave him a cool look. "As I was saying"—she gestured to the rooms again—"Each room is equipped with its own washroom and running water."

"Washrooms?" Bradán blinked. "We each have our own washroom?"

"Yes."

"And forgive my ignorance," said Connor. "But running water?"

"There is a water source in every room as well," Ariadne explained. "The aqueducts bring water into the city, and then smaller ones supply water to the buildings."

"So I can take a bath? Right now?" Bradán asked.

"Yes," said Ariadne. "If you wish."

"Well, if you'll excuse me then." He bowed to Ariadne. "I am going to take that offer immediately."

Bradán hurried past them. Connor inwardly groaned. This was not a good first impression.

"I'll leave you to get settled," said the princess. "Supper is usually served at seven, but you may request food from the kitchens at any time."

"Will you be at supper, Princess?" Connor asked. "If I'm to be a Knight of the Round Table, we should get to know each other."

Ariadne narrowed her eyes at him. "Prince Connor," she said, "I hope you know that you will be held to the highest of standards while you are here."

"Oh?" he said, a teasing smirk spreading across his lips. "And exactly how high are your standards, Princess?"

"Extremely," said Ariadne.

With that, she turned on her heel and left.

Domhnall sighed. "That could have gone better."

"I think it went well." Connor patted him on the back and headed into his own room.

Connor and Domhnall picked the rooms beside each other, and Connor had to stop on the threshold to stare. It was nearly the size of a manor house. A four-poster bed sat in the middle against the wall, with a wardrobe, a massive trunk at the foot of the bed, two armchairs and a sofa in front of the large hearth, and a writing desk in front of the window. Carpets and tapestries in red and gold adorned the room, including a folding privacy screen and a door leading to what he supposed was the washroom. He peeked inside the room and saw a large steel bathtub with faucets and a drying rack. Soaps, oils, and wash and linen towels were folded neatly on a table next to a smaller wash bin with a paste and brush for teeth.

Connor let out a low whistle. This was the epitome of luxury, and he saw now why his father wanted an alliance with Camelot. If they could afford this, a trading route with them could make Ireland a lot of money as well.

CHAPTER TWENTY-SEVEN

MORDRED

"Constantine is here."

Mordred leaned back in his chair. The figure in the fire was obscured by a hood, sitting in a nondescript room. But Mordred knew where he was. Camelot.

"Good," Mordred said. "Keep an eye on him. Make sure he does what I told him."

"He will," the figure said. "If I have to force him, he will."

"What other news?" Mordred asked. "What is Morgana doing?"

"She's been in Merlin's study mostly," the figure answered, "going through his books. I don't know what she is looking for, though."

"Find out," Mordred hissed. "She has been there for a week."

"No one seems to know," the figure snapped back. "And the damned knights won't speak of it. You should know how tight-lipped they are."

"You tried to get information from *them*?" Mordred wished he could reach through the fire and strangle him. "Idiot. You'll never get anywhere with them. Talk to the servants. They know everything. Report back to me in three days."

Mordred made to wave his hand, but the figure cried out for him to wait. He held up a large scroll of papers.

"I have something else," he said. "The architect's drawings. And a list of the castle's weak points."

Mordred's heart rate sped up. He snapped his fingers and the papers disappeared from the spy's hand and into his.

He carefully unraveled them and looked them over. "Good," he said. "Now run along."

Mordred waved his hand over the fire and the figure disappeared. He did not need distractions as he looked over Camelot's maps.

This new spy had practically fallen into his lap, angry that he felt Camelot was heading in the wrong direction. Mordred had snorted at that. More like the spoiled brat was angry he wasn't handed everything on a silver platter. Overlooked because he wasn't as talented as he thought he was. So, Mordred played into that, promising him leadership positions and boosting his ego. It worked perfectly.

Not only did he have Constantine to order around, but now this spy, who had just proved his worthiness. These maps were just what Mordred needed, especially since Merlin and Vivienne had tied the magic of the city to the damn Pendragon brats. No one could take the Camelot throne unless they were Pendragon blood, or the throne was given to them by someone of Pendragon blood Stupid decision on their part. That left it so there was no wiggle room if and when the Pendragons died out. So, the great city would fall with them? They did not wish it to thrive for generations? Mordred scoffed.

No matter. If he had to burn it to the ground to rule, then he would. The stones didn't matter to him. Only the crown did.

CHAPTER TWENTY-EIGHT

ANWIL

*A*nwil stood alone in the midst of a burned city. All that was left was the burning coals and piles of ash, still smoking. The stench of death and charred bodies hung in the air, and the only noise was the cracking and sizzling of flames still holding onto the ruins. It was so dark even with the orange glow, Anwil couldn't recognize a single building in the destruction, but he knew exactly where he was.

A heavy weight pulled on his shoulder. He looked down to see Excalibur in his hand, and he was dressed in full armor. He had never worn full battle armor before.

Crunching behind him had him whirling around, clutching Excalibur in both hands, brandishing it at whoever or whatever was coming.

Mordred. Anwil's stomach flipped. Also in full armor, grinning like a snake about to devour his prey.

"*What do you want?*" *Anwil asked, trying to not let his voice shake but failing.*

Mordred smirked. "I want what is mine," he said. "I want Briton."

"You can't have it," Anwil snarled.

"Tintagel," said Mordred, stepping closer, holding on to his own sword, "was wrongfully taken from my mother and grandmother by Uther Pendragon. Promised to my mother once again by Arthur Pendragon, who never kept that promise. Before you and your brat sister were concocted, Camelot was mine. Should still be mine. And yet...there you stand, with a sword you can't even wield."

"Camelot will never be yours," Anwil said through gritted teeth.

Mordred laughed, and the sound made Anwil sick to his stomach.

Then Mordred charged at him, sword held high. Anwil blocked with Excalibur just in time, his arms shaking under the weight of Mordred's blow. Anwil's hold didn't last long. Mordred came at him with his other hand and punched him across the face.

Anwil stumbled, falling to one knee. Before he could get back up, Mordred kicked him in the stomach. His breath lost, he fell backward, hitting his head on the hard, hot ground.

Mordred stomped on his wrist and Anwil cried out. Excalibur fell from his grip.

Mordred tossed his sword aside and grabbed Excalibur.

"Pathetic," he said. "I wasn't even trying. I had hoped you would have had some fight in you. You can't wield a sword, let alone power. You're unfit to rule a kingdom. It's over, boy. You're dying. It won't be long now until everything you love dies with you ."

Red hot anger bubbled in Anwil's veins and he shot to his feet. He rolled his shoulders to adjust the armor. "If I die, I'll drag you down with me."

Mordred lunged forward and grabbed Anwil around the throat, lifting him off his feet.

Anwil woke up with a start. Bright sunlight streamed into the bedroom through the open window. It was warm, but the breeze coming in was cool. Birds chirped and noise from outside his tower reached his ears. The door opened and Anwil shot up. Leofwine came in, carrying a tray of food and a steaming mug. Anwil's shoulders drooped in relief.

"Good morrow, Your Grace," Leofwine said, setting the tray down on the bedside table. "Shall I draw you a bath?"

Anwil shook his head and Leofwine bowed and left the room. It took Anwil awhile to compose himself and remember that it was just a dream. But the dreams were becoming more and more vivid.

He was sore, as if he had a bruise. He shook his head and managed to get out of bed. He hobbled past the mirror to get to his wardrobe, but when he glanced in the mirror, he saw Mordred looking back at him.

Anwil yelled and stumbled back, tripping over his boots. Lancelot burst into the room, sword brandished and eyes wide. He dropped the sword when he saw Anwil on the floor.

"Anwil!" Lancelot kneeled next to him. "What happened?"

Anwil shook his head. "Tripped," he mumbled, taking the hand Lancelot offered him. "Wasn't fully awake yet."

"Shall I call for Master Cassius?" Lancelot asked as Anwil steadied himself on his feet.

Anwil shook his head. "No. I'm fine."

Lancelot didn't look convinced, but he nodded and left him alone.

Anwil tossed a blanket over the mirror and hurriedly dressed, wanting to get out of his room as quickly as possible.

When he arrived in the private dining room for morning meal, he was surprised to find Ariadne and Morgana were already there.

"Good morning, brother," Ariadne said as he stared at them.

"Morning," he said slowly, glancing between the two.

"How are you feeling?" Morgana asked, pouring herself coffee.

"Fine?" said Anwil, more confused than before. "Why do I feel as if you two know something I don't?"

The two women exchanged a glance that confirmed his suspicions.

"Eat first," Morgana said. "And then we'll chat."

He narrowed his eyes but crossed over to the buffet table and loaded his plate. Morning meal was his favorite. It was the one meal that was truly private. Servants did not stay to wait on them, and there were no courtiers waiting for him outside the doors. Anwil had many fond memories of his mother and sister in this room.

"All right," he said as he sat down. "What is it?"

"Prince Connor is here," Ariadne blurted out.

Anwil nearly choked on his tea. "What? Why wasn't I told?"

"You were busy with the clergy," Ariadne said. "They arrived just before supper yesterday. And it looks like I was right about Prince Connor."

"What do you mean?"

"He went to a pub last night and only returned just before sunrise." Ariadne folded her arms over her chest.

"Who is Prince Connor?" Morgana asked.

"The crown prince of Ireland," Anwil said. "He's here to be a Knight of the Round Table."

"That leads to my next question," Ariadne said. "Why?"

"Glory? Reputation?" Anwil shrugged, annoyance growing. "Why would anyone else?"

"I don't see why King Connig would send his heir to a country on the brink of war," Ariadne said. "I think there's more to it, isn't there?"

Anwil sighed and set his utensils down. He had a feeling he wasn't going to finish his meal. "Connig originally asked for a marriage with you and Connor. I declined, and his answer was to have Connor become a knight instead."

"I had a feeling that's what it was," Ariadne said. "So why let him? This is probably just a scheme to wear me down."

"Because we need allies, and opening the trading routes with Ireland again would prove beneficial," said Anwil. "So, can you please be cordial?"

"Apparently I have to be," Ariadne said, "since he's to be my squire."

Anwil clamped his jaw shut.

"Do not laugh," Ariadne warned.

"I'm not laughing." He was trying very hard not to.

Morgana, however, did laugh, and they turned to her.

"You remind me of myself and Arthur," she said. "Forgive me. I did not mean to laugh." She turned back to her food, a smile still on her lips.

"Ari, I'm sorry I forgot to tell you about Connor," Anwil said. "But again, this could prove beneficial."

"I understand," Ariadne said. "I still hate it. And I won't marry him."

"I won't make you," Anwil said. "Now, why don't you two tell me why you're actually here?"

"I was already here when Morgana arrived," Ariadne said, picking at her fruit. "She said she had something important to discuss."

"Mirah and I have found something in Merlin's study." She pulled a book from her pocket and handed it to Anwil. "I marked the pages."

Ariadne leaned over his shoulder to read along with him.

"What the hell does that mean?" Ariadne said when she finished. "One may survive?"

But Anwil's blood had turned to ice. *Only one may survive.* They wouldn't break the tether. He would die.

"I do not know," Morgana said. "Which is why I must travel to the Otherworld to seek out Merlin."

"Isn't he mad now?" Ariadne asked. "How are you going to get answers from him?"

"I will find a way," Morgana answered. "Lady Mirah wishes to accompany me to the Otherworld. I think between us, we may get through to Merlin."

"Is it safe?" Anwil asked quietly, still staring at the page.

"She will be with me," said Morgana. "I will keep her safe."

"Jabir isn't going to like that," Ariadne said. "He's been protective of her lately."

"Go with them," Anwil suggested. "He'll be more receptive if you'll be with her."

"Nimue and Mordred are in the Otherworld," Morgana said. "They may be able to pick up on Ariadne's presence."

But Anwil did not need Ariadne hovering over him. He needed to be alone. Well, as alone as he could be as king.

"You're Morgana le Fey, aren't you?" Anwil said. "I hope if you can keep Mirah safe, you can protect Ariadne as well."

"Yes," Morgana said stiffly.

"Good," said Anwil. "When do you leave?"

"The next full moon," Morgana said. "Which is tonight."

"Anwil," Ariadne said, but he stood up.

"Ari, you'll go with them," he said. "Get answers from Merlin and break this damn tether."

CHAPTER TWENTY-NINE

MIRAH

Mirah wrung her hands together as she waited in the courtyard with her father. She, Morgana, and Ariadne were leaving for the Otherworld, and to say she was nervous was an understatement.

Mirah cursed herself for being so nervous and so scared. She could put a man's organs back into place and sew him up without batting an eye, but traveling to a world unknown, with dangers lurking? She wanted to vomit.

"Baba," she whispered as the clouds drifted away from the full moon. It was bright in the sky, a rare clear night. "I don't think I can do this. I should go back to bed."

"If that is what you truly wish," Jabir said gently. "Then I will take you to your chambers."

She knew her father was itching for her not to go. He had been furious when Mirah told him she was going with Morgana, tried to forbid her to go even, but Mirah held her ground, explaining that she needed to go, needed to see Merlin. Jabir had eventually relented.

Voices echoed behind them and Mirah turned, trembling. Ariadne, Morgana, Lancelot, and Anwil were making their way toward them.

"Are we ready?" Morgana asked Mirah.

Mirah looked back at her father. She truly wanted to go back to her room, but she would hate herself in the morning for it. She took a breath.

"Yes," she told Morgana. "I'm ready."

Jabir pulled her to him. "Be brave, my daughter. Ahura Mazda will watch over you."

"Thank you, Baba," she said, giving her father a squeeze.

"I will watch over her," Morgana said to Jabir.

He bowed and, with one more look at Mirah, he left them alone in the courtyard.

Morgana took Mirah and Ariadne to the queen's gardens. They passed by the colorful rose bushes and to the small pond that lay under a canopy of rowan trees.

"Are you all right?" Ariadne asked Mirah quietly.

Mirah nodded. "I'll be fine."

Ariadne narrowed her eyes but did not push further.

"I do not know how much time will pass in Camelot," Morgana said, stepping into a ray of moonlight. "But we should only be gone a day or two in the faelands."

She whispered in the ancient language, holding her hands out, palms up. The air thickened, filling with the faint scent of amber..

The trees in front of the pond groaned and cracked, weaving together to form a perfect circle. Morgana lowered her arms and turned back to them.

"Come," said Morgana. "It will not stay open for long. And hold your breath as you pass through the gate."

Mirah stepped through the moongate with Morgana and Ariadne. Air so thick it was like moving through water slammed into her chest. Her lungs screamed for air, but before she could open her mouth, they were on the other side.

Mirah took in a gulp of air so sweet and floral, it nearly made her eyes water.

A packed dirt path lay ahead of them, surrounded by a vivid rainbow of fauna. Happily chirping birds and the buzzing of wings filled in the air. Blinking firefly lights illuminated in the bushes and whispers of voices carried on the breeze.

"It's so beautiful," Ariadne breathed. "I've never seen such colors."

"Do not let the beauty fool you," Morgana warned, waving her hand. The moongate behind them unwound and disappeared with the groaning and cracking of limbs. "Nothing here is as it seems. Do not speak to anyone and do not touch or eat anything. Stick to the path and stay close to me."

Mirah and Ariadne heeded her words as they trotted down the path. Pixies fluttered about them, whispering, asking questions. Mirah ignored them as best she could, dodging a few here and there. Ariadne was stiff beside her, also trying to ignore the buzzing fae. Morgana just batted them away with her hands.

The trees on either side of them turned toward them as they passed, as if alive. Watching. Mirah clutched the strap of her bag. Morgana had instructed them not to take any weapons or iron of any kind. Not that Mirah had any weapons. She had a couple of daggers her father had given her, but they hung on the wall in her bedroom. She had only ever taken one down once, when she went looking for Anwil last autumn. And it had never left her belt. The only knives she was comfortable using were her surgical ones. Those were tools to help heal, not maim.

"Do you know where we're going?" Ariadne asked after a little while.

Nothing had changed in the surrounding forest. Mirah could still feel eyes on her and swore she heard soft footsteps and the breaking of twigs behind them.

"Yes," said Morgana. "We are going to see the Goddess Ceridwen. She is Merlin's grandmother."

"His... grandmother?" Ariadne nearly tripped over a root in the path. "Merlin's grandmother is a goddess?"

"He never told you?" Morgana raised an eyebrow.

"He never spoke about his family, no," said Ariadne.

Mirah bit her lip. Merlin had never spoken much of himself during their lessons, unless the story was relevant. Oh, he told stories often of his travels and the people he met, but nothing of his own personal past.

"Merlin is the son of the bard Taliesin," Morgana explained. "Who was also a great wizard."

Something rustled sounded in the trees, and Morgana halted in her tracks. Mirah froze in place, barely breathing. She gripped the strap of her bag with both hands to keep them from shaking.

Morgana eyed the bushes behind them for a long moment, but whatever was in there made no more sounds.

"We are close," Morgana said quietly. "Come."

They walked for a little while longer. And the rustle followed them. Mirah's heart beat fast in her chest, but Morgana did not seem worried about who—or whatever—was following them.

When the forest finally thinned, Mirah heard a whisper of song in the air, and the sight that greeted her was enchanting.

A two-story cottage came into view in the clearing, surrounded by flowers, a large well in the front yard, benches, animals, and fae children playing about. The children, all different fae, turned to them as they approached. A small nymph with pale green skin regarded them curiously, while the sprite with fluttering wings ran up to them. The brownies ran inside the cottage.

"Hello," Morgana said, reaching out to touch their hands. "Thank you for the welcome."

"Tell us stories," one with gray skin and large eyes said.

"Play a game!"

Morgana laughed with them as they tugged on her cloak. "Perhaps later," said Morgana. "I am here to see the Lady Ceridwen."

Some children turned to Ariadne and Mirah, giggling and tugging at their hands and cloaks. Mirah still gripped her strap, remembering Morgana's warning. Ariadne was just as stiff beside her.

"We are here as friends," Morgana said to the children. "No bargains, no offers, no promises."

"Can I give the human a flower?" asked one little one with brown skin that resembled a tree trunk.

"Only if you offer it without expecting anything in return," said Morgana.

"They are friends," said the little one, holding it out for Ariadne. "We welcome them with no malice."

Ariadne looked at Morgana, who gave permission. Ariadne reached for the blue flower, but the child pulled it away.

"She wants to put it in your hair," said Morgana.

Ariadne kneeled beside the little fae child, who carefully braided a piece of Ariadne's hair around the stem.

"Thank you," Ariadne said. "It is a lovely gift."

Another did the same for Mirah, but their attention quickly turned to a pale-skinned woman with shining golden hair and a brilliant grin who hurried through the cottage's door.

A wave of power filled the air. It was so strong, it nearly knocked Mirah over. Ariadne caught her before her knees gave out, holding her friend steady.

"Morgana le Fey," the goddess called. Her skin glittered with sunlight and her pink skirts fell around her like petals. "Welcome home, child of the fae."

"Hello, my lady." Morgana dropped into a low curtsy, and Mirah and Ariadne did the same.

Ceridwen approached them, kissing Morgana on each cheek. And then she turned to Ariadne and frowned. She cupped Ariadne's jaw in her fingers and lifted her head.

"I see a fire in you," she said quietly. "One that burns so fiercely, it threatens to consume you."

"What does that mean?" Ariadne asked. But the goddess did not answer. She let go of Ariadne and turned her turquoise blue gaze over to Mirah. She shuddered.

"Hello, Mirah of Evanshire, daughter of Nazrine," said Ceridwen, tilting Mirah's chin up with a finger. "We gods have blessed you with powerful magic, and you repay that blessing with kindness. You have saved many and will save more to come. You are a rare jewel, my child, but...I see something more for you. Do not run from it."

Mirah stared at up at her, speechless. Those were the same words The Modron had said to her when she visited Mirah at Camelot. She looked at Morgana, her heart racing, but Morgana's face was unreadable.

"Why have you come, Morgana?" Ceridwen turned to her.

"We seek answers from Merlin."

"Then you have come in vain," said Ceridwen, her eyes hardening. "Nimue's curse has damaged his mind."

"We have to try," said Morgana.

Ceridwen stared at her for a long moment. "Very well. Come."

Ceridwen waved away the crowd of fae children and led Mirah and her friends to the wood. The children stayed where they were, but Mirah discovered Ceridwen had taken them to a small clearing. Chairs and benches made from twisted vines and twigs were scattered about, and sitting on one was Merlin. Ariadne gasped. His hair was wild and gray, and his beard nearly reached his belly. Twigs, dirt, and leaves were tangled in the messy strands, and he munched on acorns, spitting them out and grimacing at the taste, but he kept at it.

Mirah pressed a hand against her mouth to muffle a gasp. Tears stung her eyes.

"Merlin?" Morgana said carefully.

Merlin jumped, dropping his acorns, his eyes wide and darting around. He spoke in gibberish, but Mirah recognized a few words in Breton and Welsh, and some French. He settled on Morgana and he screeched.

"Le Fey." He backed up a few steps. "Have you come to kill me?"

"No, Merlin," said Morgana, shaking her head.

"He is lost," Ceridwen said softly as Merlin scurried behind her. "Trapped by his own demons."

"This is what Nimue did to him?" Ariadne asked, looking horrified.

Merlin peered at them from behind Ceridwen, like a scared child.

Morgana kneeled next to him. "Master Merlin," she said. "I am not here to harm you. I only seek knowledge. Answers."

"Answers?" he said, his gaze darting from her to the ground.

"Yes," said Morgana. "Only you can answer our questions."

"Only I..." he said. "Only I can..." He looked past Morgana and froze, eyes settling on Ariadne.

He pointed at her. "I... know... you..."

"Lord Merlin," she said. "We all thought you were dead. Nimue—"

"Nimue," he hissed. "She did this!" He sputtered words in gibberish, picking up more acorns.

Ceridwen gave Morgana a hard look. "He has some moments of brief clarity, but it is no use. What Nimue did is irreversible. I fear even my powers cannot heal what she did."

Morgana straightened, looking Ceridwen in the eye. "Forgive me, my lady, but your powers are nothing compared to mine."

Mirah's eyebrows shot up. Was Morgana arguing with a goddess? Daring to say she was more powerful than a god?

"You dare be so arrogant, Morgana le Fey?" Ceridwen hissed, her eyes turning dark. The fluffy white clouds in the sky changed to a gray so dark, it was almost black. Thunder clapped and lightning flashed.

Ariadne jumped in front of Mirah.

"You know what I am capable of, Ceridwen," Morgana said quietly, venom laced in her voice. "Do not test me."

"I do not take kindly to threats, Morgana," Ceridwen hissed. More thunder. More lighting.

"I am not threatening you," Morgana said simply. "There is no need for theatrics."

Ariadne swore under her breath.

"You will not harm my grandson!"

"I will do nothing to him that he would not do to me if our positions were reversed," said Morgana. "I am here to break the tether Mordred placed on my nephew before it kills him. Merlin may be our only chance to save him. And I will not have you, nor anyone else, standing in my way."

Ceridwen stared at Morgana for a long time. Then her eyes cleared and the clouds rolled away. Sun shined again.

Mirah let out a breath of relief and Ariadne sagged against her.

"Let us talk more inside." Ceridwen whirled on her feet and stormed toward the cottage with Merlin scurrying behind her.

The cottage was an illusion. Inside was a grand manor, bigger than it appeared on the outside. Fae females with babies and children filled the manor with laughter and talk. Tapestries of the finest art, statues, and intricate furniture furnished the inside.

Ceridwen took them into a large dining room, where a feast was already laid out. The oval table and chairs bore woven woodwork with musical notes hidden in the entwined backs of the chairs and legs of the table. A worn red carpet sat underneath, and an open cabinet as tall as the large ceiling bore all kinds of knickknacks, bottles, papers, and even a sleeping pixie.

The food smelled divine and Mirah could barely take it all in. Fruits, meats, roasted and steamed vegetables, soup.

"Eat," Ceridwen said, taking a seat. "Please. This food comes at no cost."

"You can eat," Morgana reassured Mirah and Ariadne.

Merlin, who had hurried on ahead of them, was already seated, tearing into a turkey leg.

Ceridwen served them herself before taking a seat at the head of the table.

"Now, what is this about?"

"First, we must start when Nimue resurrected Mordred from the dead," Morgana said.

Ceridwen's eyes darkened again. "Go on."

Morgana took the lead to tell Ceridwen of Nimue's actions. The burning of abbeys, stealing relics, bringing Mordred back from the dead. And the tether it created between Mordred and Anwil.

Mirah picked at her food as Morgana spoke. It was the most delicious food she had ever tasted, but she had little appetite. Ariadne did not eat much either. She watched Morgana and Ceridwen closely.

"Nimue is breaking the rules of nature," Ceridwen said with disgust when Morgana finished. "I am surprised Arawn has not come for them yet."

"Who is to say he hasn't?" Morgana said.

"Arawn would let it be known," Ceridwen answered. "I know nothing of tethers, unfortunately."

"Which is why we came to ask Merlin," said Morgana, her eyes sliding back to her old teacher. He was still gnawing on the turkey leg, but realized they were all looking at him and stopped. He put the meat down and wiped at his mouth with his hand.

"We have other questions as well," Morgana continued and pulled Merlin's diary from her satchel.

Ceridwen took it and read the pages they had marked. "I know nothing of this."

"I would like to try and get through to Merlin," Morgana said. "He has the answers we seek."

Ceridwen sighed. "You may try, but it will not work."

"Merlin," Morgana said. "Look at me."

She moved around the table and knelt at Merlin's side, taking his hands in hers.

"Do not look away," she said. "Listen to my voice, and only my voice."

The air thickened and Ariadne dropped her fork, grabbing onto the sides of the table. Candles flickered and the door to the dining room slammed shut. Mirah held onto the arms of her chair. She did not like this. It felt dark.

"Morgana, what are you doing?" Ceridwen demanded.

But Morgana ignored her. "You will answer my questions, Merlin."

The candles went out, leaving the room in darkness.

Mirah's stomach churned. She clamped her mouth shut so as not to lose the little food she had eaten. Ariadne was stiff beside her, watching with wide eyes.

Merlin whimpered, never looking away from Morgana's face.

"What do you know of binding a dead soul to a living one?" Morgana asked.

Merlin's eyes were wide; his mouth opened and closed a few times. "A dead soul needs a living one if it must return to the living world," he said, his voice low and void of emotion.

"Is there a way to break it without harming the souls?" Morgana asked.

"Only Arawn can answer that question," Merlin said.

Morgana swore. "Arawn does not answer prayers."

"You must go to Arawn," said Merlin. "The Pendragon must go to Arawn."

"Why?" Morgana asked.

"Fate changed the night the twin Pendragons were born." He continued. No one moved.

They waited.

"Camelot was destined to fall with Arthur," Merlin continued. "Guinevere was never to bear children. The twins were not supposed to exist."

Ariadne let out a gasp, and Mirah put a hand over hers.

"Magic was needed to keep them alive. They are tied to the land. Their fate and Camelot's are tied together," Merlin continued, his voice stronger.

Ariadne let out a cry. Mirah gripped Ariadne's hand. Her head pounded. This was dark magic Morgana was using.

"You wrote in your diary that only one may survive," Morgana continued. "What did you mean by that?"

"I do not know," said Merlin. "Their fate is...cloudy. I see...I see...one...just one..."

"One what?" Ariadne blurted, but Morgana put up a hand and Ariadne's jaw snapped shut.

"How can we get to Arawn?" Morgana asked.

"I...do not..." Merlin gasped for air.

"Merlin, answer me!" Morgana's voice bounced around the room.

"Enough!" Ceridwen roared, shooting to her feet, and the air thinned. The lights in the candles burned brightly once again.

Relief came immediately to Mirah and she slumped in her chair, breathing hard. Merlin swayed, but Morgana caught him before he slid off his own chair.

Ariadne yanked her hand from Mirah's.

"Darkness has always been your friend, Morgana," Ceridwen sneered, rounding the table to Merlin. "No matter how you try to hide it."

Merlin groaned. "I am sorry," he breathed. "For what I have done to you, Morgana."

Ceridwen waved toward the hall, and a couple of golden fae glided in. They carefully picked Merlin up and took him away. Mirah dared not move. She couldn't bring herself to look at Morgana.

Silence filled the room for a long moment.

"You may spend the night," Ceridwen said quietly. "Tomorrow, you will leave." Without another word, she swept from the room. The pixie that had been sleeping in the cabinet zoomed after her.

"What did you do to him?" Ariadne asked quietly.

Morgana sighed. "It is called compulsion," she said. "It is not a power well liked."

"It felt wrong," said Ariadne, and Mirah agreed.

It was wrong. So very wrong to take hold of someone's mind like that.

"Sometimes the only choices we have are dark ones," Morgana said. "You should rest. I need to think..." She made to leave the dining hall, but Ariadne called her name.

"What did Merlin mean by only one may survive?" she asked, still staring at his vacant chair.

"Do not put faith in unknown prophesies." Morgana put a hand on her shoulder. "The future is often never as it seems."

CHAPTER THIRTY

ANWIL

Anwil sat on the dais of the throne room, the room filled with people waiting to bring their grievances to the king. They did this once a quarter and had since Arthur took the throne. Now that Camelot had grown twice in size since Arthur, only fifty were now selected from the hundreds who petitioned the council.

It was one of the few duties that Anwil genuinely enjoyed. Although the large crowd was daunting, he liked getting to talk to the people, even if only for a few moments. It was one of the many reasons he had visited the city so much before his coronation. He got to know the people, not just the courtiers, who were the heart of Camelot. His father had been a king of the people, and Anwil hoped to continue that legacy.

He was extra grateful for it today, as Ariadne, Mirah, and Morgana had been gone for three days and he as beginning to worry. Lancelot told him it was normal for a few days or longer to pass before someone returned from the Otherworld, but it did nothing to ease his nerves.

Lord Roland called the first couple forth and Anwil focused his attention.

"Your Grace," the man said as they bowed.

"Welcome," said Anwil, and he glanced at the scroll in his hands. "Master Bahram and Mistress Maude. Please state your grievances."

"We have a small smithy in Abbotsbury, Sire," said Bahram. "And lately, we've had a problem with our iron being stolen. We don't know who it is. We tried watching all manner of day and night, but it disappears. Every time we have a new shipment, it's gone in a day or so! We think it might be the fae, Sire, but then again, fae can't touch it, can they?"

"How long has this been happening?"

"The last few months, Sire," said Maude.

Anwil glanced at the Druids to his left. "Lord Tagh, what do you make of this?"

"I would have to see this for myself," said the elderly Druid.

"Very well," Anwil said. "We'll provide transport for you and Master Bahram and Mistress Maude. Please report back as soon as you find anything."

"Of course, Sire." Tagh gestured to the couple to follow him out of the hall, and they bowed to Anwil before they left.

Lord Roland leaned down to speak into his ear. "We've also had recent reports of iron being stolen from smithies here in the city. Lady Dindrane has her spies working on it."

"Good," Anwil said quietly. "Although the blacksmith was right. Fae can barely stand to be near it, let alone touch it. How would they steal it?"

"Fae love loopholes, Sire," said Lord Roland as the next person came forward.

They were alone, their face hidden by the hood of their black cloak. Anwil gripped the arms of the chair. Something didn't feel right. Lord Roland must have felt it too because his hand went to his sword. As did Lancelot's, on Anwil's other side.

"Good morrow," Anwil said as the figure approached. "How may we be of service?"

The figure threw off his cloak and the hall gasped. A man with green skin, green hair, and green clothing stood in front of the dais. The knights immediately surrounded Anwil, the guards pulling their swords. A few people screamed, but the green man held up his hand and a hush fell over the room.

Anwil knew this man, not from meeting him, but from the stories told, the tapestries, and from Gawaine himself. The Green Man. The Green Knight. The one who had tested Gawaine's honesty when he was just a squire.

"The crown will not make a deal," said Lancelot, stepping in front to face The Green Man.

"I did not come for a deal," he said and pulled a green sash from around his waist. "Only a reminder."

Gingalain pushed forward and reached for the sash, but The Man pulled it away. "It is not you I seek, son of Gawaine. But the Pendragon."

"I am also a Pendragon," Gingalain said with a snarl. "It was my father who passed your test."

The man ignored him and looked back at Anwil. Gingalain huffed at the cut and stomped back to his place by the dais with the other lords.

"Am I to cut off your head?" Anwil asked.

"No," The Green Man answered. "I am only here to remind you of the promise the Pendragons made to the fae. That you are our protector in this world. We gave Excalibur to Arthur because he proved worthy. Given to him to defend those who could not defend themselves. You have Excalibur, and yet you do not use it. Why?"

The question was more of a demand.

"I am not much of a fighter," Anwil admitted. "But I am doing what I can to—"

The Green Man snapped his fingers and Excalibur appeared in his hand. He held it out for Anwil, the hilt shining in the sunlight that poured in from the windows. The crowd looked at him expectedly.

He didn't even know if he could lift it in the state he was in. And if he failed in front of everyone, the trust in the crown would tumble.

"Do you think yourself Anwil Pendragon?" The Green Man asked. "Are you worthy of this heavy crown you wear? Can you wield Excalibur?"

Anwil stood from the throne and approached The Green Man. He was taller than Anwil by near a foot.

"I have done nothing to prove that I am worthy of Excalibur," said Anwil, looking right into the bright green eyes of the fae before him. "I am new in my reign and still finding my footing. If I do prove worthy one day, I will carry Excalibur with honor."

The Green Man's eyes bore into Anwil's for a moment before the fae's lips twitched into a small smile and he nodded.

"You have passed my test," he said. "Excalibur will return to you when you are ready." He snapped his fingers again, and he and Excalibur vanished. The only thing left of him was the green sash on the floor.

Gasps and screams followed his departure now that the magic to keep the crowd silent had disappeared.

Lohengrin and Lancelot took charge and, with the rest of the knights and guards, ushered everyone out. Gingalain put up a small fight to stay but finally relented after Jabir and Lohengrin gave him a few choice words.

"How did he get in here?" Brionna asked Lancelot once Lohengrin closed the door behind the final guests. They hurried back to the dais, where Anwil had slumped down onto the top step.

"Magic," said Lancelot with a shrug. "As he did before at the Yule feast for Gawaine."

"What if Nimue sent him?" Lohengrin said. "Aren't we supposed to be warded against fae just appearing in Camelot?"

"The Green Man is more god than fae," said Lancelot. "He can easily bypass any wards. And he would not align himself with Nimue."

"I thought he was a man in disguise?" Brionna asked. "Was that not the tale Gawaine told?"

Lancelot shook his head. "The Green Man pretended to be a human lord with a wife."

"Gawaine told it so many times in so many different ways, I've grown confused," Brionna halfheartedly joked. Xiang put an arm around her.

"Well, he was usually drunk when he got into it," Lohengrin said, a sad smile twitching at his lips.

"What does this mean?" Anwil interjected, shooting to his feet. As much as he hated to interrupt their memories of Gawaine, this would be the talk of Camelot for years. "Was this a threat? *Remember, you are our protector in this world.* Does he think we are not doing enough? It is illegal to discriminate against fae in Briton. The guards and knights have been handling situations every day. I've tried to make it as safe as possible, but I cannot control the people's prejudices. We just welcomed three fae refugee families after an attack in Essex. And now he takes Excalibur back. The rumors that I'm a shit king are already brewing, I guarantee it. They'll be saying I don't deserve the crown any moment now, if they aren't already."

"All right, everyone out," Lohengrin barked to the knights.

They all gave him a curious glance but followed orders, leaving him and Anwil alone.

"You said not to call you out in front of everyone." Lohengrin snatched the sash from the floor. "So, now that we're alone, that's all shit and you know it. If anything, you just proved how much more *you* deserve the crown over anyone else. The greatest men to lead are never the ones who want to. They do it because they *need* to. Not because they crave power or riches or glory. Because they see the wrongs of this world and want to make them right. *You* are that man." He shoved the sash into Anwil's hands. "So, get out of your head and quit worrying over whether or not you're worthy. Because you are. I wouldn't follow you if you weren't. None of us would."

His words hit Anwil like a stone to his chest. All he could do was clap Lohengrin on the shoulder.

"Don't make me get mushy on you again," Lohengrin said, and a laugh burst from Anwil. "And I am sorry for before. Ellyn says I still have work to do with my anger over losing Father and Lyrion."

"Perceptive, she is," Anwil said.

"Aye; it's why I'm marrying her," Lohengrin said. "Speaking of, you're officiating."

"Oh, am I?" Anwil said as they made their way through the hall. "When was this decided?"

"She decided last night." Lohengrin pushed the doors open. "Will you?"

"Of course, I will," Anwil said. "I'd be honored."

Lohengrin clapped him on the shoulder this time and they left the hall, Anwil holding his head a little higher than before.

CHAPTER THIRTY-ONE

NIMUE

"I wonder if Agravaine still looks good in his old age."

Nimue gave Mordred a look, but he only grinned and winked at her as they rode up to the castle gate. They had just arrived in Lothian that morning, traveling by horse, so as not to raise any suspicion or concern. Nimue had glamoured both of them to look like a couple of nondescript travelers, and the disguise had worked. No one had bothered them on the road. Not that many people were even on the road with Lothian's near constant rain, even in the summer.

"You men and your vanity," Nimue mumbled, shaking her head as they approached the guards at the gate.

Mordred handed them the invitation from Agravaine, and after a glance at the royal seal, they were allowed to pass.

Agravaine's castle was just as Nimue remembered: more fortress than castle. Large and meant to be intimidating. Decaying severed heads were displayed near the gate, and traps were scattered about the entryway, as well as hidden guards and war dogs. Agravaine's green and yellow banners flapped in the wind. Nimue sneered at the mud as they dismounted. She had always hated the weather up here. Always wet and far too much mud.

Standing in the doorway to the castle was King Agravaine himself, wrapped in a deep green cloak with red fox fur, and more silver in his hair than black. Nimue removed the glamour and it melted off, like peeling skin. She shivered. Mordred stretched his neck, grimacing.

If they noticed the magic, they did not react. Trained well, Nimue thought.

"So you did it," Agravaine said to Nimue as they approached. He took in Mordred and shook his head in disbelief. "You bloody well did it."

"Did you doubt me?" Nimue raised an eyebrow.

"I never will again, my lady," Agravaine said, taking her hand and kissing it before turning back to Mordred. "You look the same, you bastard."

Mordred laughed. "I wish I could say the same for you, brother. But I daresay the gray suits you."

Agravaine barked a laugh and embraced Mordred, patting him on the back.

"Come," said Agravaine. "Floree is waiting with mulled wine."

The castle was dark inside, lit only by a few sconces along the corridors, with low ceilings and old stone. The highlands were a coveted spot for fae in the human realms. It soothed Nimue a little, that there was still old magic in these lands, more so than Briton. Though she still hated the weather up here, she was more relaxed in this part of the human world than any other.

Agravaine took them to a comfortable sitting room with a roaring fire. Nimue immediately took the chaise by the hearth, hoping to dry out.

"It's been a long time, Nimue." Agravaine's wife, Floree, sat down beside Nimue and handed her a cup of wine.

"It has," Nimue said and sipped at the wine and sighed. It was good. Floree must have made it. None of the other humans could make a good mulled wine if they tried. It warmed her insides a little, and she drank more. "How are you?"

"Getting older," said Floree. "And here you both are, looking exactly the same as you had in youth."

Floree *was* getting older. Her once brown hair was gray now, and wrinkles had formed at her eyes and mouth, but she was still a beauty for a human. She possessed a commanding presence that kept her husband and boys in line. Agravaine was too much like his father, King Lot—hotheaded with a thirst for bloodshed. Floree knew how to tame him.

"Humans are ridiculous for celebrating youth," said Nimue. "Young humans are idiots."

"I thought you said *all* humans are idiots?" Floree asked with a smirk.

"They are," said Nimue. "But the young ones are worse. Too impulsive and stubborn for their own good."

"You've got that right," said Agravaine, chuckling. "I remember my sons' teenage years. They were so reckless."

"As were we," Mordred said with a grin. He sat back in an armchair, crossing a leg over the other comfortably, as if no time had passed since his last visit. "I do remember a lot of sneaking out of the castle late at night."

Floree chuckled. "Sometimes, I could say the same of you, Nimue."

Nimue shot Floree a harsh look. "I beg your pardon?"

"I admire you, you know," Floree said. "You always went after what you wanted, no matter the cost. I couldn't. I allowed myself to be imprisoned to a life of duty. Country before self. I gave up my wants and dreams ages ago when I was crowned queen."

"You shouldn't have," said Nimue. "Fuck duty." She downed the rest of her wine.

Floree laughed outright at this. "More wine," she called over her shoulder to the serving maid who had just stepped inside.

"So," said Agravaine when Nimue's cup was refilled. "War with Camelot. Your letters did not explain why you wish to continue war with the Pendragons."

"Camelot is standing in the way of what we want," Nimue said.

"And what do you want?" Floree asked.

"To take Briton back to the fae," said Nimue. "Just as we always have."

Mordred shifted in his seat and Agravaine gave him a look she couldn't quite read.

"I relish the opportunity to send an army to crush the Pendragons," said Agravaine. "But much has changed. They are far more powerful than they were when Arthur was alive. More wealthy, more allies. I need to know that I stand a chance. What army do you have?"

Nimue narrowed her eyes at him. None of his letters to her over the past couple of years had mentioned any doubt.

"We have allies," said Mordred. "Waiting to be called upon when we need them."

Agravaine raised his eyebrows. "That is not an answer."

"We have an army at Mab's court," Nimue said. "A little over a thousand, last we counted."

"That is not many at all," Agravaine said. "Camelot has at least ten thousand of their own, not counting all the men they would take from the surrounding kingdoms."

"We cannot crush them with brute force," Mordred said. "I know that. We have another plan."

"Oh?"

"Anwil Pendragon is dying," Mordred said.

"Beg pardon?" Floree asked.

"Is he ill?" Agravaine said. "Or do you have a plan to take him out?"

"Assassins?" Floree asked. "Like his bitch mother?"

"When I returned to the world of the living," Mordred explained, "I needed an anchor. When a soul comes back from the dead, it must attach to a living soul to keep it here. Normally, nothing too bad happens to the living soul, but I gave Nimue's spell a bit of my own flare. I am slowly absorbing his life force as my own. Soon, he will die, and I will no longer have need of an anchor."

"How long will it take?" Floree asked.

"In truth, we do not know," said Nimue. "No one has ever succeeded in magic of this magnitude before. But our friends in Camelot say he grows weaker by the day."

"And then what?" said Agravaine. "Wait for unrest? Storm the castle before they can crown the twin?"

"Once the boy dies, Camelot will be vulnerable. Any kingdom is after the death of a monarch. You know that, Agravaine," said Nimue. "He has no heir save for the sister—and the British kings were already reluctant with Guinevere. They are simple men. They will not want another woman on the throne."

"The girl is stronger than the boy, though," said Floree. "And Lancelot is back at Camelot, given the role of general after Gawaine's death."

"The girl is an idiot," Nimue said, flipping her hair over her shoulder. "She's arrogant, naïve, and spoiled. She's nothing to worry about."

Floree raised an eyebrow. "I hear she's a skilled fighter," she said. "and has a place at the Round Table at only twenty. She's been trained by a powerful Grecian warrior who is rumored to have learned from the gods themselves."

"She killed King Bors and Lord Cerdic," said Agravaine. "Wasn't Cerdic one of your allies?"

"A drunkard could have killed Bors and Cerdic," said Nimue. "And the Grecian warrior is no god."

"Waging war with Camelot is a risk," said Floree. "Are you better prepared this time? Exactly how many men do you have?"

"What are you playing at, Floree?" Nimue asked, growing annoyed. "Is this your roundabout way of saying you will not be joining us, then? Because if so, I cannot leave this rainy hell of a realm fast enough."

"Nimue, my love," said Mordred, putting a hand on her shoulder. "You grow impatient. Remember, Agravaine and Floree are our friends. And they are not wrong. We will not make the same mistake again."

"I am merely trying to be realistic," said Floree. She leaned closer to Nimue. "You forget. We are not you. We do not have magic to protect ourselves with. We do not have another world to run off to when the tides turn. We are mortal, Nimue. You have a habit of dismissing and underestimating humans. It was why you failed last time."

"Friends, we have been waiting for his revenge against Camelot for years," said Agravaine. "We merely want to make sure we can win this time."

"We will," Mordred said. "There is no doubt of that. Our friends have already begun the first move inside the city itself."

"And what is that?" Floree asked.

Mordred gave her a wolfish grin. "I'm afraid that is my little secret for now. But we will take Briton with a concentrated attack. First, Northumbria. Then Gwent and Sussex. With each attack, Camelot will send aid. By the time each kingdom has fallen, Camelot will be stretched so thin, it will have nothing left. And it will be ours for the taking."

"That sounds well and good," said Floree. "But you are a liability, Mordred. This tether...I do not like it. Can it be broken?"

"I do not know," he said.

"Well, I'd like to know," said Floree. "Because if Camelot knows about it, they will try everything to break it to save the king. And what if, say, he dies by something other than you taking his life? He dies in a fight, or is poisoned?"

"He needs to be alive until I have absorbed his entire life force," said Mordred through a stiff jaw. "Or else we both die."

"Then you better find out how much they know of this," Floree said.

"We will," said Nimue before Mordred could speak. His eyes had darkened in anger.

"Good," said Agravaine. "Now, enough talk of war. Let us eat and reminisce on old times, aye?"

Mordred's anger slid from his face and he grinned, following Agravaine out of the room.

Nimue turned to see Floree watching her closely. "What?"

"Nothing," she said, and Nimue knew she was lying.

CHAPTER THIRTY-TWO

ARIADNE

They left Ceridwen's at sunrise. Neither she nor Merlin saw them off, and Ariadne was grateful for that. She had slept little, tossing and turning, not able to get the old wizard's words out of her head. When she did finally fall asleep, she dreamed of her brother's death.

When Morgana woke them, Ariadne's fright had turned to anger. Fate be damned. She would not let her brother die. Neither of them would die. The gods could go fuck themselves with their destiny nonsense. She was the only one in charge of her life.

"We'll talk when we return to Camelot," Morgana said as they made their way back down the winding path. "There are too many eyes and ears here."

Mirah stuck close to Ariadne, just a few steps behind Morgana. Mirah hadn't spoken much since they retired to bed, too distraught over Morgana's spell on Merlin. Ariadne hadn't liked that much either. It felt violating. She couldn't imagine how Merlin felt.

They were nearly back to the moongate they had come through when Morgana threw out her arm, halting Ariadne and Mirah in their tracks.

Ariadne's hands went to a sword and dagger that weren't there, her senses alert. She inwardly cursed not bringing even a boot dagger.

"When I tell you to run," Morgana whispered, "you run. Do not question."

"Yes, run, run, run as fast as you can," came a cackling voice that Ariadne unfortunately knew too well.

Ariadne spun on her heel toward the sound of Nimue's voice and nearly stumbled backward when Nimue appeared right behind her. Nimue grabbed Ariadne by the throat, lifting her off her feet and throwing her backward through the air.

"Ari!" Mirah cried.

Ariadne soared and landed hard on her back, knocking all wind from her lungs. She gasped and sputtered, rolling onto her side. Stinging pain shot through her spine.

Behind her, Nimue screamed in fury. Morgana yelled something that Ariadne couldn't make out over her gasping breaths.

She tried to take deep breaths, tried to stay as calm as she could, but the sound of Nimue and Morgana fighting was getting closer.

"Ari, Mirah, run!" Morgana demanded. Her voice was strained.

If only she could. Shaking, Ariadne got to her feet, her breath coming slightly easier now. Mirah was at her side, diving to her knees.

"Relax," Mirah whispered in a shaking voice. Her hands pressed gently on Ariadne's chest. Warmth spread from Mirah's hands into Ariadne and her breathing came easier.

Flames roared. Someone screamed: Nimue.

Ariadne pushed herself to her feet with Mirah's help. She hurt all over. Her hands were bleeding, and blood tricked down her face. She leaned against a tree. Something exploded, and another scream pierced the air. A mix of pain and anger.

"We have to get out of here," Mirah said frantically. "We can go back to Ceridwen."

But then Mirah jumped and screamed. A small creature appeared behind her. It was the little fae who had given her a flower yesterday.

"Come with me!" She took Mirah's hand and pulled her through the forest with Ariadne following. The sounds of Morgana and Nimue faded the farther they hurried into the woods.

"Where are we going?" Ariadne asked the little fae.

"Safe," was all she said.

But Ariadne wondered if she was working with Nimue and taking her to her death. After a while, the forest thinned and the fae child stopped dead in her tracks. Ariadne almost ran her and Mirah over.

Mordred waited for them up ahead, grinning like a feral animal. Ariadne's blood ran cold, but she stepped in front of Mirah and the fae girl.

"Hello, cousin," he said. "Have you given thought to joining me yet?"

"Tell me you weren't expecting a yes," Ariadne snarled.

Mordred laughed, the sound sending shivers down her spine. "Tis a shame. I do like your spirit."

He drew his sword, and the child peeked out from behind Ariadne's legs. "Don't hurt them! They're friends!"

"They are no friend to you, little one," Mordred said, his voice oddly gentle. "The princess means to send us away. To hurt us."

The child growled, a loud, deep sound for someone so small. "No she doesn't!"

"Step away, child," Mordred ordered. "I do not wish to harm you."

The child stood defiantly in front of Ariadne. "No."

"Then I'm afraid I shall have to kill you, too," Mordred said, taking a step toward them.

Ariadne shoved the child back behind her. "You don't touch her."

Mirah took the child in her arms, little arms wrapping around her neck.

"How chivalric," Mordred said, his words dripping with disdain. "I shall let the gods know you were gallant till the end. But it is now time to die, cousin."

"Go!" Ariadne told the Mirah. "Go now!"

Mordred charged at her faster than humanly possible. And Ariadne gasped, the gleaming metal of the sword flashing before her eyes, but the pain never came. The blade was mere centimeters from her face.

Mordred snarled, his face red with effort. He pulled the sword away and tried again. Ariadne braced for it, but nothing came. Mordred cursed. He shot out a hand for Ariadne's throat, but she ducked and kicked his feet out from under him. He tumbled to the ground.

"I told you to leave her alone!" the fae child screamed from Mirah's arms. Her eyes glowed a pure white.

"You insolent little brat!" Mordred spat and pushed himself to his feet, running at her and Mirah.

Ariadne jumped on his back, wrapping her arms around his throat as tightly as she could.

Mordred roared and tried to throw Ariadne off like a bucking horse, but she held on, slamming a foot into the back of his knee.

He fell, and Ariadne rolled off his back just in time before the pommel of his sword met her face.

"Mirah, run!" Ariadne cried as Mordred threw himself on her, sword discarded, hands locking around her throat. She grabbed onto his wrists, bracing herself for her air to be cut off, but it did not come. Mordred's face screwed with effort and rage. But all she felt was a gentle hold.

Adjusting herself, she moved her foot outside of his, wove her arms through to lock onto one of his, and jammed his elbow, rolling them over and landing a hard punch into his nose. Bone crunched and blood sprayed, but Mordred kept fighting, never managing to land a hit.

Ariadne laughed when he tried to punch her, only to find his fist stopped an inch in front of her. His eyes flashed red.

"Whatever protection spell you wear won't last long," he spat. "But for now, I can hurt you in other ways." He shoved off of her, grabbing his discarded sword and running after Mirah and the fae child.

"No!" Ariadne raced after him. But he was too fast. He grabbed Mirah's arm, yanking her to him, sword at her throat. Mirah screamed.

Ariadne halted in her tracks, heart pounding, her breath echoing in her ears.

"Let her go!"

"If I can't kill you, I'll just kill this little witch here," he snarled.

Mirah whimpered as his sword pushed against her throat.

"Let her go," Ariadne repeated.

Mordred laughed. "I think not," he said. "She's your closest friend, is she not? How about another death on your hands, eh? I'll gladly watch the light fade from her eyes, just as I did with your little lover boy. What was his name again? Oh, right. Lyrion. That's the name Percival screamed as I killed him."

Ariadne clenched her fists, nails biting into her palms. Damn Morgana for not allowing her to bring a weapon! She took a deep breath through her nose. He was baiting her. And she would not succumb to it.

So instead, she forced a laugh—and Mordred's eye twitched. Mirah's eyes slid closed and her mouth moved ever so slightly.

"Gawaine talked about you, you know. So did Percival, and even the bards," Ariadne said to Mordred, hoping to buy Mirah time for whatever spell she was weaving. Mordred's eyebrow twitched again, and she knew she had his curiosity. Men and their egos.

"Do you have a point, Princess?" Mordred hissed.

"I just wanted you to know," Ariadne said, clocking the few jagged rocks by her feet. A slight breeze rustled through the leaves, smelling of lavender and sage. Mirah's scent. Mirah opened her eyes and gave Ariadne the smallest of nods. "And they all agree...that you're just a little bitch."

Mordred's eyes widened and he bared his teeth. A screech, piercing and terrible, filled the skies. Mordred looked up, only for a brief second, and Ariadne grabbed one of the rocks and threw. It caught him on the side of the face and his grip on Mirah loosened enough that she broke his hold and scrambled away.

"Go find that fae," Ariadne said to her. "She might be able to take you home."

"I'm not leaving you," Mirah said and whirled around, throwing a hand out. Mordred froze mid-reach. He struggled against the hold Mirah had on him.

"You cannot hold me for long, witch," he spat, laughing. "You—"

Mordred was thrown back, tumbling through the trees and landing so hard against a thick trunk, it splintered in two. Mirah stepped toward him, raising her arms. Whispering. A heavy wind swirled, picking up leaves and debris from the ground. Ariadne shielded her eyes with her arm. The wind roared in her ears.

"Return to the dead, Mordred," Mirah said, her voice overlaid with another, deeper. It made Ariadne shutter.

"You dare summon the power of The Modron?"

Mirah raised her arms higher. Dark fog rolled in through the trees, and the temperature dropped so suddenly, it was painful. Ariadne shivered, her breath coming out in icy puffs.

"It is not The Modron, I summon," Mirah said. "But Death."

Ariadne almost missed the fear that passed over Mordred's face. But he snarled at Mirah and got to his feet. He let out a weak laugh.

"You cannot summon the god of the dead," he spat. "No one living can."

Mirah flicked her wrist and the fog crawled to Mordred, surrounding him.

"No!"

Fire mixed with the fog but Mirah twisted her wrist again, and the fog smothered Mordred's fire.

"No!" he bellowed.

"Mordred!"

Something hard slammed into Ariadne from behind, and she fell face-first into the dirt.

"Mordred!" It was Nimue. "Let him go!" She ran to Mordred.

Hands grabbed Ariadne and rolled her over. Morgana, bleeding and dirty, pulled her to her feet.

Nimue shot out her hands at Mirah, but Mirah merely flicked her wrist and Nimue was sent flying. She slammed against a tree and fell to the ground, unmoving.

"Nimue!" Mordred roared. A burst of flame shot out toward Mirah and she screamed. Morgana ran to her and caught her as she tumbled to the ground. The black fog disappeared and the cold air warmed.

"Mordred!" Nimue called weakly.

Mordred glanced at his lover and then back at Ariadne. "I'm coming for you, cousin," he said and then dashed to Nimue, and they disappeared within tendrils of black smoke.

Morgana lifted Mirah into her arms and Ariadne ran to them.

"Is she—?"

"No," Morgana said. "But we must get her back to Camelot. She used too much magic."

"But the moongate is—" Ariadne cut herself off as the trees groaned. In front of them, a moongate formed.

Behind it, the little fae girl stepped out. "I can't keep it open long," she said. "Hurry!"

"Thank you," Ariadne said to her. "My friend."

The fae girl smiled up at her as they stepped through the gate. "You are welcome, daughter of the dragon."

Ariadne looked at her curiously, and she pointed up. Ariadne followed her finger, and a winged black shadow fell over them. Another piercing roar rattled the ground, accompanied by the flapping of heavy, leathery wings.

And then, there, in the break of the trees, against the now bright blue sky, the terrible face of a red-scaled dragon looked down at her. Glittering golden eyes under black horned eyebrows looked right at her, and a force so strong fell over Ariadne, she fell to her knees.

It opened its mouth, drool clinging to rows of razor-sharp teeth. Smoke rose from the back of its throat. But Ariadne did not feel afraid.

"Go, Ari!' Morgana barked.

And Ariadne was jolted from her trance. She lunged through the moongate with Morgana and Mirah as the dragon let out another powerful roar.

They were thrown to the ground as the moongate snapped closed behind them in a tangle of cracking limbs and twigs. Ariadne braced for a fall, but arms wrapped around her just as her nose brushed dirt. She was hauled back to her feet and her eyes met another pair of golden hazel, with yellow curls falling around them.

"Prince Connor?" she gasped.

They were in the queen's gardens. And they were not alone. The gardens were full of people, all gaping at them.

"Ari!" a familiar voice called, and she was pulled from Connor's arms.

"Ellyn," Ariadne said, looking into the worried face of her friend.

"We need to get to the infirmary," Morgana said, struggling with Mirah's weight. Connor took Mirah carefully into his arms.

"I'll get Anwil," Ellyn said, slipping her hands from Ariadne's. "Go."

Ariadne whispered a thank you and hurried to the infirmary, staying close to Prince Connor with Mirah in his arms.

CHAPTER THIRTY-THREE

ANWIL

Anwil ran to the infirmary, Lohengrin and Ellyn at his heels. He hadn't even bothered to excuse himself from his meeting with the barons and dukes when Ellyn had told him his sister was back and Mirah unconscious.

When he finally arrived at the infirmary, he knocked into Prince Connor, who was making his way out.

"Pardon me," Anwil breathed, looking over Connor's shoulder.

"My fault." Connor stepped out of his way. "They're in the back."

"Thank you." And Anwil slipped by him, barely registering how Connor would know where they were. But he was focused on his sister. And Mirah.

Lohengrin and Ellyn stayed outside with Connor, and Anwil hurried inside. He found them behind curtains in the back, as

Prince Connor had said. Ariadne sat on a stool, a healer bent over her as Cassius and Morgana worked on Mirah.

Ariadne was dirty, with twigs and leaves in her hair. She shot to her feet, though, when her eyes met Anwil's.

She threw her arms around him and buried her face in his shoulder. She shook hard, and sobs escaped.

"What happened?"

But she shook her head, sniffing into his shoulder. So Anwil just held her, giving her time to let it out. It was a rare form to see Ariadne cry like this. The last time, their mother had died. Anwil was worried about what had happened in the Otherworld.

"What happened?" Anwil asked, gently pushing Ariadne away to look her over.

"Mordred," she said. "He and Nimue ambushed us. But Mirah...she saved us. She somehow summoned the god of the dead and sent Nimue and Mordred away."

He looked at Morgana, who sported bruises on her face, a bloody lip, and burn marks on her clothes and hands.

"My lady," Anwil said, "should you not be looked over as well?"

"I'm fine," Morgana said. "I heal quickly. It is Mirah I am worried about. She used a lot of magic. And I do not know of any side effects when one is possessed by the God of Death."

"What?"

Jabir had arrived.

"Come on." Anwil pulled Ariadne out of the makeshift room to give Jabir privacy. She plopped down on an empty cart and Anwil asked one of the passing maids to bring a decanter of wine.

"Are you hurt?" He pulled up a stool and sat next to her.

"Not really," she said. "Mordred he...he tried. But he couldn't. His blade stopped an inch from my face; his hands couldn't choke me."

"What?" Anwil shot to his feet, carefully cradling her head to check her neck. There were no marks. He swore.

"I know," she said, and the maid returned with the wine. She poured Ariadne a large cup before leaving the rest on a small table and turning to a few patients and healers who were trying to eavesdrop. She shooed them away and took her leave, also allowing them their privacy.

"We should wait until we're alone," Anwil said.

Ariadne nodded and took a long drink. As she did, Morgana and Master Cassius ducked out from behind the curtains.

"She's fine," Morgana said. "She just needs rest. Sir Jabir will watch over her for the night."

Anwil slumped back onto the stool in relief. Morgana moved on to looking over Ariadne, but quickly gave her the all clear. Anwil took her hand and led her from the infirmary, past all the knights who had been waiting in the hall, only stopping for a moment so she could reassure them she was fine.

When they finally made it to the private wing, they discovered a maid had already drawn Ariadne a bath.

"We'll talk in the morning," Anwil told Ariadne when she protested about the bath. She looked exhausted. "Get some sleep. And don't worry about patrols tomorrow."

As soon as he closed his sister's door behind him, Ellyn came around the corner with a basket.

"I have some tea and salves," she said, gesturing to the basket. "And some fruit, in case she's hungry. But mostly, I wanted to make sure she doesn't fall asleep in the bath."

Anwil laughed at the memory of Ariadne falling asleep in the bath after her first day of training with Brionna. A maid had found her coughing and sputtering over the side of the tub. Apparently, she had slipped under the water and woken up as soon as she took in a nose full of water. Even their mother had laughed a bit at it after she was sure Ariadne was all right.

"Thank you," Anwil said. "She seems pretty shaken."

"Of course," Ellyn said. "I should also let you know that the ladies of court are absolutely in a tizzy over Ariadne falling out of the moongate and right into Prince Connor's arms."

"She's going to hate that," Anwil said.

Ellyn grinned. "I can't wait to tell her."

"Break it to her gently."

"So, I have to go to the Underworld," Anwil said once Morgana and Ariadne had recounted their time in the Otherworld to him and the rest of the Knights of the Round Table. His head was spinning. From Merlin's prophecy to Mirah being possessed by the God of Death, it was a lot to take in.

Ariadne sat next to him at the Round Table, a steaming mug of tea in her hands. She still looked exhausted, even after a full night's sleep.

"Yes," said Morgana. "Arawn is the only one who knows how to undo this."

"Do I have to die to see him?"

"I don't know," Morgana said, holding her own cup of tea. "We did not get much else out of Merlin, and Ceridwen knew nothing."

Anwil rubbed his temples. "So, what do we do?"

"Find a way to the Underworld."

"And how do we do that?" Anwil asked, his tone harsher than he intended.

"What about my mother?" Lancelot suggested.

"I could try to reach out to her," Morgana said. "Avalon is still sealed, but she should answer my call."

"Good," Anwil said. "Do that as soon as you can. How is Mirah?"

He had been itching to ask that question since the beginning.

"Still asleep," Morgana said. "She'll be perfectly fine after a few days. Sir Jabir has not left her side."

"Did she really summon a dragon?" Brom asked, and Brionna smacked him in the arm. "What? That's bloody brilliant, that is!"

Morgana chuckled. "I do not know if she summoned it personally, but yes, a dragon made an appearance and took an interest in Ariadne."

Everyone turned to her, and her cheeks turned bright red.

"If you become a dragon rider, it will be wholly unfair for the rest of us," Brom said to her. "We'll never live up to that."

"I'd rather never see a real dragon again," Ariadne said. "It was terrifying! I thought it was going to eat me."

"May we get back on track, please, children?" Lohengrin said. "Or did you not hear the part where Merlin said only one of them will live?"

"Prophecies rarely come true the way we think," said Morgana. "And many do not come to pass at all. Do not read too much into it."

"We should take it seriously," Lohengrin said. "I'd rather worry over it and have nothing happen than not worry and one of them dies because we were not prepared."

"Until we know more from Arawn," said Anwil, "let us worry over the things we do know for certain."

"I'll reach out to Vivienne tonight," Morgana said.

"I'll join you," Lancelot said. "I have not seen my mother in a while, and I have a few questions of my own."

Anwil dismissed everyone but called for Lord Roland to stay behind.

"Yes, Your Grace?" he said.

"I've written a will," Anwil said. "There are instructions for a few scenarios. Will you do all you can to make sure they are implemented if or when I am gone?"

Lord Roland's face fell, but he bowed deeply. "You have my word, Your Grace."

CHAPTER THIRTY-FOUR

NIMUE

Mordred had destroyed his chambers the moment they arrived back in Mab's castle. Nimue left him to his tantrum, needing to heal her own wounds. The bitch Morgana had gotten a few good hits in, reminding Nimue that she was still losing power. And she needed to think. She didn't need to hear Mordred's curses as he broke his furniture. She had told him attacking the Pendragon girl outright was a bad idea, that she had magic protecting her, but he hadn't listened. And now they needed to lick their wounds, and Nimue was not doing that in Lothian.

"We march on Camelot. Now!" Mordred burst into her room just as she had sunk into a bath. She was growing quite tired of him bursting through doors.

"We are not marching on anyone," Nimue snapped as Mordred paced in the washroom. "I'm injured, as are you." She spotted new blood dripping down his hands.

The glare he gave her was murderous. "We cannot wait. We need to crush them. Now."

"I am not yet healed!" Nimue snarled. "I wish to defeat them as much as you, but you must calm yourself! Your anger and haste is how we lost last time. Remember our plan."

Mordred reached for her, hand going for her throat, but she caught his wrist and twisted. "Don't you dare. We will do nothing while you are in this state. If I have to restrain you, I will."

"You cannot hold me."

"I can, and I will," Nimue hissed. "Do not test me. If I have to cast you aside and do this on my own, I will."

Mordred glared at her for a long while before stepping back. She let go of his wrist.

"Fix the door before you leave." She ducked under the water to wet her hair, and when she came back up, Mordred was still glaring at her.

"You are not taking this seriously."

Nimue reached for the washcloth and soap that sat on the small table next to the tub.

"No? Tell me, why didn't you kill them? Hmm? You had ample chance to kill not only Ariadne Pendragon, but her witch friend. But you didn't—couldn't—because you did not listen. I told you they were protected, and now look at us. We—I—need to recuperate. Once I am able, we can begin work on opening the veils—"

Mordred's lip curled. "No."

Nimue's eyebrows shot up. "Excuse me?"

Mordred leaned over her, his hands on either side of the tub. "I'm tired of pretending. I don't care about your self-righteous justice for the fae. I want Camelot's crown, and I will do anything to get it."

"You bastard." She smacked him across the face, the slap echoing.

Mordred's head jerked at the force, but he cracked his neck and then his hands were on her throat. He lifted her out of the tub. She dug her nails into his wrists, her fingers growing red hot.

He screamed and dropped her back into the water.

"Get out," Nimue hissed, and he fled..

Mordred stormed into his room, going straight for the hearth and falling to his knees in front of it.

"*Incothole*," he rasped, waving his hand over the flames.

A room materialized in the flames, as if looking through a window. King Constantine sat on the edge of the bed, head in his hands. He looked up when Mordred called his name.

"What do you want now?" the old king asked.

"The girl," Mordred barked.

"Which one?" Constantine asked. "Princess Ariadne or Lady Mirah?"

"Both," Mordred grinned, licking dried blood from his lips. "Yes, both."

Constantine's eyes narrowed. "I cannot keep betraying my country," he hissed.

"If you wish to see your daughter again, you will do exactly as I say," Mordred barked. "That was our bargain. You do as I tell you and I bring Yvanne's soul back from the dead."

Constantine's face twisted with remorse. "What about the women? What do you want?"

"Kill them," Mordred demanded.

Constantine's face paled. "I shall not!"

"You will," said Mordred. "Or Yvanne stays dead."

Without waiting for a reply, Mordred closed the connection and rolled over on his back, groaning. He was in pain. So much pain. It was getting harder to hide it. His soul itched to leave his body. His decaying body.

Mordred sat up and yanked his tunic off. His skin was turning a sickly green hue, spotted with bruises. He was running out of time. The damn boy needed to die. Why was he taking so long to die!?

Getting to his knees, Mordred repeated the spell, but this time, a different face appeared in the flames.

"Ah," Mordred said. "You finally take your hood off. I should have guessed. I could hear the similarities in your voice."

"What do you want?"

"What did they learn from Ceridwen?"

"Something about a prophecy," came the answer. "Apparently, they got Merlin to talk."

"What did it say?"

"I don't know the specifics. But whatever it is, they're worried about it."

Mordred wiped sweat dripping into his eyes. "Find out."

The face disappeared and Mordred fell back on the cold marble floor.

CHAPTER THIRTY-FIVE

MORGANA

Vivienne had not been any help. Morgana had indeed reached her via a scrying bowl, but Vivienne did not know of anyone traveling to the Underworld without dying.

After speaking with her, Morgana had tried to reach any of the gods, praying and making offerings, but no one answered.

It wasn't until the next morning that she realized how stupid she had been. So she dressed quickly and hurried to find Anwil.

"This is where I used to pray and offer to the gods when I was still a priestess," Morgana told her nephew as they swiped and yanked vines away from the old altar just inside the tree line in the woods behind the kitchen gardens. It was secluded and away from the couriers, but close enough to the growing herbs so she could pick them on her way to the altar.

It sat within a small clearing that had been planted with rowan trees and winding vines and brush. A stone altar, with three statues atop: The Modron, Morrigan, and Airmid. Morgana's personal patron goddesses.

"I tried to speak to them last night in my room," Morgana said, brushing off the last of the dirt and vines. "But of course, they would want me here. And you."

Morgana held out a small leather pouch and Anwil took it silently. He hadn't spoken much on their way here. It wasn't dusk, the perfect time to speak to and meditate with the gods; it was late morning by now, but Morgana hadn't wished to wait another day.

"Place them in here," Morgana pointed. "And light them. They'll smolder. You want the smoke."

Anwil did as she instructed and then placed one of his used quills on top of the herbs.

She gestured for him to kneel with her and to close his eyes.

"Remember to be honest," Morgana said quietly. "They know when you lie."

"What do I say, exactly?" Anwil whispered.

"Whatever you want," Morgana answered. "Once you do, clear your mind and wait. A sign should come."

"What—"

"Do not ask me," Morgana said. "Ask them."

She heard Anwil sigh. He was quiet for a moment before he spoke again.

"I am Anwil Pendragon," he said. "And I am dying. Merlin said there could be a way to break the hold Mordred has over me, but I need to go to Arawn, the god of death. Please, if there is a way, can you help me?"

Morgana reached out and took his hand, encouraging him to keep going.

"A selfless man would say I do not ask because of selfish reasons," Anwil continued, "but I do. I do not wish to die. No one does. I have not lived a long life. But I would like a chance to prove myself. And I do not wish to leave my sister alone. She's already lost too many."

Tears stung Morgana's closed eyes, from his words and the thick smoke that now wafted toward them. Heavily scented and hot, but she made no move to turn away from it.

They sat there a long while, hearing nothing but the birds and rustling from the wind and small animals within the trees.

Anwil finally shifted and sighed. "Merlin must be right," he said, his voice breaking. "Only one of us is destined for this life. And it is not me."

"Is that truly what you think, Anwil Pendragon?"

Morgana shot to her feet and whirled around as Anwil did, and both were knocked back down by the sheer power radiating from the goddess who stood behind them.

The skies darkened and wind rusted the leaves around her like a cyclone.

A tall woman with black hair that shined with hues of blue and purple stood before them, dressed in a cloak of raven's feathers. Thick black coal lined her dark blue eyes and covered her forehead. She gripped a tall staff of black, gnarled wood that wound around a jagged purple crystal. Ravens croaked and crows cawed as flocks of the birds landed in the trees above them.

"Hello, Morgana," she said with a sly grin. "It has been a long time."

"Morrigan," Morgana breathed, and bowed her head. "You honor us with your presence."

Morrigan scoffed. "Do not waste those formalities with me, Morgana. We were so very close once." She turned her gaze to Anwil, who was frozen still, staring at her as if he wasn't sure whether to run or not.

"I have heard your plea, Pendragon," she said to him. "And I have come. It was I who wrote your fate, and it was I who gave you control over it. You do not have control over it now. Rise."

Anwil shot up while Morgana took a moment, inwardly cursing her knees. She shifted closer to Anwil, noting the anger in Morrigan's eyes. Yes, she and Morrigan were close a long time ago. Closer than Morgana had been with The Modron, the patron god of the priestesses of Avalon. But Morgana had never felt a connection to her. Not like she did with Morrigan, the goddess she was named after.

Morrigan approached Anwil. As she did, her height shrank to be eye to eye with him. Morgana gripped her hands together, keeping herself from shoving Anwil behind her, away from the goddess of war, of fate, of sovereignty.

Morgana almost laughed. Of course, Morrigan would come. They should have gone to her in the first place.

"I will not tell you the future," Morrigan told Anwil. "It would ruin the surprise for you and make you complacent. It would also drive you mad, knowing no matter what you do, you will always come to the same fate. But I can give you this."

She held out a long, black skeleton key, and Anwil took it with shaking fingers.

"This will take you to see Arawn," she said. "It unlocks a path the living can walk. Do not stray from that path."

"Do I use it in any particular door?" Anwil asked.

Morrigan smirked. "Any door you like."

"Thank you," he said, "What can I—" but he did not finish his sentence. He crumpled to the ground, unconscious.

Morgana folded her arms across her chest. "Was that necessary?" she asked Morrigan.

"Yes," the goddess hissed. "I wish to speak to you. It has been a long time since you called for me, little child of the faeries."

A raven croaked overhead. Whispers carried on the wind.

"I do not pray much anymore," Morgana said truthfully. "Not since you took both my brother and son from me. You were the weaver of that fate, were you not?"

Morrigan laughed. A dark, deep laugh that reverberated around the trees. "I did no such thing," she said. "They did that to themselves. I showed you the outcomes, and they did not listen. Men never do."

"What do you want?" Morgana asked carefully.

Morrigan stepped over Anwil, growing taller as she came to Morgana.

"Nothing," Morrigan said, but Morgana did not like the smirk playing at her dark purple lips. "I just want you to remember something for me."

"Remember—"

But Morgana slipped into unconsciousness.

Morgana stormed through the halls of the castle. Her brother refused to see reason and for that, he would meet his death. Morgana would not be a part of it. Her son was the same. Stubborn to the very end. Nobles parted for her as she made her way to her chambers, throwing open her doors and scaring her maid. Morgana nearly broke the lid of her trunk, opening it and tossing gowns into a satchel.

"Morgana?"

Guinevere was at her doorway, hands on her swollen belly. Her blue dressing gown was tied under her breast, leaving her belly free, and her golden curls were loose, framing her face. It was not often Guinevere allowed herself to be seen so unpolished.

"Morgana, what happened?" Guinevere waddled inside her room. Her pregnancy had been difficult, with two babes and fate to fight.

"You should be abed," Morgana growled.

"Where are you going?" Guinevere asked, ignoring Morgana's comment.

"Away," Morgana said, stuffing more dresses and books into satchels.

"Why? What happened? Did Arthur listen?"

"Of course not!" Morgana snapped, making Guinevere wince.

The *queen slowly sat down on the edge of Morgana's bed, grimacing, holding tightly to her belly.*

"He is stubborn!" Morgana said. "Too damn stubborn. That Pendragon pride will get him killed. He thinks he can talk with Mordred, make him see reason. Mordred is well beyond reason! I—his own mother—could not talk him out of this."

"Perhaps I can speak with Arthur," said Guinevere, looking at the doorway. "Convince him to at least stay for the birth. Once he sees his children, he may change his mind."

Morgana threw her dress down. "You've spoken with him already. Another fight could hurt the babies. He believes he is doing this to keep you and the babies safe."

"Can't you keep Mordred away?" Guinevere asked. "Use your powers?"

"I am one person," said Morgana. "Against an army."

Guinevere scoffed. "Do not sell yourself short now, Morgana."

"I do no such thing," said Morgana. "I am merely tired. There are wards along the city. You should be fine."

"So you're running away like a coward?"

Morgana stilled. "A coward?" she whispered. Guinevere had hit a nerve. "A coward? How dare you?"

"How dare I? You're packing!"

"I am packing because I am obviously not wanted here. Arthur will not take my advice. He is abandoning his pregnant wife to fight a battle he will not win!"

Guinevere froze. "How do you know?" she whispered. "Have you Seen it?"

Morgana did not look at her. She could not tell her. "I cannot stand by and watch my son and brother fight each other. I cannot."

"So do something!"

"I have!" Morgana cried. "I have done all I can! And for what? Nothing! I have given all my life, and what has come of it? My mother, betrayed by Uther and Merlin, sold to Urien like cattle; Tintagel, my home, taken from me; and now Constantine sits upon its throne—"

"I told you I'd try—"

"But you didn't,*" Morgana hissed. "You didn't, Guin. I gave you children. The children you yearned for. The children we defied fate for. And all I wanted was my home. And I don't even have that. So why should I stay here where I am nothing to no one but a witch to be used for the crown's gains?"*

Guinevere's jaw dropped open. Morgana had known the words would hurt. Had said them intentionally. Guinevere's eyes filled with tears.

"So yes," Morgana continued. "I am leaving. I have given enough. Especially to the Pendragons, whom I never should have trusted."

Morgana closed her satchels and stormed out, leaving Guinevere on the bed. Blanchefleur stood outside, tears in her eyes. The look on her face said she had heard every word. Morgana brushed past her, not wanting to hear any logical words from her friend. She was done. She was done with Camelot and knights and war and magic. So she left the great city and set out into the forest and didn't look back.

Morgana came to, gasping, air filling her lungs. Morrigan stood over her as she clutched at her chest, heart racing, tears streaming down her face.

"Why?" Morgana rasped. "Why show me this? Why this?"

Morrigan crouched next to her, head tilting. "So you do not forget," she said. And with a flash of lightning and thunder, she was gone. The sun returned, the forest back to normal.

The herbs at the altar had stopped smoking, and Anwil's quill was burnt to ash.

Morgana reached over to Anwil, who was now groaning, eyes blinking open. "Are you all right?" she asked.

He nodded and sat up, pressing a hand to his forehead. "I—was that a dream?" he asked, helping Morgana to her feet.

"No," she said, brushing off the dirt and leaves from her dress. "No, it was not."

Anwil looked down at the key in his hand. "She...I did dream, though. Of—" He cut himself off, shaking his head.

"What did she show you?" Morgana asked.

"Nothing," he said, sticking the key in his pocket. "We should return and tell the others."

He was lying, but Morgana did not push. "When you do want to leave for the Underworld?"

"The day after Lohengrin's wedding," he said. "I don't want to chance not coming back and missing it."

"Anwil, we do not have much time left."

"No," Anwil shook his head. "I promised Lohengrin. You, Ari, and Mirah, were gone for a week here, yet only a night in the Otherworld. Who knows how much time will pass, or if I make it back alive? I will see Lohengrin and Ellyn married. They deserve that."

Morgana put a hand on his shoulder. He was paler than he had been earlier. "I'll make you some restorative tea when we get back. An encounter with the gods can take a toll."

Anwil merely nodded, and he led the way back to the castle. A raven flew overhead as they left the forest.

CHAPTER THIRTY-SIX

CONNOR

To his surprise, Connor was enjoying Camelot. The Knights of the Round Table had welcomed him with ease and he spent the days beginning on the training fields, sparring with the knights—mostly Sir Lohengrin and Sir Malcolm—and learning how the hierarchy worked, and his evenings in the city with Bradán and Domhnall enjoying the taverns, shops, and entertainment. The city was magnificent, with its blend of cultures and people. Connor ate food, listened to music, and spoke to people from countries and lands he had never heard of before. His uncle, Garbhan, was nowhere to be seen, which Connor had no qualms about although he was most likely tailing Connor, reporting everything he did to Connig. But Connor didn't care at this point. If he was stuck in Camelot for gods know how long, he might as well enjoy himself. His nightmares had even eased.

Which was why he was at a popular tavern in the city center, enjoying a lively minstrel band with a beautiful barmaid on his lap. He was also winning a game of cards. Although his fun was bogged down because he still had yet to have a meeting with the king, and the princess had gone missing for the week, only for her to appear out of thin air and right into his arms. And then her friend and the Lady Morgana le Fey appearing after her, injured and bleeding.

Connor had asked after them the next morning, but all he got was a one-word answer. He didn't push, though. He was an outsider. There was no reason to trust him. At least, not yet.

"That's it for me, boys." Brom, a Knight of the Round Table, tossed his cards on the table. He shook his head but wore a grin. "I'm all out of money."

Connor laughed as coins were pushed his way. "I'm only making up for last night," he said, grinning. The barmaid giggled, and he tightened his hold on her waist.

"You didn't bet your whole lot, did you?" Bradán asked.

"Oh no," Brom said. "I only bring a little with me. I'm not stupid enough to gamble my life away. Besides, strict rules on gambling when you're a knight."

"Rules? On gambling?" Connor asked.

"Oh, aye," said Brom. "Can't gamble with anyone of lower station than yourself, and you can only keep fifteen percent of your winnings. The rest you're to donate somewhere."

"But they're *your* winnings."

"Aye," said Brom. "But knights are to be an example. We are held to higher standards, yeah? We have a lot of rules to live by, being a Knight of the Round Table."

"What kind of rules?" Domhnall asked as he dealt another round of cards, skipping Brom.

"Oh, there's lots." Brom flagged down another barmaid. "But I don't want to bore the night with rules. Another round for my friends, love, on me. Thank you."

"Shall we celebrate your win, Your Highness?" the maid on Connor's lap whispered into his ear.

He was about to say yes, but Sir Malcolm had burst into the pub, heading straight to Brom. He whispered something in Brom's ear. Brom's face did not betray him, but Connor knew something was wrong.

Brom reached into his pocket and smacked a few gold coins down. "Apologies, lads," he said. "But it seems duty calls."

"Prince Connor, my lords." Sir Malcolm nodded at them before leaving with Brom.

Connor shifted the barmaid on his lap. "Another time, love," he said.

She pouted and brushed her fingers through his stubble, but sauntered off back behind the bar.

"All right," Connor said, switching to Irish. "*Dearg Corra*."

Bradán's eyes widened. "Aye," he said. "I could hardly believe my eyes when he appeared before the king. What does it mean?"

Connor shrugged and finished off his drink. "I don't like it," he said. "It's bad business, making deals with the fae."

"Aye," Domhnall agreed. "I knew someone once who did that. He wanted gold. Well. A fire took his farm along with his wife and son, and guess what? His clan chieftain gave him gold in compensation."

Bradán shook his head.

"Do you think this affects what your da wants with Camelot?" Domhnall asked Connor.

"The king was blessed by The Green Man, so Connig will want me to push even harder." Connor folded up his cards and put them on the table. "I think I'll call it a night."

After mumbling goodbyes, Connor stepped out into the dark streets, letting out a long breath. It was near madness that Dearg Corra had showed himself so publicly. Connor had heard tales of The Green Man giving one of King Arthur's knights a test, but had thought it a bard's tale. Perhaps there was some merit to it after all. Didn't the one man say it had been his father who was put to a test? Connor didn't know his name either. And what was the king worthy of? Dearg Corra had proclaimed Anwil was king, but took the legendary sword with him. What the hell did all of it mean, and what had they walked in to, coming to Camelot? Did it have something to do with the princess?

He took his time walking the winding cobbled roads, taking in the architecture under the moonlight, and the lit torches along the roads. Each building differed slightly from its neighbors, showing off the different cultures of those who built them. This, along with the cool bite of the night air, helped to clear his head. He needed to meet with the king and princess. It was a delicate matter—at least the bit about marriage with the princess, especially after her not-so-warm welcome. Connor didn't want to push them away or offend before they could establish anything.

Someone grabbed Connor's shoulder, and he reacted without thinking. The man hollered in pain as Connor twisted his arm, holding him down. Guards swarmed and yanked Connor off. He stumbled backward, heart racing, flashes of blood and battle in his mind.

"Prince Connor?" a somewhat familiar voice said.

Connor blinked, his vision coming back in to focus. Sir Lohengrin was in front of him.

"I-I'm sorry," Connor said, taking a step back. He glanced at the man he had hurt, and his stomach dropped. It was King Constantine. He knew the King of Dumnonia, had met him plenty of times in delivery trades when he was still Prince of Clannig.

"It is all right," Constantine said, rubbing his shoulder. "I should not have startled you." He waved the guards away, but Lohengrin hesitated. The king was thinner and much older than Connor remembered. It had only been a couple of years since he had seen him last, but Constantine looked as if it were decades that had passed.

"Are you sure you're all right, my lord?" Lohengrin asked him with a concerned look.

"Yes, yes," said the king, brushing himself off. "I should know better than to startle a soldier."

Lohengrin bowed and ushered the rest of his guards away.

"My lord, please accept my apologies," Connor said.

"It is all right, son," said Constantine with a shake of his head.

Connor hid a grimace. He had thought his outbursts were over with.

"I merely wished to say hello," said Constantine, "and offer my good wishes. I hear you are to train as a Knight of the Round Table. It is the highest honor in Briton. I had a seat myself with Arthur as a lad."

"Thank you," said Connor. "And you have my condolences for your daughter. She was a sweet lass. I am sorry to hear of what happened to her."

Constantine's face darkened. "Once, I thought about marrying her to you," he said, looking away. "If I had, perhaps she might still be alive."

"My lord—"

"I best be going," Constantine said. "Good to see you again, Connor."

He clapped Connor on the shoulder and headed not toward the castle, but back to the city. Connor could have kicked himself. Constantine's daughter was obviously a very sore subject. As he turned to head back to the castle, a sharp twinge hit the shoulder Constantine had touched. Connor hissed and rolled his shoulder, rubbing at it. It wasn't until he was stripping down to his bedclothes that he thought it odd for a king of Briton to be walking the streets alone at night.

CHAPTER THIRTY-SEVEN

MIRAH

Mirah dreamed of Death. Of never-ending darkness. She tried crawling out of it, raking her nails against it, but she never found the light. Whispers, familiar and not, called her name. She knew she was dreaming, but she couldn't wake up. Couldn't free herself from the dark.

Not until someone shook her shoulders, calling her name, and a wave of power washed over her.

Mirah's eyes snapped open and she jumped, her fingers gripping the arms of the person holding her. She screamed, heart pounding against her chest.

"It is all right, my daughter," a deep voice said. Someone stroked her hair. "You're all right."

"Baba," she breathed and her father held her to his chest, rocking her as he used to when she was a child.

"You're safe now," he said again. "You are safe."

She buried her face in her father's chest. And cried.

"You've been asleep for three days," Morgana said as she checked Mirah's eyes and heart.

She had fallen back asleep in her father's arms that morning and slept most of the day. When she awoke at dusk, her body felt heavy and her mind was full of fog.

"It will take some time for your body to recuperate," Morgana continued, sitting on the edge of Mirah's bed. "I've told Master Cassius you are not to work in the infirmary for at least a week."

Mirah could only nod. Her throat was dry, and she reached for the water next to the bed. Morgana helped her sit up and drink.

Mirah held the small cup with two hands, staring at her fingers. They felt and looked unfamiliar. As if they were not her own.

Morgana caught her staring.

"What is it?" she asked quietly.

"I don't know," Mirah whispered. "I feel...wrong."

"I figured you might," Morgana said. "You may have some lingering effects from Arawn possessing you."

Mirah shuddered, and a tear leaked from her eye.

"I am sorry," Morgana said. "Do you remember what happened? Right before?"

pened? Right before?"

"I called for help," Mirah said. "Like you told me. Sent a message on the wind. I guess Arawn heard it."

"I knew it was a matter of time before Arawn would come for Mordred," Morgana said, lading broth into a bowl. "I do not know why he had to come through you. I've spoken to Vivienne, but even she did not know the answer. Here." She took the cup from Mirah and replaced it with the bowl. "Sip on this."

Mirah drank, savoring the taste and the soothing warmth on her throat.

"I am sorry for what happened, Mirah," Morgana said quietly. "But you should know how brave you were. If not for you, we might all be dead. Drink all of that. And I'll send your father back in."

Morgana gently squeezed Mirah's shoulder before leaving, the door softly closing behind her.

Mirah had a plethora of visitors, much to her father's dismay. Her room was filled with flowers and baskets of fruits and well wishes.

She was arranging a few of the flowers to press into a book when someone knocked loudly on her door.

Her aunt, Anipe, was on the other side, a look of worry on her face. She threw her arms around Mirah's neck before Mirah could even murmur a greeting. The tall woman held Mirah tight, and the familiar scent of her—a musky perfume—was strong in Mirah's nose.

"I got here as fast as I could!" Anipe said. "As soon as I received Jabir's message, I raced here."

"What?" Mirah said, pulling away. "Baba wrote to you? Why?"

"Why would he not? You are my niece!" She swept past Mirah into the room, her emerald silk dress billowing out behind her. She looked as Mirah remembered. Short-cropped hair, plenty of jewelry, and kohl-lined eyes.

"It is dangerous to travel, though." Mirah closed the door and offered Anipe some tea from her pitcher.

Anipe settled onto the sofa in front of the hearth. "It was a risk I was willing to take," she said. "You were ill. Now tell me: How are you faring? Your father did not tell me what you came down with."

"Oh, just too much magic used," Mirah said, sitting in the chair across from her. "I'm much better now."

Anipe dropped a few spoonfuls of sugar into her tea and stirred slowly. "Hmmm," she said, raising an eyebrow. "Your father was tight-lipped too. If you cannot tell me, I understand. Just know that I am on your side. I will help you in whatever way I can."

"I know," said Mirah, pouring her own tea. "Thank you."

"Have you thought more of returning to Evanshire?" Anipe asked, raising her mug to her lips.

"My place is here," Mirah said. "In Camelot." *Now more than ever,* she thought.

"I don't like how involved you are with this impending war, Mirah," Anipe said.

Mirah took a breath. "Baba is worried too," she said. "But it affects all of us."

"Does it?" Anipe said. "Or is it just another warring family fighting for the throne? Court politics do not affect us much out in the duchies. You can always return home to Evanshire and wait it out. Where you are safe."

"Camelot is my home," Mirah said. "I've spent more time here than I ever have in Evanshire."

"Yes, an issue I speak to your father about frequently," Anipe said. "Mirah, you know we just want what is best for you. We worry you are wasting your life in the infirmary. Your father tells me you spend sunup to sundown there."

"I am not wasting my life," Mirah said. "I am a royal physician. I worked hard for that title and I am perfectly happy in life. Please believe me, Aunt."

Anipe shook her head. "You should be getting closer to the king," she said. "I am sure he is looking for a new bride."

Mirah choked on her tea. Anipe handed her a handkerchief. "What?"

"If you will not return to Evanshire, you should be ruling. You are of royal blood." Anipe sat her mug down. "Our grandfather, your great-grandfather, was a king, and our grandmother was the daughter of a prince. You were born for more than this."

Mirah bit back a retort before she regretted it, and turned away from her aunt. She knew her family history. Her great paternal grandfather, King Esclabor, was an exiled king and her maternal grandmother was the youngest daughter of a youngest son of a king in a small kingdom in Africa.

Both royals had fled their kingdoms. Esclabor's kingdom no longer existed and her grandmother's father hadn't wanted to stay in his. He wanted to see the world.

Anipe leaned back against the sofa and shook her head. "For the life of me, I will never understand why you turned down your chance to be queen when he proposed to you first."

"Because it wasn't what I wanted," Mirah said, tears threatening her eyes. It had been the hardest decision of her life, having to say no to Anwil.

"But it was what you deserve," Anipe said. "If I was a much younger woman, I'd do all I could to woo him."

"I—no, please, Aunt." Mirah put her head in her hands.

"I am sorry," Anipe said. "I did not mean to trouble you."

She stood and kissed Mirah's forehead and left without a word.

Mirah had not been prepared for Anipe to bring up her past feelings for Anwil. She had buried them, had spent years blocking out the memories of the secret kisses she and Anwil had shared, the meetings and all the sneaking out of bedrooms in the middle of the night. And the night she had been offered to apprentice Master Cassius was also the night Anwil pulled a ring out of his pocket.

It had broken her heart to stop him before he could ask, to see the devastation on his face. But Mirah knew that her calling was to be a healer. A queen could not spend her days in the infirmary, tending to wounds and the sick. Mirah had convinced herself that they were too young. It was only a passing fancy. So she walked away, convincing herself that her feelings would pass.

It became easier with each passing year to ignore them. The more she worked, the easier it was. And when Yvanne was announced to be his queen, Mirah was happy. She loved Yvanne and knew she'd be a perfect queen next to Anwil's king, no matter how it hurt to see them together, smiling at each other. Kissing each other. Yvanne was a perfect choice for Camelot's queen.

And then Yvanne was taken. And Mirah had to watch her throat get sliced and her blood pour from her body. And Queen Guinevere, who had become a second mother to her. Who had held her tight when she learned the news of her own mother. Who planted Nazrine's favorite flowers in her garden to honor her. Who Mirah turned to for advice when Lord Geraint, Sir Kay's grandson, had courted her.

Mirah could not save her either. Could not even remove the poisoned dagger from Guinevere's side because she wanted her to have just a few more minutes for Anwil. For Ari. For herself.

Someone knocked on door again and Mirah contemplated not answering. But she was glad she did, as Ariadne was on the other side with a bottle of wine and a basket of sweets.

"How did you know?" Mirah asked, stepping aside to let Ariadne in.

"I saw Anipe arrive," Ariadne said. "Thought you might need a little something."

"You have no idea."

CHAPTER THIRTY-EIGHT

ARIADNE

Ariadne banged on the door to Prince Connor's room. She had been avoiding him since her return from the Otherworld, using the excuse of needing time to process what had happened. Which was true. She had needed time to think, to come to terms with not only Merlin's words, but watching Mirah be possessed by the god of death. Ariadne hated to admit it, but fear crept up her spine. Fear that they were in way over their heads. Fear that they were making all the wrong decisions.

Grumblings echoed from inside the room, bringing Ariadne from her thoughts, and she banged again. The door yanked open and a very disheveled Connor greeted her. His sleep shirt was wrinkled and falling off of one shoulder. And he wasn't wearing trousers. His shirt was barely long enough to keep him decent. Ariadne sighed in frustration and kept her eyes above his head.

"Wasamatter?" he slurred.

"Good morrow to you too," said Ariadne. "Get dressed. You're coming with me to the training fields."

Connor rubbed at his eyes. "It's the middle of the night."

"It's almost dawn," she said. "Let's go."

He stared at her for a moment before mumbling something Ariadne couldn't catch and closing the door on her. Rude.

"Connor!" She banged on the door again.

"I'm changing!" came his muffled reply.

Ariadne folded her arms across her leather-clad chest. Thankfully, he didn't make her wait long. He opened the door just a few moments later, dressed in just a long-sleeved tunic and trousers and worn boots, carrying a large sack over one shoulder and holding his axe in another. His hair was still a mess, sticking up everywhere.

"What's all that?" Ariadne nodded at the sack.

"M' belts and things," he mumbled. "You wanted me fast, didn't you?"

"Let's just go," she said, ignoring the innuendo.

"What are we doing today?" Connor asked when they stepped outside into the courtyard. The orange and pink glows of the sunrise were just beginning.

"We already know you can fight," Ariadne said. "So I wanted to test some of your other skills."

Connor answered with a yawn and Ariadne took him around the back of the training fields to a giant wooden structure..

"I wanted to introduce you to The Splinter. She's a popular lady, so I wanted to make sure you got some special time with her before the others rise." She folded her arms and leaned against its side.

One of the most popular training mechanisms built by Merlin himself, it was a mess of wooden mazes with hidden traps, ropes, levers, swinging hammers, and false doors. In the center was a wooden pole with the Pendragon banner hanging from the top, worn to a shine from years of climbing. Failing any of the tasks would cause the player to fall through a trapdoor and be dumped back to the beginning to start again.

"The Splinter?" said Connor, eyes wide as he looked up at it, dropping his bag at his feet.

"It also happens to be the first step toward your knighthood. Once you pass her, you can start the first trial."

Connor said something in Irish, and while Ariadne did not speak it, she was sure he had let out a few colorful words.

"You don't need weapons for this," she said, walking up to the swinging hammers and pushing on them to get them going. "Do you wish to try it?"

Connor looked it over and shrugged. "Might as well."

She picked up the large hourglass filled with sand and turned it over. "Good. Start now."

Connor growled at her in Irish. He sat his axe down next to his bag and ran up the ramp, only to fall through the trick floor, rolling his way back to the start Ariadne laughed when his cursing continued as he moved on to the swinging ropes.

Connor cursed again as one of the giant hammers knocked him on the shoulder and sent him flying a few feet. The hammers were padded to soften the blows, but she knew how hard they still felt. He groaned from the ground as Ariadne crouched next to him.

"Not bad," she smirked. "Although I made it nearly halfway to the end of my first try. I honestly thought you'd make it farther."

She held out a hand for him and helped him up. His hands were calloused, but warm, and he held onto hers a second longer with a quick glance at her, but then brushed himself off. She handed him a waterskin, and he drank greedily from it.

"Who even thinks up something like this?" he said, tossing the skin back to her and rolling his shoulder.

"Merlin," she said. "Being a Knight of the Round Table isn't about just being good with a sword. You have to think quickly and be flexible. You can't panic or let frustration win. It's to teach us to think in dangerous situations." Something she still struggled with, herself.

Connor raised an eyebrow and shook his head. "Isn't that what all knights are supposed to learn?"

"You'd think so," said Ariadne, a few of the not-so-honorable lower knights coming to mind. "Want to go again?"

Connor glared at her but ran up the plank. A crowd formed once the morning sun had risen, but Ariadne stopped him after a particular misstep resulted in him falling from the beam, his head narrowly missing a swinging hammer by a few inches.

She crouched next to him and gave him the waterskin again. He snatched it from her and downed it. "That's enough for today. You got farther than I expected."

She helped him to his feet again and he stumbled a little. Ariadne helped to steady him, his shoulder pressing into her side. She caught a whiff of sandalwood and citrus and something akin to sea air coming from him. Not a whiff of drink on him, as she had expected, since he apparently spent most nights at the Crown and Dragon. His biceps flexed under her fingers as she helped steady him.

"Did I pass inspection, Princess?" he asked, his hazel eyes lowered to her mouth.

"For now," she said, stepping away from him. "Let's get you something to eat and then you can polish my armor for me."

Connor laughed. "Polish your armor? You jest."

"Come along, squire."

Connor ate like he hadn't had a proper meal in days. Ariadne sat across from him in the mesh hall for the guards and squires, sipping on water. This was her first time in the small hall where the knights, guards, and squires took their meals. But it had been closer than the great hall in the main part of the castle, and food and drink had already been ready. So she had taken Connor here instead.

Many waved to her or bowed, and it took them awhile to get to a seat, as a few guards were particularly chatty this morning. Ariadne found herself wishing she had brought a quill and paper to remember all their requests.

A few of the knights, such as Gingalain and Garan, one of Sir Kay's grandsons, gave her dark looks.

She ignored them.

"Tomorrow, you'll join me on patrol," Ariadne said as Connor finally slowed down after his second helping of boiled eggs and porridge.

"I've never had porridge like this before," Connor said. "It's delicious."

"We have fantastic cooks," said Ariadne. "Did you hear me?"

"Aye, I did," said Connor, wiping his mouth with a napkin. "Patrol. Aye. Will it just be the two of us, Princess?"

Connor's lips turned into a small smirk. She ignored that, too, pretending not to understand the hidden meaning.

"And all the other people in Camelot," she said. "I expect you ready by dawn."

"Should I expect the same wake-up call?" he asked, filling his cup with water. "I admit, being jolted awake by you first thing is the morning is something I'd happily get used to."

"Sadly for you," said Ariadne, "it won't be happening again. Meet me tomorrow in the courtyard."

She left before he could respond, but she heard him chuckle as she left the hall. Brionna was waiting for her in the corridor, a smirk of her own on her face.

"Don't you start," Ariadne told her.

Brionna laughed and shook her head. "I was only going to compliment you for the restraint," she said. "You didn't shove his face into his porridge. Prince Connor will be your ultimate test."

"I hate you for this," Ariadne grumbled.

Brionna laughed again and put an arm around her. "I know."

CHAPTER THIRTY-NINE

ANWIL

The key weighed heavily in Anwil's pocket. He hadn't quite recovered from his encounter with Morrigan and what she had shown him. Whispered to him. It would haunt him for the rest of his life. But it was inevitable. And he had to come to terms with it.

Someone knocked on the throne room doors and Anwil sat up, shuffling through the papers he had laid out before him on the Round Table.

"Enter," Anwil called and the doors opened, the council spilling through.

Ariadne followed them, with Prince Connor and his uncle, Lord Garbhan, behind her.

"Good morrow, Sire." Lady Sura looked at him over her spectacles as she sat down. "I wondered if perhaps we may talk in private after the meeting?"

"Of course, my lady," Anwil answered.

Lady Sura nodded and shuffled through her own papers.

Ariadne took the seat to Anwil's right as Prince Connor and Lord Garbhan hovered a bit.

"Welcome, my lords," Anwil greeted them. "Please, sit anywhere you'd like. There are refreshments and food on that cart there."

Lord Garbhan ignored the refreshment cart and plopped down in a chair.

Connor said something quietly to him in Irish as he took a seat beside him, but his uncle ignored it. Anwil saw the expressions and glances between his council.

Anwil waited until everyone was settled before making his formal opening of the meeting and introducing Prince Connor and Lord Garbhan to the council.

"Prince Connor," Anwil said when introductions were over, "you are here to negotiate opening the trade routes between Briton and Ireland once more, yes?"

"Aye, Your Grace." Connor pulled out a thick scroll and handed it down. "While the last king of Ireland had no wish for an alliance, my father and I do. We think it would greatly benefit both of our nations. My father has written up his proposal there."

Anwil looked it over; it was a well-thought-out plan that did indeed benefit both nations fairly equally. It was when he came to the last line that his eyebrows shot up.

"Am I reading this correctly, my lords?" Anwil said to them. "An alliance and trade depend upon a contract of marriage?"

Ariadne sat up, jaw dropping. Anwil gently nudged her with his knee. She closed her mouth but sent a glare at Connor.

"Aye," Connor said, not meeting Anwil's eye. "My father is a bit, er... old-fashioned. But I hope that we can see the benefits of such a match, Your Grace."

"What benefits, Prince Connor?" Ariadne asked.

Connor glanced at her. "By uniting our countries through marriage, it strengthens the ties between us. We would be family, and that would guarantee that whatever terms we come to would be continued on after our deaths through our children."

In any other circumstance, this contract would be near perfection. Anwil glanced over the proposal again. All Connig was asking for was Ariadne's dowry, and a garrison of troops—not so many that it would hurt Camelot too much.

"Don't tell me you're contemplating this." Ariadne leaned to Anwil, her lips barely moving.

He handed her the scroll, and she read it over.

"My lords," Anwil said to the Irishman, "Camelot had always been good for its word. We are more than willing to negotiate with you. However, it is not a good time to send my sister away. Nor is it my decision about who she marries."

"Not your decision?" Lord Garbhan asked. "Aren't you her king and brother?"

"I am, my lord," Anwil said. "However, Ariadne does not need my permission to seek her own husband."

Some of the council members bristled at this, but Anwil had put his foot down on it when they tried to talk to him about the subject after his mother had passed. She had had the same rule, that it was Ariadne's decision, and Ariadne's alone, adamant after she had no say in her own marriage.

"And I have no intention of marrying," Ariadne interjected.

"Your Grace, if I may?" Lord Garanwyn held out his hand and Anwil passed down the proposal.

Son to the legendary or infamous (depending on who you asked) Sir Kay, Arthur's first Knight of the Round Table and foster brother, Lord Garanwyn held a similar reputation to his father. Quick to anger and entitled, but far more clever than his father.

"Your Highness," he said to Ariadne after skimming through it, "if I may put forth my opinion, Prince Connor is heir to his own throne. As such, you would be a queen one day and Briton would have another open trading route, bringing in supplies—such as cattle—we cannot as easily get anywhere else. It would be wise to consider this."

Lady Sura snatched the paper from him. "Forgive me, but Princess Ariadne is a Knight of the Round Table. Therefore, her duty is to Camelot, not a foreign country."

"She is a princess before knight," Lord Garanwyn said. "And a princess has a duty to benefit their home kingdoms through an advantageous marriage. And there is a perfect one right here."

"Thank you, my lord, my lady," Anwil said before they could argue some more. "As I stated before, it is Ariadne's decision.

Should she decline, I hope that Prince Connor and I can renegotiate the terms of an alliance. Sister?"

"I must politely decline, Prince Connor," she said. "My duty is first and foremost to my brother and Camelot."

"I understand, Princess," Connor said, but his uncle scoffed and rolled his eyes.

"Something to add, Lord Garbhan?" Lady Sura raised an eyebrow at him.

"Seems like a missed opportunity, is all," he said with a shrug. "If it was me, I'd do anything I could to help my country defeat a fae warlord."

"Are you implying that I will not, my lord?" Ariadne said, her eyes flashing.

"I didn't say that, Your Highness." Lord Garbhan gave a smile and bowed his head.

"Good," Ariadne said. "I'd hate to see you tossed back to Ireland today if you were."

Garbhan's smile faltered.

"There is no doubt what you would do for Briton, Your Highness," Connor interjected before his uncle could respond. "And it would please us greatly to renegotiate, Your Grace."

"Thank you," Anwil said, noting the looks that passed on a few of the council members' faces. They were not happy. "I'll send word as soon as I can for us to meet again."

Connor bowed and stood, whispering something to his uncle, who begrudgingly followed him out.

"I fear you are making a mistake, Your Highness," Lord Garanwyn said as soon as the doors had closed.

"How so, my lord?" Ariadne asked him.

"Connig is a stubborn man," Garanwyn explained, "who does not like taking no for an answer."

"What king does?" Ariadne said with a scoff.

"He might retaliate," Garanwyn continued. "By either keeping the block on trade or even declaring war himself if he feels offended."

"He cannot afford a war," Anwil said. "Our men in Ireland report that his treasury is empty and they suffered a great defeat over the winter by foreign invaders. My guess is he wants Ariadne's dowry more than an alliance."

"But if he is willing to help us in this oncoming war with Nimue and Mordred, we should not dismiss the opportunity."

"We've done fine without Ireland for years now," said Lady Eneuawg, an older woman with white hair and sharp eyes. "If Queen Guinevere wanted to arrange her daughter's marriage, she would have been married by now. There have been dozens of proposals for the princess, ones much better than what Ireland proposed. Let the woman make her own choice, Garanwyn. God knows not many of us had the same."

Anwil smiled at Lady Eneuawg, daughter to Sir Bedievere, one of Arthur's renowned knights.

"It is her choice, my lady," said Lord Garanwyn. "But also her duty. Marrying to secure alliances and bolster trade is an honor and a duty to every princess."

"Then marry *your* daughter to him," Ariadne said.

"Gladly," Lord Garanwyn said.

"Enough," Anwil said. "Ariadne will not be marrying Prince Connor, and I will not hear another word about it. Now, Lady Dindrane has given me a report of suspicious movement in Lothian. Her spies say the Saxons that survived have been meeting and making their way to Lothian."

Anwil handed the report to his sister.

"We have reason to believe that King Agravaine will reignite his alliance with Mordred," Anwil continued. "Many of you may remember how close Mordred and Agravaine were, I am sure. So we should assume Mordred and perhaps Agravaine are rallying Saxons to their side by way of promising revenge on Arthur for defeating them."

"What proof do we have?" Lord Garanwyn asked.

"Not much," Anwil admitted. "But I want to be ready for it, just in case. Lady Dindrane's spies are working to get more concrete evidence."

"I'd bet my left ear," Lord Safir, who rarely spoke much at meetings, said, "Mordred is with Agravaine now. That son of a bitch has been biding his time, waiting for an opportunity to storm Camelot."

"Safir," Lady Eneuawg gasped. "Such language from you."

"Forgive me, my lady," he said. "But I know Agravaine. I accompanied Gawaine a few times to Lothian to visit his family. Agravaine is a snake. He hated Arthur almost as much as Mordred did. It is a wise choice to assume they are rallying old allies. We should do the same."

"Briton has a habit of not making many foreign allies," Lord Garanwyn said. "We're too busy fighting ourselves, and when we're not, we're trying to conquer other lands. I doubt any neighbor will come to our aid."

He glanced at Ariadne as he said this. Her lip twitched, but she said nothing.

"I have faith in an alliance with Ireland," Anwil said. "If we can offer some gold and supplies to help rebuild their northern villages, I am certain we can come to an agreement with King Connig. There is also the alliance with Byzantium currently in the works. Now, I think we are done for the day. Thank you."

Ariadne hovered behind while the others filed out, but Anwil waved her along.

"Lady Sura?" he said to the treasurer, who was almost to the door. "We can speak now."

Lady Sura bowed and returned to her seat as the door closed. "Thank you, Your Grace," she said. "I want to begin with that I know it is not my place, but there have been whispers at court. Worries, really. I know you have named Princess Ariadne as your heir, which I support, however...not many do."

"What are you saying, my lady? Are you reporting treason? Another coup?"

"No," Lady Sura bit her lip. "At least, I've heard nothing so serious. However, men tend to not like change. It was difficult for Queen Guinevere in the beginning, a woman ruling over a realm of men and warlords. There were a few tries to overthrow her, as well as a small rebellion. I do not wish to see the same for Ariadne if something, god forbid, happens to you, Your Grace."

"Are you suggesting I remarry?"

"I am suggesting that it might be a good idea to think about it," she said. "And please, I do not wish to overstep. I know this is very forward of me. But I regarded your mother as a friend. I assure you; I only have Camelot and your best interests at heart."

"I know, my lady," Anwil said. "I take it you have a list of princesses and noble women?"

"Oh no," Lady Sura shook her head. "I couldn't presume. Although...there is one woman, I think, who would be a great match and a wonderful queen. She is much beloved already."

"Oh?"

"Lady Mirah, Your Grace."

CHAPTER FORTY

CONNOR

As soon as Connor and his uncle were well away from prying ears in the corridors, Connor grabbed his uncle's shoulder and spun him around.

"What the hell is wrong with you?" he hissed. "You nearly cost us everything!"

Garbhan shrugged out of his grip. "I did no such thing."

"You insulted the princess and disrespected the king," Connor hissed. "Are you trying to sabotage this? Because you've done a good enough job already."

"I'm here to make sure you do what your father ordered." Garbhan grabbed the neck of Connor's tunic.

Connor snorted. "Well, you're doing a mighty fine job of it, then." He shoved Garbhan's hand away. "If you can't keep your mouth under control, then go home."

"I have orders—"

"Fuck your orders!"

Garbhan's jaw dropped.

"I'm going above my father's head and sending you home," Connor growled.

"You can't go above your king's orders!"

"I can and will," said Connor. "Especially when he hears how you almost ruined his plans because you couldn't contain yourself."

Garbhan glared at him but said nothing, breathing hard out of his nose like a damned bull. He turned on his heel and stormed off.

Connor ran his hands through his hair, letting off a string of curses and offending a couple of noble ladies as they passed.

"I say, sir!" one snapped at him, her face flushed red. She grabbed hold of the younger one's arms and hurried them off.

Mumbling under his breath, Connor turned down the next corridor. He would have to do damage control now, even though it was most likely useless. He couldn't see getting in the princess's good graces now. But he could try to apologize.

The meeting was still going on, so Connor went in search of Bradán and Domhnall and found them at the training fields, sparring with Sir Malcolm and Sir Brom.

"How did it go?" Domhnall asked as Connor leaned on the wooden fence.

He shook his head. "Garbhan nearly cost us," he mumbled.

"What the hell did he do?" Domhnall stuck his sword in the ground and wiped his hands off.

"Couldn't keep his damned mouth shut. What do you think he did?" Connor snapped. "Shit. Sorry."

"Can we do anything?" Domhnall asked as Brom swiped Bradán's feet from underneath him. Bradán landed hard on his back and let out out a string of cursing in Irish.

"I think I managed to recover," Connor said. "I'll have to apologize later."

"How did they take the marriage offer?"

Connor looked at him.

"Right. Not well," Domhnall mumbled. "What now?"

"Meet with the king again, renegotiate without the marriage."

"Your da's not going to like that."

"Nope." Connor opened the gate and grabbed Domhnall's sword.

"Oy, those are your good clothes," Domhnall said.

"Don't care."

Connor was in the stables—more like avoiding his uncle, really, who refused to leave Camelot—brushing his horse when he saw a blur of red hair pass through the stalls.

Connor sat the brush down and led his horse back to his stall, but not before giving him a treat and a kiss on the nose. "Good boy," he mumbled and wove through the barn to the other side, where he found Ariadne in an occupied stall.

She stood next to a beautiful beast with shining black hair and a white nose speckled with black. White hair, also speckled with black, shone around the mare's hooves. She was a good size, maybe thirteen hands, with prominent muscles under her gleaming coat. She grunted at him as he approached.

"Princess." Connor bowed and held out a hand to her horse, who gave him a good sniff. He reached into his bag and pulled out a treat. The mare gobbled it up and crunched loudly.

"Prince Connor," Ariadne said stiffly.

"I wanted to apologize," he said, rubbing the horse's soft nose. "That meeting was...not how I wished to handle things."

"Did you plan to tell me at all?" she asked, turning to him. "That you came here to ask me to marry you?"

"I did," said Connor. "I had thought we would meet with the king privately before—"

"So, you weren't even going to give me the respect of telling me first? Typical."

Ariadne stomped to the small shelf built into the wall and grabbed a brush. "Were you hoping my brother would just marry me off because you knew I'd say no?"

"No!" said Connor, offended. "Absolutely not."

Ariadne snorted.

"I wanted to present everything to your king first, as is proper," Connor said. "I didn't know that you and the entire council were to be in the room as well."

Ariadne scoffed. "Right."

"Look, I'm sorry, all right?" said Connor. "I should have...well. I'm sorry. Especially for my uncle."

Ariadne looked at him. "Your uncle is despicable."

Connor let out a weak laugh. "Aye, I can't argue with you there. I've never liked him, myself. But listen, Princess."

Ariadne raised an eyebrow.

"My father sent me here to offer marriage, yes," Connor continued. "And he won't like no for an answer, but I'm here to try and work something else out. Something he'd be happy with despite losing a marriage contract."

"Why does he want one?"

"Money, heirs," Connor said with a shrug. "To continue his line. What any king wants. Camelot—Briton—is a powerful ally to have. I'm sure you've had loads of offers."

Ariadne didn't answer, but her silence was telling.

"I know I'm in no place to be asking you for favors," he said. "But honestly, if we can open trade again, it truly would benefit us both."

Ariadne stared at him a moment before brushing again. "You're not wrong," she said, "but you need to behave. You can't tup every barmaid in Camelot and gamble your money away. Especially if you wish to be a Knight of the Round Table."

Connor didn't let the retort he wanted to make come out. He spent most nights in the pubs because it was the best place to overhear information. He had been learning about Camelot, about this threat of a fae war, and anything else he deemed useful. People had loose tongues when they had enough to drink in them. Especially the barmaids who overheard everything.

"As you wish, Princess." He winked because he couldn't help himself.

Ariadne rolled her eyes but tossed him her brush. "Make yourself useful."

She grabbed a different brush and took the horse's tail in hand, brushing gently. "This is Nerys. She's mine."

"She's beautiful," Connor said, giving Nerys's nose a rub and brushing out her shoulder.

"She also doesn't take any shit," said Ariadne.

Connor laughed. "Noted."

They brushed out the mare in comfortable silence until Ariadne led her out into the pasture.

Connor had admittedly enjoyed it and had watched the princess the entire time. She was stunning, with her wild hair and lean muscles. A brief thought of her toned thighs around his head had crossed his mind, but he shoved it away quickly, not wanting to do anything that would break their uneasy truce. If circumstances had been different, he'd be proud to have her as a wife. She was resilient, strong, intelligent, easy to smile—not for him, but perhaps one day—and mischievous. Of course, the cliché temper to match her hair, which Connor liked best.

"She'll roll around in the mud as soon as she finds it," Ariadne grumbled, watching Nerys trot toward the back of the pasture. "And there she goes."

Connor chuckled as Nerys promptly lowered herself to the ground, snorting and grunting as she rolled onto her back.

"Is she trained for war?" Connor asked.

"No," Ariadne said. "She's too small. Our warhorses are over there, in that pasture."

Connor followed her finger, shielding his eyes from the sun with his hand to get a better view. Large, stocky horses grazed and pranced around, stable-hands strewn about with them.

"My father started them," Ariadne continued. "He had a passion for them. He bred and sold them to the other kingdoms, even to other countries. I try not to get too attached to them."

Connor understood. He'd made the mistake of attaching himself to his first horse and then lost him in battle.

"I have no plans to marry, Connor," Ariadne said abruptly.

"I know," he replied. He knew from the start that she would decline the marriage, so he had secretly drawn up a contract of his own, knowing he'd face his father's wrath. He'd present that to King Anwil when they would meet again. And hopefully Connig would even let him return to Ireland after word reached him that there would be no marriage with a Pendragon.

"Good," said Ariadne. "But I will help you negotiate trade between our lands. But tell me something. Why do you want to become a Knight of the Round Table?"

Connor scoffed. "Because Connig ordered me to," he answered truthfully.

"So that's why you don't take it seriously," she said. "Well, after we agree on a new alliance deal, you can return home. I'm sure you miss it."

She pushed herself off the railing and left before Connor could reply. He hung his head and cursed.

CHAPTER FORTY-ONE
MORDRED

Mordred heaved into the pot, his throat burning. There was nothing left in his stomach, nothing to come up, but his body would not stop. The pain was getting worse. As if his insides were being ripped apart by a thousand needles. His body was decaying, inch by inch. Clothing hid the worst of it for the moment. He had tried a glamour, but the energy of the spell was too much to sustain.

Mordred heaved once more and rolled over on his side, breathing heavily. Sweat poured from his skin, but he shivered on the cold stone. It would pass in a moment. Perhaps a long moment. But it would pass.

When it finally did, he picked himself up and tore off his clothes. He called on a servant for a bath and poured a little wine from the decanter by the window.

As the Lothian servants filled the bath, Mordred peered out the window and grinned. A company of a few hundred men had arrived at Agravaine's castle just days before. Saxons. Descendants of those Arthur had killed, thirsty for revenge. Mordred would give it to them.

Once the bath was ready, he sank into it, the hot water relaxing his aching and stiff muscles. He wished Nimue were with him, if only to heighten the potency of the salves he needed to apply. He only had need of her to get the fae on his side; it was easier to kill humans with a fae army. He had learned that when he marched on Arthur in Camlann. He'd made a grave mistake underestimating Camelot's soldiers, one he would not make again.

He was better prepared this time around, with the fae from Nimue and the idiot humans inside Camelot feeding him information. So easily they turned their coats with just a few pieces of gold and a promise of power. As if Mordred would ever give it to them. Their loyalty was too fragile. He couldn't chance them turning on him.

Mordred stretched and washed himself, careful not to scrub too hard on the parts where his skin was peeling. Once finished, he dried off and dressed. He was careful to choose clothing that reflected what he wished. Morgause had taught him that clothing could also be used as a weapon.

He chose a black tunic stitched with gold under a leather surcoat and black gloves. He wore no jewelry, as he did not need to show off wealth in that way. No. He chose finely made weapons: a sword, a dagger, and throwing knives tucked into his bracers and boots.

A black velvet cloak with gold embroidery was his final piece, and he carefully braided his hair back. He did not need gaudy. That was all Agravaine, who liked to show off with shiny jewels. No, Mordred was more subtle.

He swept from the room, passing servants who made way for him, and a few courtiers who scurried away in fear.

Agravaine and Floree were already in the courtyard, talking to the Saxon leader, Uhtric.

"They caught scouts from Camelot," Uhtric was saying. "On their way here. Figured we'd take care of them for you."

"More Saxons are coming," Agravaine explained to Mordred, "from Wessex. It would seem there are many not so loyal to Camelot there."

"Good," Mordred said. "We can begin there. Send discreet scouts and a few changelings to Wessex and take down that kingdom first. It should be the easiest."

"But aren't we waiting on more fae warriors from Nimue?" Floree asked, looking from Mordred to her husband.

"We have enough gathered at Mab's court," Mordred said. "All we need to do is open the veil. We start quietly. Send assassins and changelings to the petty Briton kingdoms. Take them one by one."

"There are wards against changelings in Camelot," Floree said. "Nimue said after she kidnapped the king, they strengthened the wards around the city. If you replace their kings with fae, they cannot enter the city if summoned."

"Then they decline a summons," Mordred said. "All the better to shake Camelot's authority. Uhtric, send your best men to accompany the changelings. Make sure they keep quiet. We do not want word getting back to Camelot."

Uhtric bowed his head. "Yes, my lord," he said and returned to his camp.

"We are not yet ready," Floree hissed, grabbing Mordred's arm. "You're making the same mistake as last time."

Mordred yanked his arm from her grip and turned to Agravaine. "Are your men ready?"

"I just need to summon them," he said.

"Good," Mordred said. "Summon them. We march on Camelot soon."

CHAPTER FORTY-TWO

MORGANA

Morgana had been to plenty of weddings since leaving Camelot. They were humble, warm celebrations with the entire village out at a long table under candle and moonlight, sharing the joy, dancing around the fire to a fiddler, or raising their own voices.

She had almost forgotten what a wedding in Camelot was like. While Sir Lohengrin and Lady Ellyn had a small wedding by noble standards, the formality of it had taken Morgana by surprise. So used to the village weddings, Dindrane had to whisper in her ear a few times when she stood in the wrong place, or raised her hands to cheer. She could barely believe how many of the courtly rules she did not remember.

It was a beautiful ceremony though, officiated by Anwil, and Morgana couldn't help the tears that welled in her eyes at the love and devotion that shone in the happy couple's faces as they read their vows to each other.

Lohengrin looked so like Percival, it reminded Morgana of his wedding to Blanchefleur. It, too, had been small, with barely fifty people in the gardens to witness their handfasting, but was filled with so much love, everyone had felt it.

It was a similar feeling now. Ariadne, who stood on Ellyn's side as a bridesmaid with Mirah, grinned from ear to ear, and Mirah wiped tears.

There was a slight hiccup, as a sudden breeze took Lohengrin's paper with his vows, and a section of the roses from the archway almost fell on Ellyn's head. Both of them laughed it off, determined to go keep going.

Blanchefleur stood near her son, dabbing at her eyes with her handkerchief. Every once in a while, she would look over her shoulder, as if expecting Percival to be there, and Morgana's heart pained each time. But Blanchefleur was beaming when Lohengrin and Ellyn walked down the aisle together to lead the guests to the great hall.

"I remember the last wedding we attended in Camelot," Lancelot said to Morgana as he escorted her down the corridors. "Gawaine nearly passed out during the vows, and quite a few ladies cried for days because he was no longer available."

Morgana snorted at the memory. "I told him that ridiculous green velvet cloak was too hot for August."

She and Lancelot reminisced over Gawaine's wedding until they arrived at the great hall, where the guards opened the doors and Morgana knew something was wrong. But it all happened so fast.

The wall exploded.

Morgana was thrown off her feet with the others. Heavy stones fell, screams echoed. Dust filled the air.

Morgana groaned, lifting herself from the floor. Blood streamed down her face, and a sharp pain throbbed in her hip.

Somewhere, she could hear Lancelot barking orders. Blood and broken bodies littered the floor between the fallen stones. Her ears rang.

Morgana shook herself and grabbed a guard as he passed. His helmet had been bent and his face stained with blood, but he was moving.

"Go to the infirmary," she told him. "Tell them to lay out more beds. And return with medical supplies. Cassius has emergency bags packed in the closet. Go. Hurry!"

Morgana looked around, searching for Anwil and Ariadne. She did not see their faces in the chaos, but she did see Lohengrin holding a bleeding Blanchefleur. She rushed to them as fast as she could, limping on her injured hip.

Blanchefleur had blood streaming down her head, and she was clutching her side. Morgana yanked her handkerchief from her sleeve and held it to Blanchefleur's head wound. She inspected Blanchefleur's side, and her friend cried out as she did. Broken ribs. Morgana hovered her hand over the woman's stomach. A red light flickered under her fingers. Morgana's heart dropped. Internal bleeding.

"Take her to the infirmary," she told Lohengrin. "Be very careful with her."

Lohengrin looked at her, eyes wide. "Is she—"

"Go!"

Lohengrin carefully scooped his mother in his arms and took off as quickly as he could. Morgana looked around for Ellyn. She was bloody, her beautiful gold gown torn and stained, but helping others. So, she was fine for now.

Morgana finally spotted her niece and nephew, but it wasn't a pretty sight. Anwil knelt over an unconscious Ariadne.

Morgana scrambled to them, diving to the floor next to her niece, checking her over. She was alive, but her leg was badly broken, bent at an odd angle. Morgana inspected her head, cursing under her breath. Possible skull fracture.

"Where is Mirah?" Morgana asked Anwil.

"I don't know," he said, his own face covered in dust and blood. "She said she had forgotten something, I think?"

Morgana ripped at Ariadne's already destroyed gold gown and pressed the fabric carefully to her head.

Morgana called for Lancelot. As soon as he saw Ariadne, he carefully lifted her into his arms and carried her toward the infirmary. Anwil made to follow, but Morgana grabbed him.

"No," she said. "We go to the Underworld. Now."

"I can't leave! People are dying," Anwil cried.

"This was probably Mordred's doing," Morgana said. "They could be coming. We go now. Do you have the key?"

Anwil nodded and Morgana grabbed his hand, leading him toward the dungeon's entrance.

Anwil pulled the key from his pocket, wrapped in a cloth pouch. Morgana pulled the cloth away just enough to stick it into the lock. It clicked and the door creaked open. Morgana and Anwil stepped through.

And fell.

Morgana tried to scream, but there was no air. There was nothing except the falling. She reached out, trying to find Anwil in the dark, but she felt nothing. Her thoughts faded away, like a dream one was trying to remember, but the more one tried, the farther away it became.

Eventually, she was nothing.

Until the darkness slowly faded to a silvery light. A light so pure and warm. Morgana returned to herself as she landed softly on lush grass. Anwil was standing next to her, wide-eyed and pale. But clean of blood and stone dust.

Morgana looked down at herself. She too was cleaned and her hip no longer hurt. She looked around, taking in their surroundings.

A dark forest, not unlike the one that bordered Camelot, greeted them. Heavy clouds covered the sky, and the air was so heavy with mist, it coated their skin. Morgana felt a thousand eyes on her, as if every leaf and branch were watching her. Fog coated the ground so thickly, their feet disappeared. Twinkling lights, brighter and bigger than fireflies, surrounded them.

"Where do we go?" Anwil asked.

"Forward," Morgana said. There was an overgrown path ahead, but Morgana could make it out under the foliage.

Their footsteps were loud. Leaves crunched and small sticks snapped under their feet. The pulsing lights that had been floating around suddenly shot out in every direction.

Screams and moans echoed around them. Anwil tried to bat the lights away, but his hands went right through them. Morgana threw her arms up, conjuring a barrier around them. The pulsing lights bounced off of it. More screams surrounded them.

"They're not lights," Morgana breathed, a realization hitting her. "They're souls."

"What do they want?" Anwil asked.

Morgana had no answer.

"Is this what becomes of us?" Anwil watched the souls bounce off the invisible barrier.

Morgana was saved from answering. A black figure emerged from the trees, gliding toward them. A hollow scream pierced their ears. Anwil fell to his knees, covering his ears. Morgana's barrier burst, and she, too, fell. The souls flew away, their moans and yells fading away.

The black figure came closer, surrounded by billowing robes of black smoke. A hood covered its face and a long, black hand gestured to them.

"Come," it said, its whispered voice hollow and coarse. Without waiting for a reply, it turned and glided back to where it came from.

Anwil looked at Morgana, but they followed the black creature through the dense forest for a long while until the trees thinned and another clearing opened, revealing a large, looming castle made from dark stone, surrounded by a green moat.

Morgana raised an eyebrow at the moat with a drawbridge, but said nothing as the creature glided toward it. It stopped just before the bridge and turned around.

"Stay on the bridge," it said. "Do not touch the rails; do not look into the water."

"What's in the water?" Anwil asked.

But the creature did not answer. It turned around and glided across the bridge, disappearing through the door into the castle. Morgana followed first, stepping onto the wooden bridge. As soon as her foot touched the wood, however, the water burst to life. Hands reached out, waves splashed, screams and moans pierced the air. The bridge trembled as splotchy gray arms reached for the rails.

Morgana stumbled back off the bridge, and there was an almost immediate ease of chaos. She clutched a hand over her pounding heart. She stepped onto the bridge again and once more, arms, screams, trembling.

"Run across," Morgana told Anwil over her shoulder. "And do as the creature said. Do not look down; do not touch the rails."

He nodded and Morgana ran across the bridge, keeping her eyes straight ahead. She made it to the darkened threshold of the doorway and whirled around to watch Anwil step onto the bridge and then disappear.

All the breath left Morgana's lungs. She ran back across the bridge, calling his name. But there was no answer. The creature reappeared in the doorway.

"Arawn is waiting," it said.

"Where is he?" Morgana demanded. "Where did he go?"

"Arawn does not like to wait," was all it said.

Morgana clenched her jaw, now furious. She stalked down the bridge, ignoring the arms and trembles.

"Arawn!" she called into the darkened corridor of the castle. "Where is my nephew? Where did you send him!? Answer me!"

A chuckle. Then footsteps. Sconces came to life, illuminating a rather normal-looking castle corridor and a tall male approaching her. His pure white hair was long, the top layer swept back into an intricate braid, revealing pointed ears and moonlight gray skin. His pale gray eyes burned into her as he towered over her. He was handsome, the most handsome male Morgana had ever seen. His clothes were black velvet and leather with silver embroidery.

"Morgana le Fey," he said, his voice silky and deep. "Only you would dare speak to the God of Death so boldly."

"You didn't answer my question," she said, her voice barely even.

"No," he said. "And I will not. Not until you come with me."

Arawn led her to a small, circular study with a dark oak table in the middle. But the center of the table was carved out and filled with mist. Books lined the walls, and a worn black armchair sat in front of the hearth. The normalness of the room unnerved her.

Arawn waved his hand and a twin armchair appeared across from his. He sat and motioned for Morgana to do the same.

She did, but kept to the edge of the chair. "Are you going to tell me why you allowed Mordred to be resurrected?"

"I allowed no such thing," Arawn hissed, the mist at the table swirling. "Your son stole a small kernel of magic from me."

Morgana could not help herself. She laughed.

Arawn's eyes blazed with cold fire.

"I do beg your pardon," she said, putting a hand to her chest and catching her breath. "But you're God of the Underworld. How did he manage that?"

Arawn stood and crossed to the tall, thin window, gazing outside. "Mordred's soul had been stuck in the In-Between for some time," Arawn said. "When it finally came to me, it was burning with rage and vengeance, a part of it still reaching to go back. Part of what I do is to calm those souls so they do not disturb the peace of others. As I was trying to soothe the rage, he reached in and took some of my power. Not a lot; barely a little sliver. But enough for him to reach out and reconnect with the world of the living. I slipped. I didn't sever the part of him that was still barely connected to the In-Between. So when Nimue's spell reached its claws into the In-Between, there was enough of him for it to grab on to."

He turned back to Morgana, his eyes softening. "We gods are weakening, Morgana," he said quietly. "Our powers are not what they used to be. More and more, humans turn to the new religions and put us behind. Forget about us. It won't be long now until we are forgotten completely. Even now, our worlds are unraveling."

He pointed out the window and Morgana joined him there, following his finger to a courtyard. Filled with lush grass and colorful flora, stone statues and a fountain – and people. But Morgana looked closer. But Morgana looked closer. They were not as they seemed. The statues were chipped, broken, the flowers wilting.

And the people. They were not solid. She could see right through some of them. They wandered aimlessly, without direction. Some passed through each other.

"Not long ago," Arawn said, "these grounds were filled with life."

Morgana raised an eyebrow at him, and the corners of his lips twitched ever so slightly.

"When the dead come here," he continued, "they come here to rest. If they lived good and just lives, their time here is peaceful. If they were cruel in life...well...I'll spare you the details. The point is...once we are forgotten, so are the dead. Their souls will cease to exist."

"What happens then?" Morgana asked.

Arawn didn't answer.

"We were told you could break the tether between Mordred and my nephew," Morgana said, turning away from the courtyard below. "Can you?"

"I can," Arawn said. "But what would be the fun in that?"

Anger bubbled in her chest and Morgana lunged at him, but he was faster, stepping out of the way and catching her about the waist.

"Tsk, tsk," he chuckled. "It is impolite to attack your host. And I wasn't finished. I will give Anwil the power to break it himself."

Morgana screamed in frustration. "Why can't you, for once, just do it yourself? You know the damned consequences of Mordred being in the living world!"

"Of course I do," Arawn said. "But what would humans learn about life if we did everything for them? Anwil must find the strength within himself to break the tether on his own. Only then will he be free."

"How?" Morgana demanded, hitting him on the chest. "How the hell is he supposed to do that?"

Arawn nodded toward the window. Morgana huffed and looked out, and her knees gave out. She caught herself on the ledge of the window.

"Arthur," she whispered.

Her brother. Her baby brother. There he was, in the courtyard, looking resplendent in his favorite brown tunic, his bright red hair and beard neatly cut and shaved. He grinned up at her and waved.

A woman in blue came up behind him, long golden hair fanning out over her shoulders. Arthur slipped an arm around her waist and kissed her cheek.

Guinevere.

A sob broke through Morgana. Guinevere waved and she and Arthur parted, going separate ways.

"Wait, where are they going?" Morgana asked.

Arawn handed her a black silk handkerchief, and smiled.

CHAPTER FORTY-THREE

ANWIL

One moment, Anwil was with Morgana in the Underworld and the next, he was in a vaguely familiar stone hall. The Round Table sat in the middle and a fire blazed in the hearth. Twelve shields adorned the wall above the fire. Anwil knew all of them instantly. Sir Lancelot, Sir Gawain, Sir Percival, Sir Bors, Sir Lamorak, Sir Kay, Sir Bedievere, Sir Gaheris, Sir Galahad, Sir Tristan, Sir Palamedes, and in the middle, the heraldry Anwil knew best. Pendragon. This one had a sword attached. A sword Anwil knew well. Excalibur. It echoed in his ears. It called to him.

Anwil knew where he was now. This was the old great hall, before his mother's expansion and renovations. He recognized it from paintings and tapestries from around the castle. But how did he get here? A door creaked open and footsteps drew closer. Anwil turned around and came face to face with...himself? No.

The man he stared at was older, perhaps by about a decade, with lighter red hair and the shadow of a beard. He was stockier, more muscular.

Arthur.

His father.

Now Anwil knew why everyone kept saying how much he looked like Arthur. The nose, the shape of the jaw, the eyes, even freckles, though Arthur's were much lighter and fewer.

"Hello, son," Arthur said, a gentle smile on his face. They were even the same height.

Anwil didn't reply. He backed up a step, hand going for a sword that wasn't there. This had to be a trick. Like the one Ariadne endured when she went looking for him after Nimue had captured him.

Arthur's face fell, and he held his hands up in front of him. "I understand your caution," he said. "But you have nothing to fear from me."

"You're dead," said Anwil, shaking his head. "You're a trick. I won't fall for it."

"I am no trick," said Arthur. "Arawn merely allowed me a bit of time to see you."

Anwil narrowed his eyes, but perhaps there was a bit of truth. They were in the Underworld. Arthur would be here.

"He can do that?"

Arthur chuckled and put his hands behind his back, as Anwil had a habit of doing.

"It is his realm. He can do what he likes."

"Ariadne met a changeling who took your form," Anwil said. "How do I know you're not a changeling now?"

"What does your gut say?" Arthur asked.

Anwil stared at him. His mannerisms were familiar; the way he spoke, held himself. Anwil recognized himself in Arthur. How was it possible? He had never met his father. But he knew. Anwil knew it was Arthur. His father.

Anwil, however, didn't like how intense his father's gaze was, so he glanced around the room.

"The room is very different now," he said, gesturing with a shaking hand. "We use it as a dining hall. Mother had a new great hall built."

Arthur grinned. "Your mother is remarkable. I am sad I wasn't alive to see it, but I knew Guinevere would shine on her own. As will you."

"Why did you want to see me?" Anwil asked.

"Because you're my son." Arthur stepped closer. "And this is the only chance I could. Until your death, that is. But I do not believe it is your time, Anwil."

"Mordred, he—Nimue brought him back to life," Anwil said, looking everywhere but at Arthur's eyes. "And he is...taking my life so he can stay alive."

Arthur's jaw twitched. It was the same tell Ariadne had when she was angry.

"Yes," said Arthur. "So, I have heard. Arawn knows why you are here. And yes, there is a way to break the tether between you two."

Hope burst into Anwil's chest.

Arthur crossed the hall to the hearth, looking up at the mounted shields. He pulled Excalibur down and its song grew louder. He held it out for Anwil.

"Mordred can return to the Underworld if killed by Excalibur," said Arthur. "You must plunge it right through his heart."

"But Lancelot already did that," said Anwil. "Right after he returned."

"It cannot be anyone else," said Arthur. "*You* must be the one to do it."

Anwil laughed bitterly. "I'm no fighter. I can't win against Mordred."

Arthur put a hand on Anwil's shoulder. "You can, my son," he said. "Fighting is more than just brute strength or speed. It is also about being clever. Use Mordred's weaknesses and strengths against him. Outsmart him."

"What if I can't?" Anwil whispered. "I'm not you."

Arthur lay Excalibur down on the table and took Anwil's face in his hands.

"No, you are not," said Arthur. "And that is a good thing. You are your own man. A good man, a good brother, son, and king. Your future holds great things for you, my boy, if only you can open your eyes and see who you truly are."

"And who is that?" Anwil asked. "I've done nothing."

"You are Anwil Pendragon the First," said Arthur. "The king who saved Camelot from a great fire. Who ran into a burning building to save a little girl without a second thought. Who *sees* his people, who makes them feel safe and respected. Your mother taught you well. You are just and merciful. You do not need to be a warlord to be a great king. You already are. Besides, you have your sister to do all the fighting."

Anwil snorted at that last bit, and Arthur grinned.

"I am so proud of both of you," Arthur said, his hands on Anwil's shoulders. "But do not keep comparing yourself to me. I do not want you to be anyone but yourself. You have a good heart, my son. *That* is your strength."

Anwil couldn't bring himself to speak. He didn't trust his voice, but perhaps those were the words he had longed to hear his whole life but hadn't realized it yet.

Arthur took Excalibur and held it out for Anwil.

"How did you get it?" Anwil asked. "The Green Man took it."

"He did," Arthur said. "He took it so you can have it back at the right moment. The moment you need it the most."

"I can't wield it," Anwil said quietly. "I'm too weak. My strength fades every day."

"I think you'll find you can," said Arthur.

With a shaking hand, Anwil took Excalibur. A blinding white light exploded around them and Anwil was back in the Underworld's forest, Excalibur clasped in his hand. He fell to his knees as strength filled his body. The aching in his limbs went away and his head was clear. Excalibur was heavy in his hand, but it was not a staggering weight. He could hold it. He felt good. Better than he ever had before. And he felt strong.

A shadow fell over Anwil and he looked up at a tall figure, his face half covered by shadow. His mere presence exuded power.

"Your father gave the last of his strength to you," Arawn said. "It will not last long. Use it wisely." And the figure was gone. Before Anwil could do or say anything else, another light exploded and Anwil fell forward onto the wooden bridge.

"Anwil!" Morgana exclaimed, bending to help him up. "What happened?"

"I saw Father."

"Arthur?" Morgana asked, looking around, and then she spied Excalibur in Anwil's hand. "You have it. How? The Green Man—"

"I saw Father," Anwil repeated. "He gave it to me. He said if I use this to kill Mordred, the tether will be broken."

Morgana stared at him for a long while, mixed emotions on her face.

"I'm sorry," Anwil said. "He's your son."

Morgana shook her head. "Come. We should return to Camelot."

"How?"

"Arawn showed me the way."

CHAPTER FORTY-FOUR
CONNOR

Connor was in the training arena, helping squires with sword work, when the ground shook and an explosion rocked the north wall of the castle. Squires fell to the ground. Screams and booms of heavy falling rock came from the castle.

Connor immediately ran toward the wreckage, Bradán and Domhnall hot on his heels.

When they arrived at the site, Connor's breath hitched. Flashes of past battles came to his mind, his own warriors dead on the ground covered in blood, but he pushed those images away.

He moved stone and statue and tapestries to dig people out.

"Connor! Here!"

He ran to Domhnall, who trying to help a hurt child.

"Hello, lass," Connor knelt in front of her. She was curled up on her side, crying and holding her arm. The wrist was broken. Tears streaked down her dust-covered face.

"Can you sit up for me?" Connor held out his hands, but she ignored him. "All right, I'm going to pick you up, aye? It'll be all right; we'll get you to a nice bed, and perhaps some candies."

She sniffed and looked up at Connor, but still didn't move. He carefully slid a hand under her neck and knees, gently pulling her toward him so as not to hurt her wrist. She cried out again, calling for her mother.

"We'll find her," Connor said, cradling her to his chest. As he turned from the pile of stone, he spotted a group of nuns running toward them, carrying bulky bags.

"I've got her," one of them said to Connor when she spotted them. "Sister Marianne!" she called over her shoulder and then was hurrying off.

Connor wiped his brow on the back of his sleeve and went back to looking for more injured.

Minutes felt like hours. He was quickly drenched in sweat, moving heavy stone after stone, pulling the injured from the rubble.

Once all the victims were taken to the infirmary, Connor stayed to help clear the rubble, even though he was told he didn't have to.

Only when the worst of it was clear did Connor return to his rooms to bathe. He did so quickly, wanting to find Sir Lancelot and find out what had happened. But the exhaustion hit him hard as he dried off and he fell into his bed, sleeping almost immediately.

"Lancelot went to Avalon," Sir Brom explained to Connor the next day in the mess hall as he sat down across from him.

Brom sported a bruised eye and a broken nose. One of his hands was wrapped, and he winced when he put weight on his left leg.

"His mother is the Lady of the Lake and a healer," Brom continued as Connor pushed the pot of tea toward him. "Thanks. Infirmary is full, many in critical condition."

Connor winced. The mess hall was solemn and quiet around them. Even Bradán had barely spoken that morning. He just sat there, next to Connor, picking at his food.

"Do we know what happened?" Connor asked quietly, sipping on the bitter drink they called coffee.

Domhnall and Bradán leaned in, listening.

Brom shook his head. "No. But Lady Dindrane is questioning everyone. I'd hate to be on the wrong side of her interrogations." He shuddered.

"If there's anything I can do..."

Brom nodded. "I'll let... well, I shouldn't bother Lohengrin. He hasn't left the infirmary. His mother's there."

Connor swore under his breath. "How is she?"

Brom's face fell. "Not good."

Connor hadn't properly met Lady Blanchefleur, but she was well liked in the court, and seemed kind.

"What about the princess?" Connor asked.

"Why do you think Lancelot went to Avalon?"

His heart dropped to his stomach.

"Where's the king? Is he hurt too?" Bradán asked.

"He and Lady Morgana are on business," Brom answered carefully.

"Right." Connor downed the last of his coffee. "I'll see you all later."

He headed into the city, where the melancholy had spread as well. He listened to the talk: rumors and theories about what had happened at the castle. The main constant was Nimue and Mordred. That was the dead—or not dead—man's name, Connor remembered. Mordred. Fear was prevalent in their voices. A fear Connor knew well from the battles and raids in Ireland. His villagers felt the same fear from invaders.

Connor turned down the street of blacksmiths and approached the one he was looking for. This blacksmith wasn't known for armor and weapons. His skill was much more unique.

Connor described his idea to the tall, willowy man, and the blacksmith grinned.

"They'll be ready for you tomorrow, my lord."

Connor paid the smith and left for the Crown and Dragon to see what he could overhear.

"The usual, my lord?" The half-fae barkeep and owner smiled at him, her green eyes sparkling. They always sparkled, and it was hard not to get lost in them.

"Aye, thank you, Myfanwy," Connor said, trying to flash her a smile. "How are you doing?"

"Oh, all right," she said, filling his tankard. "Had to run off a couple of rioters this morning."

"What?"

"There's some people in the city that think all the fae should leave," she explained with a frown. "It's not new. We normally don't have many issues, but now..." Her eyes grew distant.

"I'm sorry," said Connor. "Can I do anything?"

Myfanwy smiled. "You're sweet. But I can take care of myself. I have for two hundred years."

Connor's eyebrows shot up. "Well, don't you look good for your age!"

Myfanwy smirked and patted her hair. "I know."

Connor laughed. "But tell me about this war. The knights are closed-lip about it, but I need to know if Ireland could be in danger."

Myfanwy's eyes darkened. "Nimue," she growled. "She was an Avalon priestess and was always talking about giving Briton back to the fae. But it never belonged to us. We share these lands. A few shared her sentiments, but not all. She was kicked from Avalon for killing humans and trying to open the veils permanently between realms."

"Permanently open?"

Myfanwy nodded. "If she does this, it would create a rift, an unbalance. Crops and animals could die, the weather would drastically change, water could dry up or flood; it would be a disaster. The worlds would become unlivable. All of them."

"Why does she want to do this?"

Myfanwy sighed and filled a tankard for another customer. "She has some self-righteous idea that we need to be saved. That the humans are trying to wipe us out. But it's no worse than before. Honestly, it's better, especially under Pendragon rule. Besides"—Myfanwy lowered her voice—"fae kill humans too. There's a fae queen who was banished because she liked to...well, let's say *play* with humans. Now she can't leave her own lands nor even talk to humans."

"Who punished her?"

"The gods," Myfanwy answered. "And the Lady of Avalon, Vivienne. She's part goddess, herself."

"My sister's always wanted to see Avalon," Connor said. "She's a high priestess."

Myfanwy smiled. "An honor, indeed. Now, enough of this talk. Tell me, do you know who attacked the castle?"

Connor shook his head. "I was hoping to find out something here. See if anyone knows anything."

"Well, the Knights of the Round Table will find who did it," Myfanwy said. "And I feel sorry for the poor bastard when they do catch him. They won't show mercy this time."

Connor agreed, sipping his mead. "What, er... what do the fae think about The Green Man blessing a human king?"

Myfanwy's eyes lit back up. "Oh, that's an honor. But I knew King Anwil was worthy. He's a good boy. Man, now." She shook her head, a smile playing at her lips. "All you humans are so young to me. But I watched him grow, sneaking in and out of my tavern with his sister. He'll be a good king for all. What about your kingdom, though? All my years and I've never been. I hear it's very green."

Connor laughed and humored her change in subject, giving her all the tales she wanted to hear.

"I can't let anyone into the infirmary," Lady Mirah said at the infirmary door.

"I understand," Connor replied. "But could you give this to the princess, please?"

He held out a small wooden box. Lady Mirah eyed it suspiciously.

"You can look," he said.

She sighed and took it from him, carefully opening the lid. Her jaw dropped. "Your Highness. She's going to kill you."

Connor laughed. "I expect it."

"I'll make sure she gets them, though." Lady Mirah closed the lid. "This is very thoughtful of you."

"If there's anything I can do?"

"Pray," Lady Mirah said.

CHAPTER FORTY-FIVE
ARIADNE

Ariadne slipped in and out of consciousness. In and out of pain. She vaguely recalled Mirah holding her leg and more pain. She remembered shouts and the smell of blood and smoke. Anytime she came to, Mirah was there, and Ariadne would fall back to sleep.

"Ariadne."

Ariadne woke on her back in the gardens, her mother's gardens. The gentle breeze was warm and the flowers were in full bloom. Pushing herself up, she looked down at herself. She wore a simple, undyed linen dress. She felt no pain, no fatigue.

"Ariadne."

Ariadne jumped to her feet at the whisper of her name.

"Ariadne!" It was Anwil's voice. But it was so far away.

The sunlight in the garden faded and darkness descended. She couldn't see anything. She called for her brother. She held her arms aloft, taking tentative steps, calling Anwil's name again.

She ran into something, tripping, and the light returned. But Ariadne was no longer in the gardens. She was in the city streets. People surrounded her, all staring and snarling at her.

"You killed her!"

"Lord Gawaine is dead because of you!"

Ariadne shook. The people were all yelling at her. One threw a rotten fruit that hit her in the head. She stumbled back.

"Lyrion loved you! And you led him to his death!"

"You're not fit to be a Knight!"

The people crept forward, caging her in. "No! No, Mordred—"

"You led them to their death!"

And then it was Lohengrin looking at her, his eyes red with tears. "You killed my brother and father. You killed them! I'll kill you!"

"No! No. I—"

Lohengrin kept coming at her with a rage she had never seen from him before. "No! No, you're not real! Stop it!" Ariadne blocked and blocked and blocked, but she struggled.

"Stop!" She stumbled backward and angry faces hovered over her. "I didn't kill them! Mordred did! He's to blame, not me!"

"Why?" Lohengrin asked.

"What?"

"Why is Mordred to blame when you led them to Avalon? When you took them straight to their deaths?"

"I didn't know!" Ariadne said, pushing herself up. "I didn't know Mordred would be there. I couldn't have known. I was trying to save Anwil! You said it wasn't my fault!"

"I lied!"

"No!" Ariadne shoved him away from her. "No! It was not my fault. I didn't kill them, nor did I lead them to their deaths. I didn't know Mordred was there. They chose to fight. They chose to put their life on the line, just as we do every day. That is our duty, to protect those we love! That is what they did. Percival died to save you. So did Lyrion. As I would also do for you."

Lohengrin stared at her, the rage still on his face. But he faded away, along with the streets of Camelot.

And she was back in the castle gardens. She let out a sob, falling to her knees.

"Ariadne."

She froze. That was her mother's voice.

"Ariadne."

She didn't move. The voice was behind her. No. Her mother was dead.

"Ari, it's all right."

Tears stung her eyes. "No, you're not real," she whispered, shaking her head. "You're not real, and this is torture. Go away. Please."

"Darling."

A hand fell on her shoulder and Ariadne jumped, a gasp leaving her throat.

Guinevere knelt beside her in her favorite pale blue dress. Her hair was uncovered, braided, and wrapped around her head like a crown. She looked ageless. And beautiful.

"Darling, it's all right," she said softly, reaching out. "I'm real. And I'm here."

A sob escaped Ariadne and she fell into her mother's arms. Guinevere held her tight, and her familiar rose and sandalwood scent filled Ariadne's nose.

"Mama," she cried.

"It's all right," Guinevere whispered, rocking her as she had when Ariadne was little. "It's all right."

Ariadne sobbed into Guinevere's shoulder, her limbs shaking. "I'm so sorry, Mother," she said. "I'm so sorry."

"For what, my darling?" Guinevere pulled back so she could look into Ariadne's face and wipe at her tears.

"I didn't save you," Ariadne said. "I wasn't fast enough."

Guinevere shook her head, her own blue eyes filling with tears. "That was not your fault, my love. That was my silly decision. But you saved your brother and Camelot. And I am so proud of you, my darling."

"Is it really you?" Ariadne asked.

"Yes," said Guinevere, pushing hair from Ariadne's face. "Yes, it's me. I felt you coming to the Underworld. But you must keep fighting, my love."

"Keep fighting?"

"Yes, my darling." Guinevere pulled Ariadne to her feet. "It is not yet your time."

"Am I dying?" Ariadne whispered.

Guinevere shook her head. "Not if you fight. And you do that quite well."

Ariadne let out a laugh between sobs. "Mama, I miss you."

Guinevere pulled her into her arms again. "Shhh, my darling girl. I know. But I am always with you."

Ariadne sniffed. "I wish you could come back," she said.

Guinevere embraced her again. "I know. I wish it as well. But we cannot change the past and we will not play god like Nimue has done with Mordred. Know that I am proud of you. Of you and your brother, more than words can say. And trust your instincts."

Guinevere peered into Ariadne's eyes. "And rein in your temper, yes? Don't be so quick to judge or make impulsive decisions. And never forget how strong and capable you are. You may be mocked and ridiculed and passed over by weak-minded men, but do not let their words strike you down. Do not let them take your voice, your power. You are strong. *Believe in yourself."*

Ariadne let out another sob, a warmth opening in her chest, filling her veins. She took in a deep breath, finally believing those words. She closed her eyes, and more tears fell. Guinevere wiped them away and kissed her forehead.

"I love you, my darling. Always."

"I love you too, Mother."

But when Ariadne opened her eyes, Guinevere was gone. And she was in the infirmary.

"What?" she tried to say, but her throat was on fire.

"Shhh," came a soothing voice, and a beautiful face appeared above her.

Lady Vivienne.

"Here." She helped Ariadne sit up a little and sip on cool water.

"What—" Ariadne rasped.

"There was an attack," Lady Vivienne said softly, stroking Ariadne's hairline. Ariadne relaxed under her touch.

"Where's Mother?" Ariadne whispered. "I just...I just saw her."

Lady Vivienne frowned. "You are in the infirmary at Camelot and you've been asleep for a few days. Perhaps she visited you in a dream."

Ariadne let out a small whimper, and Lady Vivienne resumed her caress.

"I'm sorry," Lady Vivienne said.

Ariadne shifted and glanced around the infirmary. There were so many people lying on cots, sporting bandages. The nuns bustled about, caring for them.

"What—" Ariadne's memory came back. The wedding. The explosion.

"What happened?" she asked Lady Vivienne.

Lady Vivienne pulled a stool over and sat down next to her cot.

"There was an explosion in the great hall," Lady Vivienne explained. "It was lucky that the wedding ceremony had run late, or it would have likely happened with all of you inside."

A sob ripped at Ariadne's chest. "Who—what—how many?"

Lady Vivienne shuddered. "Sir Malcolm is looking for whoever did it. And it was some kind of exploding powder. As for how many lost?" She glanced around. "Too many. I am sorry I did not arrive sooner."

"How are you here?" Ariadne asked. "Morgana said you couldn't leave Avalon."

"Don't worry over that for now," Lady Vivienne said. "We'll talk later. For now, drink this."

She pulled the end table toward her and poured a murky liquid from the pot into a small cup.

Ariadne crinkled her nose. "Is it the same stuff you gave me last time?"

Lady Vivienne gave her an apologetic look. "I'm afraid so. But it will help you heal faster."

Ariadne groaned but chugged the tonic, coughing. She chased it with water that Lady Vivienne pushed into her hand.

"Good," the Lady of the Lake said. "I'll take my leave of you. There's someone waiting quite anxiously to see you."

Lady Vivienne stood, and suddenly someone was lunging at Ariadne, arms wrapping tight around her neck. Lady Vivienne's smile was warm as she walked away.

"Ari!" Mirah's scent of lavender, sage, and the sweet scent of her hair oils enveloped her. Ariadne took in a deep breath, wiping at her cheeks.

She groaned. "Mirah, you're hurting me."

Mirah loosened her hold. "We almost lost you!"

"I'm sorry," Ariadne said, wrapping her own arms around her friend.

"No, I'm sorry!' Mirah pulled back. "I shouldn't have left to change my shoes."

"I'm glad you did," Ariadne said. "You didn't get hurt."

Mirah pulled away from her and sat down on Lady Vivienne's vacated stool. "We lost so many, Ari," Mirah whispered, her eyes watering.

"How many?"

Mirah shook her head. "Twenty-three. Lady Blanchefleur among them."

Ariadne sucked in a breath. No! Not her. Not the only family Lohengrin had left. Not his mother.

"Ellyn?" she asked, bracing herself.

"She's fine."

Ariadne breathed a sigh of relief, and buried her face in her hands.

"Where's Anwil?" she asked, pulling her hands from her face.

"Morgana took him to the Underworld," Mirah answered quietly.

"The Underworld?" Ariadne whispered. "When?"

"A few days ago, just after the attack."

Ariadne took in another long, deep breath and laid her head back on the pillows, trying to wrap her brain around all of it.

"I dreamed of my mother," she said, staring at the ceiling. Mirah took her hand. "I think it was real, though. It felt so real. I think I was dying. But she sent me back."

Mirah's hand tightened around hers.

"She said she was proud of me," Ariadne continued, her voice breaking. "And that I needed to keep fighting."

Mirah laid her head on Ariadne's shoulder.

"You should sleep," Ariadne told her, laying her cheek on Mirah's head. "I don't mean to be rude, but you look terrible."

Mirah laughed and playfully smacked Ariadne's arm. It was then that Ariadne noticed the box sitting on the table next to her, wrapped in a small bow.

"What's that?"

Mirah tensed and sat up. "A gift for you," she said, not meeting Ariadne's eye.

Ariadne gave her a look but reached for the box. Whatever was inside jostled together with a clear ring. Ariadne opened it and her breath caught.

"Who sent these?"

Mirah bit her lip. "Prince Connor."

Ariadne picked up one of the gold cuffs, staring at the intricate designs of knots and runes, all winding around the Pendragon rampant dragon.

"Connor sent these?" she asked.

Mirah nodded. "Had them specially made. They're protection runes."

"They're pure gold," Ariadne breathed.

Mirah bit her lip. "I should let you rest."

She carefully took the cuff from Ariadne and put it gently back in the velvet-lined box. "I'll have these sent to your room. They'll be safest there."

"Wait," Ariadne said, reaching for her, but a sharp pain in her leg had her groaning.

"Don't strain yourself," Mirah lightly scolded. "Let the tonics work. Your leg is almost healed. Thank the gods for Lady Vivienne. Your leg was so bad. Go back to sleep, Ari. We'll be here when you wake up."

Ariadne glared at her but relaxed back into the cot and soon fell back into a deep sleep.

CHAPTER FORTY-SIX

ANWIL

Anwil and Morgana returned to a castle in mourning. Anwil's heart dropped to see all the black outfits and armbands as he and Morgana stepped through the dungeon door. He had nearly forgotten the attack, but it all came rushing back when he ran to the infirmary and saw all the wounded. And the dead.

Anwil found Ariadne sitting up in her cot, talking to the Lady of the Lake. They both turned to him as he approached, and the Lady's eyes went to the sword still clutched in his hands. He was taken aback to see her dressed so plainly, with her hair braided over her shoulder and an apron over a simple blue dress.

"You have reclaimed Excalibur, Anwil Pendragon," she said. "Congratulations."

"What happened?" he asked, glancing at his sister.

The Lady and Ariadne shared a look.

"I will give you some privacy." She put a hand on his shoulder as she passed, heading toward other patients.

"Ari." Anwil dropped Excalibur by her bed and kneeled next to her.

"I'm fine," she said. "Thankfully. Lancelot went to Avalon. She saved as many people as she could. She fixed my broken leg."

"But... Morgana said she couldn't leave Avalon?" Anwil said quietly, at Morgana who was now speaking with Lady Vivienne.

"I don't know how she did it," Ariadne said. "I just woke up this morning. Anwil, it's bad. It was someone inside the castle."

Anger and betrayal bubbled in Anwil's stomach.

"Are you all right?" he asked through a clenched jaw.

"Yes. Why?"

"I'll be back." And without waiting for her answer, Anwil shot out of the infirmary. He stormed through the halls, nobles and servants alike scrambling out of his way. With Excalibur in his hands and dried blood and dust from the explosion covering him having returned, he knew he must look a fright.

The council was in the throne room, which had only been partially damaged by the blast in the great hall next to it. They all looked up, wide-eyed, as Anwil stomped in.

"Your Grace!" Lord Garanwyn said, standing. "Where—"

"Who did this?" Anwil hissed.

The council exchanged glances.

"It was a serving girl, Your Grace," Lord Safir informed him. "She said a stranger gave her money to put a small bag in the great hall just before the wedding guests arrived."

"Have we found this stranger?"

"No, Your Grace."

"Tell me the knights are looking."

"They are, Your Grace," said Lord Garanwyn. "Sir Malcolm is heading the investigation with Lady Dindrane. Sir Lohengrin is...indisposed."

"What happened to him?"

"His injuries were superficial," Lady Sura said gently. "But Lady Blanchefleur did not survive. Lady Ellyn is with him now in their chambers."

Anwil nearly lost his balance. He took a quick moment to recover his breath.

"How many others?" he asked through gritted teeth.

"All together, twenty-three have passed, Your Grace," said Lady Sura. "With nearly fifty others injured. No one save a couple servants were in the great hall at the time. Their bodies...were beyond recognition."

Anwil gripped Excalibur harder, his knuckles turning white.

"Where have you been, Your Grace?" Lord Garanwyn asked.

"Finding a way to defeat Mordred," he growled.

"Have you?"

"Yes," Anwil said. "In fact, send word that I wish to address the people in the courtyard in one hour."

Anwil turned on his heel and left the throne room. He hurried to wash himself, with Leofwine scurrying about and picking out an outfit that gave off exactly what Anwil wished to convey: a red and gold tabard with the prominent gold dragon in the center of the chest. Anwil even wore a bit of armor. As he dressed, he realized that the black markings on his chest were now nothing more than a small black dot above his heart.

Anwil strapped Excalibur to his belt and threw on his heavy red cloak and crown.

When he arrived, the courtyard was already packed with people. The Knights of the Round Table were already on the steps, even Lohengrin. Ariadne was supported by Mirah and Morgana on his right. Good. They needed to be seen beside him.

Anwil stepped to the edge of the top step and rested a hand on Excalibur and waited for quiet. It came quickly.

"There are traitors in Camelot!" he called out over the crowd. "But have no fear. They will be found and put to death. We mourn for our fellow countrymen who were murdered in cold blood on what was supposed to be a joyous occasion. But now that day has been shrouded in darkness. If anyone has any knowledge of this cowardly attack, come you forward. We will not rest until the traitors are found and dead." Anwil paused, letting the whispers circulate for a moment.

"This was an act of war," he continued. "And Camelot will answer. May the gods—the old and the new—have mercy on the souls of our enemies. Because we will not."

The crowd burst into thunderous applause and Anwil felt a rush through his veins. He stayed there for a moment before turning back to the castle. He faltered as he passed Mirah and Ariadne, both looking at him as if they had never seen him before.

"Go rest," he told his sister. "I'll tell you everything in the morning."

Ariadne called his name, but Anwil ignored her. He also needed to rest. He was exhausted, but it was a different kind of exhaustion from how he had been feeling for months.

"Your Grace." Lord Roland hurried up to him. "We need to formulate—"

"Tomorrow, Lord Roland," Anwil said, holding his hand up. "I just returned from the Underworld."

"Of course, Sire." Lord Roland bowed. "I will handle everything today. Shall I have food sent to your chambers?"

"Please."

Anwil was halfway to the spiral staircase leading to the private wing when a familiar voice called out his name. Mirah.

He turned to see her running toward him.

"Anwil," she said, out of breath when she reached him. "You need to be looked over."

"I'm fine," he said. "Just tired."

"No. I, yes, but... you look different," Mirah said, looking him over. "What happened?"

Anwil debated telling her everything, and he would, but at the moment, he wanted his bed. He needed to be at his best to handle these new issues.

"I know how to defeat Mordred now," he said quietly. He pulled her toward the staircase. "And I promise you, I'm fine. Better than before. I'll tell you everything, I promise. Tomorrow."

Mirah bit her lip. "Are you sure?"

Anwil brushed a stray curl from her face, tucking it behind her ear, surprised by his own boldness. Her cheeks flushed. "I promise."

"All right," she breathed.

Anwil headed up the stairs, but not before glancing back over his shoulder at Mirah, who had just turned away. But she, too, looked back at him. He couldn't quite read the emotions on her face, but he gave her a small smile and watched her leave.

His own heart fluttered in his chest, and memories flashed in his mind. Kisses in dark corridors, giggles, and riding off into the woods at dawn. For so long, he had ignored how Mirah made him feel, how she took his breath away, and how right she had felt in his arms. He didn't care if they had been young; he knew. Had always known. It was always Mirah. But she had turned down his offer of marriage. And he couldn't hate her for it. In fact, he loved her even more for it. She had been chasing her own dreams, making her own way in the world, and had become one of the realm's best physicians. Anwil was so proud of her. He let out a shuddering breath and climbed the stairs.

He found himself wishing there was someone waiting for him in his chambers, someone to curl up against and fall into a deep sleep with. Anwil's mind went to Yvanne, and how she had comforted him at the end of the day, her bright smile bringing him peace. He missed her and had loved her too. Anwil wondered what she would think about him and Mirah. She would have likely smacked them both and tried to play matchmaker. A small smile tugged at Anwil's lips, thinking of Yvanne's reaction. But then guilt filled his stomach. She hadn't deserved such a painful death. She was kind and honest and should still be with them. Perhaps he never should have married Yvanne. Then she would still be smiling.

It did not shame Anwil that he found satisfaction when Ariadne killed both Bors and Cerdic, especially so brutally. It was his only consolation for Yvanne and his mother's deaths. Now he had to kill Mordred.

Anwil gripped Excalibur's pommel, the sword warm and right in his hands. He hoped he could do this.

CHAPTER FORTY-SEVEN

MIRAH

Anwil came back different. Mirah could not put her finger on it, but whatever he experienced in the Underworld changed him. No longer gaunt and pale, he had a new aura about him, a newfound confidence.

Mirah touched the hair that he had brushed behind her ear. She hadn't been able to help the flipping of her stomach, the flush of her face, or the gooseflesh that had erupted on her skin when he touched her. As if she was a young girl with a fancy again. But there had been something in Anwil's eyes. The way he had looked at her so intently and how his eyes had fallen to her lips for the briefest moment.

Mirah shook her head. No. She shouldn't be thinking of those things. Not now. She mentally scolded herself. It must be the exhaustion. She still had so much to do.

She held onto the wall to steady herself as she walked down the corridors. She had barely slept the past few days, caring for the victims of the attack, and now had to prepare Lady Blanchefleur's body. Master Cassius had had to deliver the news to Lohengrin. She hadn't been able to tell another friend that someone they loved had passed, especially a mother. She felt like a coward. But she would preserve Blanchefleur's body. Mirah would do that for Lohengrin.

"Mirah!"

Turning, she saw her father hurrying toward her.

"Mirah," he said again once he caught up to her. "Let me walk you to your chambers. You are dead on your feet."

Mirah shook her head. "Baba, I have work to do. I need—"

Jabir put his hands on her shoulders. "Lady Morgana is with the Lady of the Lake in the infirmary. I just came from there. I think it is safe for you to rest."

Mirah shook her head again. "No, I need to help Lady Blanchefleur. I—"

Jabir pulled Mirah in to him and the tears broke through. He held her as Mirah sobbed into his shoulder, clutching him as if she could not let go.

"Let the other healers work," Jabir said, stroking her hair. "You need to rest, too."

Mirah sighed and relented, letting her feather take charge, if only for the moment.

Mirah slept past noon and most likely could have slept longer if Ariadne hadn't come to check on her.

"No, it's my turn to take care of you now," Ariadne said when Mirah protested her friend's offer to make her tea. "You always take care of us. Let us take care of you."

Mirah sank into the pillows of her sofa. "How is your leg?"

"Sore," Ariadne said, placing a kettle on the fire. She leaned heavily on a cane. "But Lady Vivienne said that should go away in about a week. I had forgotten how hungry Lady Vivienne's healing tonic makes you. I ate four plates of food last night before bed."

Mirah chuckled. "It is good to have her back. I can't believe Lancelot gave up his long life so she could come."

Ariadne sank down beside her. "Is that what he did?" she asked, rubbing her thigh. "Magic is mental. So many rules, and yet Lancelot can go and do something like that."

"I think being blood of The Modron lets you get away with some things," said Mirah.

Ariadne snorted. "I've officially been put on leave, by the way," she said. "For two weeks. Lady Vivienne's orders."

"You need to heal," said Mirah with a pointed look.

"She gave me a magic tonic, though!"

"Yes," said Mirah. "But your leg was bad, Ari. Really bad. I was only able to do so much myself. Besides, if you reinjure yourself, you'll have to heal on your own. Your body can only take so much of that tonic at once."

Ariadne gave her a playful glare until the kettle whistled. She busied herself making tea for them and handed Mirah a cup.

"How's Anwil?" Mirah asked and blew on her tea.

"Fine, I think," Ariadne said, sinking onto the sofa. "I haven't seen much of him, though."

"Does he...feel different to you?"

"Yes," Ariadne answered immediately. "I tried to ask him about it last night, but he was sleeping. Morgana said he has *strength anew*. Whatever that means."

"Arawn?" Mirah suggested, and Ariadne only shrugged.

"I don't know," she mumbled. "I can't believe this happened. And Lady Blanchefleur..." She cut herself off, sniffling. "I keep thinking about Lohengrin. I don't think I'd have the strength to go on if something happened to Anwil."

"You would," Mirah reassured her.

Ariadne didn't answer, and was quiet for a long moment, staring into the hearth, her eyes distant.

"Do you feel as if something bad is going to happen?" Ariadne asked quietly. "Like these are our last moments together?"

Mirah did, but she didn't wish to admit it, so she sipped her tea instead. She was saved from answering, though, by a knock on the door.

"Come in!" Mirah called.

Her father and aunt stepped inside, and Ariadne gave Mirah a sympathetic look.

"I should go," she said. Mirah wanted to beg her to stay, to not leave her alone, but Mirah knew the looks on her father and aunt's faces. They wanted to talk.

Ariadne hobbled across the room to the door.

"Do you need help, Ari?" Jabir asked her gently.

"Lady Vivienne says I need to walk," Ariadne said, giving a smile that was more grimace. "I'll be fine."

Anipe bobbed a curtsy as Ariadne slipped through the door and closed it behind her.

"Is everything all right, Baba?" Mirah asked as he and Anipe came around to sit across from her.

"Mirah," Jabir said, "your aunt and I have been talking. And there is no easy way to say this, but I think it would be best for you to return to Evanshire with Anipe."

The breath left Mirah's lungs. "What? Absolutely not."

"Mirah, please listen to what your father has to say," Anipe said.

"Camelot is not as safe as we thought," Jabir said. "The attack on Lohengrin's wedding proves this."

"I cannot leave Camelot!"

"Mirah, we are only thinking of your best interest," Anipe said. "And we think coming home is the best option for you."

"*This* is my home!" Mirah was on her feet. "Camelot has been my home since I was five, Baba!"

"Evanshire is your family home," Jabir said. "And that is where you will be safe. You will leave first thing in the morning."

"You cannot do this," Mirah said, tears of rage burning her eyes. "I am of age. I am twenty-three years old, Baba. I am not a child! You cannot force me to leave."

"You are *my* child!" Jabir said, getting to his feet. "My *only* child, and I will not see you hurt or dead! This is not your fight, Mirah."

"I am a royal physician," Mirah hissed. "I have a duty. You should understand that."

"I understand duty, daughter," Jabir said. "I understand it plenty. And my duty as your father comes before all else. You will return to Evanshire at first light and I will not hear another word against it!"

"No. Wait, Baba!"

But Jabir was through the door, slamming it shut behind him.

Mirah whirled on her aunt, who at least had the decency to look apologetic.

"He is only trying to protect you," Anipe said. "Please try to understand."

"But I don't," Mirah said, tears welling in her eyes. "He's never like this. Why is he doing this?"

"The wedding attack was the last straw for him," Anipe said. "He told me what happened in the faerie world. You almost died, and now this explosion. Mirah. These people are after the Pendragons. Not you. If you have a chance to save yourself, why would you not?"

"Because I will not run away like a coward," Mirah growled.

Anipe took a step back, eyes wide in disbelief. "How dare you throw such a word. Your father is no coward. He is only doing what he feels is right by his daughter. I'll send a maid to help you pack."

Anipe swept from the room before Mirah had a chance to reply.

She picked up a pillow from the sofa and threw it at the door with a scream.

CHAPTER FORTY-EIGHT

NIMUE

Nimue found Mordred at Tintagel. He had taken the castle with the Saxons Agravaine had given him. They were just as Nimue remembered, bloodthirsty and savage. Heads of King Constantine's leaders and court were strewn up on spikes around the courtyard and up in the turrets. His banners were burning in piles on the lawn as Mordred's banners—a two-headed golden eagle on a purple background—flew high in the ocean wind.

Tents littered the courtyard, and the Saxons drank and feasted, and some were even rutting with women out in the open. Nimue's lip curled in disgust.

She crossed the courtyard easily, the Saxons stepping back as she passed. Good. They should fear her. When she passed a Saxon taking a human woman by force in a tent, she grabbed him by the throat and sliced his genitals off. His scream was like music to her ears.

"Run," she told the girl, who scrambled away.

Nimue glared at the Saxons, daring them to run after the girl. But none of them did. She stepped over the Saxon she had emasculated and entered the old castle. The stones were ancient, filled with old magic. Nimue brushed her fingers along the walls as she wove through the corridors, reveling in the power.

Mordred was in the great hall, sitting at the center of the raised table, feasting. He looked up and grinned. It was feral. The anger she still felt for him bubbled in her veins as she approached. But she needed to rein him in. He would ruin all that she had worked for, and she would not let him.

"My love," he said with open arms. "Welcome to my home."

He embraced her and kissed her hair. "Come, sit with me."

Nimue did not sit. "When did you do this?" she asked quietly.

"A few days ago," he said with a shrug. "I was going to let Constantine keep it awhile, but then he betrayed me."

"Betrayed you?"

"I gave him orders to kill the girl Pendragon," said Mordred. "Instead, he tried to blow up both of them in the great hall, nearly killing me. So Tintagel is mine. As it should be."

"When and why did you give him those orders? And were you going to tell me?"

"Do not worry yourself, my love." Mordred brushed a piece of hair behind her ear. "I have everything under control."

"Are they still alive?"

Mordred's face darkened. "Vivienne is in Camelot."

Nimue's eyebrows rose. "She cannot leave Avalon. She is too weak."

"And yet, she has," Mordred growled, pounding a fist on the table. "Agravaine is marching on Northumbria as we speak, and his raiders from Norvegr are sailing here. We will attack Camelot within the month."

Nimue stepped back from him. "With only the Saxons and barely a thousand foreign raiders? Mordred, that is not enough."

Mordred gave a low chuckle. "Oh, my love. Mab's army is merely waiting for my word. When we march on Camelot, they will be there."

Nimue clenched her fists. She wanted to smack the smugness off his face, but she controlled herself. Now was not the time.

Mordred kissed her forehead. "You had a long journey. Have something to eat."

Nimue readied for bed alone, having sent away the maid Mordred had tried to give her. She didn't need the thing. Nimue could take care of herself and didn't need a terrified human to invade her personal space. She needed to think.

So, Mordred wanted Camelot's crown. In the back of her mind, she knew that was all he had ever wanted. Power. She was just another way of getting it. Well, Nimue would play his little game, make him trust her, and when the timing was right, she'd send him back to the Underworld.

Someone knocked at the door. Mordred. She could feel his presence. Nimue braced herself and put on a softer face.

"Enter," she called, sitting down at the vanity to brush her hair.

"My love," Mordred said, stepping inside and closing the door behind him. She took him in through the mirror as he came up behind her, the sight of him making her warm. Nimue pushed those feelings away. He had betrayed her. She would let go of any feelings she had left for the monster.

Mordred took the brush from her hands and brushed her hair. She let him. His touch was gentle, and she couldn't help but enjoy the tension leaving her head.

"I am glad you are here with me," Mordred said, running his fingers through her tresses.

Nimue didn't reply, but she turned her head in to Mordred's touch.

Mordred leaned down and kissed her neck, nibbling and sucking right where Nimue liked it. She growled and turned in her chair, grabbing his hair and pulling him to her. He met her with equal force, pulling her up and guiding her to the bed. Their clothes lay in tatters in mere seconds and Nimue pushed Mordred onto the bed, climbing on top of him. When he tried to take control, she pushed at him again. No, she would take her pleasure as she wanted.

Mordred grinned, lying back, his own eyes fluttering shut as she lowered herself onto him, riding him hard until her pleasure burst from her. Mordred's own came not long after, and she let him curl up against her under the heavy wool blankets.

"Soon, we shall have our victory," he whispered into her ear. It wasn't long before his breathing grew even. Nimue stayed awake. Sleep would not come for her. She didn't want it. Not with Mordred in her bed. But she stayed still, letting him think he was safe. That she had forgiven him. She could end him now, while he was asleep. And it would also end the boy. But Agravaine and the Saxons might not rally behind her. Especially the Saxons. Nimue hated that she needed Mordred.

So she let him sleep. For now.

CHAPTER FORTY-NINE

ANWIL

A joint funeral was held for the victims of the explosion, the courtyard tightly packed with a sea of black and dark colors. Many laid flowers at Lady Blanchefleur's pallbearers' feet as they took her coffin to the crypt to be laid to rest with Percival and Lyrion. Lohengrin was in the lead with Ellyn.

Anwil did not follow them into the crypt, letting the family have some privacy. It was a long while before Lohengrin, Ellyn, and Lady Dindrane came back out.

Both Lady Vivienne and Father Ifan prayed and sang blessings over the pyres of the others. Anwil noticed that Brother Felix was with the attending clergy and kept a constant glare on Vivienne and Morgana.

Anwil subtly nudged Lancelot and gestured toward the monk, and Lancelot nodded. The knight moved closer to Brother Felix, keeping a watchful eye over him.

A somber feast followed in the old great hall, and a bard, Captain Stout, sang of their deeds and memories. Lady Vivienne even attended the feast, though she stayed close to Morgana. Many openly stared at the Lady of the Lake, who did not have a habit of attending feasts when she visited Camelot.

"Condolences from Ireland, Your Grace." Prince Connor approached the high table with his two cousins. All were dressed respectfully in dark colors. "If there is anything I can do, please know that I am at your disposal."

"Thank you, Connor," said Anwil. "I am sorry your training to become a knight has had constant interruptions. I hope this will not hinder our treaty."

"Of course not, Your Grace," said Connor. "In fact, if I may, I'd like to speak with you more about this...threat. As crown prince of Ireland, I'll need to assess if Ireland is also in danger."

"Of course," said Anwil. "We can meet tomorrow afternoon?"

"Aye, thank you." Connor bowed, and he and his cousins rejoined their table.

"Do you trust him?" Ariadne asked Anwil quietly.

"He hasn't proven untrustworthy," said Anwil. "Why?"

"I just can't figure out what he's doing here," Ariadne said.

"A marriage to you and a trade treaty," Anwil answered. "Were you not paying attention when he told us all that?"

Ariadne shot him a look. "Yes, but...I don't know. Forget it."

Anwil glanced at the Irish table, where they were now talking amongst themselves. He and Connor had finally met the day before to work on the trade treaty. Anwil had offered them a couple of Merlin's mirrors that had not been destroyed instead of Ariadne's hand, hoping that would appeal to Connig, but they had yet to hear back from the Irish king.

It was while Anwil was glancing around the hall that he noticed that King Constantine was absent.

"Have you seen Constantine?" Anwil asked Ariadne.

She shook her head. "No, not for a while."

Anwil gestured for Sir Malcolm.

"Where is Constantine?" Anwil asked Malcolm as the knight crouched by his chair.

Malcolm looked around, the realization on his face as well.

"I don't know," he said. "But I'll find out."

"Thank you," Anwil mumbled, and Malcolm slipped out of the hall. He worried the attack might have reminded Constantine too much of the coup attempt last year.

Malcolm did not return the rest of the feast and it wasn't until Anwil was readying for bed that he appeared with grave news.

"No one has seen him since the wedding," Malcolm told Anwil. "His things are still in his chambers and his carriage is still at the carriage house. Not even his guards have seen him."

"They didn't raise an alarm?" Anwil asked.

"Apparently," Malcolm said, annoyance in his voice, "they've been so used to him not leaving his room, they figured that's where he's been."

"Some guards," Anwil mumbled.

"I sent a search out for him," said Malcolm. "We'll find him."

Anwil patted him on the shoulder. "Thank you. Let me know if you find anything else."

Malcolm bowed and left Anwil alone. Anwil changed into his nightshirt and glimpsed himself in the mirror. The mark on his chest was still miniscule.

"Thank you, Father," Anwil whispered and a slight breeze came in through his window.

Anwil was up before dawn the next day to meet Lancelot at the indoor arena. Though he and Lancelot had been meeting when he had the time, it had been a while. Anwil expected to be rusty, but when he and Lancelot began a simple sparring match, he moved with an ease and grace he had never felt before.

He blocked and ducked and swung as if he had been fighting forever. His arms moved on their own, as if he were an experienced fighter. He even managed to disarm Lancelot, surprising them both.

"You've never fought like that before," said Lancelot, slightly out of breath.

"I don't know what happened," Anwil said, looking down at his practice sword.

Lancelot put picked up his sword and grabbed a waterskin. "You said Arthur gave you the last of his strength in the Underworld?"

"That's what Arawn said," said Anwil.

"I think," Lancelot said and tossed Anwil a waterskin, "Arthur gave you some of his fighting talent as well. I recognized a few of those moves you pulled there."

"Is that what I felt?" Anwil asked after taking a long drink.

"Most likely," said Lancelot. "That will help against Mordred. He won't be expecting that. Tomorrow, I'll show you how Mordred fights. If you know what to expect, that'll be another advantage for you."

Anwil's reply was cut short, though, by Sir Malcolm bursting into the room. His face was grave. "We found King Constantine."

"It is a gruesome sight," Lady Vivienne said in the infirmary.

Anwil, Lancelot, Sir Malcolm, and Morgana were gathered around Constantine's body. Anwil held a handkerchief to his nose. Vivienne lowered the blanket, and Anwil jerked back. Constantine's body was bloated and discolored. The smell was worse.

"He was found in one of the ponds just outside the city," said Malcolm. "His dagger was found at the bottom of the spring, next to him."

Vivienne uncovered him more and Anwil stepped back as she looked at Constantine's wrists.

"No marks," she mumbled, and then peered at his neck. "Ah...looks like his throat was slit."

Morgana stepped forward, looking closely.

"Murder?" Anwil asked, his voice slightly muffled.

"I cannot say, Your Grace," Lady Vivienne said. "I would have to examine him more closely."

"Unless we find evidence around the spring, there's no way to tell," said Lancelot. "The water will have washed everything away."

"It is uncommon for someone to slice their own throat," said Morgana. "If one wishes to end their life, it is something easier. Poison, throwing themselves off a cliff, or slitting their wrists." She moved Constantine's head back, opening the wound more. "This was cut to the bone. I do not think it was self-inflicted."

"Yvanne's throat was slit," Anwil whispered. "I don't think he would do that to himself."

"I'll go back and double-check the area," said Sir Malcolm. "See if there's anything I missed."

"Don't let this get out," Anwil said before he could leave. "It was a tragic accident. And check the water supply. Make sure this pond wasn't connected to anything."

"I'll go with you," said Morgana. "I can test for any magic used."

"Lady Vivienne," Anwil said when they left, "can you examine him to find anything else?"

"Of course," she said. "If I may, I'd like the assistance of Master Cassius? I admit he has more experience examining the dead than I do."

"Yes," Anwil agreed. "And when you are finished, can you preserve his body? I'd like to have him taken back to Tintagel. They have a crypt there, and lay him next to his wife."

"I shall," Lady Vivienne answered and covered Constantine with a blanket.

"We should send troops to Tintagel," said Lancelot as he and Anwil left the infirmary. "Once word gets out that Constantine is gone, Mordred might storm Tintagel. It was Morgana's family home once, and Mordred has always wanted it."

Anwil nodded. "Yes, send a company. I'll have to call another king's meeting. They won't be happy to travel so soon again."

"Well, a man is dead," said Lancelot. "They can get over it."

"Anwil!"

Anwil halted at the sound of Mirah's voice. She was hurrying toward them. Lancelot shot Anwil a sly smile and continued on down the hall.

"I just wanted to thank you," she said. "For talking to Baba."

"You're welcome," said Anwil. When he had heard Sir Jabir was planning to send Mirah to Evanshire, he selfishly had to act. Though, there was truth to what he had said: The roads were too dangerous, and after Mirah had beaten Mordred in a fight, he would be looking for revenge. Open roads were too vulnerable. Camelot was still safer, despite the attack on Lohengrin's wedding.

"He's still angry, and Anipe even more so," Mirah said, and then bit her lip. "Especially with you."

"Well," Anwil sighed. "We need you here. You're the best physician in the city."

Mirah's cheeks flushed. "Thank you," she said.

"And"—Anwil reached for her hand, her skin soft and warm—"I admit, I did not want you to go."

She closed her fingers around his, a slight tremble in her hand.

"My place is here," she whispered. "In Camelot."

"Good," Anwil said, glancing down at their hands. They had moved closer to each other, barely an inch between them.

"Anwil, I—"

"Your Grace!"

Mirah jumped away from him, her cheeks red. She wrung her hands together as Lord Garanwyn approached.

"Forgive me for interrupting," Lord Garanwyn said, looking between the two, a curl on his lips. "But might I speak with you, Your Grace?"

"Yes," Anwil said and turned back to Mirah. "I'll see you soon."

Mirah bobbed a quick curtsy and hurried off, Anwil watching her disappear around a corner.

"What is it?" Anwil snapped at Lord Garanwyn.

The older man smirked. "It will only take a few minutes," he said. "May we?"

He gestured toward the throne room, and Anwil led him there.

CHAPTER FIFTY

It was a quiet night and King Elyion was eating with his wife and son when the summons came. Elyion sighed at the Pendragon seal, hardly wishing to open it. He did not enjoy Camelot. It was far too busy and noisy for his taste. Too large, as well. He enjoyed simple comforts. His own castle would be considered a small manor house compared to Pendragon Castle. But that was how Elyion liked it. It was large enough for what he needed. His family, a staff, and guards. Northumbria was a hardy farming and warrior country. They kept the Lothian soldiers at bay behind Hadrian's Wall and produced the most grain in Briton. It was simple. Nothing like the stress of Camelot. And he had just started to relax again in his home. So no, he did not wish to open the letter from the High King, but he did anyhow. It was his duty.

Elyion read the opening lines of the letter and nearly dropped it in his soup.

"What is it?" his wife asked, putting a hand on his arm. "Elyion."

"Constantine is dead," he said, his voice hollow. "We are to return to Camelot."

"So soon? We've only just returned," said his son.

"Edwin!" Beatrice snapped. "Have some respect."

Elyion sent his son a glare. At over thirty, Edwin was more boy than man. They had spoiled him, and now it came to bite them in the ass. They had tried to make it fair, as Edwin had been the youngest, but they had overcompensated. And when Oswald, their eldest and heir, had died in a skirmish with raiders, they had realized their mistake in spoiling Edwin.

"We must see to the funeral and elect a new king of Dumnonia," Elyion said, reading the rest of the letter. "If Constantine's nephew in Ireland does not come forward. He has no other heirs."

"He never declared anyone else?" his wife asked.

"No," said Elyion. "He was convinced his daughter would have a whole litter of boys and one of them would inherit. Might as well start packing tonight. We should leave in the morning. Edwin, that means you. You'll be coming with me this time."

"Who's going to watch over Northumbria?" Edwin asked.

"Your mother is quite capable," Elyion said. "I'm sorry, dear. I think it's time Edwin learns some responsibility."

"I agree," said Beatrice. "I'll let the staff know to ready the carriages and help you two pack. You know, I still don't understand why you refuse those mirrors of Merlin's." She stood. "Everything would be so much—"

But she never got to finish her sentence. An arrow had pierced her neck and after a heartbeat, she tumbled over, knocking into the table. Silverware clattered to the ground, her mug of half-finished ale splashing and tumbling to the floor.

Elyion and his son moved at the same time, but neither was quick enough. His son was pierced by an arrow in the back and Elyion straight through the heart. Elyion took his last breath and slumped over, knocking the soup bowl to the floor as his guards pulled their swords.

But the Northumbrian guards were, too, felled by arrows, one by one, until their bodies littered the ground. The summons slipped from Elyion's outstretched hand toward his wife. It floated down to the floor, soaking up the blood spilling from Edwin.

For a moment, it was silent. The only sound was the gentle crackle of the hearth fire.

Until the doors burst open and King Agravaine strutted in, a company of men behind him. Their heavy maille and armor swished and clanked loudly in the hall. Agravaine stepped over a fallen guard and marched toward Elyion and his family.

"Take down the banners," Agravaine ordered, tapping Edwin with the toe of his boot. He did not move. "And clean up this mess."

His men ran into action, dragging bodies away. Elyion's purple and yellow banner was yanked from the wall and tossed into the fire. Agravaine's black and yellow replaced it, the eagle now overlooking the hall.

His general approached, handing him Elyion's crown. Footsteps came up behind him but Agravaine didn't need to turn around to know who it was. He could feel the power radiating off him.

The footsteps stopped next to him and Agravaine turned to Mordred.

Mordred held up Agravaine's own ceremonial crown and held out his other hand. Agravaine handed over Elyion's crown and Mordred fused the two crowns together, blinding white light and sparks bursting from the crowns. Agravaine shielded his eyes, but it was over in a flash.

Mordred held up the now gleaming gold crown with tall, pointed jewels and handed it back to Agravaine.

"Northumbria is yours, brother," Mordred said, patting him on the back. "Don't forget your end of the bargain."

Mordred gestured for his fae archers to follow him. They leaped out of the shadows where they had been hiding and fell in line behind Mordred, leaving the castle in tendrils of black smoke.

CHAPTER FIFTY-ONE

ARIADNE

Ariadne nearly skipped out of the infirmary when Lady Vivienne gave her the all clear. Her leg had mended, and the stiffness and lingering soreness had faded. She had a list of exercises to do every morning and evening for a few weeks, but Ariadne was giddy as she dressed for patrol.

She was headed toward Connor's room in the guest wing when she nearly collided with him around a corner.

"Headed my way?" he asked.

"Er, yes." Ariadne said. "Before we begin, though, there's something I wish to discuss with you."

"All right," Connor said, following her to the side.

"I know you had a good relationship with King Constantine," she said. "And there's no easy way to tell you this. But he was found dead yesterday."

Connor's jaw dropped. "What?"

"I'm sorry," Ariadne said. "He was a good man. I only wished we had been able to help him better."

"How?" Connor asked, his voice hoarse.

"We don't know," Ariadne said quietly. "His throat was cut, and his dagger was next to his body. It looks like he took his own life, but..." She let the sentence hang in the air, hoping Connor would catch on.

Connor ran his hands through his hair and swore quietly. "If there's anything—"

"I know," said Ariadne. "Thank you. Sir Malcolm might question you. But the city is on another lockdown. So we're to keep our ears open this morning."

Connor nodded. "Aye, well, let's see what we can find out."

Ariadne wasn't sure if she was impressed or not at how easily Connor could charm people into giving him information. It was working to their advantage, yes, but he leaned heavily into the flirting and Ariadne had to keep herself from rolling her eyes at every wink and head tilt and crooked grin. After a couple hours of talking and getting free muffins from the bakery, they learned nothing significant about Constantine. The shopkeepers had only seen him once or twice, casually buying or looking. But he did not speak for long and only his guards followed him.

"I encountered him alone one night," Connor said as he finished his third muffin. "A few weeks back. I thought it odd, but didn't think much of it."

"You didn't see anyone with him?" Ariadne asked as she waved to Mistress Claudia. "Not even his guards?"

"No one," Connor answered. "I've never seen him without them. He always had a huge company of them when he came to the ports."

"Well, that might be something," Ariadne said. "You don't remember the day, do you?"

"Not particularly," he said. "Sorry."

Ariadne sighed. "I guess we'll have to wait and see if Malcolm and Dindrane can find anything out from the servants."

They stepped back to let a grain cart roll through.

"I'm sorry about your loss from the attack," Connor said as they stepped back onto the street. "Did you find out who did it?"

"No," said Ariadne. "Well, we don't know who gave the serving girl the powder. He obscured his face and voice. And, actually... come here."

She pulled him into an alleyway, ducking into the shadows.

"Princess, if you just wanted to get me in a dark corner, all you had to do was ask." He grinned at her.

Ariadne folded her arms across her chest.

Connor cleared his throat. "Right. Sorry."

"I think it might be safer if you and your cousins went home," she said quietly.

"Beg pardon?"

"With the explosion and now Constantine, I think it would be best if you went home."

Connor was silent for a long time. It made Ariadne uncomfortable. She shifted her weight.

"Look, I know you never wanted to be a knight anyway-"

"How do you know?" Connor asked harshly.

"It's obvious!" Ariadne said. "Because those who want it, *want it.* They work for it, they live and breathe it. You're far too indifferent. As if you couldn't care to be here at all."

"I've done all you asked of me," said Connor.

"I know," said Ariadne. "And look; you're a fantastic fighter. I can see why you lead your armies in Ireland, but to be honest, we cannot have the death of a foreign prince on our hands. If you're killed here, we'd have Ireland on our doorstep as well, and we cannot fight a war on two fronts right now."

"You'd think my father would wage war if I get killed doing my duty?" Connor asked, scoffing.

"You're his son and heir," said Ariadne.

Connor snorted. "You don't understand Connig." He leaned on the windowsill. "If I go back now, he'll consider me a failure."

"Why?"

"You said no," Connor said.

Now Ariadne snorted. "He's *that* angry about a declined marriage proposal? Don't you have other Irish princesses? Or what about the youngest princess of Gaul? I hear she's very pretty."

"Aye, but she's not a Pendragon," said Connor.

"What does that mean?"

"You have to know how powerful your name is," Connor said. "Briton, the new powerhouse, forged by a legendary king, surrounded by magic and might. And you're his daughter. Kingdoms would go to war just for your hand, to have children with you so their line could hold a fraction of that power."

"Of course I know that," Ariadne hissed. "It's every princess's duty to marry a foreign prince or king to benefit both countries. But I cannot. Will not."

Connor cocked his head. "What do you mean, cannot?"

Ariadne mentally cursed. She was getting too worked up. She took in a deep breath to calm herself.

"It's as you said," Ariadne said quietly. "Kingdoms would go to war for my blood. What do you think would happen if I don't live up to expectations? If I can't give them a son, or any child at all? Do you think it would be safe for me?"

Connor's face flushed with anger and he looked away.

"So no," Ariadne continued. "I cannot marry. I did think about it, once. With someone."

Connor looked at her, astonished.

"But then he died," said Ariadne. "But not before he told me that a woman's place was not to be a knight."

Connor's face darkened and he shook his head, scoffing. "A woman's place is wherever the fuck she wants it to be."

Ariadne's eyebrows shot up.

"I'm sorry," Connor said hurriedly. "You said he died. I shouldn't have snapped."

Ariadne looked away, not wanting him to see her get emotional over Lyrion.

"It's fine," she mumbled. "We should get back."

She made to leave the alley, but Connor grabbed her arm. "Princess," he said, "just so you know, you are incredible, and anyone who doesn't see that is a blasted idiot."

Ariadne blanched. "What?"

"You're too good for all those marriage proposals, Princess," Connor said, his gaze dropping to her lips, and then he looked directly into her eyes. "Even mine."

Connor slipped out of the alley before Ariadne could process his words.

CHAPTER FIFTY-TWO

CONNOR

Connor waited for Ariadne just outside the alley. It took her a long moment to appear, and when she did, she avoided eye contact and her cheeks were slightly flushed. He had not expected the vulnerability she had shared, nor had he intended to be so open with her. But something about her made him want to open up to her about everything.

And it damned well scared him.

They returned to patrol without a word and didn't talk until they heard shouting.

"That way," Connor said, pointing, and they took off.

They followed the sound to the theater street, where a crowd had formed around two men fighting.

Connor and Ariadne both jumped in, each grabbing a man and yanking them off each other. Connor's man tried to fight him, but he had his arms twisted behind him and on his knees before he could even throw a punch.

Ariadne's man was still standing, sporting a bloody nose and an already swollen eye. She held his arms behind his back, but he still glared at his opponent.

"What is the meaning of this?" she demanded.

Both men started shouting at once and tried to get out of their holds. But both Connor and Ariadne held on tight.

"If you two don't calm down, I'm going to give you an hour in the stocks," she threatened.

But the men started shouting again, accusing the other of stealing a role or lines, or maybe a woman. Connor couldn't tell.

"Enough!" Connor barked, and the two men quieted. "Your princess gave you an order. I suggest you carry on and leave each other alone."

The men looked at Ariadne as if they were seeing her for the first time.

"If I let you go," Ariadne said to the man she held, "are you going to go after him?"

The man, a tall, brown-skinned man with long hair, glared at the other for a moment before bowing his head. "No, Your Highness," he mumbled.

Ariadne slowly let him go.

"Can I trust you?" Connor asked the man he still held. He was a shorter, stockier man with pale skin and a harsh goatee.

"No," he growled.

"Well, at least you're honest," Connor said. "Listen, I'd really like to let you go. I don't want to be here all day. But if I let you go and you start fighting again, you're going in the stocks, as the princess said. Now, I don't know about you, but I've been there before and it's not pleasant. I'd rather not lock you in that damned thing."

The man blew hard out of his nose, lips pursing. "Fine," he said.

Connor let him go and he shot to his feet but did not go after the other man. Connor then turned to the crowd and barked at them to go away. They hesitantly dispersed.

"He still owes me two bronze coins!" the long-haired man said.

"Work it out without a fight," Connor said to him.

Grumbling, the man stormed off. The other huffed, fixed his doublet, and stormed off in the opposite direction.

"You all right?" Connor asked Ariadne. Her cheek was red. "I think he caught you with his elbow."

"Barely," she said, rubbing her jaw. "I'll be fine."

Connor reached out to touch her cheek, but pulled back when he realized what he was doing. "We should—"

"Your Highness!"

A guard was hurrying toward them.

"The king requests your presence in the infirmary," he said when he caught up, barely out of breath.

"Why? Is he sick?"

"No, Your Highness," said the guard. "I believe it is about King Constantine."

She glanced at Connor, chewing her lip. Connor couldn't help but stare.

"Come on then," she finally said. "If you're to be a Knight of the Round Table, you can start now."

He made to follow the guard, but Ariadne stopped him with a hand to his chest.

"But if you fuck up," she warned, "or we find out you can't be trusted, I'll make you beg for mercy. Understand?"

Connor grinned. "Perfectly, princess."

Connor had not expected to see King Constantine laid on a table in a private room of the infirmary. Nor was he expecting to be in the same small room with both the Lady of the Lake and Morgana le Fey. The king, Sir Lancelot, and Sir Malcolm were there as well. Connor hung back a little, feeling a little like an outsider.

Constantine was bare, save for the blanket that covered him from the waist down, and someone had taken great care to preserve him, though he looked more like a statue than a body.

"What happened?" Ariadne asked.

"It was Constantine," Anwil said, arms folded across his chest.

"What do you mean?"

"Constantine gave the girl the powder," he said.

"What?" Ariadne exclaimed. "No."

The Lady of the Lake stepped forward and carefully held up one of Constantine's bloated hands. She waved her own over it and it glowed a faint blue.

"This spell reveals what he had touched the day he died," she said. She turned his hand over as best she could, revealing bits of black powder on his hands. "It's the same powder used in the attack."

Ariadne took a step back, bumping into Connor's chest. Instinctively, he grabbed hold of her arms to steady her. A slight shudder ran up her arms.

"How did the water not wash it away?" Sir Malcolm asked.

"It did," Lady Vivienne explained. "But my magic can still detect the last thing someone touched. Skin holds memory, just as hair does. However, Constantine was also not in the water for long. Someone, with magic, sped the decomposition process. But they did not do it very well."

"Do we know who killed him?" Anwil asked.

"Someone working for Mordred and Nimue," Lady Morgana said in a hard voice.

Anwil hung his head. "Then we are well and truly compromised," he said. "For Constantine to have turned against us..."

Ariadne shifted in Connor's arms, and he realized he was still holding on to her. He let go, shoving his hands in his pockets. He shook his head, not daring to believe that Constantine, the kind king he had known for years, would do something like this.

"Are we sure he isn't being framed?" Connor asked and everyone turned to him, surprise across most of their features, as if they hadn't realized he was there.

"That is possible," Sir Lancelot said, rubbing his chin. Connor noticed he looked older than when he had seen him last, with more gray in his hair and beard. "Either way, Mordred and Nimue are behind this. They could have compelled or threatened him, or someone else."

"Do we have any updates on their locations?" Anwil asked, looking at Sir Malcolm.

"No," he answered. "But Lady Dindrane and I dispatched more scouts and spies to all the countries. They're either hiding, as Nimue did before, or they're in the Otherworld." He turned to Lady Vivienne.

"Both Mordred and Nimue have left the Otherworld," she answered. "I spoke with my sisters in Avalon just this morning. No one has felt their presence."

"Then we need to assume they're coming for us," Lancelot said. "We should send a call to arms."

"Yes," Anwil agreed. "Do that now. We need to be ready. And do what you can to find out their location."

Sir Lancelot and Sir Malcolm bowed and left the infirmary room.

"Do not despair, Your Grace," said the Lady of the Lake to Anwil. "Many stand with you, including the fae. Not all share Nimue's wishes."

"Thank you," Anwil said to her, and then glanced at Connor. "Connor, if you wish to return home now, we will not be offended. This is not your fight."

"I think it is, though," Connor said. "I have a feeling this war won't stop at just Briton."

"I agree," Morgana said. "Mordred yearns for power. If he wins Briton's crown, he will try to conquer further."

Anwil gave Connor a long look, but nodded. "I cannot guarantee your safety," he said.

Connor clenched his fists inside his pockets but shrugged, hoping to come off less worried than he was. "I've been in battle before. I know the stakes."

Ariadne stiffened beside him but did not speak.

"If I may, my cousins..." Connor said.

"Can they be trusted?" Anwil asked.

"Aye," Connor said. "Without a doubt."

Anwil nodded. "You may fill them in. And Connor?"

Connor had turned to leave, but stopped when Anwil called his name.

"There's something else," Anwil said. "Meet me this evening in my study."

Connor gave a short bow and was glad to find Bradán and Domhnall at a tavern. He needed a stiff drink.

CHAPTER FIFTY-THREE

NIMUE

"Successful, I take it?" Nimue said to Mordred as he sauntered into the great hall at Tintagel.

Nimue sat at the head of the table, the Northmen and Saxon leaders and fae generals surrounding her. The Saxons stayed well clear of Mab's Minotaur ambassador, and Nimue found that wonderfully amusing.

Mordred sent her a wolfish grin, and she gripped the arms of the chair. She had to hold her tongue until the time was right. Let him pretend at king for a while. Only until the veils could open. Lammas was arriving soon, and the veils would thin enough to open them. Although magic was the most powerful at Samhain, she did not have the luxury of waiting for autumn.

"Very." Mordred plucked a goblet of wine from the table. "Agravaine holds Northumbria. We'll move on Camelot in the coming days."

"When?" Nimue asked.

"As soon as Mab's army arrives at the full moon," Mordred answered. "A little less than a month."

He swiped the pear from her plate and took a bite of it.

"What kind of army does this Mab have?" asked one of the Northmen leaders. Nimue had already forgotten his name.

Mordred looked at him as if he were an idiot. Which he was. Nimue hated him. He reminded her of Cerdic.

"Fae," Mordred answered. "Warriors. Enough to obliterate Camelot."

"I am confused." The Northman leaned back in his chair. "I thought you wished to rule the city? Why burn it down?"

"It is only the crown I care for," Mordred said. "Camelot was built by Merlin and Vivienne's magic. The very stones themselves carry their power. The city will not accept anyone who is not a Pendragon on the throne of Camelot. So, we will burn it down and build a new throne."

"You speak as if the city itself were alive," the Northman chuckled.

Nimue held back a long sigh. How she wished she could flick her wrists and be done with them.

"It is," said Mordred, looking impatient. "Because the magic that built it is alive. Now, enough with the stupid questions. Are your men ready?"

"Of course," the Northman said. "As long as you hold to your end of the bargain."

"You will have your lands and gold," Mordred said. "As promised. Just make sure you do not break your promise to me, or yours will be a fate worse than death. Now, if you'll pardon me, I wish for some time alone with my wife."

Mordred shooed them away, and while the Northman and Saxons glared, their leaders gestured for them to follow.

Mordred looked at the Minotaur, who growled at him.

"If you please?" Mordred said, flashing him a grin.

The Minotaur huffed and stood, the rest of the fae following him out.

"Wife?" Nimue asked once they were alone. Mordred took the seat next to her and piled food on his plate.

"How else will they accept you as High Queen?" Mordred shrugged, digging into his food.

"I do not wish to be queen," Nimue said through gritted teeth.

"Of course you do, my love," said Mordred, and popped a grape into his mouth. "Think of the power. You will have command of your own realm. Isn't that what you always wanted?"

Nimue clenched her jaw, biting her tongue again.

Instead, she asked, "Camelot has wards protecting it not only from Merlin, but Morgana has set up her own as well. How do you plan to get past those?"

Mordred smirked. "To get past the wards, a Pendragon has to invite you in," he said. "And a Pendragon will."

Nimue laughed. "No Pendragon will let you in to Camelot."

Mordred's smirk grew. "Morgause's grandson is a Pendragon."

"Barely," said Nimue. "And why would he let you in?"

"Because he is just as disillusioned with Camelot and their high and mighty chivalric standards as we are." He sipped at his wine. "He hates his cousin and wants to see him destroyed. So, of course, I promised him power and whatnot if he were to help me, and the brat believed me."

"Gawaine's son," Nimue said, "is going to let you into Camelot?"

"Yes."

"And *you* believe *him*?" Nimue asked. "He could be feeding information to the others!"

Mordred chuckled. "Trust me, darling. He is not. He's a spoiled brat who thinks he's entitled to everything just because of his name. He's too desperate and not intelligent enough to pull that off."

Nimue took in a deep breath. "Very well," she said. "So Gawaine's son will let you in. Then what? Vivienne and Morgana are in Camelot right now, along with that little witch who summoned Arawn to best you."

Mordred's eye ticked. "Oh, I have plans for them. Do not worry. All you have to do, my love, is open the veils to let the fae flood in and I'll do the rest."

Nimue clenched her jaw. Let him do the rest? As if she would trust him to do anything. But if what he said was true about

Gawaine's son letting them into Camelot, it made everything much easier.

She was about to respond when Mordred hissed and jerked, his hand clutching at his heart. She leaped from the chair to him.

"What is it?"

"I don't know," Mordred groaned. "The boy, I think. He is...pulling at me. Fighting me."

Nimue put a hand over his heart. "It will be over soon," she said, her nails digging into his chest. "Very soon."

CHAPTER FIFTY-FOUR

MIRAH

Mirah woke abruptly, her heart racing. What woke her, though, she did not know. She sat up, looking around her still dark room. No one was there and nothing seemed out of place.

She pushed out of the covers and crossed the room to pour herself a drink of water. As she did, dread filled her stomach. Something was wrong. Terribly wrong.

She set the cup down and lit the candles in her room, looking for anything that was out of place. Nothing was. Everything was as she had left it.

As she was putting a pillow back, an image flashed in her mind. Of Ariadne and Anwil in pain. Bleeding. It was gone as quickly as it came.

Mirah dropped the pillow and threw on a dress and shoes before racing out into the corridors. She ran all the way to the private wings, her heart pounding in her ears. The guards stationed at the stairs let her pass but cast her worried looks.

She was out of breath by the time she banged on Ariadne's door. As soon as the door opened, Mirah threw her arms around her friend.

"Are you all right?" Mirah asked, looking her over.

"Yes?" Ariadne said, catching Mirah around the waist to steady them both. "What's wrong? What happened?"

Mirah shook her head. "I saw you were hurt! You were bleeding and Anwil—"

Mirah raced away, but Ariadne was hot on her heels. Mirah knocked on Anwil's door. He answered, his hair sticking up wildly.

"What is it?" he asked.

"Are you all right?" Mirah asked, looking him over as well.

"Yes," Anwil answered, confused. He looked at his sister behind Mirah. "Why? What happened?"

"I had...I don't know." Mirah shook her head and buried her face in her hands. "I saw you both hurt."

"We're both fine," Ariadne said, rubbing her back. "Did you have a nightmare?"

"No, I was awake," Mirah said, lowering her hands. "Well, maybe. I woke up. But I don't remember bamber dreaming. I'm sorry."

"Don't be," Ariadne said, pulling her in for a hug. "Do you want me to stay with you tonight?"

Mirah shook her head. "No, but thank you."

"Are you sure?" asked Ariadne, pulling away.

"Yes," Mirah said. "Seeing you both; you're fine. That helps."

Ariadne gave her a smile. "Good. Then I'm going back to bed. I have morning patrol. If you need me, though, come get me, all right?"

Mirah nodded as Ariadne slipped back to her room.

"I am sorry, Anwil," Mirah said, turning to him. "With everything that's happening, I just needed to see you were all right."

Anwil reached for her, his hand caressing her cheek. Mirah stiffened in surprise.

"I'm all right," he whispered.

Mirah didn't move, shocked by his boldness. He hadn't touched her like this in years. He looked at her with a confidence she had never seen in him before.

"Anwil," she whispered and couldn't help but lean in to his hand.

He stepped closer. Her breath caught in her throat. She hadn't come here for this, but she couldn't pull away. She should pull away.

He slid his hand down her arm and took her hand and pressed it against his chest. His heart was pounding, too, a solid beating against her palm. His eyes dropped to her lips and her logical side told her to break this moment. To return to bed. But another side of her didn't want to. She realized she had missed this.

"I should go," she whispered so quietly, she was unsure if he heard her.

"Don't go," he breathed. He leaned closer, his breath on her lips. "Please."

He looked up, a question in his eyes. He was waiting for her.

So, she did the only thing she could do. She closed the distance between them. His response was immediate, pulling her to him, but he kept the kiss gentle, soft.

Mirah sighed, slipping her arms around him. Home. That's what it felt like to have him hold her. It felt like home.

He pulled away slowly, whispering her name against her lips.

"I missed you," he said.

"I missed you, too," she replied.

And he was kissing her again. Harder this time. Desperate. As if he couldn't get enough. She matched him, holding him tight. He moved to her neck, and she tilted her head back, inviting him for more. Her breathing was hard, her heart threatening to leave her chest.

She pressed against him, clutching at the fabric of his shirt at his waist. He moaned, and she felt his excitement against her stomach. He swore in her ear.

"Mirah," he said, gently scraping his teeth against her ear. She shivered.

And then he found that spot on her collarbone.

She gasped.

"We should...we should stop." She said the words, but her body didn't comply. Mirah couldn't bring herself to pull away. She ground into him, and he growled. Her mind said they should stop. They weren't thinking clearly. Their emotions were too high, but it felt so right. As if she was always supposed to be here. In Anwil's arms. By his side.

Anwil lifted his head, his eyes dark.

"Do you want to stop?" he breathed.

"No," she breathed and pulled him back to her.

"Thank the gods," he growled and lifted her at the waist. She wrapped her legs around him and he took her to his bed.

Mirah groaned softly as she landed on her back on the soft mattress. They moved and breathed like a dance they had never forgotten. They knew where to touch, to kiss, to lick, to have both of them panting, screaming. In the back of her mind, Mirah was sure someone could hear them, but she found she didn't care. All she cared about was Anwil, and how to keep him making those sounds she so loved to hear.

Mirah woke up warm and comfortable. Something heavy was draped over her waist and she turned her head to see Anwil behind her, his face buried in her curls. He breathed steady and deep, still asleep. Memories of last night flooded back to her, bringing a smile to her lips. She curled back into him, closing her eyes, sleep taking over her once more.

When she woke up again, the sun was bright and warm. Mirah blinked her eyes open, peering at the window. The sun was high in the sky. Too high. She cursed, sitting up.

"What is it?" Anwil slurred beside her.

"It's midafternoon. Baba's going to kill us," she said.

Anwil's eyes snapped open. "I'm sorry, Mirah."

"No, you don't need to apologize," she said, scrambling out of the bed and grabbing her nightgown from the floor. "I should have left..."

"Do you...regret..."

Mirah turned to him. "No," she said. "Absolutely not. But I didn't mean to stay all night. I..." A flush warmed her cheeks. "Sorry. I don't know what to say."

Anwil laid a hand on her cheek, and she leaned into him. "I don't regret it either," he said.

Mirah grinned but pulled away to slip her dress on. She found her shoes and slipped those on, and realized Anwil was staring at her. The blanket had pooled around his waist.

"What is it?"

"I...you should know. Your name was suggested to me."

"What do you mean?" She found her dressing gown and threw that on too, but bit her lip. She'd have to walk through the castle like this. Maybe she could borrow one of Ariadne's dresses.

"Potential brides," he said.

Mirah froze "Me?"

Anwil blushed. "Sorry. I shouldn't have said anything. We should... er, you should..." He ran a hand through his hair.

"I..." The words caught in her throat. The council had chosen her? Her mind went back to the night Anwil had come to her with a ring. When she had just learned that Master Cassius wished to take her on as an apprentice.

"I'm not asking," Anwil said hurriedly. He wrapped a blanket around his waist and slid out of the bed. "You should know, though, that I..." He swallowed, looking down. He took in a breath before looking back up at her. "Mirah, I never stopped having feelings for you."

"What about Yvanne?" Mirah whispered.

"I resolved myself to never think on my feelings of you," Anwil said. "I did start to love her. And perhaps our love would have grown. At times, I felt wrecked with guilt that a part of me had wished it had been you walking down that aisle. I still do. Feel guilty, that is. Yvanne deserved so much more."

Mirah took his face in her hands. "Her death was not your fault," she said, knowing where his mind was going. But her own mind was stuck at his confession of wishing it was her he had wed.

He covered one of her hands and kissed her palm. "I know," he said. "But Mirah, I...I want to ask—"

Mirah pulled away. "Are you proposing?"

Anwil's eyes widened. "No!" he said. "No. I'm only asking if we could...give *us* another chance."

Mirah's breath hitched, heart fluttering against her chest. She put a hand on her stomach to steady herself and smirked.

"Are you asking to court me, Your Grace?"

Anwil blinked. Then laughed. "I am, yes. Would you, Lady Mirah of Evanshire, give me that chance?"

Mirah grinned and slipped her arms around his neck. "I will," she whispered and pressed her lips to his.

He pulled her to him. She heard the soft sound of the blanket falling to the floor.

And then the door burst open.

"God's fucking bones!"

Mirah and Anwil jumped apart. Ariadne stood in the doorway, eyes wide.

Anwil yanked the blanket over himself as Ariadne fled the room, slamming the door behind her.

"I've told you to knock, Ari!" Anwil yelled, throwing a shirt and trousers on.

Mirah gripped the back of one of the armchairs to steady herself.

"Well, forgive me, but you're the very last person I expected to...do that," Ariadne huffed behind the door.

Mirah giggled, and Anwil shot her a look.

"I'm offended," Anwil said, and Mirah bit her lip.

"But I need to talk to you!" Ariadne called through the door. "It's urgent, so put some clothes on, *please*!"

Anwil sighed and tucked his tunic into his trousers and threw on a belt before opening the door.

"We'll talk about this"—Ariadne pointed between Anwil and Mirah—"later, but we have a problem."

"What?" Anwil asked.

"Agravaine's taken Northumbria. Elyion and his family are dead."

CHAPTER FIFTY-FIVE

ANWIL

The high Anwil had felt when he had woken with Mirah in his arms was completely gone by the time he reached the throne room where the Knights of the Round Table were waiting. Morgana and Lady Vivienne were also amongst them, as well as Prince Connor.

As soon as Anwil stepped in front of his seat, the talk quieted.

"Who brought this news?" Anwil asked. They did not have time to waste.

"A squire," Brionna said. "He was found near death at the gates. He's in the infirmary now. Lady Vivienne revived him enough to tell us."

"They were slaughtered at supper," Morgana said, staring out the window, her face unreadable. "By fae assassins."

"Well," Anwil said, forcing himself to keep calm. "That confirms that Agravaine and Mordred have rekindled their old alliance."

"They were as close as brothers," Morgana said. "It is not surprising."

A few of the knights swore.

"This is a trap," Lancelot said with a glance at Morgana. "Get us to move north, fight Agravaine, and Mordred rides on the city."

"That is something Mordred would do," Morgana confirmed.

"So what do we do?" Ariadne asked.

"We have to go to Northumbria," Anwil said, though he didn't like it. "It is under our protection and we cannot just hand it over to Lothian."

"But that's what he wants us to do," said Ariadne. "We can't give in to that. It's a trap."

"What else can we do, Ari?" Anwil asked. "Part of being the High King is protecting the petty kingdoms. We *have* to respond."

"And Mordred knows it," Morgana said darkly. "He was Arthur's heir for a long while. He knows exactly what the High King's duties are."

"See?" Ariadne said. "We can't let him play us!"

"What choice do we have? We cannot just let Lothian take Northumbria without retaliation," Anwil said, banging his fist on the table. "What message will that send to the other kingdoms? That we will not come to their aid when they're under attack? Mordred gave us an impossible choice, but I will not—*cannot*—abandon my people."

"Can you call on the other kingdoms for help?" Prince Connor asked.

"We can," Lancelot said. "We could pick up soldiers from Mercia and Gwent and leave our best fighters here."

"We need to do something Mordred wouldn't expect," Sir Malcolm said. "Lady Morgana, do you have any suggestions?"

"I was never very good with warfare," she said, returning to the table. "But I can tell you his mind. Yes, he will want to trap you. He will expect you to take a good many fighters from Camelot to respond to Northumbria, where Agravaine is waiting, most likely with the full force of his own army. As soon as a company leaves Camelot, Mordred will probably strike."

"We have to assume he has a large fae army at his command," Lancelot said. "My mother has recruited warriors of her own, but only a few hundred. Many of the fae do not wish to fight in this war."

"How did Nimue and Mordred convince them?" Ariadne asked.

"There are parts of the fae world that are dark," Lady Vivienne said quietly. "Where the worst sort of depraved fae live. They went there."

"Great," Ariadne mumbled.

"This Mordred," Connor said. "He fights dirty, aye?"

"Yes," said Lancelot gravely.

"And because of Camelot's reputation," Connor continued, "he'll expect you to answer and fight with honor. But why not match him? Fight dirty back. Catch him off guard."

Eyes turned to Anwil, and he leaned back in his chair. "What do you suggest?" he asked Connor.

"Send assassins for the king of Lothian," Connor answered.

"He has three sons," said Lord Roland. "Who will, I assume, wish to avenge their father."

Connor gave Anwil a look.

"I won't assassinate Agravaine's family," Anwil said, catching Connor's meaning.

"Prince Connor has a point, though," Sir Malcolm said. "Do something to catch Mordred off guard."

"I am open to suggestions," Anwil said.

"Send a company," Xiang said. "Find out where their camp is. Attack in the night."

"They'll likely have lookouts," said Lancelot.

"That can go very badly if we are found out," said Brionna.

"It'll go badly either way," said Sir Malcolm. "Like Anwil said, there isn't much choice."

"Sometimes, the only choices we have, Your Grace," Lady Vivienne said, "are bad ones. You are put in a hard place, with little way out. If I may, make the decision that will be best for your country, that will save the most people."

Anwil gritted his teeth. Lady Vivienne was right. He was left with only horrid choices. Send a company and risk Camelot.

Send assassins and risk revenge; send the army to attack sleeping soldiers, risk Camelot's just and merciful reputation.

"What would my father do?" he asked Lancelot and Morgana quietly. "In this situation?"

"Arthur wasn't perfect," Lancelot said. "But he, too, had morals that he rarely wavered from. But, if he were presented with these choices, he would show that while honorable, his enemies had to fear him."

Anwil was relieved to hear that his instincts were in agreement. Mordred had trapped them, giving him little choice.

"Take a company," he said to Lancelot. "A few hundred from Camelot, and more on your way from Gwent and Mercia. If you must attack Lothian's army in the middle of the night, so be it."

"As you wish, Your Grace," Lancelot said.

"Morgana," Anwil said. "Will you accompany Lancelot?"

Before Morgana could answer, though, Lady Vivienne put a hand on her shoulder.

"You should not leave Camelot," the Lady said quietly to Morgana.

Morgana raised an eyebrow.

"You will be needed here," Vivienne said.

"Fine," said Anwil, not wishing to argue any longer. "Morgana, could you send a fast word to the kings, though?"

"Of course," she said. "I'll do that now." With a small bow of her head, she swept from the room.

"Who of us should go?" Xiang asked. "We can't send Lancelot alone."

"No," said Lancelot. "You all need to be here to guard the king."

"We cannot leave you by yourself," said Brionna.

"I'll have an entire company behind me," said Lancelot.

"I can go." Brom spoke up. While quiet, he had been listening intently. "Although I don't have actual battle experience besides the coup last summer, but the more knights, the better."

Lancelot did not look happy, but he nodded. Anwil glanced at his sister, weighing his options.

"Ari, you too," he said.

"I... beg pardon?" she said.

"You will go with Lancelot to Northumbria," he said, hating the words as they left his mouth. But if Mordred was coming for Camelot, he wanted his sister as far away as possible. It could give them a fighting chance if he lost against Mordred.

"I'm not leaving you," she said.

"I'm giving you an order," he said. "Elyion and his family were killed in cold blood. One of us must respond."

Ariadne stared at him, jaw agape. "I can't believe you're ordering me away," she breathed.

"I'll go too," Connor piped up. "I've led battles in Ireland. I'd like to help."

"You're a foreign prince, Connor, and heir to your own throne," said Anwil. "I cannot be responsible for your death."

"You won't be," said Connor. "Besides, if I'm being honest, if this all goes south, it'll be easier to get back to Ireland from Northumbria if Camelot is sieged."

Well, Anwil couldn't argue with that.

"It'll be an honor to fight by your side, Prince Connor," Lancelot said, clapping him on the back. "Your Grace, with your permission, we should leave at dawn."

Anwil nodded. "Yes," he said. "And may the gods protect you."

CHAPTER FIFTY-SIX

ARIADNE

Ariadne wasn't expecting a packed courtyard to send them off to Northumbria, but families and well-wishers stood shoulder to shoulder around the regiment. Mothers cried, wives tucked handkerchiefs into their husbands' belts, fathers gave words of wisdom, and courtiers gathered to wave goodbye.

Ariadne was already on her horse, having already said goodbye to Anwil and Mirah. She was ready to go and worried that if they delayed any longer, she would not have the courage. She didn't sleep a wink the night before, the reality of riding into battle falling on her in full force as she packed. Lancelot had given her a hastily scribbled list, and as she moved around her room, the panic had set in.

While never in battle herself, she'd heard accounts of the horror from knights and soldiers past. She saw how haunted Gawaine and Percival were when they returned from battles against raiders when she was younger. How many soldiers turned to drink to try and forget. If they returned at all.

"Nervous, Princess?" Connor asked, riding his horse up next to her.

"Never," she said, but Connor gave her a look that said he didn't believe her. She could see the tension in his jaw and shoulders as well.

"Just stick to what Sir Lancelot tells you," he said. "And there is no shame in being afraid."

Ariadne didn't answer.

"Let's ride," Lancelot called.

Ariadne looked back at Anwil one more time. He had his arm around Mirah's waist. They waved at her, and she had an urge to jump off her horse and take them both in her arms. She had a sinking feeling it would be the last time she saw her brother again.

She shook the thought, though, and followed Lancelot.

Their first stop was Gwent, then on to Mercia. Both kings had already gotten Morgana's letters and were ready with soldiers. They did not tarry at either kingdom, wanting to make good timing, though with near three thousand men marching at their backs, their movement was slow.

When they finally reached the Mercia and Northumbria border, there was no one there to meet them.

"Where do you think they are?" Ariadne said to Lancelot as they made camp for the night.

"Elyion's castle," Lancelot said. "It's a fortress. Agravaine will want to keep that high ground. We'll send scouts out tonight."

Ariadne's hands trembled as she unhooked her blanket rolls from her horse, which was not Nerys. Because her mare was not trained for war, Lancelot had given her a brown warhorse to ride. He was bigger than Nerys, and Ariadne needed a step stool to mount him, but he was sturdy and reliable, taking commands without the attitude Ariadne was used to from Nerys.

As she unpacked, tents were erected around her, along with fires and weapons racks. Pendragon banners were mounted high, along with those of Mercia and Gwent.

"You all right?" Brom nudged her shoulder.

"I'm fine," she said. "What about you? How's your legs?" She smirked at him. Brom had struggled during the ride, not used to being on a horse for so long. So when they stopped in Gwent, she had pushed Brom toward their castle healer.

"Better. That pretty healer gave me a salve," he said, popping open his waterskin. "Never realized how raw your thighs would get riding a horse. This actual knight stuff is much different than guard duty."

He frowned as he tipped the waterskin and realized it was dry.

Ariadne laughed. "A bit," she said and tossed him her waterskin.

He mumbled a thanks and drank from it. "I'll get you some more. There's a small creek not far."

"Don't go alone," Lancelot said.

Brom waved to let him know he heard him and wandered off. Ariadne went over to her tent, a small one, and rolled out her blankets. She had declined a bed, wanting to keep their load as light as possible. The only furniture they had taken was weapons racks and a table for the war tent.

Ariadne dropped her pack on her blankets and headed back out to sit with Lancelot and Jabir around a small fire. Lancelot was sharpening his sword while Domhnall spoke softly with one of the Gwent commanders.

Ariadne bit into some dried meat she had pulled from her pack. She took a moment to look out over the field they had chosen for their camp. It was colder the more north they had traveled, more open. The biggest difference she had noticed was the smell. Or lack thereof. The city had had a wide variety of smells, both good and bad. But out here, in the open, there was nothing except the occasional floral scent on the wind, or the grass after a rain. It was fresh and pure.

"Here."

She looked up. Connor was offering her a bowl of something steaming.

"Just some plain stew," he said, plopping down next to her with his own bowl. "It's not very good, but it's something different. There's more over there, Sir Lancelot."

"Thank you, Connor," Lancelot said.

Ariadne sipped at the stew. Connor was right. Plain, but she couldn't complain after days of dried meat and old bread.

Connor's two cousins joined them a moment later, stew bowls in their own hands.

"Better fighting weather than our last battle," Bradán said. "I'm not freezing my balls off."

"There's a lady present," Domhnall said, smacking him in the arm.

Ariadne snorted. "You can't say anything I haven't heard before."

"See?" Bradán smacked Domhnall back. "Quit scolding me. I told you she's not a real proper lady." As soon as the words left his mouth, realization dawned on Bradán's face. "Er... I mean. No. That's not." He let out a string of Irish words that Ariadne was sure was cursing. "I'm sorry, Your Highness."

"It's fine," Ariadne said with a shrug. "We'll just have you be our bait when the dragon comes."

Bradán's face paled. And Connor snorted.

"They have dragons?" Bradán asked.

But Ariadne didn't answer; she just ate more of her stew. Bradán looked at Lancelot, who just shrugged. Ariadne glanced at Connor, who was struggling to keep from laughing.

By nightfall, a few of the soldiers had broken out lutes and sang around their small fires. Lancelot had ordered everyone to get as much sleep as they could, but many couldn't. Like Ariadne. She had tried, but her mind was too all over the place.

She sat at one of the fires with Brom, who was singing a bawdy song with the others, though she hardly heard it.

Now she was nervous. No. Terrified. They would ride out in the morning to face Agravaine's army. Lancelot had told them Agravaine would expect them to meet in the middle of the battlefield, throw around some words, and fight the next day at dawn. But what Agravaine wouldn't know, hopefully, was their plan to attack his camp at night.

"All right?" Connor came down to sit next to her after he had wandered off for a bit.

"Fine," she said automatically.

Connor grabbed her hands, ceasing her wringing of them, which she hadn't realized she was doing. She looked down at their clasped hands. He wore a gold ring with an emerald, and a gold bracelet with runes and knotwork etched into it. His skin was warm and calloused, but his grip tense.

"It's all right, you know," he said quietly.

"What is?" she asked.

"To be scared."

"I'm fine," Ariadne said again, pulling her hands from his.

He did not look convinced but didn't press her.

"You should sleep," he said instead.

"So should you."

Connor gave a weak scoff that tried but failed to be casual. "I don't sleep before battle."

"I don't think I will either," said Ariadne.

"Here." He handed her a skin.

She sipped and nearly gagged. "What the hell is this?"

Connor laughed. "Something to take the edge off. Take a good sip. It might help you sleep."

"It might make me puke," she grumbled, but choked down a gulp. She nearly threw the skin back to him and chugged a bit of water from her own, which Brom had returned earlier.

Her throat still burned, though.

"Oy, Ari." Brom caught her attention. "Tell them about the time you got stuck in that old well for half a day before anyone knew where you were."

Snickers came from the men around the fire.

"Absolutely not," said Ariadne. "I'd rather not relive that, thanks."

"Oh, I'm intrigued," said Connor. "How did you manage that?"

"She claimed there was an animal down there," Brom said. "So she tried to go in after it. You were what, eleven or twelve?"

"Twelve," Ariadne answered through gritted teeth. "And there was, actually, an animal. I didn't know it was a rat until I fell."

Connor snorted and she glared at him. More laughter rang out from the men.

"Don't be too embarrassed, Princess," Connor said. "I once spent two nights locked in a shed after I was found with a chieftain's daughter."

"How would that make me feel any better?" Ariadne asked.

Connor shrugged.

Ariadne shook her head. "I'm going to bed."

"Princess, wait," Connor called after her. But she ignored him, ducking into her tent and shrugging out of her armor. She stretched and rubbed some salve into a few sore spots before lying down and closing her eyes, praying that sleep would come.

Ariadne wore her Knights of the Round Table tabard to ride out to meet with Agravaine. Lancelot stayed close to her as they rode, with Connor and Brom behind them. The Gwent and Mercia commanders followed with their own banners alongside Camelot's.

They found Agravaine already waiting for them on the top of a small hill, with near twenty men and his own banners flapping in the wind. So, Lancelot had been right. Agravaine wanted to gloat first.

As they approached, Ariadne was a little taken aback to see how much Agravaine looked like Gawaine, although Agravaine was much thinner than his brother had been. He also wore a crowned helm and a smirk.

Ariadne kept close to Lancelot as they stopped.

"Sir Lancelot of the Lake," Agravaine said. "Thought you were long dead. But of course, that wish of mine was not granted."

"Sorry to disappoint," Lancelot replied. "But you should know, I have no plans of dying anytime soon."

Agravaine chuckled. "It may not be today, but you will die, Lancelot of Benoic. By *my* hands."

Ariadne narrowed her eyes. She had no doubt that Lancelot was the better swordsman. Agravaine reminded her of Gingalain in the way he was all talk.

Ariadne looked over at the men Agravaine had brought. They were big men, in expensive armor, and heavy with weapons. Even their horses were bigger. She wondered if there were any fae hiding among their ranks.

"I will give you the chance to surrender, Agravaine," said Lancelot. "And you can go back to Lothian and your men will live."

Lancelot had prepared Ariadne for this. They would go back and forth with chances to surrender, deals made, but they would all be turned down. Ariadne thought it rather pointless.

Agravaine laughed. "You know me better than that, Lancelot. I do not surrender. But I will tell you this. I *am* willing to make a deal with you."

Ariadne snorted, and Agravaine's attention came to her.

"Ah, Ariadne Pendragon," he said. "I say, what a spitting image of Arthur you are. Tell me, have you inherited any of his arrogance? His weakness for mercy?"

"How sad that you mistake mercy for weakness and not strength," said Ariadne, which caused Agravaine and his men to laugh. "You may laugh, but there will come a time when you are *begging* me for mercy, my lord."

That elicited another round of laughter. Ariadne gripped her reins but kept her face cool, not giving them satisfaction.

"This can end now, Agravaine," Lancelot said. "Give up Northumbria. Go back to Lothian. You know Mordred will not honor any promise he has made to you."

"And you have?" said Agravaine. "Forgive me if I do not take well to believe the word of the man who killed my father."

"Have it your way, then," said Lancelot. "I'll see you on the battlefield, Agravaine."

"Oh, you—"

"Sleep well, my lord king," Ariadne interjected. "I'll enjoy slitting your throat tomorrow."

She gave her horse a kick and rode away, not looking behind her to see how Agravaine reacted.

"That was unbecoming of a knight, Ari," Lancelot said when their small company caught up to her a few moments later.

"Sometimes taking the high road isn't an option," she said.

"I thought it was brilliant," Connor said. "How you handled Agravaine."

"Do you have any more of that awful drink?"

"Aye?"

"Good. I need a lot of it."

CHAPTER FIFTY-SEVEN

MORDRED

Mordred's shadow warriors cut through the Wessex king and his court like they were nothing.

Like they had done to Elyion, they ambushed Wessex at dinner. And how lucky they were to find them at a court dinner. All fifty of them were dead before they even realized what was happening.

Once the court was taken care of, they turned to the servants. No one was left alive.

They did the same to Mercia, where King Caewlin was not at dinner but in his study, as if waiting for them.

"I knew you were coming," the old man told Mordred when he entered the room. Caewlin quickly drained the goblet he had been holding. "So, I am not giving you the satisfaction of my death."

Mordred snorted and sliced the old man's throat before the poison could start working.

The King of Gwent put up a fight, but he was no match for the Shadows, and he was quickly felled, falling face-first into the hearth, the flames quickly overtaking him.

Mordred left the Saxons with the kingdoms, letting them have their celebrations. Camelot was now alone, isolated. Without the kings to send troops, it would be more evenly matched. Mordred may not have the numbers, but he had deadly fae warriors who did not follow any rules or morals. And if Camelot wanted to run away to the other kingdoms for safety, they would only find their deaths.

"They're all gone?" Nimue asked when Mordred told her the good news as soon as he returned to Tintagel.

"I told you to trust me," he said, kissing her cheek.

Nimue gave him a look, but he ignored it. He did not have the energy to quarrel with her. He was in pain. His soul was screaming again, trying to break free from his body. And one of his fingers had turned completely black.

"Tomorrow," he said to Nimue as he made his way into his chambers. "We leave for Camelot. Gear up, my love. Everything we have worked for is finally in our grasp."

It was time. Mordred could almost smell the victory in the air as he mounted his horse. With the army of humans and fae behind him, and Camelot empty of her strongest knights, Mordred felt invincible.

He turned his horse one last time to take it all in and make sure they were ready to march. Thousands of infantry human and fae soldiers stood at the ready, with large siege engines towering behind them.

Mab had certainly delivered fae warriors, outnumbering the humans two to one. It was a much larger army than Mordred had had at his disposal at the Battle of Camlann, where he had failed and died over twenty years ago.

He would not fail again.

This time, Camelot would fall. And he would wear the crown.

Mordred pulled on his gorget. Memories of Camlann had kept him awake the past few nights. How Arthur had overwhelmed him, outsmarted him. Though it had been his biggest satisfaction to take Arthur's life, Arthur had also taken his. The feeling of dying would never leave him. How his body went cold, his limbs heavy, every breath a struggle. And the pain.

Mordred snarled, raising his arm in the air, eliciting a roar from his army that shook the grounds of Tintagel.

He turned his horse back around, coming face to face with Nimue. She sat on her own mount, a sturdy gray warhorse from the Otherworld. Dressed in leathers and armor of her own, she looked every inch the fae warrior she was. But she had a hard look on her face. He knew she had stopped trusting him when Mab had opened her mouth and told Nimue he had been truly dead, and not just in the In-Between. Ever since, Nimue had pulled farther and farther away. It had hurt, he could admit to himself, but he kept appearances, or tried to. He needed her to get the fae on his side. Though his father had been a fae warrior himself, Mordred had found the fae were slow to trust him, even in his past life. Even with his mother's blood, he presented more human than fae.

Perhaps it was because his mother had given him away at the first opportunity to grow up with humans in an isolated castle in the Orkney Isles. He never had a chance to know his fae side.

It was because of this that his heart was never truly in line with Nimue's cause. He did not truly care if magic was fading from this wretched realm. There was still power to take without it. Once he killed the boy and the Pendragons were out of the way, the fae could go back to their own damned world for all he cared.

"Have faith, my love." Mordred shot her a grin. "Soon, victory will be ours."

"Let us hope your impatience does not cost us," she growled.

He ignored her comment. Yes, he was going against their earlier plan, but for reasons she could not know. Unless Mordred killed the boy and took the rest of his life force soon, his soul would detach from his body and return to the Underworld.

Mordred looked over his shoulder. "We ride!"

Another earth-shattering roar came from his infantry, and Mordred kicked his horse forward to Camelot.

CHAPTER FIFTY-EIGHT

CONNOR

Battle was not new to Connor; he had seen more than his share among the tribes in Ireland and regardless of where it took place, it never changed. First, there was the stillness. Everything seemed to go quiet, so unsettling that it almost felt supernatural. Then the fear set in. It emanated from Camelot's men, fear so thick that it filled the air and Connor could almost feel it closing in on him from those around him. He didn't feel much fear in battle anymore, though. He had grown too numb. It all ended the same: Blood and bodies piled high, survivors wishing they hadn't, turning to drink to numb the pain and memories. The cries of the wounded as they slowly met their end and the nightmares that never did.

"Here's to another one," Domhnall said gravely, handing Connor a flask. They were on horseback on the front line, waiting for Agravaine's army. Lancelot and Ariadne were just ahead of them. She was in full armor and he could only see her back, but he knew she was tense. She tried to hide it; they all did, but Ariadne had not seen a true battle, had not yet stared across the field at the walls of blades and shields that could be her end. Connor had already made note of her pale face and the way her shoulders rose and fell more and more rapidly as the battle drew nearer. He could see the determination in her eyes and respected that, but he could also see the fear, and it made his heart ache for her.

A rumble of shifting plate and hard stomps alerted them to Agravaine's arrival.

He led them alone, with bannerman behind him. He halted, only for a moment. Then raised his hand. Connor was slightly relieved despite himself. At least Agravaine meant to start swiftly, and that was a blessing in disguise: there was less time to overthink and fumble a reaction.

"Shields!" Lancelot called.

The men behind Connor dropped to their knees behind their shields, forming a wall. Connor shifted his on his arm and tightened his grip on the handle.

Agravaine dropped his arm and the archers angled up and loosed their arrows, raining them down on the army. Shields raised and Connor grunted as his shield caught many. A few ricocheted off of the plates on his legs and on his horse's back.

"*Hold!*" Lancelot called, barely audible through the thuds, clangs, and screams of the volley. The archers had already begun to knock the arrows onto their bows, and as the sound of the arrows slowed, Lancelot gave the command.

"Forward!" he bellowed, and his men, Ari's men, gave a resounding roar before rushing headlong into the fray. They ran past Connor and the knights, meeting Agravaine's army with a sickening crunch as bodies tumbled together. Metal against metal, men yelling, blood spilling.

Connor gripped his reins. His heart picked up and he slowed his breathing.

Fuck. He needed a drink. More than what Bradán had offered.

Connor urged his horse next to Ariadne. She was staring at the battle, her face pale and jaw clenched so tight, Connor could see the muscles flexed under her skin.

"Princess?" he said.

She shook her head. "We should be out there, with them."

"No. Lancelot knows what he's doing," Connor replied. "Just wait for his order."

Her shoulders tensed, but she didn't respond.

Something caught Connor's ear. He turned his horse and his breath caught in his chest. He cursed.

An army of fae were coming for them from behind.

Connor yelled for Lancelot, who had also turned to see what the noise was.

Lancelot trotted up to Connor, pulling his sword. "Get Ariadne out of here," he said. "As far away as you can. Your life for hers; do you understand?"

Connor hesitated.

"Now! Go!" Lancelot barked.

Conor urged his horse. "Bradán! Domhnall, to me! Protect the princess!"

"Ari!" he called out as Bradán and Domhnall fell in line, side by side behind him. "Come on!"

"What?" Ari looked around at him, through him really. Her quick shallow breaths told him all he needed to know. She had heard nothing of the exchange, her racing heart blocking out the sounds around her despite how close and loud they had been.

"Lancelot's orders!" Connor barked.

"No!" Ariadne said. Her horse was now dancing in anxiety. "No, I'll not abandon my men!" Her voice rose with a shrillness that bordered on panic. Connor did not like the sound coming from her usually composed and confident lips.

"We can't let you die either!" Connor called as calmly as he could manage.

Arrows began to rain down again. Horses screamed, men rolled. Connor's own horse was struck in the leg by a man flailing his burning arm, and the steed bucked. Connor was thrown, as was Ariadne.

He groaned and cursed at the horses running to the woods, away from the battle. He could see Bradán and Domhnall fighting for control of their horses as they spooked and ran, wanting to follow the other now riderless mounts.

"You need to live, damnit," Connor bellowed to Ariadne as he crawled over to her. "You are heir to Briton."

"I am no coward." She shot to her feet, sword drawn. "I will stand with my men and die with them if I have to."

The fae army closed distance more rapidly than any man could.

Connor cursed again as she ran toward the fae army. He followed her as quickly as he could, catching up to her just as she broke the line with her sword.

And chaos erupted.

Ariadne swung her sword wildly through the crowd and Connor fought as the fae closed around her, trying to encircle the pair. Swinging and blocking. Trying to keep Ariadne safe as she pressed through the chaos. She was fighting off the fae with a wild determination that he would almost call desperation.

Connor gripped her backplate with one hand and fought with the other, pulling her backward just as a fae's blade fell with force in front of her and buried in the ground at her feet. He swung his axe and buried it in the fae's neck.

"I am not letting Sir Lancelot down," Connor said. "We won't win. It's a massacre. We have to go. Now!"

"No!"

"Who leads Camelot if you and Anwil die, huh?" Connor shouted.

"He's right, Ari!" Brom had made it to them. "You are our top priority. King's orders. He told us to do anything we can to keep you safe."

Ariadne didn't have time to reply, as more fae swarmed them. Connor stayed by Ariadne's side, burying his axe into any fae that came close. How the hell they were going to get out of here, he had no idea. They needed a gods damned miracle.

They kept fighting. And the fae kept coming.

"There has to be a moongate open somewhere," Ariadne called to Connor after she sliced off a small fae's head. "We need to close it."

"How the hells do we do that?"

"No idea, but we have to try!"

Connor kicked at a fae and slammed his axe into their throat. He looked around to see what direction they were coming from, but it was impossible to determine amid the frenzy.

"Wait, wait!" Ariadne called. "Look." She pointed into the distance.

Connor followed her finger and realized the fae were not only fighting Camelot's men, but Lothian's as well.

"What are they doing?" Connor asked.

"Mordred betrayed them," Ariadne said. "It wasn't just a trap for us, but Lothian as well. I need to find Lancelot."

Before Connor could stop her, she tore off. He followed her, ducking and dodging wild blades.

Ariadne finally made it to Lancelot's position, shouting all the while for his attention. By the time he had heard her voice, he had already noticed the betrayal and was calling to Brom for a signal to retreat. Brom raised the horn to his lips and blew a staccato double blast; Camelot's rarely heard signal for a retreat. Unfortunately, many couldn't hear over the supernatural volume of the fae's battle cries and the wailing of the few that lay dying. The humans were falling too fast.

Lancelot fell to a knee, hanging his head.

"What are you doing?" Connor shouted, booting a goblin in the chest and beating down the wooden shield of another with his axe. Lancelot ignored him; he was mumbling to himself, holding something tightly in his hand.

After a moment, Lancelot rose to his feet with a burst of speed that Connor and Ariadne had not expected, and with a legendary grace connected the side of his shield in an uppercut to a winged fae's jaw, leveling it instantly. The two could only blink in surprise.

"I've called for help," he said. "But I do not know if there will be an answer."

"Who?" Ariadne asked.

Lancelot didn't have time to answer as a goblin-like fae came rushing at them; Ariadne and Lancelot turned and thrust at the same time. Black blood spewed from the new holes punched into the creature and dripped from the blades protruding from its back.

The chaos continued, and every second felt like an hour. Every sword and axe stroke was heavier than the last. Brom took a hard hit to the leg and Connor hurled his axe, burying it in the creature's skull just in time to make it drop its wooden spear before it impaled his friend. Connor bolted to his side, reclaiming the axe quickly and roughly before attending to his friend.

"Leave me," Brom gasped, grasping his bleeding thigh. "I won't make it."

"Like hell you won't." Connor assessed his friend, touching as gently as he could manage, but still shifting the man's leg so he could see more clearly.

"It's deep, but the fragile artery is safe." He yanked a rag from his belt and wrapped it around Brom's thigh, and then pushed it high into his groin. He tied it as tight as he could manage, the blood making the process slick and clumsy. Connor reached with his right hand and snapped an arrow off the corpse of a Camelot soldier, muttering an apology as he did.

He pushed the shaft into the rag and twisted it, tightening the entire construct on Brom's leg as he lay screaming, but the bleeding stopped. Haphazard medicine, but effective. He grabbed Brom's hand and placed it on the arrow, and closed the grip for him.

"*Squire!*" Connor bellowed, and a terrified youngster sprinted clumsily to his side. "See to him; drag him into the woods if you must. But do not leave him. You understand?"

The youth nodded grimly, fear apparent but not crippling.

Connor gazed around himself and took it all in. It was a massacre. Fae were slaughtering humans without mercy. Connor cursed again and pushed himself to his feet. Well, if he wasn't making it out of this battle, he wouldn't die on a knee.

He hoisted himself back up, axe in hand, and ran back into the fray.

CHAPTER FIFTY-NINE

ARIADNE

Attackers were coming on all sides, and Ariadne swung her sword like a madman, trying to keep them at bay. Her shoulder throbbed from a hard hit earlier and she had rolled her ankle, but she pushed through the pain because if she stopped, she was dead.

Most of the Camelot soldiers were dead, scattered across the plains with the Lothian men.

She did not know what had happened to Agravaine—if he fled, or if this had been a part of his plan all along. Though she doubted killing his own army was his own choice. At least, what good was a king and kingdom without an army to defend it?

Ariadne screamed as something hit the ground in front of her, causing dirt to explode in her face. She tripped and fell but scrambled back to her feet, dodging more of whatever was being thrown.

When one hit too close to her foot, she fell and couldn't get back up. Her sword slipped from her hands and something hard slammed into her back as she went down. She pushed herself to roll over, her vision blurring. A dark figure stood over her and Ariadne raised her arms to deflect whatever blade came at her, but it was not a blade that came.

The figure offered their hand. Ariadne blinked away the sweat and blood that ran into her eyes. It was Connor. She took his hand and he helped her to her feet.

"What do we do?" Ariadne choked out.

Connor blew out a breath. "We keep fighting," he said. But his own voice was broken. Defeated.

Ariadne picked up her sword and adjusted her shoulders.

"You sure I can't convince you to get out of here?" Connor asked.

"I'm not abandoning the men to die while I run," said Ariadne.

"If we survive this, Lancelot might just kill you."

"I'll deal with that if we live," Ariadne said.

Connor didn't look convinced, but he gave her a nod.

"We can—" A loud horn cut him off. It echoed so loudly, Ariadne had to cover her ears. It came again, and the fae around them stopped. And looked. Men, Lothian and Camelot alike, tried to look for the source of the noise, confused.

Ariadne gripped her sword, heart pounding in her ears. Her armor was heavy and her limbs shook, but she kept her ground.

"What is that?" Ariadne asked Lancelot, who was pushing himself to his feet after a bad hit.

"There!" came a voice.

Some men were pointing toward the tree line, where a bright light shone. From the light, a rider on horseback emerged.

The horn blasted again, and the light faded.

The rider revealed was not on horseback, but unicorn back, wearing armor of green. He carried a silver and green flag, with a foliate face in the center.

A few of the fae around Ariadne let out whimpers.

The green rider raised his flag, and the horn blasted.

The ground rumbled.

And an army emerged from the trees behind him. Fae fairer than the ones on the field marched through the trees, carrying spears, swords, bows, and banners. Armor of the purest silver shone in the sunlight as the archers knelt and nocked their bows. Behind them, spearmen in armor that looked to be made of the trunks of trees raised their swords as they aimed.

The green rider lowered his flag, the pole flashing in the sunlight.

And the arrows rained.

Fae screamed and screeched. Horrid, awful sounds that made Ariadne grit her teeth.

And then they ran.

Ariadne dropped to her knees, covering her head and neck with her arms. A shadow fell over her. Connor. He held a battered fae shield over them, but there was no need.

The arrows only hit the running fae.

Ariadne slowly got to her feet as more arrows rained down, perfectly hitting their marks.

Some of the dark fae ran toward the tree lines, roaring as they went. The wooden-armored fae met them halfway, spearing them through or meeting them with their swords.

It did not go well for the dark fae.

It did not take long for the green rider's army to decimate the dark fae, and the ones that were left alive fled.

Ariadne could only stand and stare at their saviors.

As the last of the dark fae fled or died, the green rider kicked his horse and rode over to them, his flag flapping in the wind.

He pulled his unicorn to a stop and took off his green helm, revealing a green but human-looking face. Even his beard was green.

Ariadne finally realized who he was.

The Green Man.

She had heard Gawaine recount his tale hundreds of times.

Had The Green Man really come to save them?

"I heard your call, Sir Lancelot," The Green Man said as stuck his helm under his arm.

"I did not think you would come," Lancelot said.

"You are the son of the Lady of Realms," The Green Man said. "Grandson of The Modron. Of course, we would heed your call. But it was not only that, Lancelot of the Lake. It was the love you have for your king. The love the people have for this king... to inspire such true feelings is worthy indeed. And the princess..."

The Green Man turned to her. "Your commander ordered you to run. And yet you would not abandon your soldiers, even if it meant you died with them on the battlefield."

Everyone turned to her and she felt her cheeks heat. "I'm not a coward."

"It would not have been cowardly," The Green Man said, "to get to safety when you have such an important role, nor to defy orders. Your choice shows you have great honor. For that, we have come. But now, we must go. Mordred and his army march on Camelot. I suggest you make your way there."

"You won't come with us?" Ariadne said.

The Green Man shook his head. "Our presence there would neither help nor hinder. We must return to the faelands, where the veils are thinning. Nimue has already started her spell. We must try to keep them from the Otherworld."

The Green Man bowed low over the unicorn's neck and raised his flag again.

"Keep your heart, young dragon," he said to Ariadne and then turned the unicorn and dashed off.

The army retreated into the trees, leaving them on a battlefield littered with the dead, human and fae alike.

"I don't know how we're going to make it to Camelot in any time," Connor said. "Not in the state we're all in."

Ariadne looked around and her heart sank. Unfortunately, Connor was right. The men were in no shape to travel back to

Camelot. Merely a hundred or so were left of Camelot's men, and Lothian's were nowhere to be found.

"Back to camp for now," Lancelot said. "Those that can will leave for Camelot tomorrow. The rest can follow when they are ready. Wounded and tired soldiers are no use in a fight."

"Princess?" Connor came up behind her, holding out a hand as if ready to catch her if she fell. Her mind was all over the place.

"Go back to camp," Lancelot told her quietly. "I'll meet you there."

Ariadne was too tired to argue. But the walk back to camp was long. They kept having to stop to help someone who had fallen or succumbed to their injuries. But when they finally made it back, the healers were ready. Ariadne made sure those that were worse off than her made it to the tents first. She was sore and exhausted. Her hands shook and her head throbbed.

"Ari," Connor said gently when she stumbled on her own foot. "Get yourself cleaned up and rest."

"No. I—"

"Go," Connor gently urged her toward the healers' tents.

Connor helped her out of her armor with gentle fingers before he was shooed away by a healer. Ariadne was then stripped down to her undertunic so the healer could clean and tend her wounds. Ariadne let them work without protest, too tired to even think. She tried to gather her thoughts, but her mind was just a buzz.

"Salve from Lady Mirah," the healer said as she slathered it on Ariadne's ankle. "Your ankle should be right as rain in the mornin', Your Highness."

"Thank you, Tilly," Ariadne said, her throat dry.

Tilly made her drink water and a few sips of broth before leaving, and, barefoot and just in her tunic, Ariadne made her way back to her small tent, where she passed out as soon as she lay down.

CHAPTER SIXTY

ANWIL

Camelot had never been so quiet. The city was nearly empty; Anwil had given orders to evacuate, and had spent the better part of a week overseeing the massive exodus out of the city, even stepping in occasionally to help load things onto wagons and helping as many as possible to travel through mirrors if they wished. Being able to evacuate his people overrode any fears about Nimue being able to access the castle through them.

Not things typically required or expected of a king, but with the magic available to the fae—and, therefore, the enemies of Camelot—every hand was needed to speed the process. Many, unfortunately, preferred the road despite Anwil's warnings.

Eventually, the city was as empty as it was going to get. Many stayed, refusing to leave their homes and, despite Anwil's best efforts, would not be convinced to leave. Those citizens had been set up in the castle at least, and that bit of persuasion came with unimaginable compromises. Anwil placed them all behind wards that Morgana conjured, and those who were knowledge-able were ordered to help in the infirmary with the wounded. The able-bodied carried supplies to soldiers.

A scout had sent word the day before that Mordred was coming with an army near five thousand. The number had caught Anwil off guard and raised alarm bells for him and Roland. Morgana had told him to expect Mordred to play dirty, and Anwil certainly did.

Anwil assumed the spotted army was not the entirety of the forces at Mordred's command and so had posted soldiers around all entrances, old tunnels, and even the long-abandoned secret caves whose entrances had collapsed before his time. But dirt and rubble could be removed, expeditiously if magic was involved. Anwil hoped they had done enough to prepare in case Mordred snuck an attack somewhere.

As he stood with his knights and bannermen on the battle-ments, Anwil was ready to meet Mordred. Lord Roland, Anwil's most trusted councilor, stood to his right. Lohengrin was beside him, with Morgana on his left.

Mordred's army was close. They could all sense it, even though they could not yet see it on the horizon. Anwil wanted to vomit; his stomach was winding and turning in knots and he was sweating buckets under his plate armor. They all baked miserably in the sun, which had decided to come out in full force.

Excalibur was at his hip, weighing heavily on the belt wrapped tight to his cuirass, and he gripped the pommel as if it were a lifeline.

"Any last-minute words of advice, Aunt?" he asked.

"Do not lose hope," she said, turning to him. She, too, was in armor, though not a full suit, only a cuirass and iron daggers in her belt. She reached out with a heavily gloved hand to touch his forearm but stopped short and placed it on the stone crenellations.

"Camelot has defied fate before. You can do it again." The heavy, foreboding silence fell again as Morgana gazed out at the horizon.

A grumble caught Anwil's attention. It was low, barely audible. But unmistakable. An army marching. A flash of Mordred's face burst into his head, sneering, and he knew Mordred was close.

Anwil turned for a final look at the preparations they had made.. Engines of war had been deployed around Camelot in ways that had not been seen for decades, as well as a few that had never been seen before. Trebuchets and catapults had been rolled up to the ramparts of the city wall, ready for impending bloodshed. Archers were set up throughout the city, even on the roofs of shops and houses. Soldiers were hidden in places within the city and castle, ready to catch the enemy by surprise.

Lord Roland turned and barked quick, direct orders and everything went into motion. Soldiers now stood alert, ready to man the engines, or with their pikes and shields, ready for the charging enemy.

Anwil flexed his grip on Excalibur as Mordred's banners crested the horizon.

This was it. What everything had been leading up to.

Today would decide his fate.

"Remember the plan," Lohengrin called down to the bannermen and men-at-arms standing at the ready below. "We wear Mordred down before he gets to Anwil. We need to trap him."

Anwil opened his mouth to reply, but footsteps caught his attention. He glanced over this shoulder. Lady Vivienne and a handful of priestesses were making their way toward him, all dressed for battle in gleaming plate.

"They will try to break the wards first," Vivienne said.

"Can they?" Lohengrin asked her. "Break them?"

Vivienne shook her head. "No. Unless those who made them have passed, or they are invited in, they will hold." She turned back to Anwil. "Dismantle their army as much as you can when they arrive. Focus on the fae, and the men will fall quickly after. The iron projectiles in the catapults will do well."

She said the last part with a pained expression on her face and betrayal in her eyes. Anwil couldn't fathom how hard it was for her to fight her own kind. Though, men fought men every day. And yet, how different it was.

Anwil turned back to the approaching army. It was small, still in the distance. But they marched quickly, faster than a human army.

Anwil leaned over to take one last look around the city gates, at the ditches filled with wooden pikes tipped with iron. His heart pounded in his ears, and his stomach churned. He hoped it did not show on his face.

A hand fell on his shoulder.

Lohengrin. He gave a nod to Anwil and then turned, raising his sword, barking orders to the men manning the engines.

Wood creaked. Men shouted.

Mordred's army drew closer, and Anwil could now hear their distant roar.

"Steady!" Lohengrin called.

There would be no waiting, no talking. As soon as Mordred's army was in range, they would attack.

Anwil breathed hard as Mordred's army grew closer. A line of grotesque fae warriors and humans were running full speed at the gates. Anwil didn't like that. They were not led by anyone.

Anwil shaded his eyes with his hands, trying to look for Mordred or Nimue, but he could not see them.

"They're not there," he said. "Mordred."

"He's sending these in first to die," Morgana said with disgust, nodding to the approaching soldiers.

"Do you think he'll try to sneak in from somewhere?" Lohengrin asked.

"No, he'll want to be seen," Morgana said.

Lohengrin and Anwil exchanged a worried look, but Lohengrin turned back to the men.

"Ready!" Lohengrin called. Men shifted. Together, Lohengrin and Anwil stood and watched the fae approach, for they were nearly there. Anwil guessed a thousand of them approached, brandishing weapons and screaming, screeching, roaring. They grew louder. Closer.

"Release!" Lohengrin called.

Projectiles sprang from the catapults, raining over the fae and exploding in puffs of iron dust as they slammed into the ground. Enemy soldiers stumbled, screams turning into wails of pain. Fae coughed, choking on the iron dust.

Fae grabbed at their throats, their eyes, crashing and stumbling over each other as another round of projectiles soared and slammed and exploded.

Anwil wanted to look away, but he had made the command. So he watched. He looked at the horizon, where the fae were thinning.

Morgana was right. Mordred had sent these soldiers first. Most likely to test what Camelot would do and to deplete some of their supplies before the rest came in.

"Find Mordred and Nimue!" Anwil barked to the knights. "Do not let them take us by surprise!"

His orders were repeated and scouts were sent.

Lohengrin called for the catapults again, and two more giant iron projectiles exploded as they slammed into the fae on the ground. The fae that survived the projectiles stumbled into the piked ditches, impaling themselves on the iron tips and dying near instantly.

Anwil had to look away or else he'd empty his stomach on his boots.

Vivienne and her priestesses leaned over the turrets, waving their hands, and the dead fae turned to dust, the wind carrying the remains away.

"I'm sorry," Anwil said hoarsely to her.

"Don't be," she said, her voice hard. "They chose their fate."

Loud, shrill screeching rang overhead, so loud Anwil had to cover his ears. He looked up. Winged fae flew overhead from behind the castle, some large, some small. All looked to be a combination of bats and birds mixed with humanoid features. They dropped rocks down into the city that bounced off the wards.

No. Not rocks.

Heads.

Human heads.

"What the fuck?" Lohengrin said behind him.

More came, more heads raining from the flying fae. They bounced off the wards with muffled plops.

Eventually, the raining heads stopped and the flying fae landed in front of the castle, in the midst of where their brethren had died.

They did nothing for a moment, only stared up at them on the battlements.

And then Anwil heard it again. The rumble of a moving army.

The horizon darkened with the rest of Mordred's army, led by two riders. Anwil was sure he knew who they were.

"What was the point?" Lohengrin asked quietly as Mordred and Nimue led their army toward the gate. He shook his head and called out orders to reload the catapults.

"He's up to something," Morgana said.

Vivienne whispered something to the priestesses, and they ran down the battlements and disappeared through the towers to stand guard on the ground.

"Fire as soon as they're in range," Anwil said to Lohengrin, hating himself a little.

Lohengrin nodded and repeated the command.

"Cousin!"

Anwil turned to see Gingalain hurrying toward them.

"Something is wrong at the tunnels," he said, slightly out of breath.

"What?" Anwil asked.

The word had barely left Anwil's mouth when a series of booms exploded in the air. The battlements shook, men screamed. A few fell off the side. Morgana had a tight hold on Anwil, her grip stronger than he expected.

"What the hell was that?" Lohengrin cursed when the rocking subsided.

"Mordred," Anwil growled. He whirled on Gingalain. "What did you see? Why didn't you stop it?"

Gingalain huffed, the corners of his mouth turning up in a slight smirk.

"I didn't stop it," he said, his smirk growing. "Because I'm the one who planted the powder."

Anwil's whole body froze, unsure that he had heard his cousin correctly.

"What?" he said, his jaw barely moving.

"Just like I planted powder," Gingalain said, "right under your feet."

Before Anwil could react, Gingalain disappeared in a tendril of black smoke and the battlements exploded.

CHAPTER SIXTY-ONE

MORGANA

Morgana threw out her magic, slowing down the blast of the explosion. Stones hovered in the air; dust coated the air. Her limbs shook against the unsteady stone beneath her feet. Voices screamed and yelled, but they were muffled.

A faint scent of apples filled the air, and Morgana knew it was Vivienne. She let Vivienne's magic flow through her own, and with another quake that rocked the battlements, the stone repaired itself, sliding back into place.

When the last stone rejoined the rest, Morgana fell to her knees, panting. Sweat dripped down her face and her vision swam.

Her knees hit the hard stone floor and she slipped into unconsciousness.

Eventually she awoke cradled in someone's arms. Vivienne. Chaos rained around them, the battle raging in full force.

"Drink," Vivienne said, holding a small vial to her lips.

Morgana did as she was told. The liquid was slimy, and she felt it slide down her throat and through her body, waking up her limbs and mind.

"You threw out too much power too fast," Vivienne said, her own face pale and tired.

Morgana groaned, sitting up, hand to her head. "What happened?"

Vivienne frowned. "Gawaine's son has betrayed Camelot," she said as a catapult tossed an iron projectile. "He has invited Mordred's army in. The wards are destroyed."

Morgana cursed, her heart cracking in two. She was grateful that Gawaine was not alive to see such a betrayal. His own son. Morgana felt the pain of that far too much.

"Come," Vivienne said, helping Morgana to her feet. "We need to find Mordred and Nimue before they find Anwil."

"They aren't here?" Now on her feet, Morgana could see the extent of the horrid battle. Mordred's army had closed in. A company was trying to climb the walls. The Camelot soldiers were keeping them at bay for the moment.

More fae came, pulling their own siege engines.

"No," Vivienne answered. "I sent my sisters through the city to look for him. Gingalain said something about the tunnels, so we are assuming he is trying to sneak into the city."

"I will find him," Morgana said. "Stay with Anwil."

She glanced over her shoulder. Anwil stood surrounded by his knights, still calling orders. Morgana's stomach twisted as a memory flashed of Arthur at Camlann, but she shook that thought away. No. This would not end in Anwil's death.

"Be quick, if you can," Vivienne said, catching her by the arm. "I cannot hold my magic for long."

Morgana reached for Vivienne, but she was already hurrying away toward Anwil. Morgana raced to the other tower and down the tight, spiral stairs.

As soon as her feet hit the cobbled streets, she took off running, the armor biting and bumping into her skin.

I am too old for this, she thought as she wove her way through soldiers and dodged stray arrows.

She could not feel Mordred anywhere inside the city. So she took a turn into a back alley and cut through long abandoned buildings that sat just on the edge of the stone wall that surrounded the city.

Kneeling, she felt around for the off stone, and pushed. Half the wall crumbled away, revealing a dark tunnel.

Morgana listened carefully, straining over the far sounds of the battle at the front of the gate.

It was faint, but the rumbling of many footsteps could just be heard. Putting her hands on the stone, she whispered a spell and the stone replaced itself, sealing shut. This was easy, as there was no blast to contain or fight against.

She drew a protection rune where the entrance had been and took off to do the same to the next. If she could not find Mordred in the city, she could maybe keep him out. Or force him to enter where they wanted him.

If I had the time, she thought.

The ground beneath her rumbled and she fell against the wall of a shop, bracing with her arm to steady herself. When it stopped, Morgana peered around the corner, only to see Camelot soldiers running full speed through the streets toward the east end of the city.

Morgana's heart dropped. Mordred's army must have broken through somewhere. She raced to join the soldiers, and as she reached the garrison of troops now posturing in the street, she learned she was right. The east wall had crumbled and fae were swarming over the rubble like ants in a hill.

Camelot soldiers ran toward them, meeting them with a mighty clash and in a frenzy of blood and screams. She did not feel or see Mordred here, either.

"Damnit," she said. "Where is he?"

As soon as the words left her mouth, her heart sank.

Realization overwhelmed her, and she knew where he would be.

The castle.

Morgana tore off toward the castle, her muscles groaning in protest against the weight of the armor.

When she reached the courtyard, the ground was rocked with another boom, and she fell to her knees as the castle gate came tumbling down.

Her jaw dropped and heart sank as the heavy door pitched forward and fell to the ground like a drawbridge. Men poured out of the once grand doors of the main entrance like a torrential wave and flooded the streets. Many burst through the windows and leaped to the ground or flew like arrows toward Camelot's defenses.

She swore. Gingalain must have told them about the hidden tunnels within the castle. Of course he did.

Morgana got back to her feet, pulling a dagger from her belt as Mordred's army—both fae and men—stormed toward her.

But then something caught her eye. A figure at the top of the stairs.

Nimue.

They were far away, but Morgana knew. They locked eyes.

Well, if she couldn't stop Mordred at the moment, Nimue would have to do.

Morgana ran into the enemy soldiers, slashing the fae and hurling spells at the men to make her way through the crowd of bodies.

Many turned and ran from her, and she got an odd satisfaction from it. *Good. Let them be afraid.*

By the time she made it to the courtyard stairs, the fae had given her a wide berth and she made her way up to Nimue.

Nimue threw a force at Morgana, who was halfway up the stairs, but Morgana batted it away, sending it back to her. Nimue sidestepped it easily, as if expecting it, and threw another heavy gust of wind at her.

Morgana held up her hand, and instead of stopping and reversing it, she threw it over her shoulder toward the fae army behind her, hitting them with Nimue's own magic.

"You won't win, Nimue," Morgana said as she came to the top of the stairs, right in front of her old friend. "I've told you before. Your cause is lost."

"Not this time," Nimue smirked. "We have you right where we want you."

"Of course you do," Morgana scoffed. "I'll give you this last chance to leave. Leave for the Otherworld and never return."

Nimue's face turned to pure fury, her eyes white hot with liquid fire. "I will not be banished from lands we fae created," she hissed, raising her arms. "This world belongs to us. It is the humans who destroy everything in their path that must be banished."

"Nimue," Morgana warned, raising her own hand. "Leave. Now."

"Never!"

"Then so be it."

Both women threw out a spell with such force that it knocked both of them backward. Morgana tumbled down the stairs and Nimue flew into a pillar behind her, cracking it in half.

Morgana sent out her magic to catch herself, but she could already feel the bruises. Her shoulder and wrist throbbed. But she pushed herself to her feet and limped up the stairs again. She had lost her dagger somewhere.

Nimue was just getting to her own feet when Morgana twisted her hands together and threw out another spell, a ray of gold light wrapping itself around Nimue like vines and heaving her off the floor, suspended in the air.

"I don't want to kill you, Nimue," Morgana said, her voice raw and heavy. "But I will if I have to."

Nimue laughed. "Please," she scoffed, struggling against the magic holding her. "Don't give me that drivel. You never cared for me."

"You were my sister once," Morgana said. "I loved you."

Nimue snorted. "If you would have, you would have defended me against Vivienne. But you didn't. Just as the rest of them turned their backs on me, so did you. I do not care for any speeches you try to give, Morgana. It is too late. The veil is falling. We have already won."

"What?"

Another rumble, bigger this time. Enough to crack the pillars. Morgana's magic slid off Nimue and she lunged for Morgana, grabbing her around the throat. Morgana brought her foot to Nimue's chest and kicked her off; Nimue tumbled to the ground but grabbed Morgana's ankle and yanked her down with her.

Morgana fell hard on her back and Nimue crawled over her, a large dagger in her hand. She climbed onto Morgana like an insect and sat upright, raising the dagger over her head. With a burst of fear and adrenaline, Morgana rocked forward and raised her upper body enough to grab Nimue's wrist just before she could plunge the sharp blade into her neck. Morgana fell backward with the force of Nimue's thrust, struggling to keep the blade up and away from her.

"It will be my greatest pleasure killing you," Nimue growled, pressing against Morgana's hold.

Morgana tried to raise a knee into Nimue's back, hoping to slam her spine with a sharp point of the poleyn on her knee, but couldn't get the angle or force. Nimue laughed, the blade inching closer to Morgana's throat.

"I want to feel your heart stop with my bare hands," Nimue hissed, her eyes wide, feral.

Morgana groaned and struggled against Nimue. If she tried to do a spell, her grip might falter and Nimue would kill her. But Nimue was physically stronger. She had to get her off.

So, Morgana sent out a small spell, one she had learned as a child for pranks, and Nimue yelped as the magic pinched her legs, like little bites.

It was distraction enough for Morgana to shift Nimue to her side and roll her off. She scrambled to her feet, pulling another iron dagger from her belt.

Nimue got to her feet, panting, shoving loose hair from her face. "Perhaps you're right," she panted, causing Morgana to raise an eyebrow. "Perhaps I cannot win. At least, not against the infamous Morgana le Fey."

Morgana narrowed her eyes.

"Thankfully, I have help."

A hand came down hard on Morgana's shoulder and before she could react, something heavy slammed into her skull. And the world went black.

CHAPTER SIXTY-TWO

MIRAH

It was hard to take care of the injured while a battle raged just outside the doors. It had been quiet for a while, the air full of nerves and terror as they waited. Just Mirah and a few healers had stayed, along with a handful of volunteers from the city. Mirah had had a time convincing Master Cassius to evacuate. He insisted he would die doing his duty, but Mirah had finally convinced him he would be needed in the aftermath more.

"My lady, we cannot keep up," Aurelius, Cassius' new, young apprentice, said as another soldier barged his way in, carrying an unconscious man.

"We have no choice," Mirah hissed to him. "Unless you want to be out there, tending the wounded on the field?"

Aurelius shook his head frantically. His tunic and hands were covered in blood, and he was visibly shaking.

"If you wish to leave, there's a tunnel entrance near the herb garden," Mirah said as she tied off a bandage. "There's no shame in it."

Aurelius bit his lip and scurried off. Mirah did not watch where he went.

"There," she told the soldier whose arm she had just fixed. "You're good enough to go back out there."

The man looked up at her, eyes wide in terror. He had taken an arrow to the biceps, lucky that it hit nothing important.

"As I said, there's a tunnel in the herb garden," she said more quietly. "I don't care where you go, but I need your cot for those worse off."

He was silent as he moved and was replaced by the unconscious soldier who had just arrived. One look at him, with blood pouring from his stomach and leg, and Mirah knew there was nothing she could do.

"Please," the man who carried him said. "He's my brother."

"The best I can do is ease his passing," she said, plucking a small vial from her bag.

"No! You have to save him! You're Lady Mirah!" the brother said, grabbing her shoulders. "You can save anyone!"

She shoved his hands off, unable to look him in the eye. "I'm sorry," she said, moving around him to the unconscious man. She put her fingers to his neck. Her shoulders dropped. "I'm sorry," she repeated. "He's already gone."

"No!" the brother cried. "No! William! Will!" He shook his brother's shoulders, loud sobs pouring from his lips.

Heartbroken she needed to be so harsh, she left them alone and moved on to the next patient. But the infirmary was filling up fast and they were running out of room. A glance at the door told her there were many more in the halls, waiting or dying.

"Take supplies and linens to the great hall." Mirah caught one of the maids who had opted to stay. "Tell the wounded to start going there."

The maid bobbed a curtsy and hurried away to the supply closet, which was emptying quickly.

Mirah helped ease the passing of yet another soldier as the maid passed by her again, arms full of linens and bags. But she didn't make it to the door.

An explosion rocked the doorway, flames roaring through the threshold. Mirah was knocked off her feet, falling debris raining on top of her. Fae poured through the now ruined door, killing anyone in sight. Mirah crawled under a table, pain throbbing in her ankle and ribs.

A around Mirah, people screamed. And for a moment, she was frozen as the fae swarmed, brutally killing all they came across.

One of the fae made a horrifying screech, snapping Mirah out of her stupor. Her father and Morgana had prepared her for this. She pulled herself to her feet and threw out her hands, chanting the words Morgana had taught her.

All the iron daggers they had hidden throughout the infirmary flew toward the fae, ramming into them: throats, eyes, hearts.

Blood spewed everywhere. Falling fae knocked over tables and water basins. Some took out the wounded on their way down.

There was only a mere second of calm before the windows burst and shattering glass rained down. Mirah covered her neck and head, her arms taking a hit as tiny shards pierced her skin.

Small, winged fae buzzed through, their screeches shrill and sharp, their faces screwed with fury.

With a growl, Mirah threw out her arms again, power pulsating at her fingertips. She threw spell after spell at them. Bursts of flame and light lit up the infirmary as they hit each flying fae with deadly accuracy, turning the buzzing creatures to dust.

As the last of the fae were decimated, Mirah's knees gave out and she fell, grabbing a table for support. Morgana had only taught her those spells yesterday, warning her that they were draining. Killing took more effort than healing. And Mirah's head was spinning. She hated herself in the moment. So many dead because of her, and she hadn't even thought twice. She was a healer, not a killer.

The infirmary was a bloodbath. It was everywhere. Wounded soldiers, who were now dead, littered the floors. Cots and tables upturned. Most of the healers did not make it.

Mirah let out a sob, her eyes burning with unshed tears. A noise caught her attention, and she whirled on her feet, arms out, ready to shout another spell when she came face to face with a familiar healer.

"My lady?" she said to Mirah.

Mirah let out a shuddering breath and Lottie, the healer, took her into her arms. "Shhh, child," she whispered as Mirah shook with sobs. "You defended the infirmary. There's no sin in that."

She met Mirah cry into her shoulder for a moment before gently taking her face and wiping her tears.

"Come," Lottie said. "There's no more we can do here. We should get to safety with the others."

Mirah shook her head. "I will not leave," she said.

"But my lady—"

"No," said Mirah. "You go if you wish. I'm staying."

Mirah wiped her face with the back of her sleeves and picked through the rubble to find a bag and supplies. Lottie tried to protest once more, but Mirah ignored her.

So, Lottie went to work helping her pack supplies in the remnants of bags they found. There was one other survivor, a soldier with a broken arm in a sling. Other than the break, he was fine and offered to help carry supplies.

"The fae are likely swarming the castle," Mirah said, staring through the fallen doorway. A corner of the ceiling was gone, letting sunlight through. The door was a pile of rubble, of stone and wood.

"Then we should leave," Lottie pressed. "You used your energy and I cannot fight. And no offense, but Tom can't either with that arm."

Tom shrugged her comment off, taking no offense.

A boom rumbled from the distance.

"I should find Anwil," Mirah whispered.

"My lady!" Lottie cried. "Please; your father—"

"My father is out there!" Mirah snapped. She instantly regretted it, as Lottie winced. "I'm sorry. I'm going out there."

"My lady!" Lottie called after her, but Mirah was already hurrying on wobbly feet out of the infirmary.

CHAPTER SIXTY-THREE

ARIADNE

Ariadne was in a daze when she awoke the next morning. She had slept hard, barely moving, judging by the hard soreness in her shoulder and hip. She had only woken when a squire shook her, the sun already high in the sky. It had taken her a few long moments to remember where she was and that the battle had not been a just a horrid nightmare, but real. The coppery tang of blood still lingered in Ariadne's nose as she pushed the blankets away and rubbed her eyes. She almost didn't want to crawl out of the confines of her small tent and face the dreaded reality that awaited, but she knew she had no choice. It was the life of a knight, especially a Knight of the Round Table.

The realization of what horrid things Mordred could be up to in Camelot sank in and her breath hitched, her chest tightening. Battle was probably raging at the moment in Camelot, and she had no idea if her brother was alive or dead.

They needed to get home.

She began to dress, but the weight of the situation came crashing down around her, and she had to dive out of her tent to dry heave into the grass, tears streaming down her face.

When her body finally relented and relaxed, she sat back on her heels and saw Connor had joined her and was holding her hair and gently rubbing her back.

Her cheeks burned and she turned away from him, but he handed her a flask of watered-down wine. She sloshed it around in her mouth and spit it into the dirt.

"My first battle," Connor said quietly, as she took another drink, "I shat myself. I was fourteen, and not at all ready to be at my father's side on the front lines. Most relieve themselves; they can't help it. Or toss their stomachs. There's no shame in it."

Ariadne didn't respond, unsure of what to say. She wiped her mouth on the back of her sleeve and returned Connor's flask. Silently, she packed her tent, her mind replaying the horrors of the day before.

"You need to eat something, my lady," Tilly, the healer, was saying as she tied the last of her bags.

"I can't," Ariadne said.

"At least some broth?" Tilly held out a bowl of soup, but the smell made Ariadne's stomach churn.

"I'll try," she said, taking it. She took a tiny sip, and that seemed to satisfy Tilly, because she nodded and went back to the infirmary tents. They would stay until the wounded were ready to return home.

Ariadne stared into the bowl. It was just broth and vegetables, but she couldn't bring herself to even sip anymore.

"Brom's alive."

Ariadne jumped at Connor's voice, spilling the soup over her hands. She turned and found him right behind her. He took the bowl from her and she wiped her hands on the hem of her tunic.

"What?" she said.

"Brom," Connor repeated. "I just saw him. He barely made it through the night, but he's alive."

Ariadne could have cried in relief. "Oh, thank the gods," she whispered.

"You really should eat this, you know," Connor gestured to the soup.

"I can't," she said, her voice hollow.

"I understand," Connor said quietly. 'Well, at least pack something to nibble on as you ride if you feel the need."

He whistled for a squire and handed him the bowl, telling him to give it to one of the wounded.

"Lancelot said we should leave as soon as we can," Connor said as the squire hurried off. "It'll be me, you, Lancelot, Bradán, and Domhnall, riding ahead to Camelot. The rest will take their time returning with the wounded."

"So few of us?" Ariadne asked, though she had seen how empty the camp had become.

She squeezed her eyes shut, her head swimming.

"Princess—"

Ariadne huffed. "Where's Lancelot?"

Connor pointed and she followed his direction, past a few stomped-out campfires and bandaged soldiers.

Lancelot sat on his horse, talking to a soldier, but looked up when Ariadne approached. The soldier scurried away.

"We'll never make it to Camelot in time," she said. "We're at least a week's ride away. They could be dying right now and—"

"There's a moongate waiting for us," Lancelot said. "Courtesy of The Green Knight."

Ariadne nearly doubled over with relief. "When did he do that?"

"I received a message last night."

"Then we should leave now," said Ariadne. "Get back to Camelot immediately."

"Yes," said Lancelot, glancing behind her as Connor rode up with Bradán and Domhnall on horseback. A squire followed them, holding the reins of her own horse. "Before we leave, though," Lancelot continued, "I wish to apologize, Ariadne. I underestimated Mordred, and I take all blame for this battle going south. I should have realized Mordred had a trick up his sleeve."

"We knew it was a trap," Ariadne said, her voice hoarse.

"Yes, but not to this extent," said Lancelot. "I humbly ask that you receive my request of termination for my title as general."

"What?" Ariadne exclaimed. "You do not wish to be general?"

"I badly miscalculated," he said. "And I failed. The deaths are on me. I've been too far removed from battle for too long."

"It was you who called for The Green Man," Connor said. "If not for you, we'd all be dead. As the princess said, we knew we were walking into a trap. There was nothing any of us could have done."

Lancelot did not answer. He gritted his jaw.

Ariadne took the reins from the squire and mounted the horse, the back of her mind wondering how they had rounded them up, but she could worry about that later. They needed to get back to Camelot. Quickly.

"Well," Lancelot said finally, "we should expect the worst when we return to Camelot. If Mordred betrayed Agravaine, his closest friend, there's nothing he will not do."

"There's only five of us," Bradán piped up, frowning. "What hope do we have to make a difference if Mordred pulls something like this again?"

"Sometimes all it takes is one man, one voice, to change the course of the future," Lancelot said. "Though it may not feel like it after yesterday, there is still hope. And we must never lose it. Once we lose hope, well, there is nothing worth fighting for, is there?"

"Not a bad speech," Connor said with a half grin.

"Thank you, Prince Connor." Lancelot sent him a wink. "Now come; we should leave now. Be ready for anything when we come out the other side."

They followed him to the edge of the woods where the moongate awaited them, just at the entrance of the trees.

One by one, they passed through and on to Camelot.

CHAPTER SIXTY-FOUR

ANWIL

Anwil had read about battle so many times, he lost count. But nothing in the books had prepared him for reality. The copper tang of blood filled his nose as bodies fell around the city and blood soaked the cobbled streets.

The knights had kept Anwil surrounded, trying to keep him from seeing and being seen, but he could not hide.

"Any sign of Mordred?" Anwil asked when a priestess joined them on the battlements.

"No," she said, her golden skin tinged red. "But Nimue was spotted at the castle. Vivienne says he is likely there, wanting to draw you out."

Anwil hung his head. He knew he would have to face Mordred eventually. He looked up and caught Lohengrin's eye. His friend gave him a look that said he knew what Anwil was thinking.

"This has to end," Anwil told him.

Lohengrin's face fell. But he nodded and turned to the others, speaking in a low voice.

"All right," Lohengrin said, turning back around. "We'll escort you to the courtyard and draw him out. My lady"—he looked at the priestess—"can you and Lady Vivienne be with us? We'll need your magic to slow Mordred down."

"Of course," she said.

Anwil flinched as another rumble boomed farther off. "Now or never."

The knights surrounded him within a tight circle as soon as they hit the cobbled streets. Vivienne and her priestesses led them through the streets, where all around men and fae fought, screaming, roaring, screeching. The noise of clashing weapons was overwhelming.

They gained a bigger crowd around them as they moved along the city, Camelot soldiers joining the escort. Fae tried to attack, but the Lady Vivienne and the priestesses easily kept them at bay. Anwil could barely see around the bodies of his knights as they jostled through the city, but they somehow made it to the courtyard, where the grass was slick with blood and littered with more bodies.

Anwil stepped out of the circle of knights. He was breathing hard and gripping the pommel of Excalibur with white knuckles. He tried to recall everything Lancelot had told him of Mordred's fighting, but his mind was too abuzz. Too many things swirled at one time.

His heart pounded in his ear as he tried to take deep, steadying breaths. He forced himself to move with a slow caution, to put one foot in front of the other as he scanned the crowd and moved toward the courtyard stairs.

Some of the fae stopped fighting and turned to him, as if to watch. Mordred must be close.

Anwil turned his head toward the knights who huddled close behind him. He wanted to look at each of them: Lohengrin, Roland, Brionna, Xiang, Jabir, and Malcolm. His most trusted. His friends. He knew they were there, and he hoped that after today, he could look upon them again, that they would see him again. But he could not linger on heavy thoughts. There was no time.

"Anwil." Vivienne stepped up from behind him. "You need to draw him out. To challenge him. He will answer; his ego too large to ignore it. He'll want to make this a display. He'll want to kill you in front of everyone. Let his ego get the better of him and he might falter. But do not underestimate his power. I will do what I can to slow him down and wear him out. But it is up to you. You must kill him."

Anwil's hands shook, but he clenched them into fists and nodded.

"You are strong, Anwil Pendragon," Vivienne said. "Do not let doubt weaken you."

With more determination, Anwil climbed the courtyard stairs, turning to overlook the disaster. The knights had followed him, trailing up the steps cautiously, keeping an eye out.

A noise down the way caught his attention and he turned to see Mirah skidding to a halt, blood covering her tunic and dust in her hair.

"What are you doing?" She ran to him.

"Ending this," he said. "Go to safety. Now!"

Mirah regarded him with wide eyes, kissed him quickly, and ran toward her father.

Anwil pulled Excalibur from its sheath, the slide of metal against hard leather sounding like a content sigh in his ears. The blade glinted in the sunlight.

"Mordred!" he called out. "Show yourself, you coward!"

A laugh from down the corridor rang out and Anwil whirled on his heels, brandishing Excalibur.

Mordred sauntered down the corridor, a wicked grin on his gaunt face. "Forgive me," he said sarcastically. "I was merely...taking a tour of the castle. Your cousin was so kind as to show me around. I do hope you don't mind the new renovations. You see, we have very different tastes, and when I am king, this castle will not do. No; it's more palace than castle. Not as fortified for my tastes. It'll have to come down."

His grin widened as another boom shocked the castle and the east tower fell with a deafening tumble of stone and dust.

The breath left Anwil's chest.

Mordred laughed harder and drew his sword.

"Any last words, *King* Anwil?" he spat. "I'm feeling generous."

Anwil took Excalibur in both hands, vaguely aware that the knights were slowly closing in behind him.

Mordred glanced behind Anwil, and he smirked. "And you call me a coward, eh?" he said. "And yet, you can't fight me on your own?"

"I'm not stupid," Anwil said. "We both know that you are the more experienced fighter, and your powers make you stronger than ten men. It's not a fair fight. Consider this as evening the odds."

Mordred scoffed. "It's no matter. Must I remind you that I already felled quite a few of your precious knights and druids just last year?"

Anwil remembered all too well.

"No need," he said through gritted teeth. "That's why they're here."

He gestured to Vivienne and her priestesses, who each raised a hand. Tendrils of light shot from them to Mordred, wrapping around his limbs and torso.

Mordred yelled and struggled against the light. It tightened around him and he screamed louder. Something flashed and Mordred fell forward, the light fading. He retched and coughed.

"What was that?" he rasped, spittle dripping from his mouth.

"Now we're even," Anwil said, dropping into fighting stance. "Come. Stand at the ready."

Mordred let out a rage-filled roar and shot to his feet, running full speed at Anwil, raising his blade above his right shoulder and bringing it down in a hard arc. He meant to end the fight as quickly as he could, and his efficiency was brutal.

Their swords clashed with a deafening ring of metal on metal. The weight of Mordred's swing took Anwil by surprise and he almost fell to one knee under his force, but he raised his sword and put all his own strength behind his block. He deflected Mordred's blade to the side.

But Mordred swung again and again, forcing Anwil backward all the while.

Anwil managed to block every attack. Lancelot had told him Mordred would come at him fast and strong, that he liked to expend his energy quickly, thinking to overpower his enemies early and kill them quickly. He was all brute strength.

Mordred was fast and strong, but Anwil managed to match him. Whatever his father had given him coursed through his veins, keeping up with every blow Mordred brought to him.

As Anwil's foot wobbled on the edge of the steps, Mordred suddenly jerked, his blade arm dropping to his side. He snarled like a rabid dog and turned.

An arrow protruded from his shoulder. Behind him, Brionna nocked her bow with another arrow.

Anwil lunged for Mordred, but he was too quick. He batted Anwil across the face with the back of his gloved hand. Anwil stumbled, his nose spurting blood and his eyes watering.

"Give it up, Pendragon," Mordred said. "You cannot keep this going for long. You'll tire. You're weak. Camelot belongs to me."

Anwil parried and leaped to the right to avoid Mordred's blow.

Unfortunately, Mordred was right. He was tiring. But he wouldn't stop. He couldn't stop.

"Never," Anwil growled and swung Excalibur. Mordred dodged it easily, laughing.

Anwil gave the signal, and guards with iron-tipped spears rushed in from the walls and surrounded them, blocking him from Mordred.

Mordred took them in and chuckled. "Do you think this can stop me?"

The guards and knights took a step closer, closing them in even more.

"I can turn them all to ash with a snap of my fingers," Mordred said, raising his hand. "Surely, you don't wish them that fate?"

"Surely you don't wish to keep talking?" Anwil said. "Or perhaps you are too fond of the sound of your own voice."

Mordred's brow darkened and then turned into a sneer. "Enough games," he said. He raised his left hand, thumb pressed tight to his ring finger, poised to snap his fingers, but a hand appeared from seemingly out of nowhere and grabbed him around the wrist.

Morgana. She was bloodied and covered in grime, her left eye bruised and swollen, her right eye blazing with quiet fury.

"Enough, Mordred," she said. "Put down your sword. This does not have to go any further."

"On the contrary, *Mother*. It does."

He whirled around, meaning to stab Morgana. Anwil gasped, but Mordred froze. Morgana's right arm was outstretched, hand flat and emanating a bright white light, holding Mordred as if frozen in time.

"Now, Anwil!"

The guards moved for Anwil to make way, but as soon as he got close, he was blown off his feet. He crashed into Brionna and Malcolm.

As he gasped and coughed, trying to regain his breath and untangle himself from knights, Nimue roared and grabbed Morgana by the throat.

Lohengrin and Sir Jabir appeared over Anwil, dragging him to his feet.

Morgana and Nimue were fighting, and Mordred was fighting off Camelot soldiers. Fae now swarmed forward, cutting off Camelot's soldiers with a wall of bodies.

Jabir put a hand to Anwil's chest and he inhaled glorious air.

"Thank you," Anwil said, but in his next breath, they were intercepted by four large, very angry, winged fae with beaks. Jabir sent a ball of fire at them, but it only caused one to stumble. The others ran at them.

Anwil swung and thrust, but they were using their wings as blinds, and Anwil couldn't see where the faes' swords or talons were. He swiped low, hoping to take out one's knees. Excalibur bit into flesh and he heard a crack. The fae stumbled backward. Anwil pulled back and thrust forward hard, plunging Excalibur through its armor and deep into its chest.

He yanked out his blade, blood pouring out as the steel retreated and ran to help Lohengrin. He cut that fae's wings, and it let out a piercing screech before Lohengrin jabbed his sword through its throat.

Jabir's own enemy fell as Lohengrin's did. They made their way to the castle again, where more guards were stationed, ready with iron-tipped arrows, spears, and swords.

Nimue was on the other side, battered and panting. An arrow came at her, but she merely waved her hand and it burst into ash. She turned her attention to the archers on the turrets. More arrows came down, but she held out her hands and they bounced off an invisible force. She clenched her hands into fists and the archers' necks snapped and they fell.

"Fuck," Lohengrin said.

Nimue was not standing for long. A startled gasp escaped her lips as she was hoisted in the air, rigid as stone. Vivienne was beneath her, heavy bloodstains on her dress.

As she raised Nimue higher into the air, a sword burst through Vivienne's chest from the rear. Nimue fell hard to the ground and Anwil tried to run for Lady Vivienne. Lohengrin held him in place as Mordred pulled his blade from Vivienne's body and she tumbled forward to the ground.

"You'll not get away, Pendragon," Mordred said.

Anwil broke from Lohengrin's grip and stood tall, Excalibur clasped tightly in his hands.

Mordred flicked his wrist and Lohengrin went flying into the winged fae.

"Will you face me, or run like a coward?"

Anwil's jaw clenched and he placed his feet deliberately. "Let us end this."

Mordred grinned. "My pleasure." And he rushed at Anwil.

Mordred's strikes were powerful, blades sparking with every meeting. Mordred pushed Anwil farther back into the courtyard. It was all Anwil could do to keep up with the powerful swings.

Excalibur sang in his hands, leading him into parries and blocks and thrusts. With a hard block to the right, Anwil's ankle rolled and Mordred landed a hard strike on the backplate of his cuirass.

Anwil went down.

Excalibur loosened in his grip. Somewhere, someone yelled for him to get up. And Anwil rolled just in time to block Mordred's sword from his face.

Mordred stomped on Anwil's chest, pressing his boot hard.

"Goodbye, cousin." He inverted his blade in his hands and began to raise it above his head.

At the top of his attack, he grunted. The weight of his boot lessened.

Anwil slammed Excalibur into Mordred's knee and rolled hard to his left. He scrambled to his feet while his opponent roared in pain. An arrow protruded from Mordred's back.

Anwil thrust Excalibur at Mordred's chest. But Mordred caught it with his hand. The blade slowly cut through his glove and skin. Blood dripped from the leather.

Mordred's eyes were on fire.

He twisted the sword away and with a sharp yank, he pulled Anwil forward, falling face-first into the grass.

Excalibur slipped from his hands.

As Anwil struggled to his knees, Mordred kicked him over onto his back. And before he could even think, Mordred slammed Excalibur through his breastplate, through his chest.

Anwil's breath left him. Shooting pain exploded. He tried to speak, tried to move. He trembled. Someone was screaming. No, many someones. But he couldn't focus.

Mordred bent over him. "Camelot is mine."

Blood gurgled in Anwil's mouth.

And Mordred yanked Excalibur away. Anwil screamed as the sword sliced back through him.

Mordred laughed. And then slammed the hilt of Excalibur on Anwil's head. The last thing Anwil heard was Mordred's laughter.

CHAPTER SIXTY-FIVE

ARIADNE

Lancelot was right to tell them to expect the worst.

Ariadne's heart dropped to her stomach to see Camelot burning and swarming with fae soldiers. The castle had lost two towers, and buildings were tumbling to ash. Mordred's men were obliterating Camelot's army. Blood stained the ground alongside the red tabards. So much red. Just like Northumbria. A massacre.

"We have to help," Ariadne said by the stables as they slid from their horses. They had come out of the moongate just on the other side of the pasture, where the fighting had not yet reached. The horses were all gone, either let loose or had run away.

"What can we do? The city is gone," said Connor, gesturing. "You run in there and you won't get past the first gate. You'll be killed instantly."

"My brother is in there!"

"Connor is right," Lancelot said. "You cannot go running in there. Especially as how you aren't even supposed to be here."

"What does that mean?" Ariadne asked him.

"My mother Saw something," Lancelot said. "I think she Saw your death here. That is why she insisted you go to Northumbria."

Ariadne's knees wobbled and Domhnall caught her before she fell. "What?"

"I don't know for certain, but you are not supposed to be in this fight," Lancelot said. "We have to be careful. There's not much we can do, but I knew you'd wish to be with Anwil."

Ariadne nodded, tears threatening her eyes. She blinked them away as Lancelot turned to Connor, Bradán, and Domhnall.

"We'll go through the tunnels," Lancelot said. "That'll get us into the city without notice. Do not let her out of your sight."

They followed Lancelot to what looked like an old ruined fountain just within the trees. They let their horses go and Lancelot pulled away some leaves and vines to reveal a wooden door in the ground. Connor and Lancelot pulled it open and climbed down the stairs. Ariadne went in after them, with Bradán and Domhnall bringing up the rear.

The tunnel was dark and damp and Ariadne could not see in front of her.

"It's not caved in somewhere, do you think?" Bradán asked.

"No," Lancelot answered. "We cleared them for evacuation."

Someone bumped into Ariadne, and it was Domhnall's voice that mumbled an apology.

They eventually came to the other side, another door in the ground near the market. They climbed out into a small alleyway, human and fae soldiers running and fighting past the opening in the streets. Ariadne pulled her sword, the others doing the same.

Quietly, they crept along the alleys and behind buildings, over bodies, and even hiding inside buildings to make their way to the courtyard, where a large skirmish was focused.

Heart pounding in her ears and her stomach in knots, they made it to the crumbled castle gate. Heart in her stomach, they climbed over the rubble, and Ariadne stumbled when a deep horn pierced the air. Three short blasts echoed.

A figure stepped out on top of the courtyard steps and Ariadne lost all breath. Mordred came into the light, Anwil's limp frame in his arms.

"No," she rasped.

Connor caught her before she fell. She couldn't breathe. She couldn't think.

Mordred dropped Anwil's body at his feet and put Anwil's crown on his head. The fae cheered.

"Camelot is mine!" Mordred boomed, and the cheers from the fae grew louder. "The reign of the Pendragon is over!"

Ariadne struggled against Connor's hold.

"No," he snapped in her ear. "He'll kill you."

But Mordred had found them. His grin was feral. He looked at them over the crowd, wild glee in his eyes.

"Welcome home, Princess!" Mordred called, his laugher maniacal. "I have a gift for you!" He kicked Anwil's body down the stairs and Ariadne screamed.

She struggled against Connor. Lancelot now held on to her as well. But she jabbed her elbow into Connor's groin and kicked at Lancelot's knee. She broke free, yanking out her sword and running full force to Mordred.

She didn't make it to the stairs. She was thrown backward, landing hard on her back, the wind knocked from her lungs.

"Kill her," Mordred ordered.

Fae came at her, but someone stepped over her, blowing the fae away. They turned, and Mirah's face came into view. She held out a hand for Ariadne and pulled her to her feet. Lancelot, Connor, Bradán, and Domhnall surrounded them, weapons out.

Mirah pulled something from her belt—a small vial—and threw it to the ground. Smoke enveloped them. Ariadne couldn't see, couldn't hear anything. And then they were falling. Ariadne tried to scream, but her throat could not make a noise. As fast as it happened, it was over, and they landed hard on the sand. Ariadne coughed, blowing sand from her lips.

Rolling over, she saw the others doing the same, coughing and wiping sand off themselves.

A ship was docked out in the water, and a rowboat nearby at the shore.

"What's this?" Ariadne asked, her voice cracking. She got to her feet, whirling around. They were on a beach, a cliff looming over them.

"Anwil's plan for you if something happened to him," Mirah said quietly, tears running down her cheeks.

"What plan? Where are we? Why aren't we in Camelot?"

"Camelot is gone, Ari!" Mirah gasped.

"No." Ariadne shook her head. "*No*! Where's Anwil?"

No one answered her. what she saw had to be a trick. It couldn't be real. Anwil couldn't be gone. They couldn't have lost.

"No!"

"Ari, Anwil has been speaking with King Connig," Mirah said gently, her eyes red and tear tracks in the dirt on her face. "We're to take you to Ireland."

"Why?"

"Because the longer you stay in Briton, the more you are in danger." Mirah tugged at her hand. "Please."

"I can't leave!"

"Connig has agreed to aid us," Connor said, putting a hand on Mirah's shoulder. "Your brother and I spoke of it just before we left for Northumbria."

Ariadne whirled on Lancelot. "Did you know?"

Lancelot nodded. "Yes," he said. "Anwil's will was clear. If anything happened to him during this fight, we were to get you to safety. Right now, the safest place for you is Ireland."

"I can't leave!" Ariadne screamed. "I can't abandon Camelot and Briton and… and the people! I have to go back!"

"And do what, Ari?" Mirah grabbed her by the arms. "Mordred has taken over the city. We have to regroup, and you cannot do that in Camelot."

Ariadne opened and closed her mouth a few times. "But Anwil."

Mirah didn't say anything, only hugged her. Ariadne shook in her arms, hoping to wake up from this nightmare, hoping that someone would shake her awake and it would have all been a dream.

"Come, Ari," said Lancelot. "The fight is over. We will get revenge on Mordred in time. But we need to get you to safety first."

Ariadne didn't move. She couldn't.

"Ari." Mirah took her hand. "Please."

Ariadne looked into Mirah's face, Her friend's heartbreak and grief clear. And followed Mirah to the rowboat.

Once on the ship's deck, Irish sailors hurried around them, pulling anchor and shouting orders. Ariadne barely registered any of it. She was led to a small room under the ship to share with Mirah. She managed to take her armor off, but had to get out of the room. The walls were closing in. She ran to the deck. Sea salt and air sprayed at her face and she watched as the waves carried them away from Briton.

CHAPTER SIXTY-SIX

NIMUE

Nimue gazed down at her sister's body. A mix of emotions swelled in her.

Vivienne was dead.

Blood stained her stomach, her eyes were wide and glassy, staring at nothing, her hair was tangled with debris and blood. It was not a sight Nimue had truly thought she'd see. Yes, she had wished for her sister's death for a very long time, but to actually see it was something else.

Memories of long ago, when they were children, flooded her mind. They had been close once. They had built Avalon together, welcomed priestesses, the sick, the hurt, the dying. They had guarded the veils between realms together.

Nimue tapped Vivienne's body with the toe of her boot. She did not move. Nimue knelt down and pressed her fingers to Vivienne's neck. No pulse, and she was already turning cold.

She was truly gone then.

Nimue let out a shuddering breath. Tears stung her eyes. Once, Vivienne had been the only mother she had known. The Modron gave them life, but she was no mother. She did not hold Nimue when she scraped her knee, or calmed her down when her magic did not cooperate. She did not make sure Nimue ate or slept. Vivienne had done all of that.

And then Vivienne betrayed her.

When Vivienne kept looking the other way when humans hurt the fae, when humans slaughtered them, Nimue had not been able to stay silent. She could not look the other way as Vivienne had done.

So Nimue had taken measures into her own hands.

And Vivienne had banned her from Avalon, the home—the haven—they had built together. As if Nimue had no claim to it.

Nimue wiped the tears from her eyes and glanced around the fallen city. Buildings were smoking, smoldering, half gone. Rubble and dead bodies of human and fae alike littered the streets.

They had won.

Nimue was surprised.

When Mordred had decided to forgo their original plan, Nimue did not have much hope. He had acted the same way he had last time. With impatience and impulsiveness. But they had done it.

The odds had been stacked against them, and yet, the boy was dead.

When Mordred sliced him through with Excalibur, their precious army began to flee. So much for the legendary Camelot loyalty. If Nimue didn't need him dead, she'd almost feel sorry for him.

A roaring cheer came from the castle and Nimue glanced once more at Vivienne before stepping over her body and making her way through the bloodied streets to Pendragon Castle.

Mordred stood at the top of the courtyard stairs, the body of Anwil Pendragon at his feet.

Nimue shoved through the fae warriors as Mordred made a speech that she only half listened to.

Another cheer rose as she finally broke through the soldiers and made her way up the stairs.

Mordred grinned at her; the bloody Pendragon crown crooked on his head. He held out his hand and Nimue took it, letting him lead her up the last few stairs.

"Look, my love," he said, his voice dripping with glee. "Victory is sweet indeed!"

His lips found hers. She cringed. He was covered in sweat and grime, but she let him kiss her. There were far too many eyes on them for her to do anything now. So she gave him this one last moment.

"Come, my love," Mordred said, pulling her away from the stairs and into the alcove. "We should celebrate."

"How so?" she said. "You should secure—"

He put a finger to her lips. His eyes were wide, his grin feral. It unnerved her. As if he were turning wild before her eyes.

"I told you not to doubt me, did I not?" he said. "And now look. Camelot is mine. Everything we worked for. It is ours. Power is mine and now—"

He slid a hand around her waist. And froze. His grin melted off his face, and he looked down. Confused.

Nimue's dagger was sticking out of his chest. She hadn't been able to wait any longer. He needed to go.

Confusion, hurt, and then fury swam across his face as he slowly looked back up at her.

"You would have been my queen," he said quietly.

"I never wanted to be a queen," Nimue said. "I told you that. We were supposed to save the fae. I thought you understood that."

Nimue stepped out of his arms and he staggered, gripping the dagger's handle.

"I understand perfectly now," Mordred said, his face turning into a snarl. He yanked the dagger from his chest and slit Nimue's throat.

She grabbed at her neck, blood spilling over her hands. It was cold. Everything slowed in movement. Her body fell. Her vision swam. And eventually, darkness came.

CHAPTER SIXTY-SEVEN

MORDRED

Mordred looked down at Nimue's body, a puddle of blood forming under her. He had had an inkling of this, but a small, old part of him had held on to hope. He had loved her once, and they could have been great, side by side.

But no matter now. Mordred did not need anyone. He had power now. He had Camelot. He ruled Briton. And he would burn it to the ground.

He turned on his heel and made his way down the courtyard stairs. Every step was painful. His whole body hurt, but he ignored it. The fae had begun to celebrate, screeching and cheering their victory. He was on the last few steps when he realized the boy's body was gone.

"No," he growled. "No!" He looked around wildly, pushing and shoving fae out of the way.

"Where is he?" Mordred boomed. "Where!?"

The fae closest to him looked around, but none could find him.

"Find the boy's body!" he barked at the surrounding fae. "And bring it to me! Kill whoever has taken it!"

Mordred turned, and through the frantic fae, he saw his mother holding Anwil, hiding behind a large winged fae.

His blood boiled. He lunged for her, but Morgana was gone before he could even take a step.

CHAPTER SIXTY-EIGHT

MORGANA

Morgana stumbled onto the shores of Avalon, her body shaking. Anwil was heavy in her arms, her own blood mixing with his and soaking both their clothes. Her ankle throbbed with each step as she headed straight for the temple. Avalon was silent still. No priestesses were there to greet them, nor any curious animals to poke their heads out of the brush.

This was not the first time she had taken a loved one to Avalon.

She had taken Arthur's body here when he had died. Sir Bedievere had been the only one to see her, though she had covered herself in a heavy cloak to hide her face. He had let everyone assume it had been Vivienne who had taken Arthur to Avalon to clean and prepare his body, but no. It had been Morgana.

And now she had to do it for his son.

Anger bubbled in her stomach, at the sick and twisted way fate had repeated itself.

But she stumbled her way to the center of the Isle, arms shaking from Anwil's doubled weight in armor.

Finally, she made it to the temple and fell to her skinned and bruised knees in front of The Modron's altar. Carefully, she laid Anwil down and bent her head over him, taking a moment to breathe.

With tears streaming down her face, she carefully relieved him of his armor and tossed it aside. He seemed so small underneath. So young.

Shaking, Morgana lit the candles and prayed to The Modron, to Morrigan, to Arawn. To any of the gods that might listen. She tried her best to clean Anwil's wound with what was left in her bag, trying but failing to hold back her sobs.

She had failed. Again. She had failed to protect her family. Torn once again by its own blood.

"Why?" Morgana whispered. "Why must this be the way? Is this my punishment for leaving Avalon? For giving Mordred up? For leaving Camelot? Have I not atoned enough?"

A rustle startled her and she yanked a dagger from her boot.

"Who's there?" she called.

A cloaked figure stepped into the temple, leaning heavily on a gnarled walking stick. They pushed back their hood and Morgana never thought she'd be relieved and yet so sad to see that face.

"Merlin?" she sobbed.

His blue-gray eyes shone with clarity. He was clean-shaven and tidy in earthen-toned clothing and his feathered cloak. He looked just as she remembered all those years ago.

"Morgana," Merlin said, his eyes full of regret and sadness. "I have so much I wish to say."

"I don't care," Morgana said. "I failed, Merlin. Anwil is gone. Mordred has Camelot. I failed."

"Oh, my child," Merlin said, approaching them and kneeling next to Anwil. "We cannot change our destiny. Everything is done by the gods' will. What has happened was always supposed to happen, and we played our parts."

Anger bubbled in Morgana's stomach. "That is horseshit, and you know it, Merlin," she growled. "When we met at Ceridwen's, you said—"

"I know what I said," Merlin interrupted. "But I was not in my right mind. You made me say what you wished me to say."

"I did not!"

"You never learned to control minds as well as you think you have, Morgana," Merlin said sharply. "But this is not the time to fight."

He put a hand on Anwil's forehead, smoothing the red curls from his face.

"This is my doing," he said. "Uther, your mother, all of it. And I am sorry for it. I wish it had not ended this way." He put a hand on Anwil's chest. And his eyes widened. "But perhaps there is hope still left."

"What?" Morgana asked.

Merlin's blue eyes pierced into hers.

"Anwil still lives."

ACKNOWLEDGEMENTS

Realms is finally here! I know, I know. I took forever. But thank you to everyone who patiently waited for this book. What a whirlwind it has been! Going viral has changed my life and I now have an amazing core following of the best readers. Thank you to everyone who bought my books and took a chance on me!

Of course a thank you to my husband, Tim, who helped write all of the fight scenes, and kept the house going without complaint while I holed myself away in my office to write.

Thank you to my parents who have always supported my writing.

To my sister, Hannah, who hypes my book up when she can, and to all of my family. Thank you.

Thank you once again to everyone who came out to Squires Castle and dressed up as my characters so I could get promo material! Sarah, Sarah, (yes, two Sarahs) Ben, Josie, Jeff, Melissa, Paige, Jake, Jeannie, David, Leila, Mark, Carrie, Tim, and kiddo!

Than you to my editor, Susan. (I am sorry for all the quicklys!)

A special thanks to Joe and Sarah at Pretty Good Books for being wonderful with all of their support.

And a thank you to you, reader. For taking a chance on my books. You make all the blood, sweat, and tears worth it.

ABOUT THE AUTHOR

Chelsea Banning is a writer, reader, and lover of all things fantasy. Chelsea started writing in 10th grade and hasn't stopped since. She started writing Flash-Fictions that bloomed into novels. Along with writing, she has worked at Renaissance Faires on the street cast, directing fairy guilds, announcing and squiring at joust shows with her husband, and working clothing booths. She also owned a small performing business offering various fairytale and superhero characters for kids for seven years.

Also By

OF CROWNS AND LEGENDS (Book 1 in THE FIGHT FOR CAMELOT)

DAYDREAMS: A SHORT STORY COLLECTION

THE AUTHOR PLANNER

Find all of them at: www.chelseabanning.com